FRACTURED TRUST

Mike Sabey

SIDHARTA
BOOKS
& PRINT PTY LTD

Published in Australia **by Sid Harta Publishers**
ABN: 34 632 585 203
23 Stirling Crescent, GLEN WAVERLEY VIC 3150 Australia
Telephone: +61 3 9560 9920
E-mail: author@sidharta.com.au

First published in Australia 2020
This edition published 2020

Author: Mike Sabey
Title: Fractured Trust

The Producer:
Common Sense Investments PO Box 5265 Middle Park, Victoria 3206 Australia

Legal disclaimer
All characters, scenes, places and companies in this novel are a work of fiction and any resemblance to actual persons living or deceased or any organisation is entirely coincidental.

Editors: Elissa McCullum +61 418 519 010 and Bonnie Wilson; Sub Editor: Sallie Sabey
Design and Typesetting: The Creative Parrot
South Melbourne + 61 3 9690 4321
Cover design: Composite
Typeset in: Simoncini Garamond 11.5 points
Website: Smart Energy Groups - Sam Sabey
Waymore Distributors + 61 3 9801 8111

National Library of Australia
ISBN: 978-1-925707-02-1
pp 320

For my grandchildren –
James, Christian, Will, Matthew, Indie, Ully,
Coen and Ashton in the hope
that during their lives they might
leave a creative legacy that future
generations will respect and admire.

FRACTURED TRUST

Key Characters

Charles Garland
Third generation Australian who takes over the family's business and finds himself in England at the outbreak of World War Two.

Margie Childers (nee Swanson)
An English nurse who cares for her Australian uncle when he is injured and unwittingly becomes involved in a fraud.

Jessie Tyler
Margie's closest friend who becomes aware of many secrets she is forced to keep to herself.

Emilio Bestillo
Flamboyant Portuguese salesman who was sent to England during the war to sell wine.

Gregory Garland
Migrated to Sydney in the 1860s chasing a new start and fresh business opportunities.

Frank Garland
Second generation Garland, father of Charles and Alice, who continues to build the trading company.

Gertrude Swanson
Margie's cold-hearted mother, who is a distant relative of the Garlands.

Sir Kenneth Codrington
Sydney-based managing director of the Australasian Trustee Company, caught up in the scandal.

Emma Childers
Twenty-one-year-old London girl who moves to Melbourne and accidentally discovers some closely guarded family secrets.

Frank Dalton
Born out of wedlock and grew up never knowing he was adopted.

Roger Lockwood
Alice Lockwood's grandson, who manages Garland International.

1. London, 1941

The unexploded bomb had dug a crater large enough to swallow a bus.

If it had gone off, it could have demolished part of the financial heart of London.

Because it hadn't, it was now the job of one officer to disable the menacing monster, known as a "Satan", the most feared in Germany's weaponry, packing more than five thousand pounds of mass destruction.

Lieutenant Charles Garland approached the crater and proceeded to confidently descend a ladder into hell.

Seventeen seconds.

If anything was to go wrong, he knew that seventeen seconds was all the time he and his men had to bolt for their lives.

This wasn't his first bomb, but it was the biggest and certainly the most dangerous.

A distance away in the smoky shadows of the Bank of England, a small crowd peered anxiously from behind a wall of protective sandbags. They were close enough to hear when the silence was gut-wrenchingly broken by a sudden loud clunk, followed by the ugly sound of metal dropping onto rock.

To all it seemed like something going seriously wrong. Surely the extraction of the bomb's detonator should be noiseless, such was its surgical delicacy.

The onlookers held their breaths.

Then came the officer's scream, **'GET OUT! IT'S GOING OFF!'**

Two Ambulance Corp nurses crouching behind the sandbags witnessed the next seventeen seconds.

They saw the Lieutenant clamber out of the pit and run, run with his sappers the seventy-yard dash to their escape pit.

In the eighteenth second, they saw Mansion House Street explode.

The last thing they witnessed before dropping to the ground to avoid the blast was the sight of the Lieutenant diving into the pit, followed by his sappers, with a wall of dust and flame chasing them in rage.

Only afterwards did Margie Swanson, one of the nurses on duty at the Mansion House Street site, discover that the heroic officer seriously injured in the blast was her uncle from Australia, Charles Garland.

Two months later, Lieutenant Garland was presented to the King, who pinned a George Cross bravery medal to the chest of a man whose face was partly blown away and who was confined to a wheelchair.

*　*　*

Only a few years earlier, the Lieutenant could never have foreseen that he would even have been in England. The officer was Australian; his world had revolved around New South Wales' aristocracy. Over three generations since the 1860s his family had built a business fortune and had become well respected. A family tragedy had set him on a course to England where he found himself engulfed by war.

Returning from Buckingham Palace to his London flat, he received a letter from Australia that drew him into a new nightmare.

The trustee company that looked after his wealth had written to advise it had followed his instructions and sold all his shares.

The Lieutenant tried to make sense of their letter.

He had made no such request.

His turmoil grew when his London bank informed him that the proceeds from the sale had not been received. He knew his money was gone.

*　*　*

As Nurse Swanson put her skills to use caring for her uncle during his recuperation, she began to slide into her own nightmare.

Could she be unwittingly to blame for the theft of his fortune?

All she'd done was fall in love. Now both she and her uncle were facing new despair.

There were scandals racking her family.

No-one was willing to talk about it. And the consequences just kept growing and being hidden.

2. Melbourne, 2019

As the Emirates A380 flight to Heathrow via Dubai cruised at 39,000 feet towards Western Australia's jagged coast, the relaxing drum of the plane's powerful engines filled Emma Childers' senses and for a few moments erased the reason she was on board.

Easing back her business class seat that her mum had booked, she looked forward to enjoying the small bottle of French champagne that had just been put on her tray before a four-course dinner was served.

For the first time since her mother's shock call she could allow herself a moment to dream of what was ahead in London: a loving reunion with her dear mum and sister, a quiet sleep-in and a much needed catch-up with her best friend Becky, plus, if her budget permitted, a little shopping.

Uppermost on her mind was the emotional challenge of Granma's funeral and the honour the family had bestowed on her to deliver the eulogy celebrating her amazing life.

Hours earlier, the arousing aroma of freshly ground coffee from a café on the departure concourse had drawn her in for a pre-flight fix.

The latte provided the one, sure, warming lift that helped improve her otherwise sombre mood.

Perched on a stool, she stole a sideways glance in the window at how she looked.

Her stretch jeans felt nicely firm, whilst her light jacket appeared a tad loose. Her smooth, lightly tanned, English skin felt taut and to any onlooker she had a certain bounce in her step. She checked her delicate English face, her engaging hazel eyes, crowned by a flowing copper coloured ponytail that shimmered nicely in the afternoon's shards of light pouring in through the floor to ceiling windows.

Sipping her coffee, she recalled that moment when her phone rang unexpectedly beside her bed less than a week ago.

Taking that unexpected call from her mother in the early hours of the morning with her eyes half closed, she was jolted awake upon hearing the dreaded news that her beloved grandmother, Margie Childers, had passed away at the ripe old age of ninety-eight.

In shock, she peeled back her doona and slipped on a robe before shuffling towards the kitchen.

She noticed a shaft of silvery light from a full moon, which bathed the polished timber boards, that she thought must be a good omen. Was Granma perhaps providing her a guiding light?

Opening the door to the small rear garden of her South Melbourne worker's cottage, she stepped onto the dew-moistened deck, feeling its reassuring smooth boards beneath her bare feet. Looking at the moon high in the night sky she let out a distraught call for strength to help her gather her thoughts.

Tears rolling down her cheeks glistened in the soft moonlight and for a moment she feared the man in the moon might see how vulnerable she was.

In her teens Emma had suffered from bouts of low self-confidence, which sometimes prevented her from achieving what she had the talent to conquer. Margie Childers knew her weakness and flaws, and over a number of years, had been instrumental in building her inner strength to the extent it was mostly now something in her past.

Granma had always been her rock since her youngest years.

She was the one person who, despite enduring frequent personal ups and downs and her appalling war memories as a nurse, had unselfishly mentored Emma through her vibrant girlhood, her challenging school years, her parents' unsettling separation and her first tastes of love.

In the adoring heart of this vivacious girl with the world at her feet winging her way home to England, Margie Childers had always been held in the most special of places.

It had been seven exciting months since she had celebrated her twenty-first birthday in England with family and friends, then said a teary goodbye to Margie, whom she had only ever known as Granma, before flying out to Melbourne.

She had felt so excited to be starting a new life and a new job Down Under.

As the Childers' beloved matriarch, Granma had inspired Emma to do something no-one in the family had ever attempted; go and try Australia.

Granma had instilled in Emma the need to use her talents, conquer her insecurities, be resourceful, and if the occasion arose, 'crash through' barriers.

She now regretted that she had not made Granma go to the doctor a year earlier when she first suffered coughing spasms.

*   *   *

Peering out of the plane's window, Emma was entranced watching the Australian coastline disappearing five miles below. Several soothing glasses of bubbly had slowed her breathing, leading to waves of memories of Granma flooding back.

Leaning over, she removed her laptop from a carry bag and opened a fresh document to begin the eulogy.

Initially, her words came slowly, then her vivid recollections came back of happy school holiday adventures to Wimbledon to stay with Granma, where she enjoyed freshly baked muffins and long interesting chats, triggering the sentences to tumble effortlessly onto the page.

She wrote how proud Granma was of her Florence Nightingale Medal for bravery, recalling that a framed photo taken in 1942 of her receiving it had always sat on her mantlepiece.

She was reminded of the wonderful support Granma had given her during the emotional upheaval that had hit her hard when her parents separated.

Noticing her sad disposition, one of the cabin crew asked if there was anything she could do.

Emma was about to say no, but then changed her mind. In a clipped English accent she suggested, 'Yes, perhaps another champers might help, thank you.'

She prayed her eulogy would flow like a cool sea breeze over a sunbaked beach to honour Granma's life and touch the hearts of all those who attended.

As the flight droned deeper into the approaching darkness, she became oblivious to everyone around her.

Another sip of champagne liberated further memories, until

emotional waves of sadness began to engulf her, causing tears to roll uncontrollably down her cheeks, dripping onto the screen of her laptop.

Noticing her predicament, another flight attendant leaned over to offer her a tissue.

Little did Emma realise, ahead lay uncharted waters that were soon to reveal a host of never discussed family matters.

Family matters that would take her to places, people and past events holding many dark secrets, which for more than seventy years, had been swept under the carpet.

3. Wimbledon, 2019

Beneath the ominous, grey clouds over Wimbledon, muffled notes from the famous bells in St Mary's landmark spire peal across the village rooftops heralding Margie's funeral.

Inside the ancient church, its famous organ quietly plays the opening bars of one of her favourite hymns.

Fifty-four mourners rise, bashfully launching into verse.

All things bright and beautiful,

All creatures great and small …

Silently, Emma mouths the words whilst her thoughts for the moment are elsewhere. Today has arrived sooner than she ever expected.

Each little flower that opens,

Each little bird that sings …

Since her mum picked her up from the airport two days ago, she's hardly stopped. Tearful family reunions, then finally seeing her dearest school friend, Becky, has sapped her emotional reserves.

The sunset and the morning,

That brightens up the sky …

Arriving at the church, Emma was surprised how many faces she knew, including a scattering of locals and parishioners, some of Margie's former nursing colleagues from St George's Hospital and Red Cross representatives as well as the Childers family.

The cold wind in the winter,

The pleasant summer sun …

The family had requested a simple service with a few hymns, a reading and her eulogy.

The tall trees in the greenwood,

The meadows where we play …

As the organ swells majestically, the congregation launches more heartily into the final verse. Placing the Order of Service next to her handbag and taking out her tablet, Emma nervously rises, checks her new charcoal skirt and jacket ensemble, then slips elegantly from the pew. She stands tall in her heels, then bows towards the altar and the casket.

Tucked in her pocket is one of Granma's favourite lace hankies her mother has insisted she have.

The vicar in his flowing white vestments, with a reassuring smile beckons her to cross the nave's worn flagstones with him.

With a loving look on her young face, Emma passes Margie's polished coffin resting on a shiny frame, softly illuminated by the magnificent backlit, stained glass window behind the altar.

As the last verse is sung, she approaches the step leading to the 150-year-old lectern, formed by the gleaming wings of an eagle plated in gold.

All things bright and beautiful,
All creatures great and small …

Emma places her tablet on the lectern and taps to the first page of her eulogy before lifting her eyes to take in the sombre scene.

Above her hangs the famous battle cruiser *HMS Inflexible's* flag, flown in the 1916 Battle of Jutland when it sank several German warships.

As the hymn reaches its exultant climax she briefly shudders, wondering if she has the strength to do this.

All things wise and wonderful,
The Lord God … made them all.

To stop her hands nervously shaking, she grasps the edges of the eagle's reassuring wings.

She deliberately pauses, taking in the momentary silence only punctuated by the rustle of people settling into their seats on old creaking pews donated to St Mary's in the 1840s, which have been described as amongst 'the most uncomfortable in all Christendom'.

From out of the corner of her eye she notices the Red Cross flag draped coffin topped with a simple wreath of white lilies, like those Granma grew in her garden.

Before her, fifty-four sets of eyes and ears wait patiently.

She moistens her lips, stands to full height and begins with words she now knows by heart.

'Marjorie Emily Childers, who died last week of pneumonia after a short illness, was ninety-eight-years-old.

'Margie, as she was known to her many friends and family here this morning, has always just been my "Granma" since I was a child growing up with my family in Kent.

'I admired her for many things, not the least for her bravery serving so long ago as a nurse in the war with the Ambulance Service when she gave her very best, enduring unimaginable sights and horrors in the Blitz.'

'Granma was such a strong and empathetic character and many of us here will well remember her famous "strokes".

'She was a natural outdoors woman, she adored her garden, she loved her long walks and was devoted to her village community. She lived for her hospital job and was of course dedicated to her family and children.

'Margie taught me about the seasons. She made me aware of the first wafts of roses in the spring and in autumn she introduced me to the wonderful fragrance of Daphne. In my summer holidays she would take me to Brighton, where we enjoyed long walks along the pier and swimming when the sun made it warm enough to go in.'

When Emma sees many of Margie's old friends nodding in agreement and no doubt recalling their own fond memories, she feels more connected.

She continued with more confidence, 'Another of her "strokes" was her passion for cooking. I have always loved her sensational rosemary infused Sunday lamb roasts she served at Merton Hall Road.

'Marjorie Emily was the eldest daughter of Ronald and Gertrude Swanson. After finishing school she took off with her closest friend, Jessie Tyler, on an amazing adventure to Scotland to visit the Empire Exhibition in Edinburgh.

'Jessie, who despite her advancing years, has made a big effort to get here today. She recounted to me recently how she fondly recalls discovering one of Margie's "strokes" on that trip.

'For a dare in Glasgow, Margie brazenly stole a teapot from a café where they had taken tea. She bolted away down the main street with it stuffed in her handbag, excitedly screeching with joy when they got round the corner at not being followed.'

Sitting alone, unobtrusively in the middle row was an elderly silver haired lady, her body stooped by age. Hearing Emma's teapot story made her eyes well up with nostalgic joy and masked for a moment her regret and guilt that in many ways so long ago she had let Margie down.

Ninety-seven-year-old Jessie Tyler had arrived early for the service, making the journey up from Brighton by train. She had taken the news of dear friend's demise with very deep regret.

Jessie recalls fondly their very agreeable Glasgow trip, which was the beginning of their "coming out". Her thoughts turn to the unique lifelong friendship the pair had shared, despite its ups and downs. It began at school in the 1930s and blossomed unabated until the war, when they seemed to drift apart. Nevertheless, they had enjoyed a lifelong bond.

She remembers a diary that Margie had kept, of her innermost thoughts that she would sometimes read to her.

Jessie's thoughts are drawn back to Emma's heartfelt account of the lead-up to the outbreak of the war.

'Returning from Scotland,' Emma continued, feeling even more self-assured, 'in 1939 Margie trained as a nurse at North Middlesex Hospital and after the outbreak of war, transferred into the Red Cross Ambulance Service. Here, her life was forever changed by the carnage wreaked during the horrendous bombing of London.

'After one terrible night sheltering on an underground train platform, she emerged to save two injured children from a bomb-damaged house and was awarded the Red Cross Florence Nightingale Medal for her bravery.'

Emma notices a gentleman with a kind face sitting in the sixth pew, whose receding grey hair only partially covered scars on his neck, nodding in agreement.

Later at the wake, he introduced himself to her as Oliver Burrows, one of those children.

Listening to Emma, he recalls being rescued with his younger sister Lily and being comforted by Nurse Swanson after the tragic loss of his parents.

Margie had stayed in touch with them as they grew up and married, in later years playing aunt to his children.

Then he puts aside these memories when Emma relates, 'In early

1941, as the Blitz entered its fifth month, Margie learned that her Australian uncle, Charles Garland, who was visiting England had enlisted with the Royal Engineers.

'By sheer coincidence she was on duty when he was seriously injured in a bomb-defusing incident and unbeknownst to her, took him to hospital in her ambulance.

'Granma visited him in hospital and after his release, helped with his slow and painful rehabilitation.'

Emma then recounted several stories from Margie's social life in those days. 'In London's nursing social circles, Margie was considered a "dasher" and loved the endless round of parties.

'There was mention of her having a boyfriend whom she was seeing early in the war, who disappeared and was never spoken of after that.'

The mention of this boyfriend caused Jessie to reminiscence about her highly secret work during the war at Bletchley Park, which meant she could never tell Margie that her boyfriend was being watched by MI6.

She recollects several outings she went on with Margie and her boyfriend and feeling ill at ease with his flashy style and had wondered what on earth she saw in him. Then, he disappeared, leaving her at a particularly difficult time, when Margie was caring for her Australian uncle. There were also some other mysterious matters, which weren't talked about.

With the clouds rolling back outside and the sun vainly trying to peep through the church windows, the warm-hearted response Emma's eulogy was receiving helped lift her voice.

'In the early 1950s, after Margie met my grandfather, Ralph Childers, at a New Year's Eve party, following a brief courtship they married in this very church and settled into the Merton Hall Rd terrace house, a short stroll from Wimbledon village.

'In June each year during the Wimbledon All England Club's Tennis Championships, Granma would help park cars next door in St Mary's grounds to raise funds.

'As everyone knows, her favourite pub was The Dog and Fox where my grandfather used to take us for a grill and he was always careful to ensure we avoided the lounge where the street girls plied their trade.

'I am sure we all have many happy memories of that pub, whether it be attending birthdays, wedding anniversaries or my 21st party last year.

'At my party I fondly recall Granma telling me her dream summer holidays were her escapes to the Spanish fishing village of Cadaqués, where she never tired of its waterfront cafés and the galleries heavily influenced by Salvador Dali.

'I recall when I was in junior school, how exciting it was to catch a train to Wimbledon and be met by Granma. We would walk home arm in arm to enjoy her freshly baked muffins and have long chats.

'I gather when she was young, she was always up for a good prank to raise a laugh.

'I learned that for one of her nursing classes, she had to demonstrate "what you see might be an illusion".

'For her presentation, which she famously turned into a prank, Margie shopped for a small tin of fish and a little can of well-known cat food, swapping the labels after steaming them off.

'With a typical Margie smirk, she placed the two cans onto the desk for all to see and explained what was in each.

'Then opening the can with the cat food label, using a teaspoon she boldly devoured a mouthful, much to the loud disgust of her classmates.

'Offering one of her classmates seated in the front a taste only caused an even greater ruckus!

'Up there in heaven, I am sure Margie is loving it, hearing all these stories about her,' Emma adds, as the laughter swells.

Emma taps open the last page and briefly pauses.

'Each of us will have our own very special memories of her that I'm sure we will enjoy retelling down the years.

'Amongst my fondest are her mentoring and inspiring me as I grew up, especially during my teenage years. I am so much the richer for the privilege of having her as my Granma!'

With her emotions fast welling, Emma knows there are only two things left to say.

At this exact moment, a beam of sunlight suddenly breaks though the stained glass window, spreading an inspiring shaft of green, red and white tinted light across the lonely coffin and momentarily highlighting Emma's proud, loving face.

'Many might be asking ourselves at this moment what would we say to her if she was here?

'I would say … Granma, as you take your final bow, we are blessed with the joy you have brought into our lives and the wonderful legacy of your "strokes", which we will always cherish.

'As your proud granddaughter I pray that I can make a difference like you have done, giving so much to your family and the wider community through your astonishing life!'

As a subtle hum of approval sweeps the church, Emma pauses by the coffin as she returns to her pew, briefly placing a hand on it, saying under her breath, 'God speed Granma … Bon Voyage.'

As St Mary's organ pumps out the first rousing chords of "Amazing Grace", six pallbearers step forward ready to shoulder the coffin down the aisle to the blue exit doors.

Emotionally exhausted, Emma is welcomed to her seat by her proud mother's loving smile and is comforted by her hand on her shoulder as those around her convey unspoken affirmations.

With her face buried in Granma's hankie, from the corner of a tear-filled eye she glimpses the shadow of the flag draped coffin passing, causing her to look up, and seeing the stark whiteness of the lilies, knowing this is the last time she will ever be this close to her.

As the coffin passes, mourners immersed deep in their own thoughts begin to ease themselves from the pews.

Outside, they are welcomed by the warming rays of the midday sun that causes wisps of steam to rise from the wet pavement whilst above a bell peals soulfully in the belfry.

Leaving the church, Emma's grieving mother places an arm around her daughter's slender shoulders proudly saying, 'Well done, darling, you have done us all proud.'

Little does Emma know that in the year ahead, the life they had all just celebrated would be reopened with startling new revelations.

4. Sniff of Money

Seated in a waiting room in London's Belgravia business district, dressed in a dark double-breasted blazer and slacks, Emilio Bestillo seemed anxious as he nervously fidgeted with the gold latch on his satchel.

Waiting for Mr Dias to see him, Emilio ran through once more the type of loan he sought, ostensibly to finance an import opportunity he wanted to start up.

Finally, the Banco Totta manager's door opened and out stepped the smiling, dapperly dressed young Lisbon banker, who ushered him into his timber panelled, but sparsely furnished office containing a desk, two visitor chairs and a large walnut filing cabinet.

Exchanging opening pleasantries, Mr Dias soon asked Emilio what his business might be.

'Over decades your bank has been held in the highest esteem by my Oporto family,' Emilio apprehensively began.

'Since arriving in London to find additional markets for my family's wines, I have identified a profitable business opportunity that I would very much like to develop, but I need the funds to do it,' Emilio explained.

'What is the opportunity?' Mr Dias enquired.

'Importing cork products and olives from Portugal. To set it up I will need an injection of capital. I am here to enquire how I might obtain a loan from Banco Totta.'

'Mr Bestillo I can see that you have grown your family's business very substantially since your arrival,' said Mr Dias glancing at the file on his desk.

'Head Office has suggested I should make every endeavour to assist, however our lending requirements for your needs are clearly laid down.

'For a loan of fifteen million escudos, that you say you need, the bank would seek security or require a Bestillo Nacional director to guarantee it.'

Realising that obtaining the loan from the bank on these conditions would not keep his secret from his family, Emilio knew he was stumped.

'Mr Dias, thank you for that information. I will discuss it with my family and come back to you.'

Stepping out onto Sloane Street, Emilio's head was spinning.

Suddenly for the first time in his life, he had no-one to turn to.

In a confused state he walked off, feeling what he needed was a stiff whisky and a cigarette to calm his nerves and think things over.

Further down Sloane Street he noticed a quiet little tavern whose ground level windows and doors were protected by a wall of sandbags.

Breasting the bar, he was greeted by a cheerful barmaid who, seeing his worried face, quickly summed him up.

'Dearie, you look like you've just been run over by a bus,' she said pouring out a shot and sliding it over to him.

'I'm sorry if I look that awful,' Emilio replied. 'I admit you are right. I've just had a huge shock and I don't know what I should do.'

Realising her new customer probably needed time to reflect, she moved away to strike up a conversation with two elderly men further down the bar who seemed keen to catch her attention.

Meanwhile, drawing on his cigarette, Emilio was allowing the whisky and smoke to soothe his nerves.

He savoured the smooth malt gliding over his taste buds, igniting a warm inner glow.

Swirling through his mind was the dreaded reality that somehow he had to come up with the escudos by next April.

He knew he didn't possess the courage to face his parents with the truth, knowing he would be disgraced and never be able to return to Oporto.

Close to lunch time, Emilio looked up to find the smiling barmaid had returned and was poised to ask if he was ready for another.

'Have you had time to decide if you are going to tell me about whatever it was that has shocked you so?' she enquired, handing him his change.

Before his glass was empty, Emilio was spilling it out.

'I got a girl pregnant back in Portugal and now her father is chasing me for a fortune claiming if I don't pay he will go public, which would end my career in the family business and force me to leave town.'

Having heard it all before, the smiling barmaid, whom Emilio now knew as Raelene, made a suggestion.

'Love, if you don't want to marry her, then your problem isn't the girl but rather that your reputation is about to go up in smoke, unless you can solve the money problem.

'My regulars here would say you have three options … either beg, borrow or steal the money.'

Ordering another whisky, this time a double shot, the words "beg, borrow or steal" kept swirling around Emilio's slightly tipsy head.

He told himself that he had given ample thought to begging and had just tried borrowing.

Neither would prevent the scandal getting out.

If he were to take Raelene's advice, it left only the third option, but if he did decide to do that, from whom and how?

Having spent more time "peeling the onion" on the stealing option, his mind suddenly clicked into overdrive when he considered the possibility of somehow getting his hands on a little of the wealth Margie's uncle held in Australia.

But how could he do this?

It was then he recalled the part-time work he had done with the Santo Bank in Lisbon, where he was trained to handle large, complex international money transfers.

Soon all those banking procedures came flooding back, suddenly providing him with the solution.

5. Sydney, 1869

High on the cool Southern Highlands west of Sydney Town lie the lush, rolling hills and pastures of the sleepy hamlet of Bowral.

Since Australia's colonisation in 1788, successful Sydney families profiting from the rapidly expanding gold-rush colony have made their escapes here from harbour town's oppressive summer humidity.

None more so than Mr Gregory Garland Esquire, who in 1869 arrived from Liverpool with his new wife to the promise of land and an opportunity to begin an entrepreneurial business with unbridled opportunities.

Their journey aboard one the world's fastest clipper ships was only just tolerable. Despite completing the arduous 12,600-mile voyage in near record time, Mrs Garland found the passage unsettling.

Their ship, the *Marco Polo*, was one of a new breed of clippers constructed to bring well-heeled migrants to the post convict colony.

En route, the Garlands and fellow first class passengers enjoyed dining at the Captain's table, where they appreciated the lavish silver service, fine wines and convivial company.

After dinner, the Captain would thrill them with tales of his life on the high seas that helped erase some of the monotony of the long days.

Gregory Garland, recently married for a third time to the young and attractive Miss Sophie Bates, was drawn to Sydney as it offered him a fresh start and warmer climes for his wife's respiratory condition.

Having heard the availability of decent wine in the fledgling colony was problematic, Gregory had stored in the ship's holds a substantial supply of his favourite French wines.

His selection had been influenced by Emperor Napoleon III's strong preference for a select group of Bordeaux red wines including his favourite, Château Latour.

Soon after arriving and finding accommodation, Gregory

presented his wife and his credentials to the NSW Governor, Lord Somerset Lowry-Corry.

He spared not a minute thereafter to create a powerful circle of government and business contacts, which he hoped would further his personal plans for success.

* * *

By the early 1870s, Sydney Town was abuzz with the prospect of an invitation to dinner with the promise of lashings of Bordeaux wine at the Garlands' newly completed Elizabeth Bay Georgian residence, complete with its handsome stables, servants' quarters and uninterrupted views to Sydney Harbour.

Heads of government, politicians and businessmen snapped up any opportunity to enjoy Gregory's top shelf French brandies and wines from a seemingly bottomless cellar. Gregory's wines were a far cry from the rough local reds and rum that were the town's only other tipple.

Soon the Garlands' new circle of friends began procuring a bottle or two from his growing cellar on the quiet, to grace their own dinner tables, ever willing to shell out a sovereign or more for France's finest.

From these early sales, Garland Trading was established, soon after moving to a small warehouse in Pyrmont beside Sydney's busy docks. Later, Gregory opened a highly successful wine bar in the centre of town.

In January 1875, the Garlands enjoyed their first summer holiday break staying with friends on the cool Southern Highlands near Moss Vale and quickly fell in love with the region.

Secreted in their first class carriage heading back to Sydney on the train, Gregory's attention was drawn to an advertisement in the *Burrawang Times* offering a splendid 4,200-acre riverside estate, a little way out of Bowral.

Deciding to inspect the property, the couple quickly fell in love with its lush green pastures, scenic rolling hills and the meandering Wingecarribee River running through it, guarded by stands of towering red gums.

They were told that in autumn well-fattened Muscovy ducks could be seen on the river feeding on frogs and flies amongst the reeds.

Sophie pleaded with Gregory, 'I'm smitten with all this beauty which we both have come to adore. Darling, this is where I want us to create a retreat where our children will grow up and call home.'

In one of those spontaneous moments in life, the Garlands were certain this was where they would establish their weekend escape.

They named the property Latour Park, after Gregory's favourite Bordeaux wine, and set about constructing a stately country house with substantial quarters, barns and stables. Over the next decade its pastures were turned into some of the finest grazing land on the Southern Highlands.

It was here that their children, Frank William and Annabelle Grace, spent many happy years bonding with country life.

* * *

Growing into a strapping teenager, Frank was sent to board at Parramatta's prestigious King's School. On Sundays he would sometimes enjoy excursions to Lake Parramatta Reserve, where he and his friends would rent yachts and stage impromptu races.

On one of those outings in 1892, the King's boys were quick to notice a group of pretty students from the exclusive eastern suburbs Ascham Girls School across the lake.

In particular, Frank was drawn to a very attractive young lady decked in her Sunday best, who he learned was Miss Mildred Burns. Steering his yacht across to her side of the lake, he readily engaged her in some light banter before she cheerfully accepted his invitation to sail across the lake to the kiosk for an ice cream.

Having enjoyed their cones lounging on the grass beneath the overhanging willows, he sailed Miss Burns back to her group and after they had exchanged boarding house addresses, they went their separate ways.

Over the next weeks leading to months, they sent each other increasingly longer letters sharing their news, their dreams and, in time, their enduring love for each other.

During the summer holidays, Mildred became a very welcome house guest at Latour Park.

* * *

At Latour Park, shooting parties were always a gentlemen's affair with Gregory and his invited guests walking the hills and banks of the river trying to bag a plump duck or two for the evening's meal.

Before migrating, Gregory had nearly been killed in a gun accident in England. Subsequently at Latour Park he had always insisted that the most proper safety protocols be observed.

At the conclusion of one shoot, a distracted guest unintentionally had left his loaded, unbroken shotgun propped up against a stable doorframe, something Gregory would never tolerate.

Before dinner that day as the guests were assembled on the verandah sipping Spanish Fino and watching the sun slowly dip behind the verdant green hills, they were shaken by the unexpected sound of two loud blasts coming from the stables that shattered the otherwise tranquil evening.

Rushing to investigate, the guests were confronted to see Gregory in a highly agitated state holding the shotgun, with wisps of smoke rising from its twin barrels.

Suffice to say, Gregory uttered a few choice words for the benefit of the gun's highly embarrassed user.

Noting how his father had handled the matter, Frank decided in future he would make team safety one of his most important values.

*   *   *

When he finished school in 1893, Frank entered the family business as a lowly dogsbody at its Pyrmont warehouse, because his father felt his son needed to have a few acquired 'airs and graces' knocked out of him.

Gregory also wanted his son to learn the ropes from the shop floor up to ensure he gained the respect of the company's staff, so that one day they would deem him worthy to take the reins.

When the Garlands remained in Sydney over weekends, Gregory and Sophie often attended Royal Randwick, which was considered the jewel in the crown of the colony's emerging thoroughbred racing scene.

Increasingly, these occasions provided the Garlands with a grand opportunity to socialise and mingle with Sydney's captains of industry and heads of government, which Gregory used to improve his trading company's growing customer base.

Sophie became widely respected for her Victorian-era fashion sense featuring the latest narrow cut dresses, flounced underskirts finished with an exuberance of highly coloured bustles.

In the exclusive Members' enclosure, Gregory was seen as a snappy dresser, outfitted in bespoke university style wide lapel double-breasted morning coats, collared shirts and perfectly knotted Windsor ties.

Between races, viewed from the comfort of the Garland's St Leger's Stakes' private box, guests would be entertained in the Members' bar and the ladies' lounge.

By the early 1880s Gregory had become obsessed with breeding thoroughbred horses, which led him on a passionate journey towards the winner's circle.

Within a decade, Latour Park had built a name as a premier racing stud that reached a new high in 1895, when one of its sires, Havoc, won Royal Randwick's prestigious AJC Plate.

*　*　*

Through the 1890s the fledgling colony's fortunes were being fully tested when a severe drought gripped the country.

Sheep farmers threw their hands in the air in frustration at the crash in the price of wool, land values crumbled and numerous banks collapsed, leading to widespread unemployment that forced tens of thousands of people from their homes onto the streets.

However, the river at Latour Park kept flowing and the little rain that fell kept the grass in pastures going to feed the cattle.

Prices for Southern Highlands beef remained high, causing the Garlands to give thanks they had chosen a drought-resistant property.

*　*　*

Having completed his apprenticeship on the shop floor and moved through the ranks, in 1897 Frank Garland was appointed a supervisor, which meant with the small increase to his annual salary he could splash out more on Mildred.

Returning from an arduous buying trip to Europe in late 1897, one of the first things he did was call on Mildred's father, Mr Burns, whereupon he asked for his daughter's hand in marriage, which was duly granted.

Then just twelve months before the turn of the century, Gregory Garland succumbed to a severe bout of gout that was followed by further complications, which in a short time led to his unexpected demise.

His death saw Frank take over the business, together with his father's substantial share investments and Latour Park.

Four years later in 1903, Frank's wife Mildred, gave birth to a son, Charles, and two years later his sister, Alice arrived.

* * *

By 1913, the political scene in Europe was spiralling into chaos and heading towards the Great War, which was declared on 4th August in 1914.

Australia's Prime Minister, Mr Andrew Fisher, immediately promised the Motherland his country's total support, 'To our last man and our last shilling'.

Responding to the government's loud appeals for men to join up, Frank Garland was amongst some of the first to enlist at the Sydney Showgrounds.

His application to the army corps cited amongst his many qualities his general fitness and superior accuracy with a gun.

He didn't seem fazed that his first weekly pay packet of a mere thirty shillings was a far cry from the thousands of pounds a year he had been paid at Garland Trading.

After training as a private in the 8th Battalion, his commanding officer recognised his leadership qualities and promoted Frank to Second Lieutenant.

The following year his Battalion was shipped off to Egypt where it underwent intensive training. Then in April 1915 it was sent into action at Gallipoli, when Australia joined forces with New Zealand to storm Anzac Cove as part of Churchill's doomed plan to secure the Peninsula for the Allied forces.

What was left of Frank's Battalion after being withdrawn from

Sydney, 1869

Gallipoli was redeployed after a break in Egypt to the bloody Western Front, entering action at the 1916 Battle of Fromelles.

In these two blood-spattered theatres, Frank saw first hand how pompous "blue blood" British Generals, living on past glories, employing hopelessly out-of-date Boer War strategies kept issuing futile orders for our troops to 'push forward regardless', irrespective of the serious losses incurred.

After the sickening sight of so many of his close mates killed for no gain because of the insane orders, Frank never forgot his father's motto to always look after your men first.

The lack of trust he and his men now held for their British Generals was almost beyond words.

* * *

When Frank was repatriated home from France in 1917, one of the first things he wanted to do was have a heart-to-heart discussion with his son about his alarming experiences at Anzac Cove and the Western Front.

He had thought long and hard why he felt compelled to relate such horrors and what it might do to his son's impressionable mind.

Driving him was the knowledge that his father would have done the same with him.

The message he wanted to pass on to his son was about trust and about justice.

He was aware how Australian troops had proudly enlisted to serve the Empire and mother country in its hour of need.

The Government and the people of Australia had placed their unquestioning trust in Britain and its Generals in the field to do the right thing by their sons being sent to fight for them. But for Frank and his men, by the time they reached Fromelles, their trust in British Generals had been trashed after huge injustices had been perpetrated.

* * *

The opportunity to have his heart-to-heart came when the family returned to Latour Park, whereupon Frank took 14-year-old Charles out for a long walk around the boundary fences.

After reaching a grassy rise overlooking the tranquil river, the pair paused to gaze across the picturesque estate.

Frank quietly began his story.

'Charles, we discovered after we began fighting the Turks from our trenches at Gallipoli that the British General in command of the Mediterranean Expeditionary Forces, a chap called Sir Ian Hamilton, was actually conducting the campaign from the comfort of his battleship steaming a good distance off the coast to avoid the Turks' shells.

'Time and time again he would issue orders for us to go over the trenches to attack the enemy, sometimes only with bayonets, whereupon we ran directly into their withering machine guns.

'For those few of us who survived the carnage at Anzac Cove, worse was to follow when we were redeployed to the Western Front in France the following year for the Battle of Fromelles.'

'Father, were the conditions there better or worse than Gallipoli?' Charles asked.

'Initially better, then much worse. When we arrived at the front, we were billeted for several days in a delightful French village a few miles from the trenches,' said Frank.

'Talking to other soldiers there in the safety of the village café, we discovered that the British Generals issuing orders were safely ensconced in sheer luxury in Chateaux well behind the lines.

'When we finally got the call to move up to the line to fight, we were greeted by muddy, waterlogged trenches that stank of the dead. Soon after our General ordered wave after wave of us to go up and over the trenches into the face of the Germans' machine gun firewalls, resulting in catastrophic loss of lives.

'Charles, I will be forever haunted by that frightful first day's charge when we "attacked at all costs".

'I witnessed hundreds of my men being tragically cut down. That charge has since been described as the "worst twenty-four hours in our country's military history".

Sydney, 1869

'Despite now being home amongst my family, those memories will remain with me till I die.

'By the end of our time there, thousands of Australians like me realised the British Generals were guilty of serious war crimes, including sloppy planning, making wrong assumptions and employing hopelessly outdated strategies.

'What was even worse, they rationalized their many battle failures to their superiors so as to save their own necks.'

Charles asked sensitively, 'Dad, beyond the awful bloodshed you have described, did you ever get to make any friends over there?'

'Well, of course I did', Frank replied. 'One I will never forget was a fine, young Scotch College lad from Melbourne, Sergeant Alan Bishop. Our friendship grew out of fighting beside each other, huddled in the stinking trenches dug into the ridges at Gallipoli, and we went on to France to fight together.

'In that first attack at Fromelles, Bishop was caught by cross fire in No-Mans Land and was seriously injured when a bullet went through his leg. He lay in agony almost bleeding to death, waiting for the cover of night to try and crawl back to our trenches.'

When the pair reached the top of the next grassy rise Frank hesitated, slightly out of breath. He also needed to brush a tear from his eye, as the horrible memories of that bloody encounter flooded back. After a pause, he continued in a wavering voice.

'Just as Bishop was crawling back, a shell came over and exploded above him breaking his arm and taking out an eye.

'Despite his loss of blood and the agonizing pain, he somehow found the strength to hang on until he was stretchered the last dozen yards back to the trench then taken off to a field station. Sadly he was eventually repatriated to England, where he died several months later. His mother had rushed from Melbourne to be at his side.'

Walking in step with his heavy-hearted father, Charles looked into his tanned, prematurely aged face that seemed dog-tired, noticing the deep soulful eyes of a man who had been to hell and back.

As they proceeded in silence down the slope towards the homestead, Charles took in the property spread before him, and saw it with a new perspective.

He realised the good life he had been fortunate enough to be born into was the result of generations of Garland hard work and toil, and that he now wanted to ensure it would continue for later generations.

Quietly absorbing the harrowing war stories he had just listened to, little did he realise that some twenty years later they would significantly shape his values and ultimate destiny.

6. Bowral, 1920s

On the eve of the 1927 Berrima District cricket final, Charles told his father he was going to try out a new delivery he had developed at practice in the nets that evening to see how Moss Vale's top batsmen handled it.

Having read how an unknown Bowral seventeen-year-old the week before had scored a double century that helped his team secure a berth in the final against Moss Vale, Charles' competitive streak saw him set about trying to bring the lad's scoring spree to an end.

'How will your deliveries outwit him?' Frank enquired.

'I've developed a late swinging delivery that I hope will entice their new wonder boy to edge a catch to slips,' Charles explained.

*　*　*

In the weekend's hard fought final, watched by his family, Charles energetically bowled two overs of his new "swingers" to the seventeen-year-old who was batting at number four.

But the boy from Bowral stepped masterly inside Charles' menacing balls, guiding them time and again to the boundary leading to an unbeaten century.

Beer in hand after Bowral took out the premiership, Charles went up and introduced himself to Don Bradman saying, 'That was a fine knock!'

Recounting the match across the froth of their well-earned beers, Don humbly admitted Charles' swingers did bother him initially.

'Towards the end of your second over you appeared a little frustrated, so I stepped back knocking your loose ones to the boundary, knowing you would try something different.'

Asked how he had mastered his backward sweeps, Don admitted, 'It comes from many hours at home using a cricket stump to repeatedly hit a golf ball back against a corrugated iron water tank.

'Also I've discovered on coir matting wickets like the one we played on today, the balls rise more sharply, so by stepping back and glancing it behind me, I'm able to help myself to easy runs.'

This caused the pair to share a good laugh and toast each other. Before leaving the grounds they agreed to watch the next Sheffield Shield game in Sydney together, marking the beginning of a lifelong friendship.

Charles learnt an important lesson from his new friend Don, who went on to become the world's greatest ever batsman, that the first to give in when facing adversity never wins.

*   *   *

Before graduating from school in 1921, Charles considered several career options but his father had other plans.

'Your mother and I are mindful that we would like you to join the family company at some future date. In the meantime, we believe you should first obtain a university degree followed by work with other firms, that will help broaden your horizons.'

Wanting to please his parents, Charles took up engineering at University of Sydney, securing for himself between semesters an excellent part-time junior stockbroker's assistant clerk job.

At university he volunteered for the Sydney University Regiment, where, after completing officer training, he rose to the rank of Warrant Officer. On weekends in summer, he bowled for Moss Vale but with ever diminishing success.

This caused him to realise his talents as a bowler were limited, however his competitive streak left him still desperate to prove he was worthy of heading up Garland Trading.

Completing his degree in 1928, Charles returned to stockbroking as a senior clerk, cutting his teeth researching investment opportunities in blue chip companies such as Adelaide Steamship, BHP and the Bank of New South Wales.

There he watched in awe how his firm's clients' wealth had soared since the deregulation of gold in 1925. By the late 1920s the stock market boom saw share prices reach unprecedented peaks.

Further surges in the stock market were helped by Prime Minister Stanley Bruce sprouting, 'Men, money and markets', in an ambitious attempt to expand the country's population and economic potential through massive government investment.

Australia's post Great War wealth was being driven off the back of a population explosion, increased exports from the land and a surge in local manufacturing.

The growth was creating waves of high net worth Australians like the Garlands that brought about the start of a national wealth industry, the likes of which had never been seen in this country.

During this period, Frank and Mildred revised their investment strategies, deciding that upon their deaths, their share portfolio and Garland Trading assets would go to Charles, and the ownership of Latour Park and a share of dividends from Garland Trading would go to Alice.

*   *   *

One wealth management company that rode this emerging opportunity to its fullest was the Australasian Trustee Company, established in 1879, whose offices were situated in Pitt Street, Sydney, then regarded as the centre of business in NSW.

Considered by those in the know in the mid-1920s as the country's third largest trustee company, it controlled trust portfolios worth more than £30 million.

Its chairman was the highly respected Sir Kenneth Codrington, a distinguished Great War soldier, who was instrumental in significantly expanding the firm's investment and trustee activities.

Clients like the Garlands turned to well-regarded trustee companies like Sir Kenneth's to manage their many assets, which, usually upon death, would be bequeathed to their families.

As a trusted friend of the late Mr Gregory Garland, Sir Kenneth had been instrumental in setting up the Garland estate and its various investments, including Latour Park, a share portfolio and the Garland Trading company holdings.

Some 25 years later it was considered only appropriate that Frank and Mildred should continue to entrust Sir Kenneth's company to continue as their estate trustees.

In 1922, Australia's fifth edition of *Who's Who* listed Sir Kenneth Thomas Codrington KBE 1920: Born 1863 Wimbledon UK, Chairman Australasian Trustee Company 1918–1922, Ex-director

National Bank, Life Governor St Vincent's Hospital Sydney, Patron Bowral Cricket Club, The King's School, Sydney Racing Club, Royal Sydney Yacht Squadron, Australian Club, Recreation: horseracing, yachting and reading.

*　*　*

The Australasian Trustee Company's Board, comprising seven esteemed high profile directors, usually met on the second Tuesday each month at 10am.

The general manager, Mr M.C. Smithers, administered the meeting agenda, which was rarely, if ever altered.

Morning tea was always taken at 11.15am, served with Sir Kenneth's favourite hot scones, jam and cream.

With lunch booked at Sir Kenneth's Australian Club on Macquarie Street, woebetide anyone who caused the meeting to run more than a minute past 1 pm.

At his club, Sir Kenneth never failed to gaze out the windows to the harbour where his beloved racing yacht was moored at the Royal Sydney Yacht Squadron ready for the next afternoon's racing.

Around the club and his business circles he was considered an absolute gentleman, but on the harbour, with a tiller in hand and a boat race to win, Sir Kenneth never took any prisoners.

It was over lunch that the Board's real business of the day got underway, usually with potential high worth clients being invited to imbibe and smoke cigars. Guests from out of town were usually offered accommodation of the highest order upstairs.

In the privacy of smoke-filled dining rooms, deals were discreetly done and capital raised from guests with excess funds to invest.

Few Sydney citizens of the day had any idea of the rarefied atmosphere in which Sir Kenneth moved or the revered business establishment he had built into a highly respected and trusted name, run essentially as an "old boys' club".

Trustee companies of the day in Australia always appointed directors who were bastions of the business world to sit on their boards, so as to create an air of absolute respectability, and to support their "brand".

When Sir Kenneth attended his comfortably appointed chairman's chambers he usually only had contact with his general manager, Mr Smithers.

His inbound phone calls were scrutinized, his mail was pre-sorted and mundane client matters or problems were always farmed out to senior officers, which ensured Sir Kenneth didn't have to ever deal with any unpleasant situations or make difficult decisions.

*   *   *

Sir Kenneth always made time for the Garland family though, so in 1926 he warmly welcomed Frank Garland to his office where they, together with Mr Smithers, discussed Frank's wish to split his assets including Latour Park, the trading company and his share portfolio.

'Then it is your intention that your entire shareholdings in Broken Hill and Adelaide Steamship will go to Charles?' Mr Smithers confirmed.

'Absolutely,' answered Frank.

Mr Smithers advised that the new Will could be drawn up and ready to sign in a week's time.

*   *   *

Australia's 1920s boom time lasted until the Wall Street stock market crash of October 1929, which spread quickly into a worldwide depression, sweeping through Australia, causing untold business failures and massive unemployment.

Charles' stockbroking company was all but wiped out in the crash, along with most of the jobs there, including his own, leaving him no option but to go cap in hand to his father asking for a position at Garland Trading.

Assigned in early 1930 to its distribution operations, Charles put his shoulder to the wheel helping the firm weather the recession by reducing costs and creating a more efficient operating base that helped Garland Trading become financially stronger and a more vibrant business when the economy improved.

The strain of the recession took a serious toll on Frank, who, to escape, turned to over-imbibing the firm's liquor, which served to bring on crippling arthritis and cause his eyesight to fail.

Despite his worsening condition, Frank was content that the value of his share investments in Broken Hill and Adelaide Steamship had increased past the £375,000 mark.

By late 1936, with Frank's eyesight worsening, Mildred was left with no option but to drive Frank to work and on weekends down to their Bowral property.

These trips were progressively turning Mildred into a nervous wreck, as her vision was also growing weaker with her passing years.

7. The Bargo River, 1937

It was soon after eleven o'clock on a wet mid-winter's evening at Latour Park that the shrill sound of the phone roused the Garlands' housekeeper, Mrs Yeoman, from a fitful nap.

Frank and Mildred Garland were well overdue for dinner and Charles and Alice were on the Hume Highway searching for them.

The call from Charles informed her they had reached Narellan, but so far had found no sign of their parents' car.

'Is there any update from the police?' Charles asked hopefully.

'I haven't heard back from them, so I expect they are still combing the highway and haven't found anything serious,' Mrs Yeoman replied.

With the mystery of the Garlands' whereabouts deepening by the minute, Mrs Yeoman continued her vigil, topping up the kettle simmering away on the stove with the fading hope she would soon be serving the Garlands welcoming cups of tea and even dinner.

Meanwhile Charles and Alice were still on the Hume Highway, now well south of Narellan. As they headed towards Latour Park in the thickening fog, they used their torches to search on both sides of the road for any sign of their father's car.

Mile upon mile so far had only revealed endless black, damp pastures, dripping bushes and drenched trees.

Charles began to contemplate what other possibilities might have caused them to be so late. He suggested, 'Do you think they could have booked into a hotel instead of driving through this infernal fog?'

'Possibly,' Alice answered.

'But mother would have surely phoned Mrs Yeoman so she wouldn't worry.'

With the thickening fog further hampering the search, worrying thoughts continued to swirl through their minds. In silence they listened to the slap, slap of the wipers sweeping away millions of micro droplets from the windscreen, as they peered anxiously into the whiteout.

* * *

In Sydney earlier that afternoon, as a cold front swept in from the south, Mildred uneasily took the wheel of Frank's gleaming, black six-cylinder Siddeley Special for the drive to Latour Park, knowing it might be fraught.

Shortly after crossing the Nepean River as the rain eased, they encountered the first wisps of a heavy fog rolling down from the Southern Highlands.

Inside the next few miles their visibility was reduced to a few hundred yards, causing Mildred to slow, much to Frank's annoyance, as he was eager to reach the property before darkness.

*   *   *

At Latour Park, which had been engulfed in fog for some hours, Mrs Yeoman had prepared for their arrival and had put a leg of roast lamb in the oven for dinner, which was always served at seven.

As the grandfather clock in the hall chimed seven, with the fog becoming noticeably thicker and no word from the Garlands, Mrs Yeoman felt the first pangs of unease.

An hour later as she peered out into an even thicker fog swirling through the blackened trees lining the drive, she decided as it was well past their arrival time, she should check in with Charles in Sydney.

Knowing nothing, he asked her to call the Moss Vale police.

'Could you ask them to send a car down the Hume Highway to see if father's car might have possibly had a flat tyre or broken down?'

Knowing his mother's dislike of driving in the dark especially in winter, he was concerned and phoned his sister Alice Lockwood, to explain the situation.

'If the police can't find any sign of them, I think I will drive down to Latour Park tonight as they could be stranded somewhere by the road.'

Realising her parents should have arrived by now, she said she would go with him.

An hour later they met in Darlinghurst, where Alice left her car.

Meanwhile Mrs Yeoman, having followed up with the police and told they had no further news, decided to tune into the ten o'clock ABC radio news.

Other than a local fog warning, usual political goings-on and a football match result, the bulletin made no mention of any car accidents on the Highlands.

Despite feeling comforted that Charles and Alice were well on their way and that the police would soon be in touch, she could not, however, dispel the disquieting feeling that she was in for a long and difficult night.

The sound of the front door bell ringing stirred Mrs Yeoman from a fitful catnap. Standing there on the doorstep were two police officers in glistening wet coats beneath the yellowish porch light, who told her their search along twenty miles of the Hume Highway had produced no sign of the Garlands.

Returning to the warmth of her kitchen, Mrs Yeoman, feeling more worried than ever, decided to phone the Campbelltown Hospital to ask if anyone by the name of Garland had been admitted.

When the answer came back "no-one with that name", her fear that something awful might have happened out on the road was running into the red zone.

* * *

Charles usually allowed around two hours to make the drive from Double Bay to Latour Park, but this evening's slow and increasingly stressful drive was running into the fourth hour.

As his car began taking a sweeping, downhill curve, his headlights briefly picked out the Bargo River Bridge sign, which seconds later whizzed past and disappeared into the dark.

Seeing the very familiar white painted wooden bridge approaching, Alice eased back into her seat for a moment, briefly closing her fatigued eyes, fully intending to resume the search on the other side.

Nearly a mile beyond the bridge she suddenly blurted out, 'Damn, damn!'

Her sudden outburst caused Charles to lift his foot off the accelerator.

'I accidentally dozed off back there at the bridge and may have missed something!'

Despite his stress levels heading north, Charles hid his reaction, slowing down until he found a suitable spot to turn around.

Driving back, they flashed their torches into the dense scrubby bush finding nothing, which in one way was a relief for Alice.

Approaching the bridge, Charles decided to make a U-turn on the other side.

As his car swung through the turn, Alice's sharp eyes followed the arc of the headlight beams as they attempted to penetrate the whiteout.

Suddenly just before the white bridge railings reappeared, she spotted several broken saplings in the gloom that led away from the road towards the river.

'Oh God, did you see that?' she shouted. 'There's broken bushes by the roadside.'

'Heavens!' cried Charles. 'You're right.'

Reversing back up the road, he swung his headlights to follow the line of broken bushes.

'Those seem like tyre tracks,' he said in an agitated voice.

'They do,' said Alice.

'A vehicle seems to have driven off the road, flattening the undergrowth.'

'I'm praying it wasn't Mum and Dad's,' she added.

Scrambling from the car, searching the undergrowth with their torches, they began to follow the tyre marks, stepping over more broken ferns that led towards the river's slippery embankment.

Standing at its top, a dull roar filled their ears rising from fifty feet below, where the Bargo River was in flood as they peered expectantly into the fog.

Alice's sharp eyes saw something, which she quickly pointed out.

'Can you see that? It looks like a weak red light down there in the water.'

With stomachs churning, they slithered down the scrubby bank as best as they could, grabbing saplings to stop them from losing their footing.

Finally reaching the riverbank, their torches made out in mid-river what looked like a partly submerged car.

On closer inspection Charles could see the caved-in roof, the smashed front windscreen and a partially submerged tail-light burning red.

There was no sign of a living soul.

Following a quick check along the bank for its occupants, Charles removed his jacket and trousers then waded out to the car through the fast flowing river.

Approaching the vehicle, he soon recognised it as his father's and in the strong river flow he was almost swept off his feet, but he saved himself by reaching out and grasping the car's broken windscreen post, which badly cut his hand.

Using his torch he gazed inside, discovering to his horror the shocking sight of his mother's lifeless body slumped over the bent steering wheel, her eyes wide open and bloodied face partially submerged after smashing into the windscreen.

Alongside, his father's body was doubled forward, his arms outstretched as if he was trying to fend something off, half floating in the swirling water.

For a few disbelieving moments Charles thought what he was seeing couldn't be real.

But the freezing water soon brought him back to his senses and he knew he couldn't survive there a moment longer.

Somehow he garnered the strength to fight the rushing waters to wade back to the bank. Getting warm and dry was the furthest thing on Charles' shattered mind at that moment.

There, Alice stood ashen faced having watched her brother make his gruesome mid-river discovery.

Fearing the worst, she met him still holding his dry clothes, as he clambered from the freezing river knowing he was about to break the devastating news.

Seeing tears streaming down his sister's face, all he could blurt out was, 'It's their car … and they are both dead.'

8. Portugal, 1933

With Europe in the early 1930s still gripped by depression, Oporto's revered Bestillo wine family sent their eldest son Emilio, when he had completed his schooling, to the country's leading Universidade de Lisboa in Lisbon, to do a degree in law.

It was expected when he graduated he would become a fifth generation member to work at Bestillo Nacional, his family's successful fortified wine business, situated on the mighty Douro River.

Suave, nineteen-year-old Emilio, blessed with an athletic body, strong shoulders, narrow hips and handsome facial features with seductive, deep-set penetrating eyes and dark hair, was very much the eligible, worldly bachelor around town.

The teenager had never lived away from home, so it was agreed he would board with the Bestillos' lifelong Lisbon friends, Ricardo and Madalena Santo.

Their grand mansion, which overlooked the twin golden towers of Basilica da Estrela, was a short walk from the university and a few minutes by train to the city centre.

When he arrived in Lisbon, his hosts took him around the sights, including the mighty Ponte Twenty-Five de Abril suspension bridge spanning picturesque Rio Tajo Bay and Almada.

Emilio was awestruck when he walked through the ornate beauty of the historic Torre de Belem fort overlooking the bay's inviting blue waters, dotted with dozens of racing yachts with white sails.

During the next four years, Emilio discovered his place in the world whilst applying himself to law, cultivating a wide circle of friends before graduating in 1937 with honours.

He discovered a liking for poetry, listening to live fado guitar concerts and devouring fresh Atlantic sardines, which he often cooked for his friends using his grandmother's old recipe.

However, when it came to making a quick escudo, not all the Lisbon friends he had acquired had sound moral compasses.

* * *

Emilio's grandfather Aleixo had taken him under his wing since he was old enough to go into the vineyards to pick grapes.

Aleixo proudly mentored him about life and some of the inner workings of the family's wine business, taught him the basics of how to make port and make friends who could open doors for him later in life.

When Emilio reached his teens Aleixo's trust in him began to waver, having discovered his wallet usually left on the bedroom dresser was quite often lighter after his grandson's visits.

* * *

Living with the Santo family in Lisbon, Emilio often enjoyed a round of golf with his genial millionaire host, Mr Ricardo Espirito Santo, who was a very successful third generation banker.

With student jobs in Lisbon almost impossible to secure due to the poor economy, Mr Santo provided Emilio with a part-time job in one of his branches, enabling Emilio to fund his emerging lifestyle.

For many years Mr Santo mentored Emilio, showing him how large sums of money were moved, complex loans made and trust documents prepared.

Emilio made it his business to discover the workings behind bank transfers to Spain and beyond. He became very knowledgeable about opening new account procedures that required applicants to produce rate notices, tax assessments and driving licences to establish their identity and the various checks and balances that banks employed to protect their vast deposits.

He studied what few outside banking circles would ever know.

* * *

Whilst at Universidade de Lisboa, a young German student, Ernst Neumann, became one of Emilio's closest friends. He confided to Emilio that he expected to be conscripted into the rapidly emerging Third Reich army when he graduated.

For now though, Ernst was enjoying carefree student pastimes, such as Lisbon's cheap wine bars where he practised his English on young ladies.

At the end of their lazy, hazy, wine-fuelled student days in 1937, the pair went their separate ways but kept in touch with occasional letters.

Ernst returned to Stuttgart, where he was conscripted, whilst Emilio headed back to Oporto to enter the family business, confident he knew a lot more about playing the international money scene.

*　　*　　*

As a young graduate with the world at his feet and about to start in the family's business, he was unwilling to return to live with his parents, so Emilio's first decision was to find an apartment in town that would suit his intended lifestyle.

His first position with Bestillo Nacional was as a sales clerk in the bustling administration office, that he found rarely uplifting and sometimes boring.

To gain across the board experience he was occasionally assigned to other jobs at the winery that he mostly found insufferable.

One was at harvest time, sweeping up stem litter around the grape crushers and another was the cold, pre-dawn October starts in the vineyard, spent on his knees cutting bunches of grapes into metal boxes and lugging them to a cart at the end of the row.

On the other hand, he was a willing starter whenever the finance manager gave him assignments such as counting out money to pay the workers or suppliers. He was unaware that his grandfather always arranged for a clerk to keep a tab on the money.

Sensing some staff were jealous that one day he might become their boss, Emilio found it difficult to make close friends, except for Luzia Felloni, who soon warmed to his attention.

This vivacious girl was the only daughter of friends of the Bestillos, who lived with her family on the north side of Oporto.

In her early twenties, she was blossoming into a hardworking team member.

She and Emilio began taking lunch together, sitting out on the firm's wide balcony with scenic views of the river.

Portugal, 1933

On breezy days they enjoyed the colourful sight of taverner barges under billowing sails surging down from the vineyards, their decks stacked with barrels of wine to be unloaded at the wharves.

Increasingly, when she was chatting alone with Emilio, Luzia noticed she was blushing, such was the increasingly pleasant impact he was having upon her.

Given his position in the firm, she felt too shy to inquire too deeply into his life, but noticed he shared her love for the outdoors and was eager to hear more of her girlfriends' budding romances.

Hearing her speak almost enviously of the men entering her girlfriends' lives, Emilio realised she was yearning to fill a void in hers.

He found an opportunity presented itself when the firm invited all the Bestillo Nacional staff for drinks in the tasting room.

Towards the end of the very pleasant evening, Emilio managed to take her aside and ask if she would like to go out with him the following week.

Her delighted smile nearly knocked him off his feet.

'Oh yes,' she happily responded. 'But of course I will need to obtain my father's approval.'

She had never been out alone at night with a boy and knew her father would set some rules he would expect her to follow.

*　　*　　*

Having gained his permission which was a pleasant surprise, the wait for the following Friday kept Luzia awake at night. She went shopping in Oporto for a new dress, which heightened her excitement.

Thinking of Emilio merely holding her hand caused her to quiver. It was too much to hope that he might look romantically into her eyes. She dreamed he would sweep her into his arms and tell her he really liked her.

Then she contemplated something she had only read about, her first fleeting kiss, which for this innocent girl was almost too thrilling to anticipate.

Her girlfriends had often spoken of going to Oporto's famous live fado music venues.

When Emilio asked her if she knew a place to go, Luzia suggested the renowned Restaurante Mal Cozinhado she had heard of situated in the medieval Ribeira district, where beneath its ancient dingy stonewalls lay an authentic auditorium complete with hefty timber-beamed ceilings where fado could be enjoyed.

Having settled at their table and ordered wine, they savoured the Mal Cozinhado's sardines and then sat back to listen to the music that soon filled the packed space.

Feeling well pleased how the night was progressing, Emilio asked her permission to light a cigar.

Taking a long, deep draw, he exhaled and watched the smoke spiral towards the ceiling. Then with port in hand, he leant across their tiny table and looked deeply into her eyes before suddenly surprising her by breaking into a romantic sonnet:

> *'Yet love me-wilt thou?*
> *Open thine heart wide,*
> *And fold within,*
> *The wet wings of thy dove.'*

By the last line, he could see she was captivated and responding to his advances.

Leaning even closer he murmured with a smoky voice, 'Luzia, I want you to know the Fado is moving me in many pleasant ways. Is it doing the same for you?'

In the hazy lit basement, Luzia sensed she could see into Emilio's soul.

'It's just heavenly.' she responded breathlessly.

She sighed deeply, hoping her dream of being swept into his arms might be close.

Emilio rose from his seat as he donned his "Romeo" look.

He then took hold of her delicate hand and led her into the darkened space behind a thick masonry pillar. There he gently pulled her close, placing his hand behind her head.

The last thing Luzia sensed as she closed her eyes in anticipation was the heady scent of cigar smoke on his breath as his lips hovered above hers.

Then she felt the first magical moist warmth of his lips lightly brushing hers.

Pushing forward to accept his advances, she felt him tenderly press his lips closer to hers for their first breathtaking embrace.

Despite having longed for this moment since she was a young girl, initially she was shocked by its palpable intimacy.

His kiss sent shockwaves through her trembling body, unlike any she had ever known and to her surprise, they excited her.

Warming to his lingering embraces, she ardently returned them, sealing her lips to his.

She felt her body quiver and legs tremble as she almost lost her balance on her high heels causing her to seek his support.

With their bodies entwined her feelings were exploding like a shower of falling stars.

Sensing she was aroused, Emilio was encouraged to make his next move.

He raised his thumb to his lips, wetted its tip, and then pressed it gently to her glistening lower red lip.

Without taking her eyes off his, Luzia parted her trembling lips and took in his entire thumb, explicitly suggesting she was open for more.

Hearing the fado singer's tempo slow, they returned to their table and sat close, swamped by the delicious intimacy they had both just shared.

Luzia felt confused. On the one hand, she knew that she didn't want the evening to end, but on the other, her father's curfew had arrived and she was out of time.

She begged him to understand her situation, promising she would spend more time with him if he would agree to another outing sometime soon.

Luzia felt embarrassed about him knowing his was her first kiss but nonetheless she enjoyed recounting all the desirable feelings it had generated.

*　　*　　*

For their second date, Emilio took her to a quiet little restaurant by the river where they shared an intimate candlelit dinner with their conversation seemly picking up from where the evening at the fado had left off.

He was enjoying holding Luzia's warm hands, she could feel the heat between them building and he looked ever deeper into her sweet innocent eyes that seemed to sparkle with anticipation.

Emilio sensed she was desperate to be held and deeply kissed again but he was impatient to take her to the next stage.

At the end of dinner he suggested she might like to take a stroll with him to the park and he had in mind she might even like to see his new apartment.

Finishing their wines and paying the bill, they stepped out arm in arm into the crisp moonlit night, heading along the narrow cobbled street that wound past merchants' homes towards the park.

Beneath a streetlight he suddenly surprised her by pulling her close before he kissed her waiting lips.

With his taste still on her lips she swooned with excited delight as they walked on however now her feet were barely touching the pavement.

Reaching the park they discovered its heavy entrance gates had been locked for the night. Holding her close, Emilio suggested instead that they continue on to his apartment that he said was only two blocks away.

He hoped as he turned into his street that tonight his burning desire to seduce this innocent young girl might soon come to pass.

Arriving at his apartment in a fuzzy haze, Luzia only faintly heard his front door click behind her as he ushered her in, before he smoothly unbuttoned her coat and hung it on the hallstand.

In near darkness all he could see in the moonlight, filtering through a window and bouncing off the polished floorboards, was the slender outline of her torso and rising breasts. She could only just make out his towering silhouette and the whites of his eyes.

Breathless, he pulled her close and she felt the touch of his cool fingers lightly brush her bare arm as they travelled up to caress the soft, olive skin of her slender neck.

Placing his other arm around her, he drew her to him tightly, ensuring she could feel his rising member straining in his pants suggesting his fierce desire for her.

A further flurry of intense kisses caused her pulse to race madly, as he slowly worked her backwards towards his bedroom.

Reaching the foot of his bed she felt his fingers slip lightly beneath her blouse and for what seemed like an eternity, linger delightfully over a heaving breast.

She so wanted him to advance his caresses knowing they would fan the raging fire fast consuming her.

Impatiently, she took his hand and pressed it to her bare breast and hard nipple.

Indulging in divine feelings, her breath was taken away when she felt his other hand slip under the hem of her skirt. Soon she felt the heat radiating from his fingers as they trailed softly above her knee until they reached the skin above her stocking tops, where she felt them exquisitely caress her silky smooth upper thighs.

Barely able to breathe, she pressed upwards to receive even more of his caresses, slightly parting her legs, waiting for his fingers to finally discover and take possession of her most intimate mound.

At his behest, Luzia collapsed back onto the soft, inviting bed, to feel his firm body move up and over her.

She felt wave after wave of desire, until, feeling like a beautiful spring flower, she eagerly gave herself to him.

She let him expertly remove her finery until he had stripped her bare, and she lay nervously before his ravenous, manly gaze.

Kissed and caressed in places she had only dreamed of, she took a deep breath, awaiting him to begin his ardent lovemaking.

Luzia woke the next morning in his arms feeling pleased she was now a woman, and satisfied she had shared a bed with a man who held her tender heart in his hands.

Despite being tempted to sleep in, they showered and dressed to face the day.

Only then did Luzia begin to think about how she was going to explain to her parents why she didn't get home from dinner with him.

'Why don't you tell them you got caught up with some of your girlfriends at the restaurant, then having lost track of the hour and missing the last bus, stayed at one your friend's places for the night?' Emilio suggested.

Luzia was still on cloud nine with expectations that the close feelings they had shared would continue and grow.

Emilio suspected she might have long term thoughts of falling in love, which, until now, had not been part of his plans, despite the pleasures of the night. He wondered if this relationship was already becoming too complicated.

When she suggested they share lunch together the following Monday on the deck, he blurted out that he had a busy day planned and he was not sure if he would be able make it.

The following week, Luzia became increasingly upset that Emilio appeared to be keeping a restrained distance from her.

Her growing doubts turned into heartbreak three weeks later when she spotted him having lunch with another of the office's very attractive girls, who had recently joined the firm.

*　*　*

In the first years after Emilio and his friend Ernst Neumann finished university, their contact was sporadic, but after Ernst was called up to the German Army they corresponded more frequently.

Reading his letters caused Emilio to begin to take more than a passing interest in the rise of the Nazi movement. It seemed to Emilio it was more progressive and purposeful than the worn out politics steering Portugal towards an even deeper depression, and he had learnt that Germany's banking system was far superior. In his subsequent letters he expressed these sympathies to Ernst, who had been promoted to the rank of Hauptmann (captain) in 1939.

Unbeknown to the pair, the German postmarked letters being sorted at the Oporto post office had caught the eye of a British MI6 spy planted there to monitor communications. Their letters were being opened and details were sent to Bletchley Park in Britain to be placed on file for future reference.

*　*　*

By the summer of 1940, with the war raging in Europe, Emilio had been assigned a new sales role and was being sent on trips to Madrid, Cadiz and Gibraltar and returning with better than expected orders.

In August, with Portugal's economy headed even deeper into recession and unsold stocks of port clogging up the warehouse, Emilio's manager decided to send him to London to generate new customers.

As he boarded the Irish Limerick Steamship Company's trading vessel *SS Lanahrone* in Lisbon, bound for the neutral port of Dublin with dozens of cases of wine in the hold, Emilio thought about a rumour circulating the office that Luzia was with child.

With England beckoning and without a care in the world, it was the last thing he wanted to worry about.

*　　*　　*

As the *SS Lanahrone's* mooring lines were cast off, a list of its eighteen passengers and six crew was sent in code to Bletchley Park, to be checked thoroughly by MI6, in case any spies were on board or there were any other irregularities.

9. Bowral, June 1937

Following the gruesome discovery of their parents' wrecked car, Charles and Alice experienced the first waves of severe shock when they drove into Latour Park well past midnight.

The distressing sight of Frank and Mildred's lifeless bodies being carried on covered stretchers up to an ambulance, and the ordeal of giving statements to the police for the report to the coroner had emotionally drained them.

Mrs Yeoman gallantly tried to hide her grief but when she saw the blood-soaked handkerchief wrapped around Charles' hand, she broke into tears and rushed him to the bathroom where she cleaned and bandaged his gash.

Then over a cup of tea, Charles and Alice gave her an account of the night's tragic events before everyone wilted and decided to head to bed for what little remained of the night.

* * *

The next day when Mrs Yeoman had served a late breakfast, Charles sought solace by stealing away to the study, where he seated himself at his father's trusty desk to gather up his thoughts.

He pencilled a list of people to phone, in what he expected would be a very long and emotional morning.

Having completed calls to family friends and the manager at Garland Trading, there were still two more people to contact, a task he had little stomach for.

The first was to Messers T.J. Andrews funeral home in Bowral to make an appointment to plan arrangements. The second was to Sir Kenneth Codrington, whom he thought would most likely be at home, given it was Saturday.

His call was answered by Sir Kenneth's housekeeper who went off to fetch him.

Moments later a concerned Sir Kenneth came on the line.

'Charles, it's been quite some time since we last spoke, I trust everything is alright?'

'I'm sorry to be troubling you at this hour, but I am the bearer of some dreadfully bad news,' Charles blurted out with a lump rising in his throat that almost choked him.

'Last night, when Father and Mother were driving to Bowral for the weekend they encountered thick fog and had a terrible car crash. I am sorry to tell you they both lost their lives in the accident.

'Sir Kenneth, I am calling to ask if you could advise me what we might need to do next.'

Momentarily, Charles heard the line go quiet as Sir Kenneth began to process the appalling news.

'Charles, I'm shocked and devastated. This is absolutely tragic … I can only imagine how devastated you and Alice must be at this time.'

'Thank you for those kind thoughts,' Charles replied.

Then Sir Kenneth continued, 'Now, I don't want you to worry about any trust matters this weekend. I will have my general manager find your parents' Wills and ask him to determine what we will need to deal with first up next week.

'Also, when the funeral arrangements are known, would you let me know as I would like to pay my respects?' he asked.

* * *

Hundreds of mourners gathered in Bowral's St Jude's Church on the last Thursday of June 1937, in what the local *Southern Mail* paper reported the following week as 'the largest and most heartfelt funeral the town has ever witnessed'.

The paper reported a bevy of government ministers, racing identities, family friends, Garland Trading's staff and Sir Kenneth and his Trustee staff had filled the church.

Those who could not find a seat listened outside to the moving service through the open front doors.

Still in shock through the early part of the service, Charles tried to keep a stiff upper lip, supported by his old friend, Mary O'Connor, who sat next to him.

Charles began the eulogies by speaking eloquently from his

heart about how his father had successfully carried on the Garland traditions at the trading company, which had prospered under his astute stewardship.

He explained how Frank had selflessly served his King and country with great distinction in the Great War, surviving many dreadful battles that saw so many of his mates killed, returning home with a weary heart.

He spoke with great passion and insight about how his father had mentored him as a lad, teaching him about breeding cattle and racehorses. Under his father's tutelage he learned the secrets of the trading business and the importance of looking after staff.

He spoke of how both his father and grandfather had instilled in him a fear of failure that had created a driving passion to ensure the trading company continued to grow and prosper.

Alice paid tribute to her mother's rich life, giving warm accounts of her devotion to her children, her husband and her outstanding local community service with Bowral's Country Women's Association.

As she concluded her eulogy, she noticed many of those seated in the front pews were using hankies to dab away tears.

Outside the church when the funeral director, dressed in a sombre black topcoat and hat, set off on foot ahead of the hearses to lead the cortege up the road towards the local cemetery, there was barely a dry eye amongst hundreds of mourners quietly taking in the scene.

*   *   *

The Moss Vale coronial hearing into the accident held six months later received a police report which indicated Frank Garland's Siddeley Special, driven by Mrs Garland, was travelling at 40 miles per hour in heavy fog.

It appeared her vision may have been impaired when navigating a downhill bend just before the Bargo River Bridge. That caused the vehicle to veer off the Hume Highway and crash some fifty feet down into the swollen river.

On impact, the two occupants in the front seats had been thrown forcibly against the windscreen. They suffered fatal head injuries.

The Coroner brought down a finding of "accidental death".

*   *   *

In the months afterwards, Charles' grief saw him lose focus and become uninterested in life, feeling at times his loss was almost more than he could bear.

A few of his old friends, including Mary O'Connor, tried to buck him up but no-one could get around the barrier of self-pity he was putting up.

Alice was coping much better with the aftermath.

Seeing her brother's low state, she suggested to him that he needed to seek advice from a doctor familiar with his sort of grief.

Initially Charles angrily rejected her idea out of hand, but when Mary gave him the name of someone who might be of help, he finally relented.

Having completed a series of counselling sessions, a few months later Charles drove down to Latour Park.

From the counselling, he had mustered the courage to finally sit at his father's empty desk in the study and take a long hard look at his life and to honestly assess where he was heading.

He felt much of the family life he had known and taken for granted had suddenly been extinguished.

He admitted to himself he found it easy to map out the next stage of Garland Trading's growth, but from his counselling he realised he needed to put more time and energy into dealing with his own emotional issues by renewing old friendships and running the property until his sister felt she was ready to take it over.

His counsellor had made him aware that in recent years he had become a loner, obsessed with his work and, following his parent's death, he had reached a major fork in the road.

He had learnt he needed to give serious consideration as to what his personal direction was going to be, what his real future needs were and whether he should marry and start a family.

To date he'd never had a burning desire to settle down like his father had done when he had met his mother.

In fact Charles had always viewed himself as single and living a carefree life.

During counselling, he had delved deep into himself, becoming aware that at thirty-four, he had few close friends.

Yes, he had a few old cricket club mates and of course there was his good friend Don Bradman, along with a scattering of old school and Sydney business associates, but none he felt would understand the insecure feelings he was having.

He realised that he had not invested enough time in developing new friends as one by one the old ones had fallen by the wayside after marrying and settling down.

There were only a few women whose company he enjoyed socially and he had experienced just one serious love affair, with Mary, whom he now missed.

She had felt he was so obsessed making his mark with the trading company that it only left the crumbs for her.

It was such a pity he and Mary had split up.

He now knew he should have thought more about her needs.

*   *   *

In time he came to understand he yearned to break free from the very comfortable life he had been born into.

He wanted to escape the trading company and get away from Bowral and the Sydney scene to discover the world, see Europe, watch a Test at Lord's and visit his British ancestral roots.

He decided to book a passage to England and the most suitable berth happened to be on the P&O's newly commissioned 23,000-ton liner *SS Strathallan*, departing Sydney in May.

Charles also had his travel agent organise a pair of seats at Lord's to see the 1938 second Test match against Australia where he hoped to see Don Bradman play.

He wanted to avoid all the first class fuss and instead booked in tourist class hoping he might meet some more down-to-earth passengers, knowing they would be less concerned about which family he came from or how much money he had.

He hoped they would be more interested in simply enjoying his company, sharing a few meals and beers and having some good laughs during the six-week passage via Bombay and the Suez Canal to Southampton.

Should he get lucky and be introduced to a young woman on the ship who was not a gold-digger, then all the better.

10. London, 1938

As London shed its frosty mantle of winter, along the kerbs small piles of blackened snow were slowly melting, whilst in the parks, new green shoots signalling the arrival of spring searched for life-giving rays of warm sunlight.

At Ronald and Gertrude Swanson's Dulwich Village home, their daughters Margie, 18, and Lucy, 15, were considering how they would be spending their summer holidays.

Having finished school, energetic, bright-eyed Margie had been contemplating how she could break free from her strict parents, who didn't think she was old enough to make her own decisions.

Not even a looming threat of possible conflict in Europe was dashing Margie's desire to simply seize the day.

Hearing the phone ring in the hall, she raced downstairs to answer it and found her old school friend, Jessie Tyler, had quite an unexpected idea.

'Margie, now summer is nearly here, why don't we get out of dreary London and escape up to Scotland?

'We could catch the *Flying Scotsman* to Edinburgh then take in the Empire Exhibition in Glasgow.'

As Margie slowly processed her invitation, the more it sank in, the more she liked it.

'Jess, I'd simply adore going with you, but how in heavens am I going to convince my parents to let us go unchaperoned? And also how will you get yours to agree?'

'Simple', Jessie said, 'I'm going to tell mine that we intend to study the various Canadian, Australian and New Zealand Empire exhibits. It will be just like doing a world tour in a day.

'And I will assure them we will always be together and look out for each other,' she added.

*   *   *

Margie's mother, Gertrude, had always expected her eldest daughter would follow London society's protocols for young ladies by making her debut after leaving school.

However, Margie's maverick streak was driving her to abscond from what she considered was an absurd ritual.

Instead, she craved to discover what the real world had to offer and face the challenges out there.

The school she had attended through the late 1930s had adopted a modernistic teaching approach with its young ladies. It had instilled in Margie a desire to be more independent, more questioning and more forthright than her mother's generation ever dared to be. It required her to be her own person and less subservient.

It seemed to her that Jessie's Scotland escape idea had arrived at the right time and gave her a perfect chance to test the Swanson waters.

She thought to herself how exhilarating it might turn out to be, being whisked away on the marvellous *Flying Scotsman* for the ride of her life on the world's fastest train.

She conjured visions of visiting cities she had only read about, staying like royalty in hotels and spending long days roaming the city sights and exhibitions.

Then there would be evenings out on the town meeting people from all over the world and maybe some interesting young men too.

That evening, after Margie carefully had set the table, she wandered into the kitchen for a chat with her mother, who was busy stirring pots on the stove.

'Mother, do you think Father would ever allow Jessie and me to go on a trip to see the Empire Exhibition?'

Her mother's first reaction was to cough anxiously, and then having cleared her throat said, 'I've never heard of any such exhibition. What is it about and where is it being held?'

'Mother, it's being held in Glasgow and it starts in June,' Margie replied.

Gertrude's immediate fear was that her daughter was suddenly growing up too fast and that the very attractive eighteen-year-old might fall prey to some fast talking cad.

After allowing a few moments for her request to sink in, Margie reassured her mother how the educational side of the trip would be significant and that she and Jessie would be staying at the same place and always keep together.

Hearing this her mother softened slightly. 'Yes, it might be a good experience for you, but only if Jessie's parents approve and you can convince your father to agree.'

Having finished peeling the vegetables in record time, Margie couldn't wait to slip off and phone Jessie, who excitedly said that her parents had just given her permission to go.

*　　*　　*

That night an air of suspense hung over the Swanson dinner table, as Margie waited for the most opportune moment to ask her father.

Serving him his favourite dessert of apple pie and cream, she waited until he was about to enjoy the first spoonful before she struck.

'Father, did you know that Jessie's parents have given her permission to go to Scotland to see the Glasgow Empire Exhibition in June, but on one condition, that I'm allowed to accompany her?'

As the words "go to an exhibition in Glasgow" reached his ears, his hand holding the spoon froze in mid air.

The dining room went deathly quiet.

Looking to Gertrude for support, hoping she would also say no, he found nothing of the sort forthcoming and the look on Lucy's face told him he was the odd one out.

Knowing it was agreed, Margie's debut was postponed and her grand northern adventure would take its place.

*　　*　　*

On the morning of the girls' departure, Margie's mother took her aside to give her some last minute guidance.

'Darling, on this trip if you two do happen to meet some young men, please heed what your grandmother told me when I turned eighteen.

'She said I was allowed to kiss a boy, but I was to never allow his roving hands to touch me, because all men ever want from you is sex.'

Shocked by her mother's forthrightness, Margie nonetheless nodded and kissed her goodbye.

'Don't worry, I will behave and thanks again for allowing me go.'

Her father had reluctantly agreed to drive the girls to King's Cross Station to catch their train and dropped them outside the station's famous arched façade to find their carriage.

As the *Flying Scotsman* reached the open countryside and hit top speed, they were inspired by the sight of England's green, rolling hills and quaint villages flashing by at an astonishing one hundred miles per hour.

Arriving a little over seven hours later at Edinburgh's Waverley station, they caught a taxi to their budget bed and breakfast hotel on Portobello Beach.

Having unpacked, the excited pair plied their hospitable hosts with questions before heading off to discover the historic town.

The next day, whilst waiting to buy tickets to see Edinburgh Castle, Margie asked Jess if her mother had given her any special instructions before leaving.

'Why do you ask?' said Jessie.

'Because just before I left, mine told me I was never to let boys' hands touch my breasts or down there,' she confided, pointing to her skirt.

'Margie, if my mother said that to me I would have thrown up,' Jessie responded.

'Now I've left school, she knows that I am old enough to decide, if I met someone I really liked, how far things should go.

'All I can think of, is that your mother is frightened you could come home pregnant. Would the shame be too much for her to bear?' Jessie suggested.

*　　*　　*

On their second last night in Edinburgh, one of their old schoolgirl friends took them to one of the popular pubs.

Margie was not really a big drinker, and sat on one glass of lager for much of the night whilst enjoying the attention of several young men who were eager to buy her next drink.

She was drawn to one in particular, a very charming red-haired lad by the name of Stephen, whose brown, twinkling eyes and delightful manner caused her pulse to beat faster. He told her during the night he was an off duty soldier serving in a local unit.

Further along the packed bar, out of the corner of her eye Margie could see Jessie going glass for glass with a group of local university lads who were competing for her attention. A little later in the night, Margie spotted Jessie wobbling on her stool as she shared a fleeting kiss with one of her admirers who had excitedly thrown his arms around her neck.

Margie realised this might be the perfect moment to take her back to the hotel.

When she informed Stephen she was about to take her tipsy friend home, much to her surprise he rose and went to her on her stool and gave her an unexpected goodnight kiss.

Momentarily embarrassed when he asked if she would agree to see him the next evening, without thinking she said no, but she did give him her Dulwich Village address, hoping he would write to her.

* * *

Leaving Edinburgh they found the slow seventy-minute train ride to Glasgow was a far cry from their scintillating trip on the *Flying Scotsman*.

The pair had settled into a touring routine that saw Margie work out where to go using maps whilst Jessie dealt with buying tickets and places to eat.

On their first afternoon in Glasgow, they walked around town to get their bearings, before taking a bus to Bellahouston Park the next morning to take in the exhibition.

Whilst waiting in the queue to buy admission tickets, they got their first awe-inspiring sight of the 174-acre fair.

Passing through the gates that would welcome twelve million visitors over the next six months, they were both taken aback by the amazing Tower of the Empire.

Deciding to do their own thing for a few hours, Jessie wandered off to see the life-sized replica of a Highland village, while Margie was drawn to the Australian Pavilion where visitors were being invited to migrate to a country with limitless job opportunities.

An official told her about a number of nursing positions on offer in Melbourne that somehow sparked a chord, stirring something in Margie that she had never given any thought to.

Lying in bed that night she tried to dismiss the ridiculous idea of going to Australia that kept flooding back into her head. She kept telling herself she would never have the courage and anyway her mother would never let her go.

But she did update her diary with the idea and her thoughts.

* * *

After returning home and having settled back into life at Dulwich Village, Margie's mother announced at dinner a few days later that Charles Garland, a distant uncle from Australia, was soon to arrive in London to meet his relatives, see the country and take in some Test cricket.

When Margie asked how their family was related to his, her mother explained that they were all distant relatives of Thomas Garland.

In the 1860s one of his sons named Gregory had migrated to Sydney.

She explained that both Charles' parents had died in tragic circumstances the year before and that he was visiting his ancestral homeland to try and put those memories behind him.

'We understand he will be here for an extended stay and he hopes to find an apartment and see a bit of England.

'I have invited him to a family dinner after he arrives, so Margie when he comes, I want you to be here to meet him,' Gertrude concluded.

* * *

As the mercury in London headed towards its summer zenith, Margie was busily scanning the positions vacant in the papers, looking at jobs ranging from administration to nursing.

Over afternoon tea with Jessie in one of Harrods' less expensive tearooms she announced that nursing seemed to offer her the best chance to establish a worthwhile career and more importantly, escape from her mother's clutches.

'So Jess, I've put my name down with some hospitals, including North Middlesex, and I'm holding my breath waiting to hear from them.'

'That's exciting!' exclaimed Jessie, not revealing she too was job hunting and had applied for a government position at a strange place called Bletchley Park.

As the pair continued their catch-up, Margie confessed she was still waiting with bated breath for a letter from Stephen, the soldier she had met in the Edinburgh pub.

'I bet you would love to see him again,' teased Jessie.

'Sort of. I now realise it was silly of me not to see him again,' Margie admitted.

*   *   *

Six months later in 1939 on a bleak winter's morning, Gertrude fished an unexpected letter from her mailbox with a distinctive blue North Middlesex Hospital logo on the envelope, addressed to Miss M. Swanson.

Margie had all but given up hope of hearing back from any of the hospitals.

Opening the letter she read with delight that she had been offered an interview in the hospital's next nursing intake and was asked to meet with the Matron the following week.

*   *   *

Three months later having finished her training at North Middlesex Hospital, Margie caught up with Jessie again over Sunday afternoon tea at fashionable Brown's Hotel in Mayfair, for an overdue chinwag on their diverging lives.

Jessie mentioned the position she had secured with the Foreign Office, but she wasn't able to explain it was actually with the Government Code and Cypher School.

'I'm working in a mansion on a vast estate at an odd place called

Bletchley Park in Milton Keynes. There are lots of new girls like me there who are doing secretarial work and also many university types from Cambridge and Oxford.

'Much as I would dearly love to tell you what I'm actually working on, Margie, I am bound by the Government Secrets Act that I have had to sign that doesn't allow me to reveal any more. I do hope you will understand,' she pleaded.

Seeing the quizzical look on Margie's face, Jessie had to remind herself she mustn't mention anything about the increasing stream of messages coming in from British agents in Germany and Poland, pointing towards a major Nazi military build-up by the war-mongering Adolf Hitler.

'Jess, you've got to tell me something about what you actually do,' beseeched Margie.

'You are making it all sound like you have suddenly turned into a spy. Is your work in anyway related to the looming war?'

Feeling uncomfortable withholding the truth, Jessie unconvincingly tried to divert their conversation to safer ground.

'The train ride there gives me time to read a book and the office is only a short walk from the station.'

But Margie could plainly see her cover-up was in play, 'All right then, as you have to stay mum, I give up!' She sighed as she picked up her third delicious asparagus roll and took a bite before asking Jess if she was enjoying the work.

Still on the defensive, Jessie guardedly said, 'I'm still new at it and finding it very testing.'

At that moment, the waiter returned, offering to refill their teapot, which broke the tense impasse.

'So tell me about your nursing. How does it feel to be rostered into a ward?' asked Jessie.

'I do love the caring side of it and there are so many rewarding moments when I feel I'm really making a difference to people's lives.

'But my long shifts are very wearing, especially the weeks when I'm on night duty.

'And when it comes to doing paperwork and dealing with some of the cranky doctors, I'm not much chop,' Margie added.

'So when do you actually sleep?' asked Jessie.

'During the day, but I never realised how hard it is to get a decent kip with so much noise going on outside our house,' said Margie before her eyes suddenly became fixed on the expensive Brown's Hotel teapot before them on their table.

Seeing her focus on it, Jessie leant over and whispered, 'Margie, I hope you don't have designs on that? If you are about to steal it, I'm going to disown you.'

'That would never have occurred to me, but now that you mention it, it could be fun,' Margie shot back, causing the pair to laugh out loudly as they recalled the one she had swiped in Scotland.

Later walking down Piccadilly towards her bus stop, Jessie felt guilty she couldn't divulge to her best friend the truth about her real work at Bletchley Park.

They had never been confronted by such an uncomfortable situation before.

The stark reality was that her new job required her to analyse hundreds of intercepted Nazi messages, which indicated Germany had clear intentions of invading Poland.

Just thinking about it caused her to shudder.

Jessie remembered her supervisor had asked to see her the following week about a proposed transfer to the 'cypher breakers' desk, whatever that term meant.

She never imagined that many of the fine heritage buildings lining the very street she was standing in would soon be reduced to rubble beneath a tidal wave of German bombs.

Meanwhile, also strolling along Piccadilly, Margie was enjoying some rare window-shopping at Fortnum and Mason on the way to her bus stop.

She reflected on her catch-up with Jess, feeling positive about the warm bonds they still shared, but aware that since Jessie started that job, for some reason she had uncharacteristically become very secretive, which she didn't like one bit.

That night in her room, knowing that they had never held back any secrets from each other, she wrote in her diary:

What sort of job, however important, could be so secretive that Jess can't even tell me, her best friend?

After making the entry, Margie thought that some of the very personal and gory happenings she encountered in her ward were not something she should or would openly discuss with friends.

But the difference between Jessie's job and hers was that she wasn't sworn to secrecy.

*　　*　　*

As the August evenings in 1939 became that little bit chillier and the nights longer, newspaper headlines were carrying story after story of the seemingly ever-downward spiral towards war.

Jessie's new job on the cypher-breaking desk at Bletchley Park was fast becoming submerged by a deluge of highly secret reports highlighting Germany's mobilisation along Poland's borders. Each day, she deciphered reports of the massive Nazi tank and troop build-up and of German airfields filling with bombers as Hitler increased his demands on Poland to yield or face certain destruction.

*　　*　　*

The girls agreed to catch up for a drink on the first Sunday in September but Jessie phoned to cancel the day before as she had been unexpectedly called in to work.

Jessie worked on deciphering a flood of reports that indicated German troops had swarmed over the Polish border and unleashed the first blitzkrieg the world had seen.

As she finished work late on Sunday evening and was clearing her desk, Jessie realised Britain had reached the brink of war.

11. Sydney to Southampton, May 1938

Feeling the *SS Strathallan's* powerful engines accelerate the liner towards Sydney Heads as it ploughed into the first swells doing eighteen knots, Charles Garland was reminded of his sister's seasick warning.

Later as the harbour fell astern, a bell announced that afternoon tea was served.

As Charles arrived in the day lounge, he made a mental note to only take a small cake, just in case.

By sunset, Charles was huddled by the rail, wearing his warm gabardine coat with a sick bag in its pocket but getting used to the steady vibrations from the depths below.

He noticed the strong headwinds had begun to whip up a confused sea causing the ship's bow to rise and fall steadily and the laid teak decks to buck. Charles was fast losing his appetite for that night's dinner of roast pork with apple sauce, as the first waves of nausea threatened to overcome him.

*   *   *

A few days before the *Strathallan* departed Circular Quay for Southampton, the *Sydney Morning Herald* ran an in-depth feature on the new vessel. The paper gave a special insight into its state-of-the-art features and published photos of its restaurants, picture theatre, day lounges, pool, bars and library.

Having digested it, Charles realised he was about to join a thousand passengers on what he hoped would be a restful passage that would allow him to escape his worries and help him regain his lost momentum.

He was looking forward to his first days at sea without any commitments and had almost finished packing when Alice phoned to check the time she was to pick him up.

He hoped the sadness surrounding his parents' demise would be swallowed in the liner's wake and it would be the beginning of the next stage of his life's journey that might expand his interests, develop his personal life and help him get away from Sydney.

Alice and her children accompanied him to his small cabin on B deck where she presented him with a bag of coloured streamers to throw to them.

In the last hectic moments before departure, Charles felt the ship's engines burst into life, as the scene on board and on the dock quickened appreciably.

The purser announced over the public address system, "Those not travelling to Bombay should disembark immediately."

Moments later a long blast from the foghorn signalled departure, creating a further sense of urgency.

From his vantage spot on the B deck rail, Charles watched the gangplank become choked with wellwishers rushing off to find dockside spots to wave goodbye.

Above he saw clouds of black, oily, smoke being emitted from the vessel's white funnel, swirling in the wind over the ship and wharf, overwhelming the otherwise agreeable sea air.

On the deck above Charles, the first class passengers took to the rail, waving as the ship's band launched into a rousing version of "Rule Britannia" which got people singing along and tapping their toes.

From the tourist class rail, throngs of excited passengers joined Charles in waving and throwing streamers.

Finally spotting Alice below, Charles threw his streamers, which her children eagerly raced to gather then hold till the very last moment.

He could plainly see how his fragile strips of red, blue and yellow tape were adding to the amazing sea of ribbons that had sprung up to bind hundreds of people for those last precious seconds.

Then with "Land of Hope and Glory" pumping out loud across the quay, the *Strathallan* proudly sounded several loud blasts as Charles excitedly watched the black tugs ease his ship away from the wharf that caused the streamers to stretch then finally break and flutter lifelessly into the harbour.

Charles felt the 23,000-ton liner slowly pick up speed as its sharp bow began slicing east across the harbour's rippled waters towards the heads.

Over the next thirty minutes, Charles took in the panoramic view of the imposing six-year-old Harbour Bridge that had become the country's most talked about urban landmark. Around him passengers snapped photos of the magnificent sights falling astern.

Then the old convict prison on Fort Denison came into view and he observed Sydney's serrated skyline rising behind Government House, wondering when he would see it again.

* * *

Following a restful night, Charles woke to find his mal de mer had eased and he seemed to be finding his sea legs. As the sun climbed higher into the blue winter sky, he began a routine of taking meals, enjoying walks around the deck, reading and conversing with passengers.

He reminded himself of his counsellor's advice that he needed to expand his interests and embrace the new directions they might bring.

Enjoying the fresh air on deck, as the days passed he could feel the sun's rays doing wonders for his soul as the crispness of Sydney's winter phased into warmer climes.

He had discovered a favourite deckchair, where from time to time he would lift his eyes from his novel to gaze over the vast ocean beyond and the endless sky above.

He was inspired by the infinite horizon, dotted with a sea of prancing white caps that led to a graduated blue sky only punctured by clumps of fluffy white clouds, ever silently passing over him.

Studying the clouds, he began to think what the weather ahead might be and how it would affect them.

* * *

At dinner that evening Charles found himself seated next to Second Officer Rex Briggs-Jones, who explained what his position entailed.

'At sea I am in charge of the ship from midnight to four, which we call the "dead man's watch" and I also produce the weather forecasts.'

'Rex, what sort of conditions would cause the ship to alter course?' Charles asked.

'Our passenger comfort is of paramount importance,' the Second Officer explained. 'So we try to plan a route that avoids heavy seas and strong winds.'

Having noticed the heavier clouds rolling in that afternoon, Charles asked, 'What is the forecast looking like for the next few days?'

'The day after tomorrow looks like possible thunderstorms, followed by a solid cold front that might serve up strong winds and heavy seas,' the Second Officer replied.

'Rex, do you know of any books in the library on weather you can recommend?' asked Charles.

The Second Officer instead offered to lend him his latest edition of the *Admiralty Weather*, considered the mariners' "bible".

After poring through it the next day, Charles discovered two sea rules that he committed to memory.

A red sunset usually indicates good weather the next day.

Whilst a red sunrise means unsettled or bad weather is on the way.

* * *

The following morning, Charles woke to the awesome sight of a blood red sunrise flooding through his porthole, causing him to wonder if it meant they were in for some serious weather.

During the morning when the skies began to blacken over and it was announced that the afternoon's deck sports were being suspended, Charles set out to track down the Second Officer who confirmed that some bad weather lay ahead.

Finding a seat on the ship's leeward side out of the steadily rising wind, Charles was enthralled, seeing even blacker clouds roll in as the wind began to howl through the masts.

Feeling the ship lifting further by the minute, he anxiously watched the rising swell cause its bow to press upwards into the greasy grey twenty-footers that were threatening to tumble down in liquid mountains.

He watched breathlessly as the bow plunged down, flinging aside sheets of solid, angry water, some of which blew back along the decks, for the first time causing Charles to feel outside his comfort zone.

One larger wave than usual thoroughly drenched Charles, leaving him no option but to go and change clothes.

Heading to his cabin he passed grim-faced passengers, tenaciously clinging to the handrails as the pitching deck beneath their feet made getting about very difficult.

Reaching the safety of his cabin he had to keep a handhold to steady himself from being tossed around. Before changing he watched in awe through the porthole as the gale intensified towards a force ten storm.

Charles could hear the merciless howling of the wind that roared like a freight train bearing down but never arriving. His ears were filled by the fearful sound of huge crashing waves and the pitched drum of the engines battling to keep the ship on course, causing him to become rattled.

As he was in the midst of slipping a leg into a fresh pair of trousers, the *Strathallan* hit a six-storey wave that brought the 23,000-ton vessel to a shuddering halt and tossed Charles across the cabin.

The last thing he remembered before he smashed headfirst into the bathroom door was being catapulted through the air like a rag doll.

When he came to lying on the floor, he tried to work out where he was and how he had got there.

Slowly the incoherent scene started to come back to explain why his whole world was rolling and why there was blood everywhere and his head hurt like hell.

With his headache blackening his vision, he realised the storm was scaring the living daylights out of him.

From the deck above he heard the sound of crashing gear that had just broken loose.

As his fears rose, waves of nausea began to overtake him, causing him to reach for a sick bag.

As he pressed a towel to his head to stem the flow of blood, he realised that calling for help would be selfish when there might be others in greater need.

Feeling totally vulnerable, he crawled into his bed to escape the nightmare, wedging pillows against the leeboard to prevent him rolling out.

The frightening situation he was facing brought back memories of the terrifying stories his father had told him of the First World War in France when Frank's battalion had faced the full might of the German's artillery bombardments and their wall of machine guns.

Charles thought if his father could summon the courage to face those molten metal barrages, then he wasn't going to let this storm get the better of him.

When he awoke late that afternoon he sensed the storm had eased slightly.

Lying in his bed nursing his bloodied head, he stared at the pitching ceiling and could see that the cabin was rolling less and the sound of the howling wind had lessened to a more tolerable roar.

Feeling wrung out and battered, he realised he had just been through his first major storm and most importantly, he had found a way to deal with it.

From deep in his soul he suspected his fear of death had been purged.

However, it took him a while longer to venture off to the ship's doctor to have his head looked at. After having it bandaged and getting the all clear, he went out on deck to see how the rest of the passengers had fared and how much damage had been done to the *Strathallan*.

Finally, when he ran into Second Officer Briggs-Jones, he asked how much longer the storm was expected to last.

'The good news is the captain has routed us away from the worst of the weather ahead and by late this evening, the winds and sea state should be settling out.

'We encountered gusts over fifty knots and seas of thirty feet back there that caused some minor damage when a lifeboat and several hatches got loose. And we suspect the bow took a severe whack when that wave stopped us,' he added.

'So those red skies we saw this morning turned into a more intense event than you expected?' posed Charles.

'Absolutely,' the Second Officer answered, quickly deciding to try and brighten things up.

'Charles, if you feel better by tomorrow evening, would you like to join me for dinner on a table of nurses who are travelling to Bombay?'

Despite his headache and not feeling all that hungry in that moment, Charles surprised himself by accepting and the pair went their own way.

*   *   *

The next evening, Charles found himself seated next to a rather attractive and well-spoken senior Royal Melbourne Hospital supervisor, who introduced herself as Elizabeth Blow.

Sipping wine, they found themselves discussing the hot topic of the day, as to how they had survived the storm.

It was not long before Elizabeth asked about his bandaged head. Charles explained how he had lost his footing and cut his head when the ship came to that halt.

She told him it had pitched her from a chair, which had scared her witless and caused her to wonder if they would survive it.

Charles agreed it had been a scary experience, then told her about that morning's red sky warning and how worried he had been at the peak of the storm, saying how he felt like a piece of cork being tossed this way and that by the ocean.

As he was finishing his story, the waiters arrived with their main courses that captured their senses with the delicious aroma of grilled whiting, green beans and creamy potato au gratin.

Charles offered Elizabeth the pepper and salt. When she accepted with a gracious smile he did not fail to notice the animated glint in her eye.

By dessert their conversation had moved to their tastes in books and music.

Before embarking on this voyage, Charles had made a pact with himself to remain coy about giving out any of his family background.

However with Elizabeth, he already felt comfortable breaking his rule.

He spoke a little of his parents' death and why he was taking an extended holiday.

Both were becoming more than fascinated with each other,

realising their conversation had moved well beyond the first awkward, polite stage.

When the port and cheese were served, Elizabeth seemed noticeably more attentive and less reserved, confiding to him that she had divorced two years earlier.

'After I returned to nursing, my life changed direction and I really haven't looked back.

'Since I've been on my own, I've put my energies into studying for the latest certificates and was more than delighted to be invited to lead our team on this trip,' she explained.

The pair soon realised that throughout the entire dinner they had been so deeply immersed in conversation that they had not spoken to anyone else on their table. They agreed for the moment to break off and socialise with those not up dancing.

When the band next struck up, Charles invited Elizabeth to dance.

He saw her eyes light up as she replied, 'I'd be delighted!'

Her colleagues were happy to see her out there enjoying herself as they made a fine pair, tangoing elegantly across the dance floor.

As the bracket slowly drew to an end with a slow waltz, the couple's eyes romantically locked for the first time.

Charles whispered, 'Elizabeth, can I compliment you on your beautiful smile? I feel so comfortable in this moment ... and you dance so gracefully.'

Winding their way back to the table he took her hand and drew her close.

"I would consider it an honour if you would have dinner with me tomorrow night.'

Looking into his handsome eyes, her quiet reply was definite. 'Oh Charles, I would love to.'

Heading off afterwards to their cabins, Charles' head was filled with very warm thoughts of the delightful lady who had thoroughly entranced him throughout dinner and danced so wonderfully. Tomorrow he thought he would try to get to know her better and find out what made her tick.

In another part of the ship, when Elizabeth arrived at her cabin feeling flushed and exuberant, she ran into a barrage of questions from her cabin mate, Miss Kitson, asking what Charles was like and how she felt about him.

*   *   *

The following evening, Charles booked a private table for them. So immersed were they in each other, they barely noticed what they were eating or that their plates had been whisked away.

At the end of dinner, Charles rose and slid back Elizabeth's chair before he helped her on with her jacket.

Elizabeth had no idea of what he had in mind next, but as they strolled towards the lounge, he surprised her by suggesting they might go to the aft deck bar for a pleasant nightcap.

It was more romantic than she had hoped for, but first she wanted to return to her cabin to find something warmer for the cold night air and freshen up.

Half an hour later, she stepped onto the promenade deck wearing a stylish wool coat and confidently made her way towards the aft deck's dimly lit bar.

Here, Charles welcomed her with a beaming smile and a warm outstretched hand as he beckoned her to a stool.

Asked what nightcap she might like, Elizabeth answered, 'Champagne would be perfect.'

While Charles went to place the order, Elizabeth realised how much she had missed the attention of such an attractive gentleman.

Waiting at the bar, Charles wondered if he was taking things too quickly with this very attractive thirty-six year-old, who seemed to be enjoying his attention.

He asked himself were he and Elizabeth simply two romantic "ships passing in the night" and wondered what it all might come to.

Having filled their glasses with champagne, they raised them to each other and then quietly sipped the bubbles whilst gazing out into the night.

Both were thinking to themselves how wonderful it was to be alive and here in this moment.

Beyond the ship's rail, they could feel the cool salt-laden night air swirling aft and listened to the steady slap of waves coursing past the ship's sides that ensured their endearing words were audible to no-one but themselves.

Looking astern as they held hands, they saw the *Strathallan's* silvery, moonlit wake trailing off into the enveloping darkness.

As the wine softly worked its magic, Charles impressed Elizabeth with stories about his family, his business, his love of farming at Latour Park and having made friends with Don Bradman when he met him playing cricket at Bowral.

Suitably impressed, Elizabeth moved the discussion to a critical question bothering her.

'Charles, you seem to have led such a charmed life. Am I permitted to inquire if there is anyone special in it at the moment?'

'Sadly, there isn't, but that could be about to change,' he boldly replied.

Suddenly the tension, which had been building all evening, became more palpable.

Positively sparkling, Elizabeth wondered if their night was about to take a new turn.

'Charles, why don't we toss a coin to decide which cabin we should retire to to finish our champagne?' Elizabeth suggested devilishly.

'Tell you what, if I win, we can drink it in mine with Miss Kitson with whom I'm bunking in with … most likely she will already be there.'

Deciding he didn't much care for Elizabeth's option, Charles picked up the ice bucket and bottle in one hand and her arm in the other and began leading her towards his cabin, saying, 'My little cabin is probably more private and more importantly, we won't have to share our champagne.'

As they headed there walking arm in arm, Elizabeth had a few moments to ponder the many long years she had yearned for the passionate warmth of a man with whom she could enjoy intimate togetherness.

Entering his cosy space, Elizabeth could see there was barely room to dress. The cabin had a small bathroom with a mirror and the porthole was cracked open to allow air in. Other than a chair, she noticed the only place to sit was on the double bed. As the champagne continued to unwind her, she hoped there wouldn't be too much sitting.

They sat together on the edge of the bed.

Ever the gentleman, Charles felt unsure where things might be headed.

Topping up Elizabeth's glass, he raised his for a second toast to her.

Taking a slow, deliberate sip, she locked eyes on his, leaned closer and with her moist lips lightly kissed him.

Charles responded by placing a hand around her slender waist to draw her closer and with the other put aside their glasses.

Looking more deeply into her eyes, Charles ardently returned her kisses as years of denial melted and his hands began to explore her and she began to feel a deep need arising.

Breathlessly she unbuttoned his shirt so she could glide her fingers through the manly hairs on his chest.

Glancing over Charles' shoulder in the half-light, she caught a glimpse of herself in the mirror that showed she still looked firm, trim and desirable.

The moment her skirt and silk blouse fell to the carpet, she wanted him more than anything in the world and eagerly gave herself to his ardent advances.

*　*　*

Having held each other close through the night of unbridled passion, with the sun well up and the coast more than 500 miles over the horizon, they found the energy to make love again.

Strolling into breakfast, they soon felt the knowing glances from the others as they approached their table.

Regardless of their stares, they felt very happy. Elizabeth agreed to go to dinner with Charles again that evening.

She returned to her cabin to collect her thoughts, begin her day and pick up where she had left off, wondering if it was possible that after only one night of lust she could feel such positive feelings for this amazing man who had completely swept her off her feet.

She asked herself if this was a whirlwind romance or if it could in time lead to love.

*　*　*

Searching for a deckchair on the sunny starboard side, Charles settled in to read his novel and from time to time would check how the day's weather was turning out after having slept through the sunrise.

Despite the best of intentions, his mind kept returning to their amazing night of lovemaking and how wonderful it felt to be tightly held by Elizabeth.

He was now really glad she had been eager to progress things, yet ultimately she demanded he take the lead. Was it just desire or was there something more between them that he was now feeling?

But with only four days until the ship reached Bombay, he was sure Elizabeth and he would not want to leave a stone unturned as their fledgling shipboard romance blossomed.

Before the ship berthed, Charles reminded himself he needed to write to his uncle in London, Ron Swanson, to seek his advice as to where to find a suitably furnished flat handy to transport and a village that might meet his needs.

*   *   *

On their final night, as they glided across the dance floor, Charles saw Elizabeth looking deeply into his eyes, and she seemed to be beckoning him closer.

He drew her close so she could feel him, causing her to passionately yearn for him one more time.

Days and nights of shared feelings, unspoken words and mutual desire spilled into a lingering embrace at the end of the band's last set.

Charles' strong arms enveloped her so closely she could feel his chest heaving and his heart pounding.

He leaned down and breathed into her ear, 'Promise me Elizabeth, that we will never let what we have created ever end.'

Her eyes lit up and her pulse raced.

Her look of sheer delight as she lovingly rested her head on his shoulder and squeezed him tighter was the only response he could have ever asked for.

After their exquisite shipboard romance, the pair parted in Bombay on an emotional high fuelled by the wonder of what their fledgling relationship might hold when they next met.

Charles promised to write often and pledged to see her in Melbourne upon his return.

She decided to wait until she next saw him, whereupon she would tell him her deeply held feelings would know no bounds.

*　*　*

Amongst a parcel of letters awaiting Charles in Bombay was a surprise one from Don Bradman saying how delighted he would be if they could catch up after the Test at Lord's for dinner and a chance to chat about how Charles was faring after the death of his parents.

As the *Strathallan* left the Arabian Sea behind and passed through the Suez Canal, the much warmer days were making life on board even more relaxed and pleasant.

During Charles' many hours on deck, reading and daydreaming, his mind frequently turned to how delighted he was to have met Elizabeth and what joy she had brought into his life, if only for a handful of precious days and nights.

12. Dulwich Village, London, 1938

After weeks at sea relaxing with few worries other than trying to work out who the culprits were in his novels, Charles felt he had begun to sort through some of his emotional turmoil emanating from his parents' deaths.

The trip had given him time to expand his range of interests, as he had been advised to do in his counselling sessions.

He had always taken a keen interest in the weather at Latour Park, but at sea he realised there was a whole lot more to learn.

At this point in his life he had always felt confident he could conquer most challenges.

As the storm had loomed, despite his initial bravado, he discovered surviving it was another matter, and that made him realise he was actually quite vulnerable.

Having deliberately left the door ajar to make new friends, who should walk through but Elizabeth. She exceeded his need to discover a love interest, she wanted to share more of his journey, and he felt so much richer that she had entered his life and looked forward to many happy times with her upon his return to Australia.

Standing at the *Strathallan's* rail on the final morning, he watched with some excitement as the hazy English coast slowly emerged from beneath the depressing grey skies.

As the ship passed the Isle of Wight's chalky cliffs leading into the choppy Southampton Waters, Charles saw only a few craft moving about.

Arriving in the port of Southampton he watched the tugs gingerly nudge the *Strathallan* into the wharf, whereupon its lines were secured and the pilot on the bridge ordered, "stop engines".

For the first time in many weeks, the steady throb of the ship's engines died and now Charles itched to get ashore to stretch his legs.

Some of the returning passengers were greeted by excited relatives but most, like him, were strangers in this country with no dockside welcoming committee.

The trip to London by train seemed a blur as Charles found himself engrossed watching the lush green countryside flash by, punctuated by oddly named stations and rivers.

Finding a taxi outside Waterloo Station he loaded his bags and asked to be driven to a Marylebone bedsitter, which he had booked.

After introducing himself to his Baker Street landlady, he was shown upstairs to an old-fashioned sunlit room on the third floor, where through the open window he immediately smelt the fragrance of climbing roses. She drew his attention to meal times, noise rules and doing his laundry.

When she left, he noticed two letters waiting for him beneath an antique lamp on the bedside table.

The first from the Swansons was an invitation to dinner.

The second, bearing a Bombay postmark, was more than a surprise. Taking a seat he eagerly tore Elizabeth's letter open.

> *Dear Charles,*
>
> *I hope this letter finds you safe and well and my letter was there to greet you at the Baker Street address you gave me.*
>
> *I want to again wish you well for your stay in England. I do hope your meeting with relatives is rewarding, that you find a comfortable flat, your reunion with Don Bradman goes well, the Aussies win and that your travels refresh you.*
>
> *Our Royal Melbourne nurses shone at the surgical conference and we were shown a number of recovery procedures that the hospital will be very interested in hearing about when we get home.*
>
> *When we waved goodbye, my heart was in my mouth as there was still so much to say, but no time left to do it.*
>
> *So I decided I would write to you before I leave here, to express how wonderful it was to meet you and spend surprisingly romantic hours together on the ship.*
>
> *You have made a wonderful impression on me, despite us only sharing a few short days getting to know each other. It's my hope you might find a few moments in your busy schedule to write me a line in due course.*
>
> *Yours sincerely,*
> *Elizabeth*

Dulwich Village, London, 1938

Her loving words in beautiful handwriting seemed to float up from the lightly fragranced paper. Charles' eyes began to fill with tears, which caught him by surprise because until this moment he had failed to grasp how much he really needed to hear from her.

After unpacking and settling in, he sat down to put pen to paper …

Dearest Elizabeth,

What a simply delightful surprise I had when I discovered your letter from Bombay awaiting my arrival in London.

Thank you for your chatty news and I hope my letter finds you safe and well now you are settled back at your Elwood home. Is your weather getting colder with June upon us? I hope all is well at the hospital. My passage to Southampton after you disembarked was a lot less pleasant than the leg we shared together to Bombay.

Whilst I have not been at all unhappy these last several weeks, I need to admit that a light in my life seemed to go out after we waved goodbye from the dock and I watched you disappear.

I've been invited to a family dinner next week with my uncle and aunt whom I told you about. I'm looking forward to meeting them and I will tell you more when I write next.

Until then, keep smiling and I hope you might find time in your busy life to write to me, soon.
Yours,
XX Charles

*   *   *

The following week, his taxi pulled up in front of a modest two-storey attached house in Dulwich Village. The cheerful red front door was opened by Uncle Ron and upon entering, Charles was soon distracted by the tantalising aroma of a herb-infused roast coming from the kitchen.

Hearing voices in the hall, Aunt Gertrude emerged, followed by Margie and Lucy.

Enjoying a glass of sweet sherry, Charles recounted some of the highlights of his passage to his two nieces, who listened engrossed, interrupting only to ask about shipboard life, which led to him admit he had enjoyed the company of Elizabeth from Melbourne on the leg to Bombay.

Following forty-two days of ship meals, he pleased his aunt no end when he told her he was very much looking forward to a proper home-cooked roast.

From the head of the table Ron carved, whilst plates of baked potatoes and steaming greens were passed around, followed by the gravy boat.

After dinner, Charles brought up something on his mind. 'I keep reading in the papers that Hitler is making more worrying threats that appear to be further eroding Europe's political stability.

'What's the general feeling here?' he inquired.

He was slightly surprised when Gertrude spoke up and said, 'Our Prime Minister keeps telling us the government is doing all it can to appease Germany, but we are worried where it all might be leading.'

Margie, the older and more outspoken of the daughters, chipped in. 'Uncle, a soldier I met in Scotland told me as the situation with Germany gets worse, his battalion has increased the number of training manoeuvres and they are taking in more recruits.'

Impressed with her comment, Charles added, 'Margie, before I left I heard my old Sydney Uni Regiment had been sent out on serious joint exercises with other battalions.'

Attempting to brighten up what she thought was becoming a depressing conversation, Lucy decided to change the subject.

'Uncle, do you know that soldier Margie spoke of is called Stephen and she had her first kiss with him? Ever since then she's the first to the letterbox to see if he's written!'

Hearing Lucy's revelation, Margie abruptly rose, collected the plates then headed to the kitchen to hide her embarrassment, followed by Gertrude who wanted to know more.

As the pair disappeared into the kitchen, Charles heard his aunt asking, 'Margie, you told me nothing had happened on that trip. Now I discover you were kissing boys! What else happened that you haven't told me about?'

Meanwhile in the dining room, the men finished their clarets and began discussing various suburbs with flats that might suit Charles.

When Margie returned somewhat humiliated, to change subjects, Charles asked her what career path she was thinking of pursuing.

'I am hoping to go into nursing and I'm searching for a training placement with several London hospitals,' she replied less than confidently.

Before the very pleasant evening drew to a close Charles asked Margie if she would accompany him to see the Trooping the Colour at Buckingham Place the following week.

Then he raised with Ron the matter of the next Ashes Test.

'I'm going to see my good friend Donald Bradman lead Australia against England. Even though I realise you would want to barrack for the Poms, I have a spare seat if you would like to come as my guest,' he suggested.

Ron realised it had been many years since he had been to a Test and with a little prompting from Gertrude, he accepted. 'Charles, that would be splendid, thank you.'

That night in her room Margie entered the upcoming trip to Buckingham Palace with her uncle into her diary and added how much she had enjoyed meeting her new Australian relative.

*　　*　　*

In the taxi on his way back to Baker Street, Charles ruminated on the very warm and rewarding evening he had spent with the Swansons and their spirited daughters.

He noticed his aunt seemed a little over-protective of the girls and wondered what else was said in the kitchen about the kiss.

Regardless, he felt drawn to Margie, who spoke her mind and appeared to have plenty of "get up and go". He hoped her move into nursing would turn out for the good.

The dinner with the Swansons made him realise that for too many years he had avoided family gatherings like that in Sydney and he resolved he would do more when he got home.

Until that evening, he thought he knew Alice and her children, but as their uncle, he now realised he had put scant effort into getting to know them and had instead put all of his time into his work.

Before heading up to his room, Charles stopped to buy *The Daily Telegraph* newspaper to read the preview of the Lord's cricket match.

It predicted that after the first drawn Test, a result in the second in England's favour was on the cards and for the first time ever, something called "television" whatever that was, would be covering play.

Turning to the front page of his paper, he read yet another headline about the threat of war.

The article, written by a young journalist, Clare Hollingworth, reported that Britain was being left flat footed by Germany's provocation.

A few pages on, a small article reported that English factories had begun delivering tens of thousands of civilian gas masks. It made Charles realise that if there was a danger of people being gassed, clearly the government was not being truthful about the serious risk Germany posed to the people in Britain.

13. Outbreak of War, 1939

Over many years Charles had enjoyed seeing cricket at the Sydney Cricket Ground, but none prepared him for the spectacle that awaited him at Lord's, the iconic home of cricket.

Emerging from the St John's Wood Underground station, he and Uncle Ron heard the sell-out crowd's excited hum.

Passing through the turnstiles, they purchased scorecards with the player names and numbers then rented a pair of cushions to ease the prospect of sitting for hours on the hard timber benches.

From the food stalls scattered on the lawn came a pleasant mix of aromas. They resisted stalls selling delicious asparagus rolls, frothy ales and iced lemonade, but couldn't go past the one with freshly baked scones.

Once seated, Charles was overcome with the magical sight of Lord's hallowed, lush green ground that contrasted with the straw-coloured pitch in the centre being given a last minute hand roll by three perspiring groundsmen.

Then he noticed the famous scoreboard waiting for the player numbers to be slid into place and at each end of the ground stood white sightscreens manned by attendants dressed in black.

Ron pointed out the Victorian red brick Members' Pavilion that boasted the famed Long Room and the players' change rooms with their small balconies.

'Unfortunately, when Tests are on we can't visit the trophy room to see The Ashes urn,' Ron explained.

Through binoculars Charles could see members puffing away on pipes and enjoying pre-match champagne. Wearing a variety of hats, many were decked in gaily-coloured red and gold-striped jackets, adorned with loud, red and yellow club ties.

Around the oval's packed stands was a sombre, grey hue rising from tens of thousands of anxiously waiting smokers.

A hand bell was heard from the Long Room, announcing the start of the day's proceedings.

An expectant murmur swept through the stands, as ten thousand pairs of eyes followed the arrival of the two imposing very upright umpires, who strode purposefully out of the boundary gate onto the turf.

Wearing traditional black brimmed hats, long length white jackets with oversized pockets and contrasting dark slacks, they were initially greeted with a scattering of polite applause that increased as they reached the wicket.

The crowd was eager to hear the first exciting clunk of ball on willow and the cries of "Howzat".

Seeing England win the toss and elect to bat, Charles' excitement mounted when he saw Don Bradman, resplendent in his baggy green cap, with a determined look, lead the Australians onto the hostile ground.

For the next few hours the ever-present military threat looming across the Channel was forgotten.

At day's end, they retired to a tent behind the grandstand for an ale where Ron surprised Charles when he asked about Elizabeth.

'From the little you told us, you appear to be more than a little drawn to her.'

'Yes, more than a little. But for the moment we are worlds apart and I fear Hitler might keep us that way for much longer than I would like,' Charles admitted.

Taking a long, deliberate slow sip of his ale, Charles thought how her first letter had certainly kept his fire for her burning brightly.

*　*　*

After the Test had ended in a tense draw, Charles caught up with Don for a quiet pub dinner in Marylebone.

He noticed that Don deliberately chose a seat facing away from the bar, hoping to avoid any unwanted attention. In that moment, Charles fleetingly wondered if his friend had become a prisoner of his own fame.

Regardless, they had much to catch up on.

Charles confided that at his sister's insistence after his parents' death, he had sought help to deal with his grief. The sessions had unlocked many personal matters which he had begun to deal with, but he still had moments where he felt lost and all "at sea".

Charles then told him about meeting Elizabeth, divulging they had since begun writing to each other.

* * *

A few days later Charles received an unexpected letter from Don thanking him for shouting dinner and encouraging him to pursue Elizabeth for all he was worth.

Don wrote he could see she was causing him to worry less about himself and to learn about caring for another, adding that he hoped to meet her when they were all back in Australia.

Charles wrote back saying he would take his advice, then penned a letter to Elizabeth telling her of the cricket match and his dinner and Don's subsequent letter.

* * *

Two months later in September, whilst Charles read his morning paper over a cup of tea, he came across what seemed like a more reassuring page one headline.

"Munich Agreement promises peace in our time" declared Britain's Prime Minister Neville Chamberlain, who claimed Hitler had conceded to Britain's demands at a meeting in Munich.

Pausing to let the news sink in, Charles still held considerable doubts. He recalled Hitler's clear expansionist threats these last years, suggesting this week's agreement with Britain was only on paper and may well prove useless.

With many having seen the frightening new H. G. Wells' film based on his novel, *The Shape of Things to Come* that depicted the Nazis dropping high explosive bombs and poison gas on London, only added to the nine million residents' deeply held fears.

As the Munich Agreement drama played out, more than one hundred and fifty thousand Londoners fled to Wales, prompting the government to attempt to head off a wave of panic.

* * *

Nine months later in June 1939, the conversation at the Swansons' dinner table inevitably turned to the threat of war.

'Do you think now might be the time, before peace in Europe as we know it spirals inevitably into a bloody argument, that the German force should be met by British force?' posed Charles.

Seeing his uncle nod in agreement and about to answer, Gertrude interrupted.

'Here in Britain, we have put our faith in Mr Chamberlain, who maintains we will avoid a war with Germany at all costs. Your uncle and I still happen to agree on this.'

Following the plates being cleared, Charles asked Margie about her nursing and busy social life. With her parents out of earshot, she confided that she suspected her best friend Jessie was doing undercover work for the Foreign Office at a place called Bletchley Park.

'Jess tells me she works extremely long hours and is handling a flood of radio messages from Europe. She had to swear to keep everything she does a secret and had to sign some sort of hush-hush legal agreement.

'Uncle, don't you think that's a bit strange?' Margie queried.

Hearing mention of floods of messages, Charles realised they would not be the regular diplomatic ones from friendly embassies.

'More than likely, they are reports from agents observing Hitler's military build-up,' he suggested.

Conscious of being a guest in a household steadfastly supporting "Peace in our Time", Charles tried to be diplomatic.

'I do agree with you Margie, her job sounds odd, but let's pray you are wrong. If you are right, then at least Britain is getting first-hand reports on what is actually taking place that gives your government the opportunity to prepare for the worst,' he concluded.

*　*　*

Thinking later about Jessie's Bletchley Park job and the continuing threat of a war, Charles asked himself what his father would have done if he was facing the prospect of a major conflict.

There and then he promised himself that should Australia join Britain to take on Germany, he would make enquires about serving.

Maybe he could join the British Army, rather than travel home to enlist, only to be sent back to Europe.

However, this would create two problems.

The first would be that his company would have to manage without him.

Secondly, his return to Australia to see Elizabeth and further their budding relationship could be scuppered.

He wondered whether he should write to Elizabeth to explain his decision, or wait and see how the fast developing crisis turned out before he broke her heart.

With London's newspapers in the latter part of August 1939 printing headlines heralding the build-up of German troops along its border with Poland, it seemed to Charles the "tipping-point" had almost been reached.

* * *

Several times Margie had tried unsuccessfully to meet Jessie in August but each time she said her job had gone into overdrive and she didn't have a spare moment.

With Germany poised to strike Poland, Ron confided to Gertrude that it was clear the Prime Minister had badly miscalculated the Nazis' intent and that meant very bad news for Britain.

Gertrude admonished him for changing his position, insisting there would always be peace in their time.

Her hopes were swept aside when the *Telegraph* broke the dreaded news that Hitler had invaded Poland. Cities across England introduced nightly blackouts.

Britain's ultimatum to Germany to cease its military operations in Poland and withdraw was being ignored, prompting the Prime Minister to address the nation.

At eleven o'clock on Monday 3rd September, a number of Baker Street residents, including Charles, filed quietly into the boarding house's dining room.

When Mr Chamberlain came on at eleven-fifteen am, London's streets had emptied and a deathly hush had descended across the city.

In the dining room, Charles saw fearful faces all turned anxiously to the radio to listen. Some wrung their hands, most like him fidgeted nervously, preparing, like millions across the country, to hear what could only be the worst.

Then speaking in a wavering voice, their Prime Minister wasted few words.

"This morning the British ambassador in Berlin handed the German government a final note stating that unless we heard from them by eleven o'clock that they were prepared at once to withdraw their troops from Poland, a state of war would exist between us.

"I have to tell you now that no such undertaking has been received, and that consequently this country is at war with Germany."

Around the Baker Street dining table, women broke into tears, fearing the unknown. Men, who had earlier maintained a stiff upper lip, were quivering at the thought of having to enlist and fight.

Charles was caught up too in a groundswell of shock and confusion and he wondered how long it would take Australia to join Britain.

At the end of the broadcast, the BBC announced that people should stay tuned for further announcements about war preparations, which will be made throughout the afternoon.

Soon the alarmed chatter in the room turned to where to find the nearest air raid shelters.

Few had the stomach for lunch.

It was only after hearing war declared that Charles' landlady realised the unopened crate in her hall delivered the previous month contained gas masks, which seemed like a very bad omen.

Upset by the morning's news, Charles excused himself, collected an overcoat then set out for the park to think matters through.

Walking beneath trees dropping autumn leaves along near empty paths, his father's advice from all those years ago came flooding back, that it was a man's duty to serve his king and country should they need him.

The question now wasn't if he would serve, but when it would come to pass.

At this moment he wished Elizabeth could be with him, because his decision was going to wreak havoc with their fledgling romance.

He thought by now it would be evening in Melbourne and he

expected she would have heard the same awful announcement from Australia's Prime Minister, Robert Menzies.

Charles realised that he would have to write to her about what he felt duty bound to do. But first, he had to sort out how he could go about volunteering his services.

*　　*　　*

That same morning, Margie's father summonsed the family to the sitting room to hear the Prime Minister's address.

Seven minutes after it concluded, they heard the frightening sound of air raid sirens being tested across South East London. This sent the Swansons and millions of frightened citizens fleeing in panic to the nearest air raid shelters.

*　　*　　*

Londoners soon heard news reports that dozens of German U-boats had been mobilised to the English coast, with orders to sink British warships and merchant vessels.

That same night in the Irish Sea, a German U-boat torpedoed the *SS Athenia* en route from Liverpool to Belfast carrying 1,303 passengers and crew.

On Baker Street, the air raid sirens caused widespread apprehension as anxious residents dashed to the nearby underground rail shelters in case the alarm was genuine.

That Monday night all of London went into its third successive blackout, however few realised the horrendous years of darkness that lay ahead.

14. Royal Engineers, 1940

The following month, Charles went to see an enlistment officer at the London Officer Cadet Training Unit to sort out what would be involved if he volunteered his services.

He had read that the government was introducing conscription, but he was advised that since he held an Australian passport, he would not be called up.

In light of his previous military service and engineering qualifications, he was told the Royal Engineers might be keen to offer him a place.

Knowing little about the British Army, he took away some forms should he decide to apply.

* * *

Instead of enlisting immediately, he decided to look at developing an import opportunity he had spotted after noticing there were widespread shortages of butter and wine on shop shelves, due to supply problems from France.

He telegrammed Alice, in her capacity as a Garland Trading director:

```
DEAREST ALICE HOPE YOU ARE ALL WELL STOP
HERE IN LONDON I HAVE IDENTIFIED A PROFITABLE
OPPORTUNITY TO IMPORT BOWRAL BUTTER AND HUNTER
WINES TO MEET GROWING SHORTAGES STOP
HOPE YOU AND THE BOARD AGREE STOP
PLEASE ADVISE STOP
LOVE CHARLES STOP
```

Awaiting her reply, Charles made some long-distance phone calls to his old friends at the Bowral Fresh Food and Ice Company, which produced butter, and to friends who owned Tyrrell Wines in the

Hunter Valley. Both expressed interest in these export opportunities, subject to binding letters of agreement.

Later that week a reply from Alice arrived:

```
DEAREST CHARLES PLEASED ALL IS WELL STOP
HAVE DISCUSSED YOUR PROPOSAL WITH DIRECTORS WHO
AGREE TO YOUR EXPORT PROPOSAL STOP
PLEASE MAIL US MORE DETAILS STOP
LOVE ALICE STOP
```

Charles then advised the directors of the Bowral Fresh Food and Ice Company and Tyrrell Wines that he had his board's approval for the proposal and that his company would handle the various shipping arrangements and permits with both governments.

He then set to convince the Australian authorities that Britain was desperately short of butter and that NSW's struggling dairy farmers in Bowral needed new markets. They agreed that exporting Bowral's excess capacity would provide a positive boost to the town's shrinking economy.

With the Hunter Region also suffering an economic downturn, Charles successfully argued that incremental exports could only benefit the struggling district.

Further discussions with a London-based grocery house led to him appointing a distributor who assisted with securing the necessary UK import quotas.

He placed orders for two tons of packaged butter, ready to go onto near empty shop shelves and fifty cases of wine to launch the new import business, firstly in London and later in other cities.

Needing a space to operate from, Charles set to searching for a furnished "gentleman's" flat in Marylebone, from where he could run the business. He was fortunate to find one on the second level of a set of pleasant terraces in Ashland Place.

He had a preference for this suburb because of its friendly village shops, transport options and almost everything he required.

The flat had a comfortable sitting room with a pleasant view over a small leafy park and enough room for a desk, filing cabinet and phone, providing his landlady would agree to the connection.

It was a far cry from his managing director's suite in Sydney but despite its modest setting Charles felt happy with it, because in it, he felt private.

With the considerable time required to establish the London import operation, and with so little action happening on the war front and as he faced his first wet and very cold British winter, he decided not to rush his enlistment.

Except for the initial shock sinking of the *Athenia* at the outbreak of war and scattered reports of Germany consolidating its gains in Poland, he read little of Allied European activities in the papers.

Many in Marylebone were muttering about the difficulties caused by widespread blackouts and he heard that some who had fled London when war was declared had since returned.

He regularly tuned into the BBC news, which was reporting air force sorties dropping millions of propaganda leaflets over German cities, which his local shopkeepers described as useless "confetti raids".

There were news snippets that more troops were being sent to France, but little else was heard. With so little happening in the public domain, some were now calling these first quiet months a "phoney war".

*   *   *

Returning from his trip to Scotland to hunt down where his family had once lived, the London papers carried dramatic news that German troops had marched into Belgium, bringing a conclusive end to the "Phoney war".

Soon after, Prime Minister Chamberlain, who had lost his party's support, was forced to resign and the King had no alternative but to call Winston Churchill to Buckingham Palace to invite him to become PM.

Charles was inspired by the new Prime Minister's first address to parliament, in which he announced that a new War Cabinet had been formed, which included the Opposition, to create national unity.

Mr Churchill roused the nation behind him saying, "I have nothing to offer but blood, toil, tears and sweat. For without victory, there is no survival."

*   *   *

Later in May, Charles came to realise England was on its knees after he read the damaging reports from the Battle of Dunkirk where the German army was relentlessly driving the totally disorganised Allied forces back to the French coast.

Then in early June, the War Office announced its decision to rescue more than 300,000 stranded British troops in an amazing cross Channel seaborne operation dubbed the "Dunkirk Evacuation".

Afterwards, Charles was initially delighted to hear that, "Hitler was absolutely furious that so many British soldiers had escaped from right under his nose!"

But reflecting on it more deeply, he realised that the Nazis would respond with massive force that could involve widespread bombing of Britain's ports and cities ahead of a seaborne invasion.

He realised that no-one, including himself, was safe from the Germans.

With the war clearly intensifying and the PM's call to fight, Charles was driven to dig out his enlistment papers and begin applying.

He signed the last page, folded and inserted the application forms into an envelope and took it to the mailbox. Here he paused, asking himself one last time, if he was doing the right thing.

He feared the dire consequences when he told Elizabeth, but knowing his father would have approved, he found the strength to slip the envelope into the slot realising that now, higher authorities would decide his future.

With trepidation his fingers let it disappear into the bowels of the bright red box and it flopped into the bag barely making an audible slap.

Charles then sent a telegram to Sydney asking the managers to hold the fort at the trading company in the event of him being accepted and to keep a close eye on his newly established export business.

Then he sat down to write the most difficult letter to Elizabeth, a task he had been dreading for a very long time. Words did not come easily as he knew the effect his decision would have on her.

6th June 1940
My Darling,

I do hope this letter finds you in excellent spirits even though Melbourne's renowned winter is fast closing in and I pray you are not as yet gripped by days of grey, dreary wet weather like the many months I had to endure here during our winter.

I had a happy smile on my face when you wrote in your last letter that you had purchased the latest copy of the Country Women's Association cookbook, more so when you said that you had been busy baking Anzac biscuits and successfully trying out several new recipes for lamb chops and even an exotic pavlova on your nursing colleagues.

I can imagine you there in your Elwood kitchen in a floral apron, happily "cooking up a storm".

I do hope when I visit you will try a few of those recipes out on me too.

The export plans I wrote about previously for butter and wine are progressing well. I am awaiting the first shipments, due to land this month, providing those awful German U-boats in the North Atlantic don't sink the freighter our goods are in.

My recent visit to Scotland, especially to Edinburgh, was a wonderful escape from the pressures of war and the unseasonal warmish weather was a blessing.

I successfully located my great-great grandfather's family plot at the Glasgow Cemetery and paid my respects.

When I last wrote, this war was moving at a slower pace than expected, but since my recent return from Scotland, its pace has significantly accelerated, especially following the disaster at Dunkirk.

I now fear Britain is preparing for an invasion. Some say this might well begin with the Germans bombing London.

My darling, I have previously written how often your sweetness and your smile occupy my every thought, and how I long to hold you close, to feel your warmth seep into my otherwise slightly empty soul.

Much as I have promised to visit you in Melbourne upon my return to Australia, in my heart I now know with this war right upon us, I cannot simply sit here in London as a mere spectator, with the threats engulfing Britain.

I need to tell you that a while ago I had preliminary discussions with the recruitment people at the London Officer Cadet Training Unit, who suggested that I might consider nominating for a position in the Royal Engineers.

I've since established that they actually don't fight the enemy face to face, but rather build bridges and infrastructure to support the front line troops, alongside a wide variety of other duties.

Subsequently, and with enormous regret, since I know the effect this news will have upon you, I have decided I must serve our King and Empire by enlisting.

It seems to make more sense to do it here in London, instead of returning to Australia, only to be shipped straight back here.

Darling, I know my decision is dashing your hopes and I anticipate you will be more than a little dismayed that I have reached this difficult decision.

But the talk in shops and on the street is that the war should be over within the year and things will soon get back to normal.

That being the case, I promise you here and now I will book a ticket on the first available ship leaving for Melbourne, just as soon as I am able.

I so hope and pray that upon my arrival, you will be at the wharf to greet me with that loving smile and those flashing eyes of yours, which as you so well know, totally captivate me.
All my love and wishes,
Yours,
Charles

*   *   *

In the weeks after he posted his letter, he routinely checked his mailbox for a reply from the Army and any response from Elizabeth, although hers might be months away.

On a summer's evening in the second week of July, over dinner with the Swansons, Margie announced that she and some nurses at North Middlesex Hospital had been invited to a function in September at The Dorchester being put on by the Wine Association of Portugal.

Knowing Charles' interest in wine, Margie suggested he might like to go with them.

Gracefully he declined saying he would be out of London that week.

Returning to his flat, he found an official looking envelope with an embossed round gold seal depicting King George's Crown, two inset letters "G:R" for George Royal and an inscription "Royal Engineers".

He rushed upstairs, knowing what he was about to read was going to change everything.

Scrambling for his key, he uncharacteristically fumbled as he opened the door, stepped breathlessly inside and turned on the reading lamp.

Before sitting down and opening the envelope he crossed the darkened room to the sideboard, where he poured a stiff shot of whisky into a tumbler and took it to his leather armchair to calm his nerves.

Taking a deep breath, he took a slow swig, then his excitement got the better of him and he tore open the envelope, being careful not to rip the letter.

In the weeks since lodging his application, Charles had hoped he might be invited to join the Royal Engineers, possibly as a Commissioned Officer.

Instead the letter contained a surprise.

The Commanding Officer who signed it indicated his office had made enquiries in Sydney as to his University Regiment experience as a Warrant Officer and noted his engineering qualifications were of the highest order.

The letter indicated that subject to him passing his medical and after having successfully completed the preliminary training, the Royal Engineers might send him to officer training.

Charles felt quietly dumbfounded and rather chuffed.

The letter requested he present himself at the Officer Cadet Training Unit the following Monday for three days of induction. He needed to bring the letter plus an overnight bag with personal items and running gear, some of which he had to go out and buy.

*　*　*

Meanwhile, the letter Charles had posted to Elizabeth in June spent seven long weeks on the water before it reached the Melbourne General Post Office.

He worried day and night how she would take his enlistment news, realising their fledgling relationship had far too quickly reached a major crossroad.

*   *   *

That August at the Royal Melbourne Hospital, Elizabeth Blow's long working days were taking a toll on her spirits and nerves.

On her way home by bus, she frequently saw smartly dressed servicemen and groups of young women in frocks happily entering St Kilda's popular George Hotel. Despite the blackout, it kept beckoning her in for a well-earned end of work reward.

Defying the temptation, she maintained her weekday rule that sweet sherry was only to be enjoyed at the week's end.

As her dimly lit bus slowly made its way towards her Tennyson Street stop, she was looking forward to seeing if by chance there was a letter from Charles. Being kept in a state of constant anticipation for his letters made her feel happy and very wanted.

Opening her picket gate she peeked into the letterbox just in case.

To her delight, despite the gloomy light, she could see it contained a slightly damp envelope with a London postmark and Charles' familiar handwriting.

She clutched it close to her chest as she rushed inside, desperately tearing it open before even shutting the door or sitting down, so eager was she to devour every precious word.

With her eyes wide open, her heart pounding and feelings of great anticipation she breathlessly began to read …

My Darling … Noticing immediately he had never been so familiar but she liked him addressing her this intimately.

Hanging on every word, her mind swirled at a whirlwind pace. Her emotions rose as she became totally absorbed by every nuance of his letter.

The first couple of paragraphs caused her to sigh happily, made her laugh when he referred to her newly acquired baking skills and she was intrigued hearing of his visit to Scotland.

Then on the second page, her mood began to slide, when Charles wrote of his deep fear of England being invaded and that he could not just sit there and watch it all happen around him.

Reading down further, it was if she had just been hit by a bus.

She encountered something she had never wanted to read:

Charles has enlisted

The shock overwhelmed her and in rising waves of panic all she could think was she wouldn't see him again, she would never be in his arms or feel the excitement of his kisses should he be fortunate enough to survive the war.

In her distraught state, Elizabeth completely missed what he wrote towards the end his letter, about expecting the war to only last a year.

Her eyes blurred with an uncontrolled deluge of tears that streamed down her reddening cheeks, dripped onto the pages in her shaking hands, causing his words to smudge into murky, ever widening inky lines, flowing this way and that, into bluish wavy patterns.

Sinking heavily into the sofa, Elizabeth was at a loss as to how she was ever going to cope never seeing him again.

Seeing herself in such a state in the mirror on the wall, she let out an anguished cry that was probably audible to everyone in the nearby units.

'Oh my God! How could he do this to me?'

15. Wine-tasting, September 1940

Life as a passenger aboard the trader *SS Lanahrone* en route from Oporto to Dublin in early September 1940 for Emilio Bestillo was in stark contrast to what he had read in travel ads promising sheer luxury on fast, stylish liners.

With the war on the high seas worsening and an increasing number of U-boat attacks being reported, few passengers attempted sea voyages.

Even fewer chose to travel on ships like the Limerick Steamship Company's very small trader, even though it sailed under Ireland's neutral flag and displayed neutral markings in the hope it would escape becoming a German target.

Emilio's cabin offered few comforts other than a compact dresser, a tiny hanging space and a narrow shelf for his case.

He was shocked his bunk had raised timber sides to prevent him rolling out in rough weather. Initially he was concerned it offered little opportunity to entertain should he meet a woman during the three-day passage, but none were on board.

*   *   *

Before his departure, Bestillo Nacional had alerted its wine agent in London of his arrival and plans to spend several months promoting the family's brand, hoping a surge of new orders might clear its overstocked cellars.

His arrival coincided with his firm's sponsorship of a Wine Association of Portugal's gala event on the fifth of September, to which many VIPs and industry leaders had been invited and at which Emilio had been asked to speak.

*   *   *

Soon after the *Lanahrone's* departure from Oporto, its crew and passenger list had been sent to Bletchley Park, where Miss Tyler immediately noticed a "person of interest" to British Military Intelligence (MI6) was on board.

She alerted her supervisor that the passenger, a Mr E. Bestillo, identified as a possible Nazi sympathiser, was about to arrive in Dublin.

*　*　*

Nine hundred miles over the ocean to the north, in London's Dulwich Village, unbeknown to Emilio, an attractive young nurse, Margie Swanson, was excitedly looking forward to going to the tasting with several nursing colleagues and her best friend Jessie Tyler.

*　*　*

When the *Lanahrone* berthed, Emilio arranged for his samples in the hold to be shipped to London. He then set about boarding a ferry to Liverpool and from there he took the train to London where his agent would show him to his hotel.

Standing unobtrusively on the dock, leaning against a parked truck, was a nondescript MI6 operative. With the brim of his hat pulled down he quietly smoked a cigarette, but his eyes didn't miss Emilio walking down the gangplank.

*　*　*

The Swansons' 1920s modest bathroom in Dulwich Village was cramped at the best of times, but for two young women preening themselves for the wine gala that evening, space mattered little.

Margie had waited months for this evening to arrive, having been well-primed by Charles, who due to his own importing interests had become interested in Bestillo Nacional.

Before the night, Margie had promised herself a hundred times not to make the same mistake she had innocently made in that pub in Scotland with Stephen the soldier. She had really liked him, but she had fobbed him off, all because her dominating mother had warned her off being with men.

For Jessie, tonight was her first opportunity in months to escape the intensity of her demanding work at Bletchley Park, which had her slaving week in and week out, dealing with the flood of coded messages arriving from across the Channel.

A night out like this on the town, at the swank Dorchester, was their first in over a year.

They were having so much fun, taking giggling turns before the small steamed up mirror to brush their hair and powder their faces, applying touches of rouge and eyeliner from small containers balancing around the rim of the basin.

'I've snuck a hip flask of sweet sherry in my make-up bag. I know your parents would never approve,' Jessie, ever the risk taker, confided.

Enjoying heady sips, they happily completed last minute checks, then brushed out their bobs, emitting peals of high-spirited laughter which echoed through the house to the kitchen where Mrs Swanson was busy preparing dinner.

'Girls, your bus leaves in fifteen minutes,' she called.

This produced more excited, slightly tipsy shrieks, as the modest A-line dresses were pulled on in the bedroom, new fangled zips swished shut and stockinged feet slipped into pairs of new high heels.

'Come on Jess, let's fly, goodnight father, bye mother ... Don't wait up,' yelled Margie, as the divine looking pair burst from the bedroom, threw on their coats and noisily toddled out the door, banging it behind them.

One moment it seemed like sheer pandemonium, then in a flash they were gone, leaving the house stone silent as Ron and Gertrude sat down to eat.

Getting off the bus at Park Lane they had a short walk to the swish, blacked-out Dorchester Hotel. Up the stairs, through the grand doors and into the brightly lit foyer they went. A smartly dressed dinner suited manager ushered them towards the magnificent ballroom's VIP receiving line, where they were announced to the Wine Association's president and his wife as well as several industry leaders.

Lastly, they shook hands with a dashing young gentleman, who was introduced as Mr Bestillo from Portugal.

Margie quickly appreciated his tanned Mediterranean good looks, dark swept back hair, confident penetrating brown eyes and near perfect English.

Wearing a suave, dark three-piece suit of obvious European style, he simply took her breath away.

As they entered the ballroom, Margie excitedly took a quick glance back, noticing Mr Bestillo was noting where they were heading.

Whilst searching for her friends, Margie said under her breath to Jessie, 'Mr Bestillo appears very eligible, don't you think? I wonder if he is single.'

'He appears too swarthy for my liking. I actually prefer my men to be more English,' Jessie countered.

Finding Margie's friends, conversation was soon raging, assisted by copious glasses of champagne, which kept flowing until the president stepped up to the microphone and asked for quiet.

The association's latest news soon bored Margie who suggested to Jessie they retire to the powder room.

Returning a while later, they discovered Mr Bestillo had been introduced as the evening's guest speaker and was proudly talking about his fine Douro River wines whilst his flashing eyes swept the room.

'Tonight I invite you to taste the romance of our most special family port we now export worldwide, which has been widely judged as one of the world's finest.'

When his speech concluded, a waiter with a tray of glasses filled with Douro port glided up to Margie and Jessie. As they were about to take a sip, a familiar voice from behind them asked, 'Would you two beautiful ladies mind if I join you for a toast?'

Turning her head, a thrilled Margie responded, 'Why Mr Bestillo, we would be simply delighted,' as they re-introduced each and raised their glasses.

His unexpected presence caused her heart to nearly miss a beat.

Jessie seemed less forthcoming, saying little, instead taking a sip of the deep red port, then another, discovering she very much liked its enticing fruity taste.

'Would you consider it presumptuous if I enquired as to how you ladies found your way to our function tonight?' Emilio asked, with eyes only for Margie.

'Not at all Mr Bestillo', replied an all too willing Margie. 'Some nurses and I received invitations and my Australian uncle, who actually imports your wines, urged me to come.'

Realising he was spending too much time chatting alone to Miss Swanson, whom he was finding very engaging, Emilio reluctantly saw the need to move on. 'I am afraid that much as I would enjoy talking with you longer, I must do my duty and move on to meet more industry leaders.

'Perhaps Miss Swanson, you might consider an invitation to take afternoon tea with me sometime soon,' he suggested looking deeply into her eyes.

Asking for her phone number, which he quickly wrote in a notebook, he said he would be in touch.

He bowed and slipped away to speak to those in the room eager to hear about his special September clearance offers.

Jessie, who had moved away to another group on the other side of the room, noticed Margie weaving towards her with her face simply glowing and cheeks flushed.

'Are you quite sure that smooth Mr Bestillo you have spent half the evening with hasn't made a line for you?' Jessie blurted out when she arrived.

'Not quite so. How could you ever suggest such a thing?' Margie spluttered. However she knew full well she had just shared a very warm conversation with him and he had said he would call her.

Returning fire, Margie challenged her friend.

'Have all those ports I've seen you downing gone to your head?'

Later, chatting endlessly about their night as their bus, lit by a waning moon, headed towards Dulwich Village, Jessie lapsed into deep thought.

Bestillo, Bestillo ... that name seems to ring a bell.

She decided when she got to the office on Monday she would check.

*   *   *

After meeting the very charming Mr Bestillo, Margie wanted him to take a chance with her. So eager was she to see him again, she wrote "Emilio Bestillo" five times in her diary to get used to its foreign spelling.

She then went on to describe for almost a page how handsome and engaging she found him and that he had unwittingly caused her heart to miss a beat.

*   *   *

On the first Saturday in September, following Charles' promotion to Lieutenant, he was released from barracks for a rare day off. When he arrived at his flat he eagerly checked his mail for an update on the arrival of his second butter and wine shipment.

His London distributors had placed unexpectedly large orders, which had put a broad smile on his face and provided a welcome diversion from the grind of his army training and the looming threat of action.

In the cool evening light his Marylebone apartment's mailbox contained several letters, including one with Elizabeth's very familiar and much loved handwriting.

He was looking forward to receiving it, but was very unsure of what she was about to say:

My dearest Charles,

I hope with this horrible war raging in England that my letter finds you as well as you can be, and in good spirits.

I think I am mostly managing and have immersed myself in my work at the hospital these last turbulent months.

Melbourne, like London, is also blacked out at night. There are no streetlights, petrol is rationed and we have to use vouchers to buy food. Sugar has become in short supply so I am doing lots more homecooking than before.

A few of my friends whose husbands have been caught up in the war go out to tea on Sundays, and I join them as it keeps our spirits up.

Since I received your last letter about your surprise enlistment, I feel like I've been on one of those rides at Luna Park.

Sometimes the ride is rather scenic, the next moment it's quite frightening when my car hurtles steeply down into a darkened tunnel and I have no idea when it will ever end.

Darling, if I say that your June letter shattered my heartfelt hopes we would soon be together again to create a beautiful shared

*future, my words fall short of the actual feelings of devastation
I feel.*

*My anger that you have put our King and country ahead of
me has lessened slightly, because I fully realise you are a noble
man with the best of intentions.*

*It is just that I knew we had discovered something we had
both been looking for, for a very long time and I was so happy
that we seemed to have a chance at a splendid future together.
Now with the outbreak of war and your enlistment, everything
has changed.*

*I inquired if I could book a passage to London to see you
and was informed that citizen travel was not possible without
government approval.*

*So I don't know if and when I might be able to see you again.
Yours with love,
Elizabeth*

Putting down her letter, Charles took a deep breath then leaned
back in his armchair to think.

His enlistment had dashed her hopes and caused her to all but
give up on him.

He wondered what in heavens he could do to save their
relationship.

16. The London Blitz, 1940

With his letter of appointment and a small overnight bag containing a clutch of Elizabeth's letters for good luck, in August, Charles presented himself at the Royal Engineers' Officer Cadet Training Unit.

If his seven weeks' passage on the *Strathallan* had done one thing, it had brought Charles down a notch, to rely less on his family name when meeting people. So when he arrived at the Training Unit early one warm Monday morning, he was aware he was just one of sixty-two inductees.

Once his group had its documents processed, they were sent back to the parade ground to wait.

After what seemed like an eternity, the large imposing door of the induction office opened. Out onto a landing overlooking the inductees stepped a very confident Captain Smith, smartly dressed, with a leather "swagger stick" neatly tucked by an elbow to his side, gleaming in the last of summer's warm sunlight.

'Stop the talk … form up in three ranks,' the Captain barked.

His stark orders brought back for Charles memories of his 1930s military training with the University Regiment in Sydney and how the Non-Comissioned Officers (NCOs) relentlessly drove discipline into his disparate fellow students.

During the three days that followed, Charles and the recruits were kept busy with assessments of their skill sets, health, fitness and suitability to serve and they were also measured for uniforms.

Charles completed two interviews, one with an officer from the Royal Engineers explosive unit that held much appeal to him, and a second with the Intelligence unit, which he concluded seemed too much like a boring desk job.

On day three as the recruits lined up on the parade ground, Captain Smith curtly addressed them. 'Gentlemen, thank you for volunteering to serve your King and country.

'In due course you will receive a letter from HQ with the result of your application. Good luck with your new regiment … now … right turn … and … DISMISS!'

*   *   *

As the first nippy London mornings of autumn foreshadowed the approach of a bitterly cold winter, Charles received his final papers, ordering him to serve in the Royal Engineers' Explosive Ordinance Disposal (EOD) Regiment with a posting to the Bomb Disposal section, located just outside London, commanded by Lieutenant Colonel E. Stanton.

His initial reaction was one of shock as the thought of defusing bombs simply terrified him. He believed by joining the Royal Engineers it would be significantly less dangerous than facing the enemy in battle and that this might in some small way appease Elizabeth.

On the other hand, he sensed the posting meant on his days off he could escape to the sanctuary of his Marylebone apartment, which would be a pleasant change and a chance to keep abreast of Garland Trading's UK import business.

Meanwhile, in the skies above Britain the Luftwaffe had just gained air superiority, winning the first bloody stage for the Battle of Britain.

*   *   *

As his training got underway, Charles learnt that the EOD Section would be responsible for defusing unexploded bombs and incendiary devices.

What no-one knew at the time was that Germany was about to commence saturation bombing of England's major cities and that in the next eight months, tens of thousands of unexploded bombs would need to be rendered safe.

For millions of Londoners, like those training at the Royal Engineers barracks, the seventh of September 1940 marked a nightmarish turn in the war.

That Sunday afternoon London was shaken when waves of German bombers swept over the city just before five o'clock in the first devastating air raid of its kind.

It only lasted two agonising hours and shook London to its core.

Residents had no idea the raids would continue every night under the cover of darkness for the next eight long and very frightening months.

Grabbing his helmet and gas mask, Charles joined his fellow recruits, who raced across the parade ground to the safety of an air raid shelter.

Unlike the endless practice drills, this one contained a new element: the ominous roar of German planes approaching, the fearful crump-crump of bombs exploding and the steady return fire from the city's scant anti-aircraft emplacements.

A horrifying new edge had been added to what war meant in England.

Tucked inside their shelter, fifteen men in Charles' Section gathered in a corner to await the orders they would carry out once the raid had ended.

Reports were being received that London's Thames Dock area was being hard hit. Charles sensed that his newly formed Section might be sent there after the Luftwaffe departed.

He knew after that afternoon's first attack that this war had well and truly begun.

*　　*　　*

London's frightened residents had little option but to adapt quickly to a new routine of eating before the evening sirens rang out to alert them that the Luftwaffe was on the way to bomb the daylights out of them.

When they heard the planes, people raced to shelters, which were mostly in underground railway stations.

On the poorly lit platforms, they bravely endured the thunderous sound of hundreds of bombers flying above. It became their worst nightmare. When the planes had passed overhead, they would hear the terrifying whistle of free falling bombs raining down, followed by exploding thuds, some frighteningly close.

The dreadful possibility of a bomb exploding above was a lottery no-one wanted to win. With explosions close at hand, people could feel the very air being sucked out from where they hid, followed by massive shockwaves as the ground around them trembled and shook.

Then followed the sounds of falling rubble, burning fires and hapless cries from the badly injured and dying that created a commotion nobody could shut out.

*　　*　　*

Charles' new Section comprised four sappers and an officer. As officers were considered more highly educated they were considered better suited to undertake the highly dangerous defusing tasks.

In their training sessions, they were taught that every unexploded bomb could have a slightly different detonating system, making every defusing task a "life or death" operation.

Charles realised if he graduated from the disposal course and officer training, he would be the one making these "life or death" decisions and it would be his life that would be on the line.

The word around his unit was that several officers had been killed defusing unexploded bombs in recent weeks.

News of this rattled Charles, but on reflection he promised himself that he would find out exactly what mistakes they had made and ensure he didn't make the same ones.

They were briefed that direct hits had accounted for as many as nine hundred deaths on some nights, with countless more injuries. Hundreds of thousands of homes were being obliterated as the Luftwaffe mercilessly targeted London, dropping over a million tons of bombs.

The rapid surge of bombings through September resulted in thousands of unexploded bombs that created a desperate shortage of trained defusing personnel, so it wasn't a complete shock to Charles when he was informed after completing his officer course that he had been promoted to Lieutenant in charge of his Section.

He learned that the type of bombs the Germans were dropping ranged from SC 112 pound general purpose thin-cased devices that could bury themselves ten feet or more into soft ground, right up to 4,400 pound monsters nicknamed "Satans" that could level a city block.

Charles and the trainees were briefed that the enemy was also dropping massive numbers of incendiary bombs, designed to ignite widespread raging fires as well as light up the target area for the bombers following in the rear.

In addition, they were warned that bombs with delayed fuses were being dropped. These ticked for a prescribed time before detonating, causing widespread panic and disruption, as whole city blocks had to be sealed off and evacuated as a precaution.

Ordnance experts explained in great technical detail how the bombs were fitted with transverse fuses located on the side of the bomb's casing.

Dangerous, almost surgical procedures were necessary to disable a fuse's delicate electrical detonating system.

Some of the equipment Lieutenant Garland's Section was issued with was demonstrated in hands-on sessions.

Their kit included a device called a Crabtree, used to defuse type 15 bombs. It was fitted with two prongs that depressed the fuse's electrical plunger that led to the fuse being deactivated.

When the Crabtree was inserted, the officer tied one end of a long reel of string to the fuse. He then unwound the reel to the nearby escape pit where once he had ducked into it, he could safely pull very firmly on the string to extract the fuse.

*   *   *

In October, Charles' apartment building, like many in Marylebone, had sandbag protection at street level around its doors and windows. But it was not sufficient to save it from some damage when a bomb crashed through the roof of the adjoining premises without exploding and smashed through three floors, before lodging itself in the basement, badly cracking the party wall.

Despite the widespread terror, plus the massive loss and carnage, Charles admired how Londoners had adopted a very stoic "Blitz Spirit", proclaiming they would never succumb to Hitler's attempts to rattle them.

Nearly a quarter of the Nazi bombs were failing to explode, so by the end of the first month of the Blitz, nearly 4,000 live bombs lay around London waiting to be rendered safe. Most had to be defused where they landed, because moving or blowing them up was out of the question.

*   *   *

On an early morning training visit to a London suburb that had been flattened overnight, Lieutenant Garland's Section observed a team defusing a 1,100 pound unexploded bomb. They saw first hand the extreme dangers the mission presented, especially for the officer undertaking the deadly task.

The Lieutenant was held spellbound watching the sappers work in appalling conditions, as they dug down into the muddy crater, carefully removing soil around the bomb casing with trowels. He watched as sheets of old roofing iron and loose timber were used to shore up the crater's sides, whilst sappers dug out soil and rubble to reveal the bomb casing inch by inch until they exposed the fuse mechanism on its side.

Their next task was to identify the ordnance, before establishing the type of fuse and the method to defuse it.

Deep in the crater, almost out of sight, the officer could be heard calling out the details, which were smartly relayed to a sapper who had moved back to the "escape pit", dug a safe distance away. When the fuse was safely recovered it was placed in a timber box and sent off to the School of Mine Warfare for analysis.

Unknown to the Lieutenant, amongst a small crowd of onlookers was a Nazi agent, noting the measures being employed that morning. This vital information would later be radioed in code to "The Abwehr", Germany's feared military intelligence operation, which would forward it to bomb factories, with orders to alter the fuse operation so that when a "Crabtree" was inserted the bomb would explode.

* * *

Later that day, the aroma of early dinners being prepared was carried on the breezes blowing down London's war torn streets as millions of fearful but resilient residents readied to eat early. They had become used to preparing for another terrifying night of wailing sirens and worse.

In his apartment Charles decided to write to Elizabeth about how the Blitz was creating widespread upheaval.

25 September 1940
My dearest Elizabeth,

It has been two long months since you last wrote and I'm praying you are well and that a letter from you might be on its way soon.

Since I took in the sight of the first waves of German bombers in the skies over London eighteen days ago, the papers are reporting the bombings have taken hundreds of lives. They have caused widespread devastation, and appear to be a tactical shift by Hitler to take Britain after our successful Dunkirk retreat.

I feel compelled to write as we are now under siege and one's safety is far from guaranteed, despite residents taking refuge during the raids in the crowded underground stations.

The bombers come soon after dark, and somehow you can sense from the quick, bitter firing of our city's defence guns that there is not a shell or moment to be wasted.

After we hear the sirens wail there's the grinding sound of the planes overhead. Some nights when I am off duty, from the safety of the Underground I feel the shake from the seemingly endless explosions tearing buildings apart and setting rows of houses on fire. They are not so far away and I pray they will not come any closer.

Last night I ventured up from the Underground for some badly needed fresh air and was appalled to see London ringed with fire. It was a simply terrifying sight.

While I watched, batches of falling incendiary bombs flashed terrifically before they quickly simmered to pinpoints of dazzling white light that soon caused ferocious fires.

My defusing training is now complete and I have been commissioned a Lieutenant with my own Section.

I have been assigned a batman by the name of Lance Corporal Kirk. He told me his colleagues call him "Buzz" even though his name is Benjamin and he will drive my vehicle, support me and carry out a multitude of tasks.

I will post this to you now whilst I have the opportunity and of course I will eagerly await the arrival of your next letter.
All my adoring love,
Yours,
Charles

17. Bomb Disposal Section

Britain's War Office was in crisis by the end of October 1940 with so many of London's streets cordoned off due to hundreds of bombs waiting to be defused.

This created a massive demand for more disposal teams, but few volunteers were coming forward, given the life expectancy for this work was a little over twelve weeks.

Subsequently, army recruits were being sent regardless to the Royal Engineers on the understanding that if they managed to survive six months, they could seek a transfer out.

Lieutenant Garland's newly formed No. 1 Bomb Disposal Section was placed on active duty in mid-October, under the eyes of a wily old sergeant. They were initially assigned to defuse the smaller, lower risk bombs, fitted with less complicated fuses to build their expertise.

One morning soon after sunrise, the Lieutenant and his Section were dispatched to a site in London's East End Docks.

Driven by Lance Corporal Kirk, the men were equipped with their basic kit, comprising hammers, spanners, chisels, an older version Crabtree discharger, rope, blocks and tackle, picks and shovels, plus a small stash of explosives.

They carried with them the Section's unwritten prayer that nothing would go wrong.

The sappers in the Lieutenant's Section, whom he was still getting to know, included Private Norry Smithers who had completed six months' training. He was a driven soldier, itching to make his mark fighting the enemy, but he had been assigned instead to the Royal Engineers because of his mechanical background.

Then there was the chain-smoking Private Tubby Jones, the son of a Welsh publican, who had volunteered to join the Royal Engineers and had quickly become the platoon's joke master. He stood five foot five in army boots, with a slightly ruddy face, hinting he enjoyed a pint or two of ale.

The third was Private John Lawrence from Portsmouth, a schoolboy cycling champion, who having turned eighteen in February was able to enlist, in spite of his parents' opposition. He was never allowed to smoke at home and the Lieutenant had noticed he had an unpleasant habit of picking his nose when stressed.

When their van pulled up at the docks, the scene that greeted the Section was one of smouldering, blackened warehouses. Nearby a bulldozer was busy pushing burnt beams and concrete rubble aside to clear an area around an unexploded bomb that fell two days before.

An acrid smell of exploded TNT mixed with the oily fumes of hundreds of bales of burnt wool rose eerily from the wreckage to fill their nostrils.

The site was cordoned off and guarded by civilian defence workers to keep spectators away.

The sergeant took up a position from a short distance to ensure the correct procedures were being followed.

Nonetheless, the Lieutenant, as he stooped beneath the cordoning ropes and crossed the broken ground to the bomb, found his first live assignment highly stressful.

There he surveyed the explosive nightmare lying in an eight-foot pit, which was slowly filling with vile smelling groundwater.

Peering more closely at the bomb, his eyes narrowed at the sight of its green painted tail fin jutting from the pit, which suggested it might only be a 110 pounder, which the manual stated contained 46 pounds of high powered explosives.

Down the side of the casing he spotted the fuse situated midway across the bomb, set in its screw locker with a locking ring.

His anxious face became a picture of concentration knowing he had only one chance to get it right.

Following procedures to the letter, the sappers secured the pit head and shored its sides up with timber before the ladder was re-lowered to enable the Lieutenant to scramble down to complete the identification and form his defusing plan.

Meanwhile, a short distance away the sergeant ticked off points from his clipboard, added notes, saying little, but ready to correct any possible mistakes before they proved fatal.

The sergeant watched intently as the Lieutenant climbed down the ladder to inspect the lower part of the bomb pointing downwards at seventy degrees with its nose buried in the foul water.

Using a stethoscope, the Lieutenant placed the listening bell against the bomb's casing to hear if there was any sound of mechanical ticking, which would indicate its fuse had been activated.

Nothing was heard.

Then he wiped layers of mud from the casing with a rag so he could read its telltale markings.

Gripped by a mixture of fear and not knowing if the Germans had fitted an anti-defusing device to the 46-inch long SC 110 pounder, he found himself sweating heavily beneath his steel helmet and buttoned up jacket, despite the crisp morning air.

Returning to the pithead he held a short conference with the sappers. Then he ordered Private Jones to the safety pit to assist, Private Lawrence to take down notes and Private Smithers to bring the tool kit and rope down into the pit to him.

Re-entering the pit, as he reached the ladder's bottom rung just above the murky water, he knew his moment of truth was close at hand as he surveyed the bomb one last time.

He paused for a few moments to collect himself.

Briefly he thought of Elizabeth and felt reassured he had left her a farewell letter in the event he did not survive the next hour.

Then fleetingly his mind turned to his late father, who had faced life-threatening moments like this in the Great War and hadn't shirked his duty.

The Lieutenant then called, 'Smithers, bring down the ropes and tools'.

'Sir,' came his sharp reply, but Smithers left his bravado at the pithead when he saw the extreme danger below.

After Smithers had climbed out and given the all clear, the Lieutenant placed a foot onto the flooring strut that had been run from the ladder's bottom rung to the pit wall.

He had to wriggle around behind the bomb to make a closer inspection of the fuse pocket and its locking ring, situated around a third of the way up from the nose cone.

He recalled being told during his training that should the bomb be accidently activated, he had only seventeen seconds to escape.

Sizing up his situation, the best he could hope for was to scramble out and dash to the safety pit, protected with rows of sandbags, that his sappers had built some thirty yards away.

Now with his face less than twelve inches from the devilish device, again he listened through the stethoscope for any new ticking sounds.

Thankfully, there was none.

He took a large cold chisel and a hammer from the bag and began gingerly tapping the fuse's locking ring in an anti-clockwise direction to delicately unscrew the mechanism.

A dozen more solid taps later, he paused and re-applied the stethoscope to listen for any ticking sounds.

Hearing nothing, he resumed his tapping.

Twice he missed the chisel, causing the hammer to hit the metal casing.

After each missed hit, the Lieutenant re-checked for any new sounds.

Breathing heavily, with his adrenaline pumping, he kept his mind on the task that he had practised so many times.

Finally, with the fuse ring unscrewed, he applied the Crabtree to do its magic. As it slowly extracted the detonator's firing mechanism, a smile began to crease his apprehensive face.

The Lieutenant carefully slid the assembly from the fuse pocket, making sure it didn't touch the sides and cause an explosion.

Having removed the fuse he unscrewed the "gain" that he knew contained enough penthrite wax to kill him.

With the assembly safely in hand, he climbed the ladder and handed it to the very anxious Smithers, suggesting humourlessly, 'Private, try this for your dinner tonight.'

Then the Lieutenant tied the rope around the bomb's fin and fed the end through a block and tackle that had been placed over the pit, that enabled the sappers to hoist it onto a truck to be taken away to be exploded.

*　*　*

Returning afterwards to barracks, the Lieutenant ordered his batman to stop off at a local pub where he shouted his men a few ales to mark the occasion of their first successful assignment.

That evening in his private quarters, Charles' batman, Lance Corporal Kirk, thought about their day and felt fortunate to be serving a Lieutenant who was so caring of his men, so careful to get things right the first time and so calm in the face of adversity.

The Lance Corporal hoped that should he gain a commission, he would become a trusted and inspiring leader like Lieutenant Garland.

*   *   *

That night, before the return of the hated bombers and the ensuing dash to the shelter, a very tired but relieved Charles penned a caring letter to Elizabeth recounting his day.

> *October 1940*
> *My dearest Elizabeth,*
>
> *I so loved reading your last letter and wish to reassure you that come what may, when this awful war is over all I want is for us to be together again to share those many things we both enjoy.*
>
> *I very much understand your feelings surrounding my enlistment and its impact on our future, but darling I could not bring myself to refuse the call to serve our King and country in this time of desperate need.*
>
> *I have been brought up knowing I have a duty to serve in these circumstances, like my father did in the Great War.*
>
> *Since my last letter, as we leave summer behind and enter the cooler days of autumn, the intensity of the war in London has increased, with the widely held fear that Hitler might invade when his infernal bombing has done its job.*
>
> *Earlier this month I was very proud to receive my commission as Lieutenant and I was able to celebrate it with the Swansons who seemed delighted too.*
>
> *I have been assigned to lead the Number 1 Bomb Disposal Section and for several weeks we have been undergoing rigorous training in preparation for being sent into active duty.*
>
> *Suffice to say, before I go out to lead my men, I always pause to think of you, which helps settle my fears, before focusing on the task at hand.*

I wish I were able to return to the safety of your arms that I miss more so as every day goes by.

But for the moment this is not to be.

Be assured, I am in good spirits.

Do keep up your grand work at the hospital and pray that the only news you hear of me is good news.

Till my next letter, all my love and sweetest wishes; chin up through all this my darling!

My adoring love,

Charles

* * *

By late 1940 in London with the Blitz causing widespread havoc, the need for thousands of additional civil defense workers escalated dramatically.

Typically, they held down day jobs. Then in the evenings, they would deal with bomb incidents, fight fires, treat the vast number of injured, enforce the blackout regulations, run rest centres and canteens, assist the rescue of bomb victims trapped in the mangled ruins of city buildings and homes, and remove the dead to the mortuary vans.

* * *

London's Ambulance Corp had put out a desperate call for trained nurses and Margie Swanson was amongst a handful from North Middlesex Hospital to apply.

Having recently obtained her driver's licence, Margie was one of those selected and was assigned to drive an ambulance.

There, she spent most nights in London's Underground train shelters, tending to huddles of frightened families wrapped in blankets, taking refuge.

By morning light, when the bombers became an easy target for the defence AA guns and had slunk back across the Channel, the welcome "all clear" sirens were heard.

The ambulance crews would emerge from their shelters to begin the unpleasant work of tending to the injured rescued from the burning rubble, which a few hours earlier had been rows of homes and shops.

Carrying out her angel's work night after night, she proved an unflappable figure in her crisp uniform with its distinctive white bib, light blue shirt with sleeves rolled up above the elbows, black stockings, black lace-up shoes and tin helmet, which contrasted sharply with her soft facial features.

During the Blitz, many a night she was unsure if she would survive to see another dawn. She had one recurring thought that kept her looking forward to each new day, the prospect of the handsome Mr Bestillo calling her.

18. First Kiss

The Swanson home phone rang three times in the third week in October before being answered.

Margie had worded up her sister and father that she was expecting a call, and they promised to be accommodating. The last thing she wanted was for her mother to answer Mr Bestillo's call.

When she had told her Emilio had invited her to tea, all she heard was a strong reminder about the dangers of foreign men like him, who held few scruples when it came to a young woman's virtue.

In fact, Gertrude's advice didn't stop there.

She brusquely reminded Margie that sex outside of marriage was not an option in the Swanson household and she expected the highest standards from her elder daughter, who needed to set an example to her impressionable sister.

Hearing the phone ring, Gertrude rushed from her kitchen to get it.

'Good evening ... the Swanson residence ... Mrs Swanson speaking ...'

'Good evening Mrs Swanson, this is Emilio Bestillo. I am hoping to speak to Margie.'

Gertrude immediately felt uncomfortable having a foreigner on the line and worse, he was asking for her daughter.

'Margie won't be home until late. I will give her a message you called,' she curtly replied.

'Would you be so kind as to let her know that she can reach me at the Tavistock Hotel?' he asked.

"I will pass it on, good evening to you now.'

Upstairs, having skipped out of her bedroom, Margie only managed to hear the tail end of the conversation and from the landing she glared down with a growing fury.

'Mother!' she yelled. 'How dare you do that to me? Was that Emilio? Did he say where he was?'

'My dear, I have every right to decide whom you can speak to when they call my household,' Gertrude hissed.

'No, you don't. I'm no longer a schoolgirl so my calls are my private business.

'Tell me where is he staying or I will have to knock on every hotel door in town to find him.'

Seeing how upset she had become, Gertrude backed off, saying, 'The Tavistock.'

With tears of dismay streaming down her face, Margie stormed down the stairs with her purse, grabbed her coat and bolted out the door, slamming it hard in her wake.

As she raced down the road to call him, she made a decision in light of her mother's actions.

If Emilio was prepared to take a chance on her, she was ready to take a chance on him!

At the phone box, she looked up the Tavistock's number in a battered directory.

Whilst waiting to be put through to his room, she saw that her hand was shaking. It was quickly forgotten, when, to her great relief, his warm voice came on the line, causing her heart to miss a beat and a broad smile to spread across her anxious face.

After exchanging pleasantries, Margie came straight to the point.

'Emilio, thank you for trying to call me. I'm so very sorry that my mother made your call so difficult and I want to apologise for how poorly she treated you.

'But if you were calling to see if I still wanted to see you, I would like you to know my answer is yes.'

Despite being slightly stunned, Emilio quickly regained his composure.

'Margie, if I had been given the opportunity earlier, I would like to have said how delighted I was to have met you and your friend Jessie at The Dorchester.

'Given we are now past that conversation with your mother, yes I would very much like to see you. May I suggest we take afternoon tea when you are next free?'

Margie paused trying to remember what her work schedule looked like for the week ahead.

'I have the day off next Friday. Does this suit you?'

'That will be perfect. Why don't we plan to meet outside the London Bridge train station's ticket office at 3 pm? I am sure we can find some tearooms nearby,' he suggested.

Swept off her feet with the prospect, Margie tried to sound calm. As she accepted, her cheeks became redder than the phone box she was standing in and her heart was beating fast.

'Emilio, that will be simply perfect,' she said, thinking as she hung up that next Friday could not come quickly enough.

*   *   *

Despite his frosty encounter with Margie's overbearing mother, Emilio thought that this delightful English rose seemed eager to see him again, which very much suited his growing desire for her.

In the meantime, he had a number of orders to send off to head office and a letter to write to his old Lisbon university friend, Ernst Neumann, who was asking about life in London and how he was surviving the bombing raids.

*   *   *

Returning to her desk at Bletchley Park, Jessie Tyler searched through the "B" files for the surname "Bestillo" and soon one turned up, which indicated he had been flagged as "a person of interest".

His file showed he had been shadowed by a MI6 operative from Dublin to London and his subsequent movements seemed to confirm he was going about his wine business, as his arrival papers had indicated.

However, several letters that had been intercepted by MI6, which were sent to Mr Bestillo from an officer serving in the German army, suggested he might be overly supportive of the Nazi war efforts.

The most recent letter from the officer asked Mr Bestillo to tell him about the effects of the German bombing on London.

There was also mention in the file of a scandal Mr Bestillo had left in Oporto. A former girlfriend of his was pregnant. Her enraged father was chasing him for a sum of fifteen million escudos, which

Jessie estimated was close to £70,000. The girl's father had warned Mr Bestillo that should he refuse his demands, he would take the matter to the newspapers, alerting the whole town as well as his well-respected family of his outrageous deeds.

Jessie added her own note on the Dorchester night to the file, recording that she had attended and been introduced to him during the evening, noting that he had spoken about his wine interests and appeared to be well mannered. She omitted making any reference to Mr Bestillo appearing to take more than a passing interest in her best friend.

Returning the folder, Jessie prayed Mr Bestillo would not follow up and contact her, as she didn't want Margie being recorded as a known associate of his in the MI6 file.

*　*　*

On the first Friday in October, feeling poised and looking radiant in her peach-coloured dress with a smart matching woollen jacket, gloves, felt hat, sheer stockings, her newest high heels and a flouncy hair style she had copied from a film magazine, Margie arrived early for her three o'clock station rendezvous.

It gave her a few precious moments to re-check her makeup and hair in a nearby shop window. As the hour arrived, she positioned herself in front of a pillar so Emilio Bestillo could easily spot her from the hundreds of people entering the station.

Keeping a keen eye over the entrance from where she expected him to arrive, she was suddenly startled by a pair of hands being gently placed around her narrow waist from behind, as a voice with a Mediterranean accent said, 'Miss Swanson, I do believe?'

Turning, she was shocked to discover the hands and voice belonged to the beaming Mr Bestillo.

'How lovely to meet this way,' Margie exclaimed, 'but sneaking up like that was a huge surprise.'

'I hoped you wouldn't mind … I came in the other way, saw you with your back to me and thought that it gave me the opportunity to catch you napping, which was just too tempting,' he said.

'Now if you are starving, we should head off down London Bridge Road to Sainsbury's tearooms which I think will be private.'

'Emilio, I missed lunch so I'm ravenous,' said Margie. 'We need to walk quickly or I might embarrass you when my tummy rumbles.'

Offering his arm, the pair strolled off happily towards Sainsbury's.

Over tea, they shared scones topped with jam whilst their conversation flowed as easily as the whipped cream he was spreading over them.

Margie asked about his university days, his family in Portugal and his job and he wanted to know more about her ambulance work and whether her mother knew she was seeing him today.

'For obvious reasons she does not know we are meeting. I told her I am catching up with friends and I changed at the hospital so she would not see me in this outfit,' Margie confided.

Looking at her beaming across the small table, Emilio leaned forward.

'If my eyes don't deceive me, you appear even more beautiful than when we first met!'

The flattering compliment was music to Margie's ears and made her swoon.

With their afternoon disappearing fast, Emilio suggested they catch a bus to his hotel for an aperitif, before the bombers returned, which would force everyone to take shelter for what would be the fifth consecutive week of nightly raids.

Half an hour later, seated in the Tavistock Hotel's fashionable lounge, Margie was thoroughly enjoying a second champagne, a pleasure she could never afford on her meagre wage.

Seated opposite her, Emilio lit a cigarette, drew deeply and slowly exhaled before taking a further sip, appearing in his element and at ease for the first time.

She was in pure heaven, more so whenever she looked into his deep, dark brown eyes.

Secretly she wondered if their first exciting date would end with a kiss.

Many a night since they met, she had tossed in bed, dreaming of being swept up in his arms with his lips pressed to hers.

'Margie, I have something special I want to show you. Would you like to accompany me to my room to see it?' he casually suggested.

'I love surprises. Of course I would.' Margie replied, feigning virtuousness whilst her heart beat faster.

Her answer delighted Emilio, causing him to feel surer of himself.

As they walked across to the lift, Emilio sensed she appeared suitably entranced and hoped she might accept a tender kiss before long.

Leaving the lift on the fourth floor, he took her arm as they headed down the hallway's lush carpet towards his suite.

Still feeling the warmth of his arm, Margie felt thrilled to enter his private space but she also felt pangs of guilt, knowing her mother would never approve of her being there.

Emilio resisted sweeping her up in both arms there and then.

Instead he purposely made her wait, adding fuel to her already breathless anticipation.

He invited her to sit next to him on the sofa, then picked up a book from a small side table celebrating Bestillo Nacional's first hundred years of winemaking.

Handing it to her, he watched in silence as she studied the photos before he answered her questions. Sensing the moment had arrived, he moved even closer to her until he could feel her warmth.

Putting the book aside, he turned back to look more deeply into her wide, innocent brown eyes. Taking her soft, slender hands in his, he drew her towards him until his moist lips brushed hers leading to their first perfectly timed kiss.

Immediately she tasted his tobacco-tinged lips that soon swept her off her feet.

She could feel his passion was igniting a fire in her that she had never known before.

The kiss soon turned to a second, then an even more passionate third one, each seemingly longer and more arousing than the one before.

She hoped their newly discovered intimacy would never end. Nothing she had ever read in all those romantic novels compared with the absolute thrill of being in Emilio's arms and receiving his passionate embraces.

Emilio well suspected Margie was most likely a virgin and even if she wanted to, this afternoon was never going to be the right time to ask if he might make her his woman.

His thoughts strayed momentarily back to his messy Oporto office affair with Luzia and how the ugly problem had followed him to England.

He promised himself he would avoid making that sort of mistake again.

'Margie, your kisses are like the sweetest wine, so special, so romantic and so beautiful,' he murmured in her ear.

'Do you know ever since that night we met, I have longed to hold you like this? I had no idea until this moment the feeling was mutual.'

If she thought she had been carried away in the phone box calling him, it was nothing like the flood of passion that was fast engulfing her here on the sofa.

She felt ready to take their passion further, but time had run out and unbeknown to her, his next move was more calculated.

'With it almost 6 o'clock, I should be putting you on your bus, before the bombers return and you have to explain to your mother how you came to spend the night with me in an air raid shelter,' he said.

With her pulse racing and out of breath, Margie sat up, flushed from their passionate kisses and embraces.

'Yes, that would be a little difficult to explain, as she has no idea I've been here … but I have simply loved being held and kissed by you.'

As her bus pulled into the stop, Emilio drew her close for one farewell embrace that she never wanted to end. His last words echoed through her head all the way home.

'Margie, I feel I'm ready to see where things might go between us. When I see you next, can you let me know how you feel about us?'

*   *   *

That night in bed in a corner of the Swanson's cellar, still in high spirits after her amazing experience, Margie updated her diary with the headline:

Today Emilio kissed me!!!!

She allowed some of her innermost thoughts to flow effortlessly onto the page to record her breathtaking afternoon.

She decided she couldn't wait to give him her answer on how things might go and as she drifted off to sleep, she was no longer sure if she was going to be strong enough to resist him the next time they kissed.

But in the cool of the following morning, she decided she wanted for the time being to keep him guessing.

Nonetheless, she could not get out of her mind a rising desire for Emilio's passionate kisses, his arousing hands and firm body.

Despite her mother's pleas to the contrary, she now better understood how a girl in her situation experiencing such strong desires could be tempted to want to quench her passionate fires.

*   *   *

The same evening, when Emilio had finished dinner and taken some fresh air on a short walk to Russell Square Park, he returned to his room to await the air raid sirens. His mind kept returning to Margie's exquisite lips and embraces, which were so much more than merely agreeable.

In fact, he felt she was a very special girl with so much to offer and he was looking forward to exploring her offerings, whatever they may be, when the proper occasion presented itself.

He was in a hurry, but did not want to rush things merely to satisfy his immediate urges.

He reminded himself before dropping off to sleep that tomorrow he must deal with the letter of demand from Luzia's father, which was sitting unanswered on his desk.

It was proving to be a larger problem by the day.

19. Waterloo Park, 1940

When Emilio Bestillo's firm asked him to extend his successful London stay, he secured a short lease on a modest Baylis Road flat directly opposite Waterloo Park.

In the following weeks he gained considerable pleasure rearranging the furniture to make the living room more comfortable and improve the view from the bay window.

He enjoyed shopping for various household items at a local second-hand store, which he hoped Margie would appreciate.

Emilio felt more comfortable entertaining her here in his flat because it was more private and proper than the hotel, which was in plain view of the nosey reception staff with their prying eyes. Should things work out, she might even choose to make use of his flat as her city base.

* * *

When Friday finally dawned, he rose early, shaved and showered and meticulously ironed his slacks and a shirt to go with his new reefer jacket.

For lunch he went to the grocer for some cold treats. Then he uncorked a bottle of the prize-winning Bestillo claret he had saved for a special occasion and placed it near the heater to take the chill off it.

Emilio wondered if Margie would be as excited to see him as he was to see her.

Their mutual hunger for something other than lunch might need to be met with first.

* * *

Margie had chosen to wear a knee length figure hugging skirt, expensive silk stockings and a black cashmere cardigan over a crisp white cotton button-up blouse under her winter coat.

On the bus to Waterloo, she was surprised that she was such a bundle of nerves and found herself breaking into cold sweats despite the sleety, grey day.

In her bag there was a house-warming gift of two crystal wine glasses, which she hoped Emilio would like.

Whizzing past the rain-splattered windows was a blurry, endless landscape of dull grey, colourless buildings and people.

Her mind drifted back to the liberating thoughts that had coursed through her excited head after their first romantic encounter which had her, on the one hand, wanting to throw herself at him, but on the other hand, feeling the need to act demurely.

These opposing thoughts kept confusing her.

Strangely, in the days following their first kiss, her wild desires had slightly diminished. In their place were more responsible thoughts, which were now making her feel slightly nervous as to how her visit to see his flat might turn out.

It was hard to imagine it could be even more exciting than her first one in his hotel room. From the bottom of her heart she hoped it would be.

She was still undecided if she should only allow him to lightly embrace her and share a kiss or two. Or would she be tempted to want much more?

*   *   *

Meanwhile, as he set the table in his flat and enjoyed a last cigarette, Emilio jumped when the phone rang unexpectedly.

'Hello, oh it's you Margie … Where are you?'

'I'm on the corner of Baylis Road and the park. How much further along the road is your flat?' she eagerly asked.

'If you start walking down it, I will come out to greet you. I'm in a blue reefer jacket and I promise I won't creep up and surprise you from behind!' he told her.

Stubbing out his cigarette, he raced excitedly downstairs, buttoned his jacket, checked his tie and started walking briskly towards her, hardly noticing the sleety drizzle drifting down to form a light sheen on his eager face and jacket.

From a distance Margie had little difficulty spotting his suave figure, and despite wearing heels, she broke into a run.

At fifty paces, their eyes locked on each other and with faces filled with anticipation they broke into a mad dash that ended when Margie leapt effortlessly into his outstretched arms to receive his welcoming kiss.

As their hungry lips met in an emotional embrace and their bodies moulded tightly together, neither cared one hoot what anyone watching may think.

They were oblivious their romantic scene had delighted several residents waiting for the postman. One elderly woman muttered under her breath that a movie director would have been thrilled to create an amazing scene like that.

They disengaged out of breath and Margie straightened her attire.

Arm in arm, they walked, enthusiastically chatting towards his flat.

Enjoying his firm support guiding her and relishing his intoxicating kiss, she turned more than once to look intensely into his face.

Reaching the top of the stairs, short of breath and flushed, Margie told him, 'I am really looking forward to seeing your place.'

Despite wanting to take things slowly she knew she was on the verge of being carried away. Playing for time she suggested, 'First, you must show me around.'

She was surprised how comfortably furnished it was, with a large sofa and a cosy day chair with padded arms looking out the windows, a partly filled bookcase, a swivel chair and small desk that was neatly arranged with pens, folders and beside it a leather briefcase. She took in the intimate little dining table set for lunch, quickly imagining herself seated there on one of its bentwood chairs against a delightful leadlight bay window, with a splendid view across the park, made more cheerful by red winter flowers in the window box.

On the table she saw that he had lit a candle that flickered romantically in the warm eddies rising from the wall heater that brought a smile to her happy face.

Feeling warmer and more settled, he helped her off with her coat.

Margie was impressed to see his small, welcoming kitchen bathed with soft grey window light, with an old-fashioned stove, scrubbed pine table and chairs, complete with a bowl of apples and oranges, plus a little wall cupboard with plates, glasses, biscuit tins and bowls.

Next Emilio showed her the bathroom and last of all he opened the door to his bedroom. Modestly she only took one step in, taking in the inviting double bed, a side table with a novel and reading light and windows screened by partly drawn curtains.

Slightly anxious at the sight of his bed, the thought crossed her mind that she might end up in it sometime soon.

With the electricity between them becoming palpable, she turned to him, 'It's so peaceful and private in this half-light, I'm sure you find it very restful.'

Waiting behind her at the doorway, Emilio was impatient to hear her answer to the question he had posed when he put her on the bus ten days earlier.

'I have opened a special bottle of wine and lunch is prepared when you feel hungry.'

Returning to the living room Margie took a present from her carryall.

'This is my house-warming gift. I'm hoping you will like it and will find a use for them.'

Carefully removing its wrapping, a broad smile spread across Emilio's face as he set down the superb crystal glasses on the table, noting how they sparkled in the soft light.

'You shouldn't have gone to so much trouble, they are perfect, thank you,' he replied looking appreciatively at them, before pouring wine into each glass.

Then he proposed a toast, 'To my beautiful Margie … may we, with your exquisite glasses, share innumerable pleasures!'

Flushed by two glasses of wine, she felt her legs begin to tingle. The room suddenly seemed much hotter.

Noticing change in the colour of her cheeks, Emilio took her into his arms more intimately to thank her for the gift.

Drawing her close he noticed her racing pulse as they held each other more tightly, moulding into one.

Their heavy breathing and passionate kisses made everything else insignificant.

Margie could feel a sensuous longing rising in her, like the time before. She suspected this time she was approaching the point of no return.

Emilio was pacing himself to be sure she felt ready and he had her permission.

He need not have worried, she was offering it without having uttered a word, but he needed to be sure.

Pausing, he looked into her eyes and asked, 'Do you recall that question I asked the last time we met as to where things between us might go?'

'Of course I do,' she quietly responded. 'I am ready and want to be with you.'

Obligingly, he deftly swept her off her feet, and she found herself falling backwards on the sofa still balancing her wine in one hand and holding the back of his head with her other.

Emilio rescued her glass and placed it aside before he knelt before her slightly open legs and smothered her hungry lips with further kisses that moved to her cheeks, then swept down the velvet white skin of her neck.

Then she felt his confident hand go around her slender waist, drawing her ever so slowly towards him. Then a hand began to caress upwards over her soft blouse.

Soon his eager fingers reached the firm outline of her small, rising breasts. It only ignited an even fiercer fire deep in her that she knew only Emilio could quench.

As they embraced, she tenderly held his head in her hands as his fingers slipped beneath her bra to hover over a heaving breast, causing her to utter an even louder pleasurable sigh.

Never taking his eyes from hers, he leaned back and deftly began to unbutton her blouse from the top, one button at a time.

Each release became more breathtaking than the last as her entranced eyes followed his deft fingers.

Offering another inviting kiss, he tempted her to lean forward as he slipped her blouse over her head and unclipped her bra, which was soon tossed towards a nearby chair.

For the first time in her young life, her pert breasts were set free in front of a man, causing her to feel completely liberated.

When he moved forward between her now spread legs on his knees to kiss her sweet lips and caress her bare breasts, she felt his aroused body pressing.

She liked him moving over and down on her, caring little that her skirt had ridden up, exposing her stockingless upper thighs.

With each successive thrust she could feel his firm swelling pressing ever closer onto her. Unwittingly she edged out further so she could receive more of him, which was new and exhilarating.

Margie wondered if he was going to take her here on the sofa.

Was he going to ask permission?

What if she said no to his advance?

Instead, the wild child in her seemed to take over. Her state of high arousal, her increasingly deeper groans of pleasure told him she wanted him to take the lead.

His passionate kisses continued to devour her breasts and further arouse her nipples causing more sighs that only further encouraged his lips to meander lower past her navel to her soft heaving mound.

He had thoughts of carrying her to the bedroom but he realised she was more than comfortable where she lay and seemed to welcome his every move.

Never taking his gaze from her innocent, brown eyes that seemed to be saying yes, he smoothly unzipped her skirt and feasted his eyes on the bare young woman before him except for one last item of underwear.

Modestly looking away, instinctively she raised her hips to enable him to slip them off, revealing to his hungry eyes the splendour of her smooth upper thighs above her stockings, her soft mound and flat tummy below her awakened breasts.

Now she needed to feel more of his skin and run her hands over his chest.

Without asking she began unbuttoning his shirt before sliding her hands up his torso.

She then removed his shoes and felt no sense of guilt as she commenced undoing the buttons down the front of his slacks.

Down to his underwear, he leaned over her reclining form to

erotically kiss every inch of her rising from her toes to her head as her moans only encouraged him to continue.

He looked into her loving face and saw her pretty lips softly open and her eyes closed, as she absorbed the cloud of ecstasy that had enveloped her.

Past the point of no return, to Margie's absolute surprise, his sure fingers continued to pleasure her deeply until her breathing quickened that caused her hips to rise and the small of her back to arch upwards as waves of release catapulted her into orbit.

With his desire unquenched, in the breathless, sweaty moments that followed, she was aware of him slipping on protection before she felt him gently enter her.

Then, encountering some resistance that soon gave way, he moved deeper still commencing a wonderful rhythm that caused her to gasp aloud.

He kept moving until she felt his torso stiffen and he moaned aloud announcing his pulsating release, before their bodies fell exhausted into comfortable depths of the sofa, enveloped tightly in each other's perspiring arms.

Waking in a dream-like state, she wondered where she was until the memories flooded back and she became aware of the light patter of rain on the windowpanes. Cocooned in his warm embrace she felt far from the starkness of war and she gave scant thought about the chance she had just taken with him or where it might lead.

Instead she wondered if her tummy rumbles might mean her appetite had returned.

*　*　*

At home that evening in bed, still wearing a contented smile, Margie wrote in her diary beginning with the bold headline:

Emilio made perfect love to me today! I am now his woman.

20. The Rescue, 1940

On one particular night in November, the exploding bombs seemed closer and heavier than usual in the Earl's Court Underground shelter. One explosion that rumbled overhead had felt perilously close.

Margie Swanson and her colleagues emerged from the Underground after the all clear had been given, donning gas masks. They were greeted by spine-curdling screams of children trapped in a house nearby that had received a direct hit.

Refusing to wait for the fire brigade and protected only by her heavy coat and helmet, Margie and a fire warden dashed courageously into the smouldering ruins to find the youngsters.

Gingerly climbing down into a wrecked basement, they discovered amongst the charred beams the gruesome sight of two dead people who had been killed by the falling debris whilst using their bodies to save their children.

Beneath them lay two terrified kids whose fearful, wide eyes said it all.

Margie extracted the first of the children, wrapping her coat around the boy before carrying him in her arms to the ambulance, comforting him as she went.

Behind her, the warden carried the distressed little girl.

They were given first aid for their burns before Margie noticed one of her legs had been burnt.

Despite it hurting, she insisted on driving the ambulance to the hospital through lurid clouds of red smoke and burning buildings.

Arriving at casualty, she briefed the nurses on the children's injuries and made sure the doctor on duty saw them as a matter of urgency.

In the flurry of the rescue, she hadn't noticed a Metropolitan Police sergeant had arrived on the scene and witnessed Margie heroically emerging from the destroyed home with the injured boy.

The sergeant made a note of her name, which he obtained from

Margie's colleague, before writing a recommendation to his district commander that she be nominated for a bravery award.

*   *   *

Several days later, Margie made a visit to the hospital to check how the children were recovering and to enquire what else she could do.

Still sedated and covered in bandages, their faces lit up when they spotted two small teddy bears Margie had brought for them.

She discovered they were Oliver Osborne, aged five, who told her he loved British fighter planes and his sister Lily, aged three, who kept asking when she was going to see her mummy.

*   *   *

In the heady days following Margie's thrilling visit to Emilio's flat, her emotions ranged from sheer ecstasy to being uncertain where it might all be heading, but she didn't feel a single pang of remorse.

Her mother kept asking if she was seeing that foreigner and she wondered what she would say to Jess, whom she knew would not approve of the most recent developments.

Yet, she admitted she was enjoying being on cloud nine, being wanted and desired and hopefully loved by the man who had made her a woman.

For the moment, she was declining his invitation to use his flat as her base, knowing all hell would break loose at home if her mother found out.

Over the next few weeks, the couple enjoyed frequent daytime trysts, full of unbridled passion and lust.

*   *   *

By November 1940, retail supplies of fine wine in England were becoming more difficult to find, which enabled Bestillo Nacional to fill the gap, with larger monthly deliveries being shipped from Oporto via Dublin.

*   *   *

Turning his full attention to Mr Felloni's letter of demand, Emilio decided to propose paying a yet to be agreed sum in three months' time. In the meantime he offered to send a monthly allowance, which he could manage from his pay packet.

He had in mind to offer five million escudos (around £23,000) to settle the matter, which admittedly was well short of the amount Mr Felloni was demanding.

The burning question was where he was going to lay his hands on such a hefty sum by the end of March should his proposal be accepted.

Amongst his options was enquiring whether his family's bank in Oporto might provide a loan or he could ask his grandfather for one. He realised both these options could unravel, resulting in the scandal sweeping through his close-knit family and worse, through his hometown.

Lying in bed at night, his restless mind kept churning over his dilemma. Ever the optimist, he was confident that he could somehow find a solution, although he was not looking forward to Mr Felloni's next letter.

In the meantime, he consoled himself with the thought that Margie had become the delight of his life. She had turned out to be such a passionate and willing diversion, he knew she adored and needed him, but he wondered how long their tryst would last.

21. Letter from Melbourne

By late 1940 it was taking up to ten weeks for letters sent by sea between London and Melbourne to reach their destinations, meaning that at any point in time, several of Charles' and Elizabeth's might be on the water.

*　　*　　*

Melbourne's war economy resulted in widespread rationing that was forcing everyone to adapt. With food and petrol becoming scarce, people walked instead of drove, renovated forgotten backyards to grow vegetables, kept chooks and encouraged fruit trees back to life.

At night in the suburbs, volunteer air raid wardens patrolled the streets to maintain the blackouts and alerted residents of accidental blackout breaches.

*　　*　　*

Having not heard from Charles for nearly two months, by November Elizabeth was fretting. She was surprised she had not heard from Charles for her birthday, causing her to wonder if he was all right.

Also, her brooding was being driven by something that happened on the way home the previous week when, feeling in need of a pick-me-up, she had dropped into the George Hotel where she knew some girlfriends were kicking up their heels.

Sipping sherry and enjoying many laughs, she was introduced to a dashing air force Group Captain, who, as the evening developed, took more than a passing interest in her.

Visiting the restroom, she noticed her cheeks were flushed in the mirror, hopefully from the sherry, but more likely from his undivided attention.

When he asked if she would like to go to the dance at the St Kilda Town Hall, which had become famous for attracting American servicemen and dozens of young, single women, she declined.

Instead, she took herself home, feeling more than a little guilty that she had been tempted, but sensed there was something missing in her life and that something was obviously her darling Charles. She was yet to admit she was struggling and did not have any idea what she should do.

A week later, she received an invitation that had been delivered to the hospital from the Group Captain asking if she would like to have afternoon tea at the Windsor Hotel with him on Sunday.

It set her mind racing.

*   *   *

Through London's dark and wet months of November and December, the bombing continued unabated.

The War Office estimated more than fifteen thousand tons of bombs had been dropped on the city since September.

Charles' defusing Section was being overwhelmed with tasks and every able soldier was working long stretches without breaks.

The School of Mine Warfare was regularly issuing Charles' Section with updates about the types of bombs and fuse systems the Germans were employing.

One such report indicated a reason quite a number of bombs were failing to explode was in part due to the Czech prisoners of war being used by the Germans as slave labour in their bomb factories, deliberately sabotaging the fuses.

*   *   *

On the night of Sunday the twenty ninth of December, the most notorious and destructive raid since the Blitz began took place, causing what was soon called London's "Second Great Fire".

In just a few hours it took the lives of one hundred and seventy people, devastated hospitals, government buildings and homes across large parts of the city.

The morning after, before he reported for duty, Charles phoned the Swansons to check that they had survived the night.

'It was an awful night, but we are miles from London and we felt more or less safe in our cellar, despite the racket in the distance of wave after wave of bombers,' Gertrude told him.

'I am worried about Margie though. She did not come home last night and we haven't heard anything from her, but I suppose she knows how to look after herself. Also, I am more than apprehensive that she seems to be seeing that foreign salesman far too often.

'Would you like to speak to Ron who can tell you about the great fires he saw from the loft?' she asked.

'Yes, please,' answered Charles, who had spent the night in his barracks' shelter. Gertrude handed the phone over to Ron.

'Good morning Charles, what a night we have all had,' he began before asking how he had survived it.

'Yes, I'm safe and sound but shaken nonetheless,' answered Charles.

'Aunt Gertrude just told me about you watching London go up in flames.'

'Charles, it was the greatest fire I have ever seen,' said Ron, taking a deep breath.

'The flames whipped hundreds of feet into the air, illuminating pinkish white clouds of smoke that were ballooning upward, especially around St Paul's Cathedral, which I am sure could not have survived.'

'Amazing,' said Charles.

'Immediately above the flames the sky turned red and angry. It was like there was a low ceiling in the heavens made of pink smoke dotted with hundreds of brilliant specks, which might have been anti-aircraft shells bursting around the German prey', he added.

'You were fortunate to be outside the targeted area,' said Charles.

'From our barrack's shelter, I could hear the distant whistle of bombs as they fell, followed by muffled detonations. I also heard the metallic tinkling of incendiary bombs igniting.'

*　　*　　*

Charles read later in that day's *Telegraph* that the War Office estimated over one hundred and twenty thousand bombs and incendiary devices had been dropped from St Paul's Cathedral to Islington.

The Germans had cunningly planned the raid for low tide on the Thames, which severely impeded efforts to pump water to fight the fires.

Charles also read that Mr Churchill had urged St Paul's be saved at all costs, which resulted in hundreds of "Cathedral Watchers" climbing bravely onto its roof during the attack to quell dozens of spot fires.

Other articles reported widespread ruptured gas mains, severed sewer lines, burst water pipes and electricity being cut. Across the city lay hundreds of unexploded bombs, surrounded by corpses, entombed in destroyed houses and buildings.

That morning at first light, every available man was ordered out to deal with hundreds of new unexploded hazards.

Leading his four-man Section Lieutenant Garland was sent to a road in Islington where a small, unexploded device had lodged in a row of demolished houses.

Arriving at the site, his Section went through its usual procedures of setting up and preparing the plan to defuse the bomb.

After carefully removing the bomb's fuse ring and hearing nothing ticking, the Lieutenant extracted the fuse mechanism. When he had it safely in hand, he re-checked the empty fuse pocket cavity with his torch and was surprised to see a rolled up note at the back.

Opening it he was amazed to read, in roughly pencilled text:

WE MAKE SURE THIS DOES NOT GO OFF

The Lieutenant presumed it was written by a gallant Czech slave labourer who had not only risked his life to save theirs, but also had the courage to let them know who did it.

Climbing from the pit with the message tucked in his pocket, he knew his commanding officer would be tickled pink when he got to see it.

* * *

Following the arrival of the 1941 New Year, having done nearly three weeks' straight duty, the exhausted Lieutenant was sent on leave.

Walking slowly home from the Underground, he picked up some supplies, including a bottle of whisky. He was looking forward to relaxing, knowing more than likely most of his cold winter nights would be spent in the nearby air raid shelter.

Amongst a small pile of mail his landlady was holding for him was a much anticipated letter in Elizabeth's handwriting, which sent pleasant shivers of excitement through his wrung out body.

He poured himself a double shot of whisky that soon began to smoothly caress his weary senses, as he began to pleasantly anticipate reading her sweet, loving words.

Before opening the envelope he paused to realize how much her letters meant to him and how he sorely missed her warm embraces, her trusting smile and soothing voice.

Settling deeper into his armchair, he began to read:

November 1940
Dearest Charles,

As I write I still wait patiently for any further news from you and pray every day you are still safe.

Our papers are full of the war raging over London and how brave you all are. I often find it difficult to sleep at night knowing what dangerous work you are undertaking dealing with those horrid bombs.

My life in Melbourne is such a long way from the stark reality of life and death you are facing, but we are experiencing many hardships nonetheless as part of our war effort.

I would like to wish you a Merry Christmas and a Happy New Year.

I hope your celebrations are as pleasant as can be made possible considering the circumstances England finds itself in and perhaps you are able to celebrate with your kind relatives in Dulwich Village.

Charles, I do so miss you and given it's now 70 long days since I received your last letter, I rather despair if I am ever to hear from you again. Since we met, my life has been on hold, patiently waiting for you, and now this uncertainty and not hearing from you is making me feel more than low and perhaps unloved.

Recently I met an air force officer who later invited me to take Sunday tea with him.

Of course my first reaction was to decline.

However, if you have met someone special over there in London who is able to take my place, to nurture your soul and love you to bits then I will fully understand. If this is to eventuate, then I may feel inclined to accept the officer's next invitation.
Yours truly,
Elizabeth

Never for one moment since they met did he ever expect to read Elizabeth had come to doubt his love or commitment to her, let alone have her admit she was thinking about going out with someone else.

With his mind churning like a wild Atlantic storm, Charles poured a third, then a fourth even stiffer whisky to drown his rising fear that he might have lost her.

*　　*　　*

Twelve thousand miles across the globe in Melbourne, Charles' inbound letter arrived just days after Elizabeth had posted hers.

Reading his latest letter full of news and his absolute love for her, Elizabeth felt absolutely disgusted with herself that in a moment of selfish weakness, she could have ever doubted his love.

Little did she realise the devastating effect her November letter was about to have on him.

22. Mansion House Street

When his leave was over Lieutenant Garland returned to duty at Princess Gate, Kensington, late in January 1941.

His Section was promptly assigned to central London to defuse a very large unexploded bomb that had narrowly missed the Bank of England.

Overnight, bombs had hit the nearby Underground killing more than one hundred people in it.

Driving to the site, Lance Corporal Kirk had noticed his Lieutenant's distracted state after he had to repeat several briefing matters they had been told of earlier.

On the way, the Lieutenant's mind kept drifting off to Elizabeth's letter that had shocked him and made him jealous that an air force officer might be lying in her arms, instead of him.

He promised himself that when he returned to barracks, he would telegram her to reassure her of his undying love and promise to be at her side as soon as the war ended.

When their van pulled up in Mansion House Street, the Lieutenant quickly observed that the site was covered in debris from fallen buildings and the nearby roads were cluttered with ambulances, emergency workers and vehicles.

He reminded himself that today's operation would just be like others they had previously completed.

They all understood what was at hand, knew the risks and without fail, everyone meticulously set about carrying out every aspect of the defusing as though it might be their last.

In the nearby smoking ruins, dozens of civilian volunteers continued searching for survivors.

The Lieutenant ordered the sappers to go ahead and have the site prepared and to let him know the type of bomb at hand.

After confirming that it was a Satan bomb in the pit, he returned to the van and began nervously thumbing through his manual to refresh his memory on every aspect of this new type of high explosive, which lay a few hundred yards away.

When he was advised it was shored up and ready for inspection, he headed across the site to the crater's edge to be greeted by the ominous sight of the grey bomb with its white-stencilled markings.

It was intended to destroy the nearby historic Bank of England, the centrepiece of Britain's banking system, situated a hundred yards down the road.

The bomb lay nose down, tilted at twenty-eight degrees, on top of what appeared to be unsteady rubble.

Whilst the device was now reasonably accessible, deciding how far away to locate the three-foot deep escape pit lined with rows of sandbags presented more of a challenge.

The manual indicated that should its four thousand, four hundred pound payload go up, it could kill anyone within a hundred yards and take out an entire block. In view of this, instead of the usual thirty yards Lieutenant Garland briskly stepped out seventy oversized paces from the crater and ordered his sapper to dig the escape pit where he had ground the heel of his boot in the dusty rubble.

He also carefully noted that the thirteen foot long Satan SC 2500 MAX was fitted with forward and aft fuse pockets and contained an explosive combination of Trialen and Amatol, which was a mix of RDX, TNT and aluminium.

Beyond a safety rope that had been erected a safe distance around the bombsite, a number of support rescue workers crouched behind walls of sandbags.

Amongst them were two Red Cross nurses who, having parked their ambulance around the corner, had been assigned to the Mansion House Street operation.

One was Margie Swanson who was dog-tired after enduring a gruelling twelve-hour shift.

From their position the nurses had no real opportunity to get a close look at the officer carrying out the defusing.

When the Lieutenant left the van to face a life or death situation, he put Elizabeth's disturbing letter out of his mind and made a point of striding confidently to the pit's edge where Private Smithers waited.

Private Jones was instructed to stand well back from the bomb, ready to relay observations along the line to Private Lawrence, who would write them down from the safety of the escape pit.

Climbing down the ladder into the crater's depths, the Lieutenant squatted beside the massive bomb to listen with his stethoscope for any internal ticking.

Hearing nothing, he called to Smithers to bring the tool kit and gear down, then ordered him to leave.

The first step of the defusing procedure was to unscrew the bomb's fuse ring in a circular direction by tapping it forcibly with a hammer and chisel. He began tapping and continued for several minutes with the ring moving only a few turns until momentarily his concentration was distracted when Private Smithers asked how far the fuse ring had to go until it was unscrewed.

The lapse caused his hammer to miss the chisel head and instead thump painfully into his thumb, causing him to drop the chisel that fell with a clunk under the bomb and disappeared.

Angry at having made such a stupid mistake and with his thumb hurting, the Lieutenant bent down to pick it up but he could not see where it had fallen so he climbed lower to search with his torch.

Taking a foot off the ladder's last rung, he placed it onto a large slab of rubble, unaware it was also supporting the four thousand, four hundred pound bomb.

His additional one hundred and seventy pounds on the rubble caused it to shift, resulting in the bomb's nose suddenly dropping further into the pit with a loud, sickening clunk.

Shocked by the bomb's unexpected slip, the Lieutenant whipped the stethoscope from around his neck and pressed it to the casing.

He was horrified to clearly hear that the fuse mechanism had started ticking.

Suddenly he realised he was out of time.

He knew everyone had less than seventeen seconds to live unless they could escape.

Tossing the hammer and stethoscope aside he began climbing for his life.

As he reached the pithead he screamed, **'GET OUT! OUT! IT'S GOING TO GO OFF!'**

Scrambling over the crater he grabbed Private Jones, who was momentarily frozen and started running in the direction of the escape pit, some seventy yards away.

With his words still echoing across the site, those watching threw themselves to the ground as best they could, whilst the Lieutenant and the sappers tried to escape.

From their sandbagged wall, the Ambulance Corp nurses witnessed the next dramatic seventeen seconds.

In what seemed like slow motion, they saw the Lieutenant desperately clamber from the pit and run, run with his sappers towards the escape pit.

Despite his age, the Lieutenant easily outran Jones and Smithers as they sprinted for their lives.

The dash seemed to be taking an eternity.

In the eighteenth second, the nurses watched Mansion House Street literally explode.

A wall of flame and dust chased the three soldiers in rage.

The Lieutenant was last seen diving headfirst into the escape pit, ahead of Smithers, with Jones somewhere behind.

Like a rugby player attempting a "try", Smithers dived over his Lieutenant, who in his final conscious seconds heard the train-like roar of the blast overcome his ears. Even with his eyes closed in fear, he saw shards of vivid blue light. The Lieutenant's face and body felt crushed by a massive pressure followed by a wave of searing heat.

Flying debris and grit sandblasted his torso, tearing his helmet off and shredding his jacket to his bare skin.

He felt an excruciating burning sensation across his face and neck, an arm ached agonisingly and blood was seeping from his eyes.

His life seemed to spin before him. Briefly he had visions of Elizabeth, then he knew nothing.

Writhing in the pit beside the Lieutenant lay Private Smithers who was so badly wounded that the skin on his back was peeling off.

Private Jones, who was the slowest runner, had almost reached the escape pit when he took the explosion's full force and died instantly.

As rescuers raced to tend to the injured, they smelt the stench of burnt TNT and gas leaking from burst mains.

The Lieutenant and Private Smithers were placed in Margie's Red Cross ambulance to be raced to the nearby St Thomas' Hospital.

It was only when Nurse Swanson was completing her paperwork and checking their identity tags at the hospital that she discovered that the shockingly injured officer on the stretcher was her Uncle Charles.

When the ambulance had left, the Lieutenant's batman collected a green tarpaulin from his van and covered Private Jones' headless torso.

The blast had blown debris more than two hundred yards down Mansion House Street, badly damaging the Bank of England's façade, but leaving its vaults unscathed.

*   *   *

In barracks that evening, Lance Corporal Kirk removed the Lieutenant's final letter addressed to Elizabeth from where it had been taped to a mirror.

He took it to his Commanding Officer, who told the Lance Corporal that earlier he had sent a telegram to Elizabeth with the grim news that the Lieutenant had met with an accident and lay badly injured in hospital.

23. Rehabilitation

Lying on his back in St Thomas' surgical ward heavily sedated with his face covered in gauze, leaving only his left eye and mouth exposed and with his arm in plaster, Lieutenant Garland, when he came to, tried to make sense of where he was.

Two beds along the ward, filled mainly with Blitz victims, Private Smithers lay face down with angry lesions over his burnt back.

The only unburned skin was where the narrow webbing of his shoulder straps and trouser belt had covered him.

The Lieutenant's broken right arm had been set in plaster and in his other arm a saline drip kept him hydrated.

For the time being, visitors were not being allowed. Unbeknown to him, a get well card and small bunch of flowers in a vase from the Swansons sat beside his bed.

Still shocked from the events that had unfolded at Mansion House Street, Margie had badly wanted to see Charles, but the nurses insisted doctor's orders were to be kept.

From what little she had learnt, her uncle was very lucky to have survived the blast.

His doctor said his face may be permanently disfigured and there was doubt he would regain sight in his right eye.

* * *

Shortly after the Blitz began, King George VI realised the critical importance both the civilian and military efforts made to the war effort at home and instigated a gallantry award called the George Cross.

It was struck to recognise acts of great heroism, bravery or conspicuous courage in the face of extreme danger that was "not in front of the enemy".

When the papers broke the news of the Lieutenant's gallant defusal attempt, the King thought he appeared a most worthy recipient and had his Private Secretary make enquiries.

* * *

Almost a week after the explosion, when a doctor shone a pencil light beneath an eyelid, the sleeping Lieutenant gave his first response to the fuzzy world around him. Very slowly he regained consciousness and became aware of the extent of his injuries.

He was awake for only short periods, which the doctors said was a good sign, given the trauma he had suffered.

In addition to the flowers and cards beside his bed were two telegrams that he asked Margie to read to him.

The first was from Alice wishing him a speedy recovery and saying that his commander was keeping her family informed.

The second was from Elizabeth who said how deeply shaken she was to learn of his injuries. She pleaded for permission to come to his bedside.

His commanding officer and batman visited him, as did Gertrude and Ron, who were shocked at the extent of his injuries.

Overcoming her aversion to the pungent smell of her uncle's septic burns, Margie promised when he was released that she would help him in every way she could to make a speedy recovery.

'I really appreciate your offer,' he responded, trying not to show his deeply held fear that he might be disfigured for life and never regain full sight in his right eye.

'Margie, there is something you can do for me,' he suggested.

'Could you take down a telegram to Elizabeth then get some money from my wallet there in the drawer and have the post office send it?'

```
DEAREST ELIZABETH
THANK YOU FOR YOUR SWEET TELEGRAM STOP
MY ARM IS KNITTING WELL STOP
BURNS ARE REPAIRING SLOWLY BUT MY RIGHT EYE
REMAINS A PROBLEM STOP
AM RECOVERING AND EXPECT TO BE SENT HOME SOON
STOP
SUGGEST NOW IS NOT THE BEST TIME TO COME OVER
STOP
ALL MY LOVE CHARLES STOP
```

Putting away her notepad and looking more closely at Charles, Margie saw he had closed his eyes and was slumped into the pillows looking exhausted.

She was aware he was struggling to come to terms with the shock of his disfigurement and other injuries that were obviously causing him considerable self-doubt and worry.

As she willed him off to sleep, holding his pale hand, all she could feel was his fragile pulse.

*   *   *

With so many new Blitz victims being admitted to St Thomas', the hospital was desperately in need of beds, which resulted in Charles being released ahead of time.

Proud and wanting to regain his independence, he assured his doctors he would be more than able to look after himself when he was released and to assist, he had a relative coming in to do some cooking and shopping.

On the morning he was leaving, Charles went to the bathroom for a shower and shave.

The person he saw in the mirror shocked him.

Yes, he had a broken arm that he kept reminding himself would soon heal.

True he had only one good eye and he might be that way for life, but it was the swag of bandages covering his burns that he knew would be too much of a shock for Elizabeth.

The ghastly image he saw made him wonder if she could love him looking so dreadful.

He told the character in the mirror he wasn't quite beaten yet and certainly wasn't going to throw in the towel.

*   *   *

Charles' landlady warmly welcomed back her injured "hero", cheerfully opening his door and handing him a pile of mail that had built up.

She kindly suggested she could bring his meals up to him and do some of his ironing in the weeks ahead.

While he settled in his day chair to peruse his letters, Margie slipped down the street to do some shopping, returning with fresh fruit, newspapers and some chocolate, which she knew he always loved.

Surprisingly, it failed to spark him up.

Her uncle then indicated he wanted to have another rest before dinner, so Margie and her father tidied up and bade him good evening.

*   *   *

In the days following, Charles observed that his wounds were not responding to treatment and they had begun to emit an unpleasant odour that made him even more despondent.

Confined to a wheelchair, still in pyjamas and a dressing gown, he remained a far cry from the strapping Lieutenant who confidently led his Bomb Disposal Section a few weeks earlier.

Margie could see her uncle was much frailer than he was letting on and sensed there must be more to his injuries than the medical notes she had read at the foot of his hospital bed.

He still looked shell-shocked and gaunt, and more recently she had discovered he seemed hard of hearing. Having the use of only one arm and with his face covered in bandages, his movements remained limited.

*   *   *

An outing to the Woolwich Odeon picture theatre gave Jessie and Margie a badly needed opportunity to escape the grind of their jobs and a rare chance to enjoy the film of the month, *Kitty Foyle*.

They eagerly took in the romantic melodrama starring Ginger Rogers as an attractive secretary caught up in a love triangle with a struggling doctor and her philandering husband.

It tickled both the girls' fancies, but for very different reasons.

Over afternoon tea afterwards, Jessie explained, 'I would never have allowed a philandering husband of mine to hoodwink me like he did Kitty Foyle. And worse, after they slept together, that very common girlfriend of his ended up needing an abortion!'

Desperately trying to discover true love and knowing how her emotions and heart palpitated at the very thought of finding it, Margie thought differently.

'I'm all with Kitty. When the skeletons in her husband's cupboard were exposed, she had no alternative but to go out and find real love.'

With Jessie firmly holding her ground Margie changed the subject, asking how she was coping with her demanding work at Bletchley Park.

Jessie offered her usual sanitised explanation trying to keep her best friend off the trail.

Margie only briefly mentioned the tough times she was experiencing with her ambulance work. She glossed over rescuing the children from a bombed house that had left her having nightmares, before steering the conversation to Charles' tragic injuries and its impact on her family.

At the mention of how Gertrude had reacted when Margie began seeing Emilio, Jessie said she had always been wary of her mother after the kerfuffle she kicked up when she heard about that Scottish soldier kissing Margie. Jessie asked if her mother was showing any signs of accepting Emilio.

'You know, she took a huge disliking to him at the outset simply because he's foreign and maintains none of them can be trusted,' Margie confessed.

'I really think, Margie, it's more about what her friends would say if they found out her daughter's boyfriend came from Portugal,' said Jessie.

'She's told me several times she doesn't want me seeing him and with me going behind her back, it's making me feel uncomfortable. And she has actually threatened to disown me if I do. But Jess, I'm really fond of him and I think he likes me and we are getting on so well together,' Margie added.

'Oh you poor thing, what an absolute fix you have got yourself into,' sighed Jess, realising things must have well and truly developed further between the pair.

'How long is he staying in London and also where do you see him?' Jessie enquired.

'His company has extended his visit because of his excellent sales,' Margie explained.

'He has taken a pretty little flat in Waterloo Park which I've been to quite a few times. But Mother has put me under the threat of death if I should ever sleep with him, so staying the night is still one step too far.'

'You mean you have gone with him!' gasped Jessie.

Returning her glare, Margie honestly replied.

'Yes, I have.'

'How could you have been so rash? What about his dubious background?' asked Jessie, getting angry, then quickly regretting she had mentioned that last bit.

Seizing on it, Margie came back hard.

'What do you mean by his dubious background, Jess? Is there something I should know you have not told me?'

Rattled by her blunder, Jessie choose her next response far more judiciously.

'Well no, not entirely,' Jessie said hesitantly, grabbing at straws.

'It's just that we all know that eligible foreign men like him have built quite a reputation for being too fast with English ladies, and as my best friend the last thing I ever want is to see you get hurt.'

With daylight fast fading the girls paid the bill and headed off, each with their own thoughts occupying their minds for their separate trips home.

On the bus, Jessie thought that should Margie ever find herself in any sort of trouble with her new boyfriend, then that very difficult mother of hers will more than likely have the final say.

Approaching her Dulwich Village stop, Margie wondered if Jess was hiding something about Emilio. She seemed rattled when confronted and suddenly became decidedly cagey at the last moment before changing the subject.

24. Visit to the Park

Sitting at his desk, oblivious to the golden shards of late afternoon light filtering through the leafless trees across the lush, green park lawns opposite his flat, Emilio Bestillo reread Mr Felloni's latest letter.

With Luzia's child now a toddler, Mr Felloni had tentatively agreed to Emilio's proposed monthly payments with an April settlement. However, he insisted that the fifteen million escudos was not negotiable.

Emilio still believed he could negotiate a lower figure, but regardless he still had to somehow dig up a huge amount of money. He thought about raising a loan from his family's bank. In the meantime he sent the first monthly instalment by wire to Oporto. He intended, in the next few days, to write to Mr Felloni again, claiming he could only fund a lower amount and if agreement could not be reached he would hand the matter over to his solicitors.

*   *   *

Charles was caught off guard when he received a phone call from Lieutenant Colonel Stanton, expecting he was enquiring about his recovery and when he might be ready to return to barracks. But after a cursory query into his progress, his Commanding Officer informed him that the War Office had advised the King may award him a George Cross bravery medal. He suggested Charles should keep an eye out for an announcement in the *London Gazette.*

*   *   *

When Margie told her uncle she had a new boyfriend who was making her extremely happy, she hoped he would be more accommodating of him than her parents.

Charles suggested she should bring Emilio to meet him when she came next.

On this occasion she found her uncle in considerably improved spirits, helped by his arm aching less and his painful burns slowly starting to heal.

However, the sight in his right eye had not improved and he tired quickly.

She noticed his blotchy, reddened skin on his troubled face and thought she got a whiff from his seeping wounds that suggested he was fighting an infection.

But knowing how determined her uncle was, she was confident a healthy diet and exercise could overcome it.

Dressed smartly in a dark reefer jacket, freshly pressed shirt and slacks, her uncle received Emilio very cordially, much to Margie's considerable relief.

Emilio proudly showed him his family's winemaking book and Charles quietly told him about the third generation firm he headed up in Sydney.

Charles was anticipating his niece taking him out to the park for a little fresh air and their customary afternoon tea.

Before arriving at her uncle's, Margie had explained to Emilio she wanted to do this on her own, as it gave her an opportunity to better assess how he was really progressing.

When the time came, she helped Charles into a warm coat then she and Emilio assisted him down the stairs to his wheelchair, which she began pushing down the road.

Nearing the Paddington Street Park gates Charles looked up at Margie. 'I've been thinking that's a very bright, young chap you brought with you today,' he said.

His words were pure music to her ears, something she had yearned for since she had begun seeing Emilio.

'Thank you Uncle, those kind words mean an awful lot to me. I had hoped you might like him as you both have quite a lot in common.'

A smile creased her face as she discovered new energy to push his wheelchair through the park's famous towering, cast iron gates.

'Emilio's helped me discover a lot more about myself and seems really keen on me too. You know, since I met him he has helped me to feel more confident about so many things.'

Visit to the Park

Realising Margie had fallen in love brought back sunlit memories of when he fell for Elizabeth, but Charles felt out of his depth expressing this to Margie. Instead he asked, 'Isn't it about time we head to the tearooms? I'm ravenous and I hope you are too.'

* * *

Playing second fiddle to Margie whilst she was away pushing her uncle around the park wasn't any bother to Emilio.

He wandered upstairs to wait and killed time by reading some of the newspapers on Charles' desk.

After a time, he put the paper down and allowed his gaze to travel out through the windows to the park beyond, where he hoped he might see Margie returning, but there was no sign of her.

Visualising her slender body and recalling her warm kisses caused a flurry of lustful thoughts of wanting to hold her tightly, then, after they had kissed deeply, tossing her onto his bed to enjoy more. But the visit here today meant that afterwards there wouldn't be time for any such afternoon delights.

Bored with the paper, he decided to make a cup of tea.

Walking around the desk, he noticed a stack of papers in a wire basket. Leaning closer he noted they seemed to be about Charles' investments.

The document on top showed he had a very substantial holding in a company called Broken Hill Proprietary. The statement indicated the Australian Government had frozen its share price soon after the outbreak of the war and that his parcel was worth over £480,000 Australian.

As he waited for the kettle to boil in the kitchen, Emilio wondered what the conversion rate might be between English and Australian pounds.

As a matter of curiosity, he thought he should look it up.

* * *

Having returned and settled Charles into his day chair with a rug and book after the park visit, Margie bade him goodbye and she and Emilio left to catch their bus.

Turning to shut the gate, Margie noticed some letters had been delivered to Charles' mailbox and impulsively decided to race back upstairs to give them to him, failing to notice one carried an impressive gold logo.

As they began walking towards the bus stop she took Emilio's arm and leaned contently closer, suggesting daringly, 'Darling, when we get to the flat and before I go on duty tonight, I need to spend some time in your arms. You know what I mean,' she whispered, in case anyone was within earshot.

Squeezing her arm in mutual agreement, the sultry look in his eyes told her he needed her too.

After the couple had made furious and passionate love, Margie drifted blissfully off to sleep, oblivious to Emilio lighting a cigarette and exhaling blue smoke over her head, which he dispassionately watched spiral towards the ceiling.

He felt satiated and intoxicated with their ardent lovemaking.

His mind was almost at rest, except he couldn't prevent Mr Felloni's payment demands returning to haunt him.

He promised himself in the morning he would go and see the family's bank in London to ask about a loan.

Beside him, Margie looked blissfully fulfilled, but Emilio feared she was becoming smitten and knew she might soon want to ask where their love was heading.

*   *   *

When Charles opened the letters he was surprised to find one from Buckingham Palace.

BUCKINGHAM PALACE

Lieutenant Charles Garland
Royal Engineers
No. 1 Bomb Disposal Section

Dear Sir,

I am pleased to request your attendance at
an investiture ceremony to be conducted at
Buckingham Palace at 10am on 17 March 1941,
whereupon The King will present you with the
George Cross Medal as recognition for your
bravery in the face of immense danger in January
this year.

Yours sincerely,
Sir Alan F Lascelles GCB GCVO CMG
Private Secretary to The King
RSVP

25. Instructions to Sell

Emilio had surprised Margie when, out of the blue, he suggested he would like to accompany her when she next visited her injured uncle.

He told her he hoped to get to know Charles better and had an idea how Garland Trading might increase its imports of Bestillo wine.

She loved the thought of them visiting her uncle as a couple and hoped this indicated Emilio was wanting to spend more time doing things she liked instead of mostly meeting in secret at his flat.

She innocently had no idea he had an ulterior motive.

*   *   *

Prior to going, Emilio had given some thought as to what excuse he could come up with so he could be left behind at Charles' flat while Margie took her uncle out for a walk in the park and afternoon tea.

'Darling, I have an overdue sales report to finish so I'm just as happy to stay behind which will allow you time with your uncle,' Emilio suggested.

'Then perhaps, afterwards I could join you at the tearooms?'

*   *   *

Upon their arrival at the Marylebone flat, Charles was delighted to see Emilio again, which pleased Margie. Leaving for the park, Charles suggested to Emilio he could use the desk for his report, although he might need to clear some papers out of the way.

'Thank you, Mr Garland,' he responded. 'Given it's such a sunny day, I'm looking forward to joining you both at the tearooms.'

'Emilio, please call me Charles,' he suggested holding onto Margie's arm as he gingerly made his way slowly down the stairs.

Emilio apprehensively watched Margie push her uncle off in his wheelchair, hoping he had sufficient time to find what he was looking for.

Taking a seat at Charles' desk, Emilio spread out his report papers.

Then, placing the tray of Charles' investment files beside them, he began scanning months of company statements, letters and reports.

He jotted down Charles' principal contacts at the Australasian Trustee Company, including its chairman, Sir Kenneth Codrington and its general manager, Mr M. C. Smithers, its Pitt Street address and phone number.

He recorded details of Mr Garland's Broken Hill Proprietary Limited shareholdings, including the account number, noting that the November 1940 trustees statement indicated the shares were valued at £490,309.

Then he searched for correspondence between Charles and the Australasian Trustee Company to shed light on interactions between the parties that might prove to be of future use.

He found a condolence letter from Sir Kenneth Codrington, written two years earlier at the time of the tragic loss of Charles' parents, correspondence involving Garland Trading setting up in London, lunch invitations to Sir Kenneth's Australian Club and general information about the Garland's Latour Park estate.

Finding a document with Charles' signature proved much more difficult.

Searching through the drawers he finally discovered an Australian passport containing his signature and decided to have a duplicate made.

Instead of returning the passport, he slipped it into a large envelope he had brought, along with several other letter and papers he was borrowing, hoping with Charles' limited eyesight, that in the next few days they would not be missed.

Deciding it was too risky to take the most recent Broken Hill Proprietary Limited statement, he rummaged deeper down the pile and drew one out from eight months earlier, which he added to the envelope.

He noted Charles had an account at the Commonwealth Bank of Australia's London branch in Ludgate Hill. He decided he would go there to open a new account but use a different address.

He also found a useful letter from Charles' Royal Engineers' commanding officer confirming his commission as a Lieutenant, which he borrowed.

Noticing how much time had passed, he realised as he packed everything away that he was due at the tearooms.

Striding down the path towards it, he saw Margie rise from her patio seat to call him to their table.

He greeted her with a self-satisfied smile and a brushing kiss, but not all of it was from seeing her. She asked him if he had finished his report, to which he nodded.

On the bus going home, Margie took Emilio's hand and looking into his eyes asked what he would like her to cook for dinner, suggesting first they could have a snuggle.

At that very moment he turned to absently gaze out the window with his thoughts hundreds of miles away. His mind churned over the extraordinary stash of documents he had secreted away in his bag.

After they had finished their lovemaking, Margie sensed his heart hadn't been in it. She wondered if he had lost his burning desire for her.

"Darling, is everything all right with us?' she innocently probed.

"Why do you ask?" he brusquely retorted, before realising she had picked up on his brooding disposition.

'Because, when we made love, our usual spark was missing,' she honestly said.

Endeavouring to allay her concerns, he drew her close and, looking deeply into her questioning eyes, whispered, 'It wasn't you my sweet … you were sensational … it's just that I was distracted by some matters I have forgotten to put in my report.'

*   *   *

The following morning, Emilio returned to the tavern off Sloane Street to speak to Raelene.

'Love, you're back,' she said dryly. 'Will it be a single malt that you are after?'

'That will do nicely,' he replied.

His eyes followed her filling a glass and watched it as she slid it across the bar to him.

As he picked it up, she asked if there was something else he needed.

'Well, sort of,' he answered after taking a slow sip.

'And what might that be?' she casually probed.

Pausing for another sip, he checked unobtrusively if anyone was watching or listening, before leaning forward and taking out a £10 note that he folded and put under an ashtray then slipped to her.

Watching her eyes carefully, Emilio said, 'The other day you gave me some excellent advice, which I am considering acting on.

'To this end, I am wondering if you are able to put me in touch with someone who could help me with a small passport problem I need dealt with?'

Momentarily, a smile creased her face that turned to a wry grin as she absorbed his generosity and the implications of his request.

'Only if you promise with your life that if I give you a phone number, it never came from me.'

'Agreed,' he said easing back on the stool to take a long draw on his cigarette and take another sip as he watched her slip the folded note into her bra.

She made him wait a few agonising minutes before returning with the phone number on a piece of paper.

Emilio then caught a bus to the Marylebone Post Office to organise a post box and he rather liked the number 388 he was given as it ended with a pair of eights, which he hoped would bring him luck.

Returning to his flat, he phoned the number on the piece of paper.

The gruff man who answered seemed distant and unhelpful.

'Someone we both know suggested you might be able help with a small passport problem I need attended to,' said Emilio, unruffled.

'I dunno what youse is talking about,' said the gruff man, obviously playing for time, but not hanging up.

'Guvnor, you 'av got the wrong man …' he suggested, but remained still on the line.

Thinking fast Emilio suggested, 'Can we meet at the tavern where I can buy you a drink and we can have a little chat?'

Five days later Emilio took possession of the new passport, complete with his photo, in the name of Charles Garland. It had cost him an outrageous £110 in cash.

*　　*　　*

Later that week, Emilio visited the Commonwealth Bank branch in Ludgate Hill to update Mr Garland's contact details and to open a new account, into which he deposited £150 that was duly stamped into a shiny new blue passbook.

*   *   *

Needing to find the quickest way to send a letter to Sydney, he visited the Australian Consulate on The Strand.

Dressed with a black eyepatch, face bandages and a sling on his right arm, masquerading as Lieutenant Charles Garland, he was ushered into a small meeting room by a young army corporal assigned to the embassy to deal with enlisted personnel queries.

He produced a letter from his Royal Engineers' commanding officer confirming his appointment as Lieutenant, together with his new passport.

All this quickly convinced the corporal to bend over backwards to help get his letter to Sydney. Emilio was advised that it could be sent in a diplomatic bag by air that would be delivered a week later.

With the plan almost in place, that evening Emilio wrote to the Australasian Trustee Company.

8 February 1941
Sir Kenneth Codrington, Chairman
Australasian Trustee Company Pty Ltd
Pitt St, Sydney, Australia
Re: Customer number – CF Garland/1868

Dear Sir Kenneth,
I trust this letter finds you in good spirits despite the ravages of war.
Having previously advised you of my enlistment in the Royal Engineers, I have more recently had the misfortune to incur an injury that has quite set me back.
Because of my need to rehabilitate I have decided to stay on longer here in London. Therefore I have decided to repatriate the

proceeds of my Broken Hill Proprietary Limited shareholding, held by Australasian Trustee Company at your earliest convenience.

Shareholder number: BHP 4945FG
Number of shares: Estimated 218,468

Can you advise the selling price for my shares, which I understand has been frozen by the Federal Government?
I hereby request that following their sale, the funds be remitted to my Commonwealth Bank account at Ludgate Hill London.

To credit of: Charles F Garland
Account number: 21-774

Sir Kenneth, would you be so kind to confirm by telegram to my Marylebone Post Box 388 your acknowledgement of having received my letter?
Can you advise a date I should expect the funds to transfer?

Yours sincerely,

Charles F Garland
Charles F Garland
Post Box 388
Marylebone, London UK

Having posted the letter, Emilio turned his thoughts to how he could quietly return Mr Garland's borrowed papers before he discovered they were missing.

26. Phone Call from London

'*I very much regret we have not acknowledged your instructions, Mr Garland,*' said a highly embarrassed Sir Kenneth Codrington from his Australasian Trustee Sydney office over the phone to the firm's high valued client in London.

'*No, the sale has not been finalised as yet,*' he admitted, getting more flustered, with his brow breaking into a cold sweat.

'*Yes, I assure you we will sell those Broken Hill shares today,*' Sir Kenneth added as he waved to Mr Spratt, his senior trust clerk, who had just arrived with the file, to take a seat.

'*Yes, I agree we should have acted more promptly and I do apologise for the delay,*' Sir Kenneth admitted, trying to quell the torrent blasting from the earpiece.

'*Yes, yes, we should have the funds wired to your account within days,*' Sir Kenneth said, becoming frustrated by the very poor quality line that was making it difficult to hear.

At the London end of the line, trying to put on an Australian accent, which Emilio muffled by speaking through folds of a handkerchief, he recognised the call was going better than he could have imagined.

At this very moment he was aware he had Sir Kenneth "well and truly on the ropes".

Proud of maintaining his "hale and hearty" reputation with his major clients, Sir Kenneth, on the other hand, carefully avoided conflict like this at every opportunity.

With the client file now in front of him, he noticed that attached to Mr Garland's eighth of February letter was a brief note from the senior trust clerk expressing his reservations about making the sale.

In spite of it Sir Kenneth told his client, '*Yes, certainly Charles, we will wire the funds to your Ludgate Hill bank account as soon as they arrive and yes, I assure you we will telegram you when this has been done.*

'Also, I assure you everything will be finalised as quickly as possible. And thank you for your call!' he disingenuously added, looking drawn as he hung up from the bad-tempered client.

Wiping his brow then leaning over the desk, Sir Kenneth stared angrily at Mr Spratt, asking why the sale hadn't been finalised earlier.

For more than fifteen years, Arthur Spratt had progressed through the trust's ranks from junior ledger clerk to senior trust officer. He had rarely had reason to be called to the chairman's office or exposed to hostile calls like the one that he had just heard.

Mr Spratt tried to placate his hopping mad chairman.

'Sir Kenneth, for your information the sale documents were completed a week ago and sent to Mr Smith for his signature.

'I had rather felt, as this transaction was unlike those we usually handle, we should check with Mr Garland's London bank to ensure everything was in order,' he explained.

'Bollocks!' retorted the now furious Sir Kenneth, who realised the call had made him half an hour late for an important client lunch at his Club.

'Spratt, I don't give a damn what you think, you should not have dilly-dallied.

'I'm directing you to sell those shares immediately and make sure that a telegram confirming it is sent to Garland.

'I don't want to ever give him another reason to call me in that frame of mind,' Sir Kenneth added bluntly, before storming out of the office.

*   *   *

The following evening, a still humbled Arthur Spratt closed his gladstone bag and left for a quiet weekend, relieved the week had ended and Mr Garland's money had been wired to London.

Before leaving he pinned a note to the file with a reminder to write a "Completed Sale" letter on Monday to Mr Garland, but he needed to resolve whether to mail it to his old Marylebone address on file or to his new post office box number.

*   *   *

On 17th March, the Swansons were thrilled to be attending Buckingham Palace to witness the King present Lieutenant Garland with the George Cross Medal.

Since being injured, Charles simply wasn't enjoying the cards he had been dealt one little bit and was feeling consumed by his injuries and hopeless situation.

On the sunny, cold spring morning, dressed in their Sunday best, the family, with the Lieutenant in his wheelchair and his batman arrived outside the palace gates.

Being invited to meet the King was something Charles had only dreamt of and his depressive bouts, seeping wounds, headaches and listlessness, for the moment, were set aside.

Having shown their invitations at the guardhouse, the batman pushed the Lieutenant's wheelchair, while Margie walked alongside with a camera hanging from her shoulder.

Passing through an arched entrance they were ushered into a majestic ballroom.

No-one could have been more proud of her hero uncle than Margie, who was hoping to take a roll of photos for Charles and her family's album.

As she took her seat, Margie was politely informed by a Gentleman Usher that cameras should not be used during the investiture, but she could take any number of photos afterwards.

She had been bitterly disappointed when Emilio had phoned that morning to say he was ill and unable to join her on such a special occasion.

Seated in the third row, the Swansons nudged each other excitedly hearing Charles' name called.

They watched in awe as his batman wheeled him forward. The Lieutenant looked resplendent in a new uniform but he still had bandages that covered part of his face and he had a black eyepatch.

His wheelchair came to a stop before the King, who was standing attired in full military regalia on a dais beneath the velvet-covered throne canopy.

As the King's Private Secretary read out the Lieutenant's bravery citation, a discernable jolt rippled through the audience.

The Lieutenant sat unmoved.

The King stepped forward and leant down to affix the medal to his chest and as he spoke a few brief words to him, the audience applauded politely.

Returning afterwards with Margie to his Marylebone flat, Charles felt fatigued.

He stopped at his mailbox before Margie helped him wearily climb the stairs. Inside he slumped into his chair and looked over the mail.

He was intrigued by an unexpected letter stamped with an Australasian Trustee Company's logo.

With the cheery sounds of the kettle whistling in the kitchen, Charles took from the desk's top drawer his prized gold-plated map-reader that his father had given him when he returned from the Great War and used it to read:

Australasian Trustee Company Pty Ltd

Pitt St, Sydney, Australia

19 February 1941

Mr C. F. Garland

301 Ashland Place

Marylebone, London SW1

Re: Customer Number – CF Garland/1868

Dear Mr Garland,

We hereby confirm that the Australasian Trustee Company has completed the sale of your lot of Broken Hill Proprietary shares as per your instructions in your letter of 8th February this year.

The sale proceeds being £484,300 were wired to your London account on 16th February and as per the attached documents, you will note we have deducted the broking and transfer fees as detailed.

Thank you for trusting your investments to our esteemed firm and we hope that on some future occasion you will find it appropriate to deal with us again.

Yours sincerely,

A. G. Spratt

A. G. Spratt
Senior Clerk
(Attachment – Sale of Shares document)

Initially Charles was utterly shocked and confused.

For the life of him, he could not believe what he had just read.

He thought some sort of mistake had been made.

He took a nervous sip of tea from the cup Margie had placed on his armrest and using the map-reader anxiously re-read it again, trying to understand how or why the trustees could have done it without his authority.

Noticing his ashen face, Margie took a seat opposite, asking, 'Uncle, the letter seems to have upset you. What is it about?'

'Something has happened to our family savings,' he said.

Unable to speak further, he passed it to her to read.

'What do they mean when they wrote, "We have completed the sale as per your instructions in your letter of the eighth of February"?

'Uncle, you were recuperating at home then and couldn't have written any such thing. How could they have ever got those instructions?' she asked.

'I wrote nothing of the sort,' he grimly retorted.

Realising something was very amiss Margie tried to console him. 'I can't believe that they would ever do such a dreadful thing. There must be some sort of a mistake. But cheer up, the money will surely have arrived in your account by now, so all you need to do is check it's there.'

Knowing his bank would not take calls until after ten the next morning, Charles knew he was in for an extremely restless night worrying how the trustees could have got it so wrong.

Trying to settle him as best she might, Margie finally bade him good evening, pecking him on the cheek and giving him a squeeze, saying, 'Uncle, everyone was so proud of you today, you were such an inspiration'.

Her words caused him to think back on his extraordinary day and where he had been, which momentarily brought a satisfied smile to his face.

On her way home sitting in the bus, Margie remembered she had felt slightly off colour that morning, which left her unable to eat breakfast. She had put it down to Emilio's disappointing call.

Walking up her road in the partial moonlight, she listened to her leather heels clacking and soles slapping on the smooth concrete pavers, reflecting on all that had happened on this memorable day. She had enjoyed an exhilarating experience at the palace but quite unexpectedly the day was ending very poorly.

She was afraid that things were not adding up with the trust company.

Seeing the staggering amount of £484,300 in the letter was more than she had ever known, so it was little wonder Charles was worried.

Arriving at her front gate, she still felt a little out of sorts, believing perhaps now it was the shock of the news of her uncle's problem with the trustees.

But more thoughts kept swirling through her mind.

For some weeks, she felt Emilio had been acting strangely.

Much as she needed to be with him, of late he had not wanted to see her as frequently and more often than not had declined to make love to her, citing something about his many "business distractions".

*　　*　　*

Following a restless night, Margie woke in a haze. Soon her thoughts turned to her first true love, Emilio, whom she adored.

Feeling unwell again, she began thinking about several out-of-character happenings with him in the last month.

She began to wonder after that last occasion they were at her uncle's flat, when she had raced back to get a scarf on the way to the park, why Emilio had looked rather guilty sitting there at the desk.

And what were his so-called "business distractions"? When she had asked, he had bluntly brushed her off, saying he didn't want to worry her with them.

Tying her robe, she suddenly felt waves of rising nausea that caused her to make a sudden dash to the bathroom.

The noise of the door slamming behind her prompted her mother to call out that her breakfast eggs and bacon were nearly ready.

Bathed and dressed but still feeling fragile after throwing up, Margie wondered how she was going to explain for the second day running she wasn't all that hungry.

*　*　*

Margie had put off calling Charles until almost midday, partly because she was still feeling nauseous.

Finally she dialled his number and trying to be cheerful asked, 'How are you this morning?'

She heard him take a deep, purposeful breath before answering.

'Thank you for calling. Unfortunately things have only gone from bad to worse after I spoke to the bank. I really don't want you to worry about this, but they informed me that my money has not arrived in the account. They said they will look into it to see if there is a hold up somewhere.'

Hanging up shocked, Margie wondered how she could help.

When she broke the news of this worrying development to her parents, Ron and Gertrude had a sense something was deeply wrong.

27. Prime Suspect

Emilio was not answering his phone. Margie had tried many times to call him.

His silence was starting to break her heart.

Now here she was, sitting in the doctor's waiting room, worrying she might be pregnant. Would she see Emilio again?

If she were pregnant, would he marry her?

What would her mother say?

What would her friends say?

What would her uncle say?

What would she tell work?

Suddenly the receptionist announced that the doctor was ready to see her.

Seeing this young women anxiously sit down on the edge of the chair and not wearing a wedding ring, Doctor Rose realised the news he was about to give was not what she would be hoping for.

'Miss Swanson,' he said. 'The test shows you are pregnant.'

Despite suspecting that her morning sickness pointed to this, quite unintentionally Margie let out an audible groan, then buried her face in her hands, hoping what she had just heard wasn't true.

* * *

Jessie Tyler had not spoken to Margie in over a month and she felt it was time they got together. From the moment she came on the line, Jessie sensed Margie was subdued, but she seemed to brighten up after they set a time to meet.

* * *

On his third, more desperate call to the bank in Ludgate Hill, Charles was advised that they had been in touch with Sydney, who advised, "No transfer had been arranged or was pending".

Those few words caused Charles' fragile world to turn upside down as he suddenly feared the worst.

The reality sinking in was that someone other than him had authorised the sale of his shares.

The loss felt like a spear being thrust into his back, painfully ripping apart his insides, causing him to gasp for breath.

Wounded, he felt the first waves of guilt for having lost three generations of Garland sweat and endeavour.

Despite vague assurances to the contrary, he was terrified that the bank might not be able to trace the money or the police recover it.

Feeling gutted, he agreed to go to the bank the next day and meet with the police.

* * *

Arriving early at the Kensington tearooms with restful views across the park, Jessie selected an outside table on the patio bathed in sunlight.

The wait gave her a few moments to think about Mr Bestillo's MI6 file, which Jessie had been tempted to read but then had thought better of it because it would only create a conflict, and seeing Margie was what mattered most.

Spotting Margie heading towards the tearooms, Jessie noticed her characteristic "I'm going somewhere" walk was absent and in its place was someone bearing a load.

'So lovely to see you … what a beautiful outfit you have on,' Jessie exclaimed as they hugged as only old friends do.

'Jess, you look so well. Tell me how you are and what's been happening in your life.'

Deciding to give Margie time to order and catch her breath before probing what the trouble was, Jessie asked, 'Tell me all about the Buckingham Palace investiture and how exciting it was.'

Before she could answer, tears started streaming down Margie's flushed cheeks.

Half an hour later, Jessie's mind was reeling from having learnt that her best friend was pregnant, the father was nowhere to be seen and her uncle's fortune had been taken. She also realised that Margie's mother would soon be on the warpath.

* * *

Having been told the money was in the throes of being wired to his account, from the moment Emilio Bestillo hung up from the call to Sydney he realised his days in Britain were numbered.

His fondness for Margie had been steadily increasing and at times she was warming his heart.

However, his dread of being disowned by his family and having his reputation in Oporto condemned was a much greater concern.

He had no option but to walk out on his relationship with Margie. However much he might like her, he had to quickly put miles between himself and London.

He transferred the funds from Sydney when they arrived into a new Madrid bank account he had opened in the name of Garland. He knew he could only temporarily use this account, as the money trail to it would be easily traced.

He was well aware that not a single bank in any country was going to hand over hundreds of thousands of pounds in cash to a stranger like him.

So for his next move he would open an untraceable account, in the name of an unrelated third party.

To meet this end, the name of his old university friend Ernst Neumann came to mind and Emilio decided this would suit perfectly.

He needed to revisit the passport contact Raelene had put him onto to organise a German passport in the name of Oberstleutnant E.G. Neumann.

With £1,000 in notes in his pocket, he knew this new identity and passport was going to cost an awful lot more than the first one.

Emilio opened the new account with a bank in Lisbon and then arranged to transfer the funds into it. This meant that should the police trace the money to Lisbon, they would never be able to get in touch with Oberstleutnant Neumann, who was a major serving in the German Wehrmacht, presently at war with Britain.

*   *   *

Margie went with Charles to the meeting at his Ludgate Hill branch of the bank with the police.

Whilst she read patiently in the waiting room, in the manager's office Detective Farrow Jenkins from Scotland Yard's fraud squad, whom the bank had called in, plied the bank and Charles with questions.

The branch manager proved less forthcoming with his replies than Charles had expected.

He told the detective that some four weeks earlier, Mr Garland ostensibly opened a new C. F. Garland account with a post box address.

Detective Jenkins asked the manager if the bank could describe the person who came to the branch.

The manager then called the teller who had opened the account to answer some questions.

Asked by Detective Jenkins if the gentleman in the wheelchair sitting opposite looked like the person he had dealt with, the teller quickly replied, 'Definitely not'.

The teller then recounted that the man who opened the account was tallish, in his late twenties, wore a dark-coloured reefer jacket and pressed slacks and had bandages over what appeared to be a head injury, wore an eyepatch and was European in appearance.

The bank manager admitted to the detective that the records showed when the funds arrived in the new account, they were transferred days later by Mr Garland to a bank account in Madrid.

'Given the enormous amount of money involved, did anyone at the branch make contact with Mr Garland at his Ashland Place residence at any stage?' the detective asked.

The bank manager looked at the teller, then reluctantly replied no, realising the serious oversight.

The detective asked Charles if he knew of a person fitting the description the bank teller just provided.

'No-one immediately comes to mind,' Charles answered.

The detective then asked the teller to look through a folder of suspect photos he had brought to see if anyone looked like the person who had opened the account.

Taking his time, the teller skipped through dozens of photos then went back to one that he looked at again, this time more carefully.

'None of those others look close, but this one of a thin, dark European bears some sort a resemblance,' he offered.

'Mr Garland, is there anyone you know of or have met that resembles this person?' the detective asked as he passed across the photo.

Studying it, initially Charles said he couldn't recall anyone.

The detective suggested he needed to give this more thought, inferring there must be someone he may know who dresses smartly.

Absorbing the "smart dresser" cue, suddenly the penny dropped.

Charles' face turned ashen grey and the meeting fell silent, as he grimly admitted, 'Now I think about it Detective, my niece's new boyfriend bears some resemblance.'

Sensing the new development, the detective asked Charles to describe him.

'He's around five foot ten tall, in his late twenties, tanned and comes from Portugal. If I recall, when I first met him he wore a smart reefer jacket, which might have been navy blue,' Charles said.

'At anytime could your niece's boyfriend have gained access to any of your investment or banking records?' the detective posed.

'He could have had a number of opportunities to read them as they were sitting on my desk when my niece wheeled me off to the park,' Charles admitted, remembering the hours Emilio had spent alone there in his flat.

'What's her boyfriend's name and where does he live?' the detective asked.

'It's Emilio Bestillo and I understand he has a flat in Waterloo Park, but I will have to ask my niece for the address.

'Detective, when I break the news about Mr Bestillo, I know it is going to be very upsetting for her. So if it is all right with you, I would like to use this office to tell her and ask for his address,' Charles proposed.

When he invited Margie to come into the office for a minute, Charles felt sickened with the thought that what he was to tell her was going to break her heart.

Seeing her uncle looked dreadfully fraught, Margie clearly sensed something big was up.

She knew he was livid at the bank's incompetence, but she was totally unprepared for the bombshell about to be dropped.

'Margie, there is something you need to know,' he said, calling on what little emotional strength he had left.

The seconds of silence that followed made her wonder what on earth could be worse than losing his fortune. She waited with bated breath.

'The police have said they consider the fraud was possibly an inside job,' Charles explained.

'The bank have revealed that a bogus account was set up in my name by someone who claimed to be me.

'This next piece of information that came out was very hard for me to stomach, but Margie, I know it is going to be far more upsetting for you.'

He paused to clear his throat, momentarily noticing his adored niece, sitting upright, perched opposite, whose usually soft brown eyes had suddenly developed a twitch.

'The teller has described the person who opened the bogus account as male, tall, thin, European in appearance, in his late twenties and wearing a dark jacket.'

Hanging on every word, at first Margie disbelieved the dreadful possibility that she knew this person.

She kept telling herself, no, no, never.

My Emilio would never do anything of the sort.

But the evidence she was processing suggested otherwise.

Her uncle gravely explained, 'From a file of photos the teller was shown, he picked out one that from the teller's description looked like your boyfriend.

'Detective Jenkins asked me if anyone in recent months resembling the man in the photo had any access to my private papers or bank statements.

'Having carefully considered the consequences of his question, I had no option but to tell him the answer was yes.'

As the bombshell exploded, waves of shock began to engulf Margie.

Her initial reaction was total disbelief that the man she trusted and had come to love could be a criminal.

Suddenly Margie's growing feelings of disillusionment overcame her as she realised that Emilio's strange behaviour these last few weeks had been pointing to this.

Her face turned pale and she felt dizzy.

All she could manage in that moment was to provide Emilio's address before turning away in shame and burying her face in her hands.

Enveloped by the growing humiliation that Emilio might be a crook and feeling guilt for having introduced him to her uncle in the first place, she burst into a flood of tears.

Anguished at the sight of his devastated niece, Charles placed a supportive arm around her shoulders. When she seemed to have settled, without a further word, he wheeled himself out of the office to give Detective Jenkins the address he was waiting for.

*　*　*

The Australasian Trustee Company chairman took the urgent phone call from his upset London client.

Earlier, Sir Kenneth Codrington had been summonsed from lunch at the Australia Club to speak to Charles Garland.

Sir Kenneth's ears went pink upon hearing Charles spit out, 'What do you mean you took a call from me last month, hurrying up the sale of the shares? I did nothing of the sort!'

Sir Kenneth quickly realised his firm was in deep, deep trouble.

It had been defrauded and all hell was about to break loose.

He realised that if a whiff of this reached the ears of any of his wealthy clients at the Club or down Pitt Street, his company's good name, built over nearly one hundred years, was finished.

'Charles, we've only learnt in these last few minutes that someone other than you had written to us, under your signature, instructing us to dispose of your BHP holdings and transfer the proceeds to your account at Ludgate Hill,' Sir Kenneth proffered, hoping to reduce Charles' state of anxiety.

Charles knew that the fastest way to get action from Sir Kenneth was to threaten to expose the matter.

In his mind, Charles felt badly let down and shocked by the firm and Sir Kenneth, who had been a loyal and trusted friend of the family for over fifty years.

He could not believe how the situation with the trustee had turned out so awfully.

'Sir Kenneth, my London bank has called in the Scotland Yard fraud squad to investigate and I've given them a statement,' Charles announced.

'What has been revealed is that the signature used to create a new account in my name was a forgery and that the proceeds you sent to it have been withdrawn and transferred to a bank in Madrid, which the police are trying to track down.'

Looking down at his perspiration-soaked desk blotter, Sir Kenneth noticed it was looking as though he had tipped over a glass of water. The handkerchief he was using to wipe his brow was barely stemming the flow.

'Charles, on behalf of the firm, I acknowledge the messy situation that has arisen', Sir Kenneth blurted.

'I am about to call the board into an urgent meeting to see what can be done to sort out this problem and I will get back to you afterwards.'

Charles hung up feeling empty, knowing three generations' worth of the family's hard work was gone.

He asked himself why on earth the trustees hadn't called him to verify the letter's instructions.

Why didn't they at least telegram his London bank to check everything was in order with the account?

How could they have been so easily duped?

28. Gertrude's Rage

Emilio being named the prime suspect tore Margie apart but she knew she couldn't possibly withhold this dramatic turn of events from her parents.

After blurting it out, she recoiled when she saw her mother's face redden in a fit of anger.

In one of the nastiest moments witnessed at the Swansons, Gertrude seized on the revelation to launch a stream of ugly profanities.

'Where has the crook gone?

'How could he be so low, to steal from a war hero?

'I'm so angry I could slit his throat!'

Little did Gertrude realise that matters concerning her daughter's ex-boyfriend were about to worsen.

*　*　*

After several days of Gertrude maintaining her wrath, Margie realised she could no longer keep the news of her pregnancy a secret.

She approached her parents with trepidation, asking if she could turn the radio volume down to announce something, before seating herself opposite them.

Primly clasping her knees, hoping this position might protect her from what was to come next, she nervously began.

'As you both know I have been off colour in the mornings of late. I have been to see Dr Rose for tests and he's told me I am … *expecting.*'

The word had barely left her lips when she saw Gertrude's nostrils flare.

Her cheeks turned red with rage and she took on a murderous expression.

'I never expected a daughter of mine could bring such shame upon our good name!' Gertrude screamed.

'I am very sorry, Mother,' Margie said.

In shock, her father leant over to pacify his wife, but she angrily knocked his arm away, as she spat out, 'Have you been sleeping with that foreigner behind my back?'

With her head hung low, Margie nodded.

'God forbid, with that criminal?'

'How many times have I told you the likes of him want only one thing from nice girls like you?' Gertrude said viciously.

Gesticulating violently, Gertrude knocked her cup of tea off her armrest. In a fit of indignation she picked it up still dripping from the rug and hurled it at her daughter, narrowly missing her.

Ron's shocked silence after the cup shattered on the sideboard suggested he was more understanding of Margie's plight. As Margie turned to him for solace, he headed out the door to the garden unable to get a word in on account of his wife's outrage.

Gertrude recalled that years earlier when the eldest daughter of a good friend had a child out of wedlock bringing shame upon the family, she had decided if a disaster like this ever befell her family, it would be kept secret at all costs.

The following ten minutes seemed an eternity to Margie as her mother read the riot act, finally announcing what would be happening next.

'None of this must ever get out,' she said threateningly as her daughter sobbed in shame.

'I am going to call my sister in-law in Plymouth to see if there is a place she knows for your confinement. Then when your baby is born, it is to be adopted out,' she concluded.

When she had finished with Margie, Gertrude went out to the garden to remind her husband of the scandal their daughter had already caused by introducing that foreign crook to Charles.

Ron realised how distraught Margie was and felt they couldn't desert her.

'Despite your anger dear, we are both still her parents and in her hour of need, we should support her. If we don't, she could walk out of this house.'

'I don't give a damn if she did. She should have considered the dire consequences before she slept with him.

'The most important thing now is that everything must be kept hush-hush,' Gertrude said, leaving Ron with the feeling there was little else he could do.

* * *

When Margie reached the top of the stairs Lucy came out of her room and bailed her up. 'What was that all about? I've never heard Mother screaming like that before.'

Then Lucy noticed the tears streaming down Margie's sullen face that told her something huge had happened.

* * *

Desperate to see Emilio one final time before she caught the train to Plymouth, Margie took the bus to his Waterloo Park flat.

After repeatedly ringing his bell, she returned downstairs and knocked on his landlady's door.

'I'm sorry to bother you,' Margie explained, 'I'm wondering if you have seen my boyfriend in unit nine of late?'

Recognising Margie, who had become a regular visitor, the landlady told her he had not been there in more than ten days.

'He came to me saying he had suddenly been called home and asked if he could keep his flat going, giving me two months' rent in advance before disappearing.

'I told the police the same thing when they came knocking last week.'

Margie thanked the landlady and turned to make her way home, knowing in her heart she would probably never lay eyes on him again.

* * *

Feeling in an even more vulnerable state that evening, Margie opened her diary, not caring if her snooping mother might get to read her day's thoughts:

20th March 1941

Today a chapter of my life came to an abrupt end, but not the way I had ever imagined it.

I do not regret for one moment my deep and unquestioning love for Emilio.

Through him I have discovered my true self, and revelled in how he valued my uniqueness, which gave me such confidence.

Together, we reached unimaginable heights and I entrusted myself to him, believing he would always be true to me.

But now my world has come crashing down.

Mother is banishing me to Plymouth to have the baby and she has gone out of her way to make me feel like a slut.

What cuts even more deeply is that Emilio left town without saying a word before going.

How could he be so cruel after everything we had shared?

In the stillness of her bedroom, her tears began to smudge the newly written page. Putting down the pen to read what she had written, she gave up and left the diary open to dry.

Snuggling into bed she could hear muffled thuds of bombs exploding in the distance. She hoped for a much better day tomorrow. Her last thought before nodding off was that being sent to Plymouth was never going to heal the huge rift that had opened up with her mother.

*   *   *

The thoughts rolling around Jessie's head after her disturbing tearooms conversation with Margie at the tearooms was what could she possibly do to help her best friend.

She was devastated Margie was pregnant, but realised this was wartime and the rules of purity and virtue that would usually have applied to young women had long been thrown out the window.

She knew that Margie's mother would be ruling the roost and there was very little she could suggest or do that would help.

Then there was the matter of Mr Bestillo.

It now appeared that he had committed a serious crime on British soil that required her to inform her Commander and MI6 as well. She was devastated that there was no way now she could keep Margie's serious relationship with Mr Bestillo out of the file.

At the meeting with her Commander, the Bestillo file was reviewed and the Garland fraud details were added as well as Margie's relationship with him.

Jessie noticed a more recent update that Mr Bestillo had booked a passage on a freighter from Dublin, which had sailed the week before, arriving in Lisbon several days later.

Then she read that MI6 were in the throes of organising with Scotland Yard's fraud squad for Mr Bestillo to be apprehended by the Lisbon police.

29. The Cover-up

In Sydney, Alice was distressed her brother remained physically and mentally incapacitated. With him being so far away and the war preventing travel, she fretted there was very little she could do.

She had made further enquiries with the Australasian Trustee Company on his behalf but had run into a deafening wall of silence.

Even when she was able to arrange a meeting with Sir Kenneth Codrington, she got short shrift.

'The firm is doing all it can,' he flatly told her and stubbornly refused to consider any interim compensation.

He bluntly informed her the trustees' insurance would be unable to cover the loss until the police investigation had been concluded and a determination made in any subsequent court case.

Hearing this made Alice's blood boil.

Undeterred, she continued her enquiries by switching tack.

It occurred to her that over the many years she had conducted business with the trustees, on most occasions Sir Kenneth had passed her over to Mr Spratt to handle any matters.

On those occasions she always found Mr Spratt most professional, always ensuring her best interests came first.

She assumed Mr Spratt had also handled her brother's matters. If so, she wondered if he could have become ensnared in the fraud.

Realising she couldn't phone and ask him such a sensitive question, she decided if by chance she happened to accidentally run into him, she might be able to unearth some answers.

She had heard that on board meeting days, Sir Kenneth took the directors to lunch at his club.

Was it possible that on these days Mr Spratt might afford himself a slightly longer lunch hour?

It didn't take Alice long to find out the date for the next board meeting.

*　　*　　*

As the town hall clock peeled 12.30 pm on the day of the meeting, Alice positioned herself across the street from the Australasian Trustee Company's front doors, to keep a close watch.

Soon after one o'clock, Sir Kenneth led the directors out through the doors and towards his Pitt Street club, with a cheerful, hungry look on his face.

Then her waiting game began.

After twenty minutes, having seen dozens of office workers stroll out into the coolish afternoon, there was still no sign of Mr Spratt. Alice began wondering if he might have brought lunch from home and was not going out.

Finally, a tallish gentleman appeared through the doors, busily buttoning up his coat and taking off at a fast pace down Pitt Street.

Beneath his felt hat, Alice saw enough of his face to recognise it was Arthur Spratt.

Determined not to let him out of her sight, she stepped off the footpath almost into the path of a fast moving furniture van.

Feeling like a sleuth, she didn't care if he discovered he was being followed.

A few hundred yards down the street he turned a corner, causing her to break into a dash to keep him in sight.

She then saw him enter the tearooms.

Reaching the window, she looked in to see him take a corner table seat and unfold a paper.

Seizing the moment, Alice entered and went to the cashier, where she placed an order and asked to have it brought to Mr Spratt's corner table.

Then summonsing every ounce of feminine charm she possessed, she breezed casually up to his table and, avoiding eye contact, casually asked if she could use the spare seat.

Caught momentarily offguard, Mr Spratt politely half rose saying, 'By all means.'

Alice then made a point of looking at him directly in the eye, and declared, 'If I'm not mistaken, it's Mr Spratt from the trustees.

'What a surprise to find you here, this is one of my most favourite tearooms.'

Hearing his name, Mr Spratt rose more fully, for a moment slightly unsure who the well-dressed woman joining him was.

After she re-introduced herself, the sight of Mrs Lockwood brought back some of Mr Spratt's worst memories of the Garland fraud and Sir Kenneth's obvious cover-up to save his own skin and the firm's name. How the managing director had botched the sale, lied to the police and kept him and the staff in the dark would in later years give Mr Spratt frequent nightmares.

He was unsure how much she knew of it, however felt sure she wouldn't want to discuss it anyway as they waited for their lunches to arrive while they exchanged pleasantries.

Alice was coy about why she was in town and after tea was served, she observed Mr Spratt appeared more relaxed than when they had first met.

Then she very delicately mentioned her brother. 'Mr Spratt, my family is very proud of my brother, who as you may have heard, was awarded the George Cross Medal after he was injured.'

'Indeed, we did read the very good news about his award,' Mr Spratt replied, not realising he was being gently drawn into a trap.

'I was very sorry when I heard he had been so badly injured. I haven't had any updates of late, how is his recovery going?'

This was the lead-in Alice so desperately needed.

'His news, I am afraid, is not all that good. The fraud has taken a terrible toll on him, happening just when he was so low and unable to cope with a financial disaster of such magnitude,' she answered.

'Mr Garland's swindle was such a terrible matter and I admit it has caused me many sleepless nights,' confided Mr Spratt.

'Should I assume you somehow got caught up with it when it happened?' Alice asked gently, not wanting to point the bone.

'Mrs Lockwood, at the time, I was handling his file and the fraud gave the firm a huge fright.'

'Mr Spratt, given the huge sum involved, my brother still doesn't understand how the firm failed to check with him or contact his London bank before proceeding to sell his shares and then transfer the proceeds,' Alice said.

'Mrs Lockwood, just between the two of us and this must never get out, that's exactly what I had advised Sir Kenneth we must do.'

'So what actually happened?' asked Alice.

Before answering, Mr Spratt paused to allow his thoughts to churn back over those dreadful events that had left such an emotional scar on him and his firm. He never fully understood how Sir Kenneth was able to influence his good friend, the NSW premier to have the police prematurely close their investigations, how he got the newspapers to not publish the scandalous news of the fraud, and why shattering his client's trust in the firm was less important than saving his own skin.

Ever since, he had always thought Sir Kenneth was a self-serving, bumbling, spineless coward.

With these thoughts in mind, Mr Spratt decided not to reopen a can of worms.

'Mrs Lockwood, as I understand it, Sir Kenneth was completely deceived by the bogus phone call and letter from Mr Bestillo and overrode my advice, instructing me to proceed with the sale of the shares forthwith to keep faith with his valued client.

'It was only after I sent the letter to Mr Garland advising we had followed his instructions and completed the sale and bank transfer, that I was absolutely shocked to hear the firm had received a call from the real Mr Garland saying he had never instructed us to do any such thing.'

This admission cemented what Alice feared were Sir Kenneth's motives to blatantly cover up the fraud and push back every attempt by her brother and herself for redress.

'Did the NSW police interview you about your knowledge of the circumstances of my brother's loss?' she enquired.

'Yes and no,' answered Mr Spratt. 'Initially I helped them by providing copies of the fraudulent letter and the bank transfer details.

'Then some days later, Sir Kenneth told me off-the-record that the matter had been hushed up and I had nothing to worry about. Also he said that I would not be hearing from the police again as they had been informed Scotland Yard was dealing with everything.'

'Mr Spratt, when the fraud took place, would you say Sir Kenneth was on top of his game or were there things distracting him?' Alice posed.

'It's not for me to say, but Mrs Lockwood, there had been some loose talk in the office that Sir Kenneth had been noticed returning from lunch in a somewhat jolly state and on those days, he tended to go off at the slightest provocation.'

'Are you suggesting he might have had a drinking problem?' asked Alice.

'That is not for me to say, but our Chairman, who is getting close to retiring, still doesn't seem to think Mr Garland has been treated all that badly, despite the fact that the fraud went close to destroying the firm's reputation.'

'What do the others in the office say about it?' Alice asked.

'Everyone refers to it as that "*near death experience*".

'What worries me the most, and the reason I have been open with you today Mrs Lockwood, is that Mr Garland has been treated very unfairly,' Mr Spratt disclosed.

'Are you saying an injustice has been done? Alice asked, shocked by his admission.

'I only hope that one day he receives due justice,' Mr Spratt concluded, feeling he might have divulged more than he should have.

Realising the time, Alice checked her watch then stood to leave. 'I have always appreciated how professional you have been in all our dealings. What you have told me today is no exception and I want to thank you.'

*   *   *

Telegramming Charles afterwards with a brief update of the meeting with Mr Spratt, Alice asked if she should approach the NSW police to speed things up.

He sent back his agreement, and informed her to the best of his knowledge Scotland Yard had never told the NSW police to leave things as they lay because the fraud had taken place on Australian soil. He also requested that she should act on his behalf.

*   *   *

When Alice provided this new information to the NSW police fraud squad sergeant handling the matter about the senior clerk's account of the trustee's cover-up, it resulted in them reopening the file with a new line of enquiry that the firm may not have divulged all of the facts leading up to the crime.

A week later, she read with great interest a small article in the *Sydney Morning Herald* about the fraud but it provided no names.

When Alice called the fraud squad sergeant for a further update, she was appalled to be told that "someone with a lot of pull" had brought pressure to bear that had resulted in the investigation of Emilio Bestillo's fraud being spiked.

In other words, there was a cover-up, Alice concluded.

Not giving a damn about Charles and Garland Trading, the trustee company had cunningly and unethically used its influence to ensure its gross negligence would never be revealed. Alice's disgust knew no bounds.

*   *   *

Early in September 1941, frustrated by the injustice, Alice sought advice about transferring her investments with the Australasian Trustee Company to another firm.

When she advised Sir Kenneth of her intentions by phone she was very upset when he dressed her down.

She responded by writing a strongly worded letter to the trustee's board complaining about Sir Kenneth's arrogant behaviour towards her and the firm's incompetence, which had led to the loss of her brother's fortune.

In the short run her letter was not answered, but sometime later she was delighted to read in the paper that Sir Kenneth Codrington had been stood down and the firm was undertaking a search for a new chairman.

Regardless, the firm still kept the Garland scandal a secret.

There was still no justice.

For several months, Alice had corresponded with Margie for updates on her brother's rehabilitation.

After reading of Sir Kenneth's dismissal in the paper, Alice decided she would write to Margie and offer her help if she could find a way to settle the score with the trustees.

30. Bottle of Pills

Adding to Charles' woes, Margie's cheerful visits, which he had enjoyed so much these last months, had suddenly come to an abrupt end when she unexpectedly moved to Plymouth.

Until now, he hadn't realised how much he looked forward to the positive and youthful energy she brought through the door.

The shock of losing close to half a million pounds had caused a massive setback to his recovery, which was further affected by the lack of progress being made by the British and New South Wales police who seemed unable to bring the prime suspect to heel.

To Charles, the Australasian Trustee Company were making the right noises but it seemed more interested in keeping the scandal out of the papers than seeing justice done and refunding his money.

He was unable to draw a salary from Garland Trading as he had taken an extended leave of absence and due to the tough economic conditions brought on by war, his firm was barely holding its own, with any profits made used to sustain the business.

The wine and butter export business to Britain was doing well without his day-to-day involvement, but that income was offset by a drop in Australian sales.

Garland Trading's bank, upon being informed of the sale of the shares, took note but having recently re-valued the company's assets and in view of its solid trading position, scrapped the requirement that his shares be used as security.

However, when his annual £12,250 dividend cheques came to an end, Charles immediately felt the loss as he watched his bank balance dwindle.

He was becoming increasingly anxious about whether he would have sufficient money to meet his costly medical and living expenses, but he loathed the idea of asking his sister to assist, even though he knew if he did, she would.

For Charles, his loss of dignity was becoming too much to bear.

* * *

By late October, Charles finally summonsed the courage to write a very overdue letter to Elizabeth:

October 1941
Dearest Elizabeth,

I am sorry I have taken an inordinate amount of time to reply to your several letters, but I continue to find it an effort to put pen to paper, partly because I only have limited vision in my good eye and also my writing hand is still weak and continues to give me grief.

As you suggested, I discussed with my doctors the prospect of being repatriated home, but given my poor condition they have insisted I remain here for the time being.

More importantly, I now fear the prospects of me regaining the full use of my arm and right eye appears bleak and the lesions on my face are refusing to heal.

Since March, I have missed the visits from dear Margie, who had been an inspiration since I was hospitalised.

She suddenly upped and left to take, what I presume is, a position in Plymouth and she says she can't get back to London, which saddens me very deeply.

There is little good news emerging relating to my fraud that I informed you happened earlier this year, which shook me considerably.

The last word from the trustees indicated the Lisbon police are still investigating Margie's boyfriend, but they haven't updated me for quite some time and I now hold out little hope of ever getting any money back.

I have to admit I am concerned that in my present poor state of health I feel I am not well enough to return to manage the trading company, which is a worry.

Since my shares dividend cheques ended I am struggling to find sufficient funds to cover my living expenses, which is causing me considerable despair.

Some might also say my mental state has been affected and I have to concede this may be true.

Over the last few months I have taken account of my prospects and much as you have always believed I will soon get back on my feet and return to my old self, the fact is this is not going to happen in the near future.

> *I fear I would only prove a burden to you, which I cannot accept.*
>
> *Elizabeth, it is therefore with an extremely heavy heart, that I implore you not to wait for my return.*
>
> *I think it best if you put me into the background, step again out into life there in Melbourne and seize the next exciting opportunity you so richly deserve.*
>
> *My thoughts are with you and I pray you will accede to my heartfelt request.*
> *My best wishes for your journey,*
> *Charles*

*   *   *

Despite the wonderful home care the British Red Cross nurses provided Charles during their visits, by late 1941 his health and mental wellbeing had further declined.

Whilst he managed to get around his flat with a walking stick, for outings he still needed a wheelchair.

He gained comfort that his father's map-reader helped him read the papers and mail, especially from Alice and Garland Trading, which sent monthly board reports he always looked forward to.

From time to time when he happened to glance at the George Cross Medal on the mantelpiece, it would buck him up, but it was of little help when it came to his increasingly dire health issues and financial situation.

*   *   *

Suffering an increasing weariness he was unable to shrug off and continued poor spirits, Charles contracted a bad dose of influenza in early December, which set him back even further.

Later that month his doctor admitted him to the Queen Alexandra Hospital in Smallfield with pneumonia, where his condition continued to slide.

In his final days the next of kin were called and many old friends visited his bedside, including his commanding officer, his former batman and his Marylebone landlady.

The Swansons were shocked when they saw how badly Charles had wasted away since the last time they had seen him and noticed his will to live had all but evaporated.

Having returned to London after giving birth to her baby, knowing he had only hours to live, Margie lovingly sat by her uncle's side hour after hour holding his pale weakened hands, reassuring him she would always be there for him whilst privately shedding tears as everyone prepared for the worst.

She found it unsettling to smell the unpleasant odours his infected wounds were emitting and had to work at putting them out of her mind.

Having refused to eat and with further complications setting in, he began slipping in and out of a coma. Just before Christmas Day, several hours before sunrise, alone in the darkness, he drew his final breath.

After his lifeless body was placed on a trolley and removed, a nurse stripped his bed and took the old linen out to the laundry. Soon after a cleaner came in to scrub and prepare the room for the next patient. Mopping the floor she noticed out of the corner of her eye an empty pill bottle lying on the floor beneath the bed.

Without giving it further thought, she picked it up and as she was leaving the room with her bucket and mop she ran into Margie, who had arrived to collect Charles' belongings.

Shocked to see an empty bottle of sleeping pills in the cleaner's hand, Margie asked where she had found it, then hearing the answer she promptly took it from her saying, as she slipped it into her pocket, that she would report it.

*   *   *

At Charles' private funeral in the Dulwich Village parish church, attended by a small gathering of family and friends, his commanding officer paid a glowing tribute to his former Lieutenant.

On Charles' coffin draped with the Australian and Royal Engineers' flags and adorned with his George Cross Medal gleaming in the soft, grey light, lay a simple wreath of red roses from Elizabeth, with a card attached expressing her devotion for her departed lover.

Ron Swanson read a heartfelt telegram from Alice in Sydney, and then added a tribute on behalf of his family.

A squad of sappers from Charles' Royal Engineers solemnly carried his coffin out to a waiting hearse, then formed up and marched proudly behind the funeral cortege as it pulled slowly away from the church steps.

Silently watching the cortege depart, Margie was consumed by pangs of guilt that Emilio's cold-hearted swindle of her uncle and its far reaching effect on his terrible injuries, had no doubt triggered the tragic events leading to him ending his life.

Margie left the service leaning on Jessie's arm, feeling utterly devastated, which was not helped by her mother having refused her requests to deliver a eulogy for her adored uncle.

She later found out Gertrude's reason was that it would draw unwanted attention to the family and risk questions being asked about matters she did not want raised.

*　*　*

Soon after the funeral, Margie received a letter from Charles' sister that spoke of her loss.

Alice felt devastated that her suffering brother had died without seeing Emilio brought to justice or the trustees held accountable for their part in the fraud. Despite her attempts to obtain more information about the investigation, they had remained secretive.

The letter said that the Garland legacy had been all but destroyed and it wasn't looking like she would ever see it restored. All she could now hope for was that somehow someone, somewhere, could find a way to "square the ledger".

Given there was no justice, Alice offered to assist if anyone could help settle the score with the trustees.

31. The Cough, 2019

In her ninety-eighth year, Margie Childers invited her granddaughter for a special afternoon tea, something the pair had not done for quite some time.

Emma Childers, now twenty, had been caught up with her work and hectic social life.

Nonetheless, Margie had something she had been waiting a long time to give her.

It had taken more than a decade, after giving birth to Frank, for Margie to find the strength to begin to try and find a way to forgive her mother for how abominably she had treated her.

When Gertrude died, she left Margie a beautiful 1920s wristwatch, which was worth a considerable amount. However she refused to wear it and instead kept it locked away.

A few years ago she had given it away to rid herself of what should have been a treasured heirloom, but which she hated.

However, she had kept its little leather case, hoping one day to give it to Emma with something special in it.

Sitting in the living room, as Emma savoured the aroma of freshly baked muffins wafting from the kitchen, she marvelled that her Granma still loved to bake them. In front of her, she could not but notice the small case sitting on the coffee table.

She was distracted when she heard Granma suddenly gripped by a coughing spasm.

"Are you all right?' Emma called.

'It's nothing really, just a silly little tickle, don't you worry,' replied Margie.

Recovering her composure after several sips of tea, Margie beamed with anticipation.

'I have an inspiration I want you to think about.

'If you open that little case, there is something in it that I have kept since a trip to Glasgow when I had just left school.'

Removing a very old travel leaflet from the case, Emma immediately noticed its dated format.

'When I was a little younger than you, my dearest school friend, Jessie Tyler and I went on holiday without our parents to Glasgow to see the Empire Exhibition, which was our first escape from home,' Margie explained.

'We found the exhibition simply amazing, especially the Australian Pavilion that really captured my attention, where I was told there were plenty of opportunities for English nurses in Australia.

'But at such a young age I didn't have the courage to take up what might have been the adventure of a lifetime.

'However it did spark my interest in nursing, which became a major part of my journey in life,' she added.

At the mention of Australia, Margie saw her granddaughter's eyes light up.

'Down the years, Emma, there have been so many times that I have regretted not having gone there.

'For some time, I have wondered if you have ever thought about going off on an overseas adventure like that.'

'Granma, would you believe a little while ago on my galleries tour of France, I met a guy who was backpacking around Europe who came from Melbourne.

'He told me a lot about his remarkable country and he promised if I ever decided to go there he could help me find somewhere to stay and find a job.

'Ever since then I have been too preoccupied to give the idea any further thought,' Emma explained.

'Dear, if you still happen to be at all interested', Margie proposed, trying to suppress another pesky splutter, 'I have put aside some money to buy you a return plane ticket.'

'Oh Granma, how kind of you! I had thought about going there, but part of the reason I never have, was I didn't have the money.'

Emma finally agreed it would be a great experience, and after accepting the offer, promised to write often about what she saw and did.

As she kissed Granma goodbye on the way out the door, Emma suggested, 'You need to have your doctor check that cough.'

*　　*　　*

Six weeks later, as Emma's plane climbed majestically into the burnt red evening sunset west of Heathrow, heading towards Australia, below in a small Wimbledon garden, having checked the time on her antique clock, Margie Childers watched it fly overhead.

With a few small tears in her eyes she wondered how many years she had left to wind her clock up every week.

However, at this moment she had so much to look forward to with Emma on her way to discover a whole new world and life.

Margie was very much anticipating the thrill of reading her letters describing what Melbourne was like and how a job interview she had secured turned out.

She wanted to hear more about that young backpacker, Alex, whom Emma spoke of. She pondered whether anything between them might ever eventuate.

These thoughts steered her mind back to the early years of the war when her longing for a boyfriend led to her exuberant, headstrong fling with the wine salesman, that ended in grief and inflicted so much pain on her family, her uncle and of course herself.

Margie still shuddered at the thought of Emilio.

In part she blamed herself for not heeding Jessie's warnings, but at the time she desperately needed to escape her mother's clutches. For her, Emilio was, at the time, a ticket to womanhood but she wondered now at what price.

Margie had never forgotten how the Plymouth Hospital had been so mean not allowing her to take any photos of baby Frank, to treasure next to her heart, before they took him away.

The guilt of giving up her baby had come back to haunt her far too many times. She used to stare at young schoolboys on their way to class or playing rugby in parks. Then she watched young men on their way to work, wondering if one of them might be her son and if so, would she be able to recognise him.

* * *

A month after Emma arrived in Melbourne, Margie was delighted to receive her first letter from Australia and could scarcely wait to read it.

Dearest Granma,

I have arrived safely, which I hope Mum has passed on to you. The flight was long and a little tiring but from the moment I set eyes on this vast country from the plane window, I knew it was all going to be worthwhile.

It was so unlike England's expanse of rolling, lush, green countryside.

Australia is agonisingly dry. Its ranges flow down to plains of sun-bleached fields that are dotted with huge "gum" trees and dry creeks.

The light here is so different to what I've ever known. When I walked along St Kilda beach yesterday it was bluer, clearer and noticeably more intense, which dramatically amplifies the earthy landscape. It's so bright you need "sunnies" when you venture outside.

I was met by Alex, that backpacker I told you about, and one of his friends and stayed in their share house in Brunswick, which is near the city.

Since then I've found a little cottage in South Melbourne and I will be moving into it on my own very soon.

Next Monday I have a second interview for a position with a firm of recruiters in Melbourne's business district, which sounds really exciting.

Thank you again for inspiring me to decide to come here and for the very generous ticket.

I asked Mum, when we spoke last week, about your cough and she didn't know anything about it. So I'm hoping you have seen your doctor to have it looked at.

All my love and hugs from sunny autumnal Melbourne. I am so excited to be here and I have a positive feeling great things are about to happen!
All my love,
Emma XX OO XX

As she brushed away small tears of happiness, Margie felt enormous pleasure that her wonderful granddaughter was fulfilling a dream that had eluded her.

With decades of rich thoughts swirling through her mind, Margie's gaze was attracted beyond the window to the rustle of a change in the weather with the first drops of rain splashing down on the path and bouncing off the green bushes in her garden.

Suddenly the silence was broken by another troublesome cough.

The visit to her doctor that Emma had insisted on had led to tests and X-rays which had not produced good news; quite the contrary. She now faced the difficult task of telling the family of her dire prognosis.

*　*　*

Down the years, Irene Childers had watched with great pride how her mother, Margie, had bonded so instinctively with Emma, especially mentoring her through the ups and downs in her teens.

She'd seen the pair develop an inseparable bond and some in the family had commented that Emma seemed to have inherited many of Margie's finer traits.

On more than one occasion, Irene wondered why her mother had not mentored her like this when she was growing up.

She rationalised it might have been that her mother didn't have the money at the time or the energy.

More recently she wondered if, as Margie aged, she wanted to ensure that her lost opportunities were made good through Emma.

*　*　*

Wondering how Emma's experience in Australia might be working out, Irene hoped now she had left home that it would improve her resilience and finally put her many talents to full use.

Irene remembered that she herself had only really stood on her own two feet after she went off on that infamous "Contiki Tour", partying all the way from Paris to Prague with all the young Aussies, who were so much fun.

She had been looking forward to hearing from Emma, when early one morning her phone unexpectedly rang.

'Irene, it's your mother here, how are you?

'Have you got any more news from Emma about that position she was interviewed for?' Margie asked.

Disappointed it wasn't Emma on the line, Irene coolly replied, 'Oh, it's you Mum, I thought it was Melbourne calling.'

'Darling, I want you to know that in that newsy letter I received from Emma ten days ago she reminded me I needed to see my doctor about a niggling cough I've had for many months.'

Finding it hard to choose the right words Margie continued, 'I saw my doctor last week and had some X-rays and other tests done. This morning when I saw the doctor to hear the results, he gave me some horrible news.

'The tests revealed I have a tumour on my lung. He now wants me to see a specialist but I'm so upset I can't bring myself to make an appointment.'

As the shock of her mother's news sank in, Irene's face went deathly white.

'Oh Mum, what ever can I say? That's simply dreadful news.'

As a small tear formed in her eye, Irene suddenly began to feel terribly guilty.

'Mum, if only I'd known I would have taken you there today. I'm on my way over, please put the kettle on.'

* * *

Gripping Margie's hand in the specialist's rooms, they listened as the oncologist explained her tumour was too advanced to operate on.

Knowing the news couldn't get any worse, Irene took a deep breath before asking what her mother's prognosis was.

The oncologist suggested possibly six months at best, and six weeks at the worst.

Shattered with the bitter hand that Margie had been dealt, mother and daughter left the appointment completely gutted.

In the car about to drive home, Margie somehow summonsed the grit to rise above the cloud of sadness that had just enveloped both of them.

'Let's face it Irene … I'm ninety-eight … I have had an amazing innings … And when I'm gone, everyone will, of course, find a way to carry on.

'Now I certainly don't want you or anyone in the family spilling tears over me,' Margie bravely announced.

'If it's all right with you, when we get home I would like to discuss a few ideas I have got for my funeral.'

On the way home Irene glanced across at her uncharacteristically subdued mother and was dismayed by the sight of her looking a shadow of her usual chirpy self.

'When I go, I would like the funeral to be at St Mary's,' Margie began quietly, then as Irene turned into her street, she said, 'Do you think Emma would be up to it if she was asked to do my eulogy or am I expecting too much of her?'

32. The Will

With tears rolling unashamedly down her distraught face, in silence, Emma watched the hearse carrying Margie's coffin slowly make its way down the driveway of St Mary's Church.

As it passed from view through the gates, she let out a quiet gasp then turned to her grief-stricken mother to give her a knowing hug.

Afterwards a few close friends came up and offered their condolences.

About to get in the limousine taking them to the wake at Margie's favourite pub, the 19th century Dog and Fox, the undertaker presented Irene with the signed attendees memorial book.

Emma's best friend Becky had given her great support, taking her aside at one point to tell her what a stirring eulogy she had delivered.

For Emma, the wake soon turned into a blur as she and her mother were swamped by a sea of faces and memories.

Emma had girded herself for the service, but afterwards she had little remaining energy for the emotional drain of having to meet so many of Margie's old friends, who wanted to share their fondest personal memories.

Reflecting afterwards, she vaguely recalled meeting Margie's younger sister Lucy, who spoke of the sad rift her sister had with their mother.

Then there was an elderly gentleman in his eighties who had introduced himself as Oliver Osmond, saying he owed his life to Margie after she rescued him and his sister from a fire in the Blitz, for which she was awarded the Florence Nightingale Medal.

She recalled the sweet-faced elderly lady who was sitting alone in the middle pews during the service, who introduced herself at the wake as Jessie, one of Margie's old school friends, however her surname escaped Emma.

She recalled, as the last of the mourners were leaving, a gentleman in his seventies, dressed in a smart blue suit, who had introduced himself as Frank.

He complimented Emma on her eulogy then quietly told her how saddened he was with Margie's passing, adding, 'I wish I had known about those "strokes" of hers when she was alive.'

Emma asked her mother where she thought that gentleman who introduced himself as Frank fitted into Granma's life.

'He seemed to me to be more European than English, how do you think he knew her?' she asked.

Sensing this was not the moment to explain something very complex and important from her mother's past, Irene intimated that many people came up to her whom she hardly knew, telling her how they had known and come to love Margie.

'I suppose Frank would be one of them,' Irene said before subtly changing the subject.

'Emma, with all we have had to deal with this last week, I haven't had a chance to mention that your grandmother's solicitor has suggested we should make a time to visit his chambers in the next few days for the reading of her Will,' she said.

*   *   *

Feeling at first she was being dragged along to merely hear the Will being read, Emma had to remind herself that her mother needed her support at this time.

With preliminaries dealt with as they sat in the solicitor's chambers, the lawyer perfunctorily opened the folded Will and began in a monotone voice:

> "I, Margie Emily Childers, hereby revoke all former Wills and declare that the proper law of this my last Will shall be the law of England and Wales.
>
> I appoint my daughter Irene Childers to be my Executor.
>
> I give the following legacies:
> - To my daughter Irene Childers ten thousand pounds and all my jewellery
> - I give to the Red Cross ten thousand pounds

- I give and bequeath all my real and personal property, including my Merton Hall Road home in Wimbledon, my car and shares of whatsoever nature, to my Executor to sell or dispose of as she pleases
- Except for my antique mantle clock, which I bequeath to my granddaughter Emma Childers."

Warm memories of being a little girl, winding up Granma's clock, soon flooded back to remind Emma of how special it was.

'Oh, how wonderful. During Granma's life, I always loved how it imposed a sense of time in her living room,' she exclaimed.

Pausing on the way out to collect her copy of the Will and sign several documents, Irene realised she had an awful lot of work ahead tidying up her mother's estate, getting the Merton Hall Road house ready to sell and dealing with her furniture, clothes and effects.

Driving home she suggested they might go to Wimbledon the next day to get things started.

Knowing she had to fly back to Melbourne in a few days, Emma reminded herself this would probably be her final visit to Granma's home and it would mean a lot to go with her mother.

'Of course Mum, it will be a chance for both of us to say goodbye to the place and I can pack the clock to take on the plane with me.

'You know, having it will always remind me of Granma every time I check its time.'

33. The Clock, Melbourne

Suffering jet-lag after returning to her Melbourne weatherboard cottage, Emma crawled from beneath her doona and struggled into her dressing gown before padding sleepily out to the kitchen to put the kettle on.

Waiting for it to boil, she went to the hallstand where she remembered she had left the clock.

Bringing it into the kitchen, which was being warmed by early morning sunlight filtering through two smallish, creeper framed windows, she placed it on the table.

Then, snipping at the bubble wrap and brown packing tape that was partly covered by customs stickers, she was dying to hear the comforting sounds of its hundred years old *"tick-tock"*.

Removing the wrapping, she carefully eased the heavy piece from its mahogany case and opened its small glass front door.

Retrieving the brass-winding key, she began to slowly wind it, then delicately shifted its hands to read 8.45am.

Turning the clock around, she opened a small brass mesh and silk covered door and, peering in, saw a complex set of shiny sprockets connected to what she thought looked like the pendulum.

Emma tried several times to get it to swing, but to her consternation, it refused to budge.

Knowing her Granma would never allow a small inconvenience such as this get the better of her, Emma grabbed her phone and Googled *"How to make an antique clock tick"*.

Her screen filled with heaps of suggestions, but none she tried got the pendulum to swing.

Almost checkmated, she decided to text Alex, her backpacking friend, having recalled him saying his mum ran Zacher Antiques in Albert Park.

He messaged back:

Try Colman's in Malvern, who are horologists. They will be able to fix it.

Her phone call to them was answered by a Michael Colman who suggested she bring it in for him to look at.

* * *

Emma had visions that being antique clockmakers, Colman's would be a fusty old-fashioned establishment.

Alighting from her tram she soon realised Colman's was more contemporary than she had expected, nestled amongst a cluster of stylish interior design studios, crowded cafés and antique dealers buzzing with interesting shoppers.

Stepping through its front door she entered a world of high-end, superbly polished, collectors' pieces.

Many were ticking and a number chimed at intervals.

Some were small, others large, quite a few hung from the walls, twenty or more were behind glass and a dozen stood in long cases along the walls.

From the rear workroom appeared a friendly, bespectacled, middle-aged man with a discerning face wearing a well-loved brown cardigan. His attention was drawn to the fine English piece Emma held.

'Good morning, I presume by the clock you have there, you are the young lady who wants to find out why it won't tick.'

'Yes, I'm Emma, we spoke earlier,' she replied.

Removing it from the case, Mr Colman adjusted his glasses to assess its attributes and workings.

Moments later he looked up with a reassuring smile. 'This is a very good example of a beautiful late 1800s Victorian mahogany bracket clock, made by Barraud and Lunds of Cornhill, London.'

Turning the piece around he opened the rear door and continued his examination.

'This might be your problem!' he exclaimed after he discovered the pendulum had been set to travel mode.

He explained that the pendulum should have swung after it was released and might have been damaged in transit.

'Emma, if you leave this I will have the suspension link replaced, then I am confident it will work perfectly,' he reassured her.

Walking from Colman's, Emma felt her clock was in the best of hands, but remained frustrated it still wasn't ticking.

She reminded herself when checking its time she needed to say a word of thanks for her gift.

* * *

The following Saturday, Emma was up bright and early, eagerly waiting on the footpath outside her cottage for Alex, who had kindly offered to drive her to Colman's.

Arriving, Mr Colman told her, 'We had a good look at your piece which is now working perfectly. Our records indicate it's rather valuable, so we would suggest you have it insured,' he said.

But having to take leave without pay to fly home for the funeral meant Emma was down to the last hundred dollars credit on her card. The expense of insuring it was beyond her means for now, at least until she was next paid.

'Mr Colman, I will get back to you about the insurance,' she replied politely as she paid for the repair.

Waiting for the sale to go through, he reminded her she needed to wind the eight-day clock once every week on the same day and try not to let it get down to the last day, otherwise the loss of tension in the mainspring will cause it to lose time.

'Also the key for its rear door was missing and we were on the verge of cutting a new one, but when we gave the clock a polish, we discovered this small panel here on the base moves.

'When we tapped it this secret drawer sprang out, which as you can see contains the missing key, plus a little surprise.'

Sliding it open, it revealed a set of folded pages tied with a fading red ribbon.

Emma looked quizzically at the bundle before taking it out and untying the ribbon.

About to begin reading the handwritten pages, she suddenly remembered the insurance matter.

'When I insure it, Mr Colman how much should it be for?' she asked.

Leaning across the counter Mr Colman said privately, 'We would suggest at the very least for $18,500.'

Hearing such an unexpectedly high figure, Emma almost fainted. 'Can I check … You said $18,500 … Are you quite sure?' she asked.

'Absolutely,' he said.

Distracted by her shock windfall, the bundle of pages were fast forgotten as she slipped them back into the drawer, fully intending to look at them later.

* * *

Heading home in the car to South Melbourne with the clock on the floor held safely between her legs, Emma agreed to Alex's suggestion they should pick up a bottle of champagne to celebrate her windfall.

Emma texted her mother with the thrilling news, then invited her work colleagues to drop in to celebrate.

In all the excitement she did not give a moment's thought to the parcel of red ribbon-tied pages in the hidden drawer.

34. Hidden Pages

Emma spent the next day recovering from her impromptu "windfall" party hangover.

It was only after she got home from work on Monday, when her clock chimed seven o'clock, that she remembered she hadn't had a proper a look at the notes in the drawer Mr Colman had shown her.

Taking the clock into the kitchen and placing it on the table, she tapped her fingers along the side panel until she felt a discernable click that enabled her to open the little drawer. She then took out the bundle of pages.

Becoming excited for the first time about what they might contain, she carefully untied the ribbon and flattened out the yellowed sheets, immediately seeing dated entries and ragged edges that suggested they may have been torn from a diary.

On closer inspection, she realised they were in her Granma's distinctive handwriting.

<u>Wednesday 26 March 1941</u>
Woke after a patchy night's sleep being sick again.
Feel so sorry for Uncle Charles after he was swindled out of his fortune and he's tried to break up with Elizabeth.
How awful for him.

<u>Friday 28 March 1941</u>
Today is my worst ever, after my doctor told me I am pregnant.
Had huge fight with mother when I told her. She doesn't understand me.
Saddened beyond words with Emilio as he refuses to answer my phone calls.
Am now feeling very alone and helpless.

<u>Sunday 30th March 1941</u>
Have discussed my plight with Jess, who seemed supportive, but I sense there is something she is holding back.
Mother is giving me the "cold shoulder" treatment.
She told me I'm being "dispatched" for the sake of the family's good name.

<u>Monday 31st March 1941</u>
Uncle's earth-shattering news that Emilio is the prime suspect is too much to swallow on top of him ignoring my calls.

<u>Tuesday 1st April 1941</u>
Went one last time today to Emilio's flat to see him and was told he has disappeared, I presume home to Portugal.
My sister pulled a joke on me before breakfast when she set fire to some oily rags outside the bathroom window and yelled, "fire". About to take a bath I smelled the smoke and ran into the hall, to be greeted by Lucy who called "April Fool" something I was not in the mood for.
Am beside myself as I leave for Plymouth in a few days.

Putting down the last page, Emma looked up and stared out of the kitchen window into the moonless night to process what she had just read. The only sound breaking the stillness was the steady, reassuring "tick tock" from her clock.

Emma asked herself why they might have been hidden in the drawer and who would have torn them from Granma's diary.

Always believing that Granma had only given birth to her mother and Aunt Peggy, Emma was quite certain there had never been any mention of a third child.

She asked herself why Granma would have gone to Plymouth given she had a vitally important wartime job in the ambulance corps.

Then her questions turned to the brief mention of Uncle Charles' swindle. Why had the family never made mention of it to her and what was that all about?

And what about the reference to Granma's boyfriend Emilio, who seemed to have left her in the lurch?

The pages there on the table suddenly raised so many puzzling questions, for which there were no explanations or answers, but obviously something very important had been swept under the carpet for most of her life.

Facing a quandary, she decided to text Alex:

Have just read the pages in the clock drawer. They appear to have been torn from an old diary. Unsure what they all mean but they raise heaps of family questions.
Talk soon. XX Emma

To clear her mind before heading to bed, she noted down the four burning questions that were eating away at her.

Try as she might to get to sleep, the questions just kept dancing over and over in her mind.

Before finally dozing off, it occurred to her that perhaps no-one in her family would know all the answers. If so, what could she do then?

35. Seeking Advice

Following a restless night's sleep, before she headed off to work, Emma decided to text her best friend in London for her advice:

Becky i hope u are well?
Am struggling with some family matters that i have just discovered.
It appears someone tore some pages from granma's war diary and hid them in that old clock she left me.
Am unsure what they mean and don't know who to turn to.
Also have just discovered granma might have had a child before she married, that has never been mentioned in our family.
Love Emma

Later that day, Becky's reply came in:

Great to hear from u. Yes all is well and am enjoying the warmer spring days and extra daylight.
Re your questions … you should ask your mum who will surely be able to tell you all?
Love Becky

* * *

Having scanned through the pages, Alex agreed they were more than intriguing.

'Yes, I agree your mum will know a whole lot more. But before you ask her, maybe there is someone in Australia who might know something.'

'Probably not, unless that Melbourne lady friend of Charles my mum told me about could throw some light on it,' said a doubtful Emma.

'Emm, from what I gather, that romance was over seventy years ago so she may not still be alive,' Alex said.

'Alright, if I was to ask mum, how do you think I should approach her?' posed Emma.

Alex watched her take a long, slow sip of her juice before answering.

'If I was you, I would use a more oblique approach. Firstly, text her to let her know you have discovered something about the family and that you are going to call her.

'Don't be too specific, as she may well have her reasons why these matters have not previously been aired,' he concluded.

'Do you think she might suspect I have found something awful?' Emma asked.

'Well, when you call, why don't you use the line that while you are out here, you thought you might make contact with Charles' lady friend. Then ask her if she remembers Elizabeth's surname and where she lived.

'If she asks why, say you have discovered some notes hidden in the clock that mentions her,' Alex suggested.

'What about the other questions?' Emma asked, taking another nervous sip of juice.

'Don't mention the diary for the moment, just ask one question at a time. The answer to one question may well lead you to uncover the next,' Alex suggested.

'That makes perfect sense, Alex. Can I ask you one more favour? How would I go about finding how many children Granma had?' Emma asked.

'In Australia that sort of information is kept by the Births, Deaths and Marriages registry. England will probably have a similar service.' Alex supposed.

'Look, I'll Google our Births and Deaths for you.'

Downing the last of his mouth-watering burger, he showed her the Births and Deaths home page that indicated she would need the full name and the correct dates to begin her search.

*   *   *

The first thing Emma did when she got back to her desk was text her mum, saying she would phone her the next day, not elaborating why.

A reply soon came back:

Looking forward to hearing all your news,
Love mum.

* * *

Emma punched in her mother's number and settled back with a notepad, waiting to hear her familiar voice.

Before dialling, she had reminded herself to only ask about making contact with Charles' former Melbourne lady friend.

Several rings later, she heard, 'Darling, how wonderful you have called. How are you?'

'I'm settling in really well and everything is fine with me,' Emma answered, as she anticipated her mum's next question.

'I hope you are eating properly?' her mum asked.

'For heaven's sake, don't worry, I'm having really healthy meals,' said Emma, before coming quickly to the point.

'Mum, I remember Granma sometimes spoke of her Uncle Charles, the war hero, who had a love affair with a woman who I recall lived in Melbourne.'

At the other end of the line, Irene thought it more than strange that Emma had suddenly become interested in something from so long ago.

'Do you think, if she is alive … I think her name was Elizabeth … would she have any interest in meeting me? asked Emma.

'Dear, I expect she will have died years ago,' Irene answered, not knowing where this was leading.

'Do you recall her surname?' Emma queried.

The question caused Irene to take a deep breath before she responded.

'From memory her name was Mrs Elizabeth Blow, who was a nurse when Charles met her on the ship coming over to England.

'Why are you so interested in their romance?

'While I'm here I am trying to trace some of our Australian connections,' Emma replied airily.

Hanging up from the call, Irene looked pensively out the kitchen window at the clouds scudding across the sky. She couldn't help wondering why Emma seemed so cagey about suddenly wanting to make contact with Uncle Charles' lady friend and that she seemed overly happy when she told her the name.

* * *

Reaching the office the next day, Emma ran a time-consuming, often frustrating, but finally rewarding search on Elizabeth Blow (nee Darby) whom she learned was born in the Windsor Avenue Hospital in 1902.

She married in 1925, divorced in 1936, and then married Mr M. Jenkins in 1943.

She died in 1982 in Sandringham, aged 80.

The eldest of her three children was John Kirkhouse Jenkins, whom Emma figured could still be alive.

Her initial phone directory search for J. Jenkins produced more than seventy results but she whittled this down to four when she just typed in "John Jenkins".

On her third call she reached a Mrs Jenkins in Sandringham, who said her husband John was at golf and before hanging up mentioned that his mother's name was Elizabeth.

Emma couldn't wait for him to ring her back so she could find out how much he knew.

* * *

Then Emma began a computer search of the English office of births, deaths and marriages, the General Register Office for England and Wales.

She entered Margery E. Childers (nee Swanson) born February 1920, died 2017.

The initial certificate showed only that she had married Ralph Childers in 1955 and had two daughters, Irene and Peggy.

Recalling Margie's diary mentioned she was being "dispatched to Plymouth", Emma tried her maiden name of Margery E. Swanson and the City of Plymouth.

There were no results for 1940, but 1941 revealed information, which changed Emma's understanding of her family's history.

To her amazement there was a birth registered in October that year at Plymouth's City Hospital of a boy named "Frank Swanson", whose mother was Miss M. E. Swanson, but there was no mention of the father's name.

With her pulse rising, for the first time Emma was sure Granma had borne three children and now understood the firstborn, Frank, who hadn't grown up as part of the Childers family, had been given up for adoption at birth.

This was the first concrete answer to emerge from the diary pages.

*　*　*

Several days later when she hadn't heard back from John Jenkins in Sandringham, Emma was getting mildly exasperated.

Seated on a crowded tram on her way home, trundling past the Clarendon Street shops, she only just heard the muffled ringtone from her phone buried in her handbag.

Fumbling amongst the clutter she managed to get in a "hello" before it rang out.

'Is that Emma? This is John Jenkins whom you asked to call.'

'Oh, Mr Jenkins thank you for calling back,' she answered.

'I am doing some research into my family, and I'm particularly interested in a late uncle who was a close friend of your mother's.'

Seeing several passengers eagerly listening for what she was about to say next, Emma continued.

'I am afraid it's quite a long story that I can't share with you right at this moment as I am on a tram. Could we arrange to meet, perhaps at a café near where you live so we can discuss this further?'

Mr Jenkins, who was a retired bank manager, was becoming intrigued with Emma's interest in his family.

He insisted she come to his Sandringham home, where, over afternoon tea he could show her an old album.

'If that is what you prefer, it will be perfect, thank you,' said Emma. 'Would next Sunday suit?'

'Absolutely, and in the meantime, I will have a closer look through mother's old photos and papers to see if there is anything there that might be of interest to you,' Mr Jenkins concluded.

*   *   *

Waiting for Sunday to arrive, Emma decided to send Becky a screen shot of the diary pages and her list of unanswered questions.

She asked Becky if she could check through the phone directory for a certain Frank Swanson.

If that failed, could she phone the Plymouth City Hospital where he was born and ask if they could provide any more information about his adoption.

She also told Becky that she now had suspicions that the gentleman who had introduced himself to her at Granma's funeral as "Frank" could well turn out to be Granma's secret firstborn child.

*   *   *

Walking from the station down Sandringham's streets lined with flowering gums on Sunday afternoon, past rows of freshly renovated Edwardian homes, Emma looked for Abbott Street, then Mr Jenkins' number.

Stepping onto the house's generous porch, with two solid brick pillars supporting the substantial red-tiled roof, she knocked on the front door, wondering what her afternoon would reveal.

Mr Jenkins opened the door and welcomed her with a warm smile. 'It's a delight to meet you, please do come in.'

Entering the living room, she noticed it was furnished in a similar style to Granma's, with floral covered sofas, polished antique furniture and an array of framed photos, mostly of family, on the sideboard.

From the kitchen came sounds of Mrs Jenkins preparing tea as Emma took a seat and Mr Jenkins began telling her that his mother had remarried several years after Mr Garland's untimely death. John showed her a photo of his parents on their wedding day.

Emma sensed Mr Jenkins was becoming absorbed in her research, so she decided to tell him about finding the diary extracts and a little of what they contained.

'Mr Jenkins, there was a mention in the pages that Uncle Charles lost, what I suspect, was quite a sum of money. It happened around the time your mother knew him.

'She, of course, had no involvement but he might have written something to her that might throw some light on the mystery.'

Flipping through an old photo album, Mr Jenkins told Emma that when he was a young boy he asked his mother about the army officer in one of her albums.

He showed one of Mr Garland to Emma, with a brief caption.

Mr Jenkins said if his recollection was correct, his mother had told him the officer was from Sydney and the photo was of him in his British army uniform during the war and that he had died in England after being badly injured.

Asking Emma to call him "John" he continued, 'I had no idea why you wanted to talk to me, but since we spoke, I've made a more thorough search through several cartons of mother's old papers in the loft and found an old shoebox with Mr Garland's letters.

'These might be a good starting point.'

'Oh John, how perfect!' Emma exclaimed.

'Why don't we each take a batch to see what mention Mr Garland makes of having lost his money?' he suggested.

Emma began with Charles' early ones to Elizabeth and John examined the later ones, which covered the outbreak of war and his active service.

The silence in the room was occasionally punctuated by the rustle of a page being turned, as two pairs of eyes delved back into twenty-four months of Charles' life that were initially full of hope and memories of the first flush of love, but when war broke out, turned to increasing levels of despair that was to change their lives for the worse.

As Emma read on, she felt herself being drawn into the Jenkins' history dating back two generations.

John quietly read out to her how Garland Trading and the British import business were progressing and the odd mention that Charles' said his BHP shares were doing rather well, until the outbreak of war when they crashed, leading to the Australian government freezing share prices.

Emma was fully absorbed reading letter after letter, which highlighted Charles growing attachment to Elizabeth.

It was abundantly clear she was far from happy when he announced his enlistment after having promised to come home and pick up where they had left off.

John then came across the fateful telegram, sent from Charles' Commanding Officer in January 1941, breaking the dreadful news that he had been badly injured in a bomb defusing accident.

Handing it to Emma, she immediately saw there were tear stains etched deeply into the yellow slip of telegram paper that must have left Elizabeth feeling helpless being so far away.

Then the next letter, in handwriting she didn't recognise, probably because Charles' writing arm was still in plaster, spoke of his return home from hospital and only lightly touched on his injuries.

It did speak of his excitement and pride at receiving the George Cross Medal from the King and revealed a little of the trauma he was going through, having discovered his BHP shares had been fraudulently sold without his approval by the Australasian Trustee Company. She read further that this had left him in dire financial straits.

Emma broke down when she read Charles' heartbreaking telegram refusing Elizabeth's plea to come to his side, reading between the lines he couldn't stand the thought of her seeing him so badly disfigured and being hopeless.

John then showed Emma a letter from October 1941 and watched her upper lip quiver as she read that Charles, despite knowing how deeply he loved Elizabeth, sensed he was about to lose her and suggested it best if she put him in the background and step out into life there in Melbourne.

She looked up to discover John had put his letters down and had become aware of her state, handing her a tissue to dry her eyes.

'Emma, do you know how many shares he held in BHP?' John asked.

'I gather it was a very large holding,' Emma replied. 'But I have no idea how many he had.'

'If you are interested I could make enquires through my old bank,' John suggested.

'Yes, that would be of interest, but please don't put yourself to any trouble', Emma gratefully replied.

As her train made its way back towards the city, Emma gazed from the window, over the rows of leafy quarter acre backyards abutting the line, filled with shrubs, umbrellas, overgrown lawns and leaf strewn swimming pools.

Having just read Charles' insightful letters, she realised it was only one half of the story. She wondered if her mum or Aunt Peggy had kept any of Elizabeth's letters to Charles.

If so, there was another side still to be learned.

*　*　*

Two days later, Mr Jenkins called Emma telling her he had some interesting news.

'The bank successfully tracked down the details of that 1941 sale of Mr Garland's tranche of shares. Would you believe at the time it was worth £487,000?

'That in today's money, if you are sitting down, would be worth over $16 million in Australian dollars.'

'That is just staggering,' Emma said faintly, lost for words. She thanked John for going to so much trouble, with her head swimming with the magnitude of the fraud and the stench of scandal surrounding it.

Emma suddenly realised what appeared on the surface to be an innocent set of missing diary pages had suddenly taken a whole new twist, maybe for the worse.

36. Peeling an Onion

Instead of Granma's clock bringing back warm memories, hearing its steady ticking now reminded Emma of the skeletons that kept coming out of the cupboard since the discovery of the hidden pages.

More than once she had wondered if she should just let things lie and not "rock the boat".

But the diary pages seemed like an omen that kept nagging her to keep burrowing for the truth.

It made her wonder if it was Granma egging her on to continue "peeling the onion" until she got to the centre of what had been swept under the carpet.

Deciding to try and clarify the questions swirling around her head, with a pen and notebook she began writing:

> *Unanswered questions:*
> *Q1: How did the torn out diary pages find their way into the clock's secret drawer?*
> *What is known? Very little – I need to ask my mother.*
> *Q2: Did Granma have an illegitimate child?*
> *What is now known? England and Wales records show a Frank Swanson was born in late 1941 to Granma, but very little else is known about what happened to the child.*
> *Am hoping to contact the gentleman who introduced himself as "Frank" to me at the funeral. Becky is presently trying to establish his possible whereabouts and family link to Granma. Either Mum or her sister will surely have the Guest Register from the funeral. That needs to be checked.*
> *Q3: Why had she never heard anything of Uncle Charles' grand swindle?*
> *What is known? – ask my mother*

Q4: Granma mentions Emilio in her diary. Who was he and why was he mentioned, what did he do and what happened to him?
What is known? – need to ask someone.

* * *

Having decided she needed to ask her mother about the first three questions, she suspected that after Becky got back to her with information about Granma's war baby, there might be more.

Emma decided to contact the Australasian Trustee Company mentioned in Charles' letters, to see if someone could throw any light on Granma's boyfriend "Emilio" who, after being named a suspect, had fled London.

She expected that if she phoned them there was no doubt the trust company would refuse to assist, citing its privacy clauses.

* * *

Deciding to use a different tack, she called Alex to get his thoughts on a wild idea she had thought up. Over the next thirty minutes he helped her concoct a story that she would spin to the trustees.

She would tell them her family had been contacted by the police about an account they had discovered containing a certain amount of money that had a paper trail leading back to a Mr Garland in London.

'Emma, if you are lucky enough to bluff your way into speaking to a funds manager who has the authority to reopen the Garland file, try using the "police enquiry" line and see how far it gets you,' Alex suggested.

'In the process, they might unwittingly provide you with Emilio's surname,' he added.

'Alex, that's so cool. Before I ring them, I think it would be worth my while asking Mr Jenkins if he has any suggestions about how to identify who is the right person,' Emma added.

* * *

When she called Mr Jenkins and outlined her intended approach with the Australasian Trustee Company, he enthusiastically offered to contact them first to ascertain who to speak to.

The next day, he left a message for her suggesting she should ask for the senior trust manager, a Mr Maxwell Marshall, whom he had managed to speak with, alerting him of her intention to call.

He also suggested she could check online for backdated copies of the *Sydney Morning Herald* in 1941 to see if there were any press reports on the Garland fraud.

*　　*　　*

Deciding that evening to do the newspaper search, she began looking for the Fairfax media conglomerate on her laptop, but quickly found it was of no help.

Looking further down the Google page she saw a link to a site she had never heard of called "Trove".

When she entered "Sydney Morning Herald, May 1941" it brought up a scanned front page that seemed a perfect start for her needs.

The broadsheet's bold front page, set in old-fashioned typeface surprised her, as there were no photos amongst tightly laid-out columns of "classified" advertisements and surprisingly very little mention of the war raging across Europe.

In her search, she tried the "Australasian Trustee", "Garland" and "fraud" but nothing of interest came up.

Then it occurred to her to try "police reports", which brought up a short four-line item on page six in a late July edition that grabbed her attention:

The NSW Fraud Squad has been asked by the Sydney family of a prominent London-based Australian serving in the British Army to investigate an alleged fraud involving a well-known NSW firm, which the police are declining to name.

Having saved the article, she searched through to the end of 1941 and found it very strange there were no further mentions and wondered what it could mean.

*　　*　　*

She then decided to try to contact a descendent of the Garland family to see if they could throw any light on where the 1941 NSW police enquiry had gone.

Initially Emma was at a loss as to where she could find a descendent.

Inspired by her Granma's dogged tenacity, she thought more deeply.

Then the penny dropped.

She recalled Garland Trading was mentioned in Charles' letters to Elizabeth.

Despite her beloved clock chiming one o'clock in the morning, for the first time in a long time, Emma felt inspired.

She reopened her laptop and began a search for "Garland Trading".

A broad smile creased her strained face when up popped several entries including a 1950s mention, and an even more recent 1990s business report that the firm had relaunched itself as Garland International, "purveyors of imported fine wines and exporters of leading Australian wines and gourmet dairy products".

Noting the North Sydney head office phone number, she decided she might call it later in the week, after she had looked up *Who's Who in Business* for the latest information on Garland International's recent history and who its current directors were.

*   *   *

Armed with the name "Roger Lockwood", a grandson of Charles' sister Alice, who had been appointed Garland's chief executive officer in 2012, she was now more determined than ever to get to the bottom of what the company could reveal of Charles' swindle.

Expecting to be given the usual run-around by Mr Lockwood's personal assistant, instead she decided to try his golf club, which was listed in *Who's Who in Business.*

Speaking to the club's general manager, she told him she had recently arrived from England to follow up some important Garland International's family matters and would like to contact one of the club's esteemed members, Mr R. Lockwood.

'Would it be too much to ask for the club to kindly pass on my request asking him to call me about this matter?'

*   *   *

'Emma, your message came as a complete surprise, but I assure you it's a pleasure to see if I can help,' said Roger Lockwood from his Garland International office. He asked her to tell him more about the matters she had raised in her message.

When he learned it was about his grandmother's family and a possible fraud, he told her that when he was quite little, his grandmother had shown him war photos of her brave brother who had died from his injuries in England in the early 1940s. This was the same brother who was swindled out of a fortune.

'Sadly, grandmother went to her grave deeply affected by the whole grubby affair. It apparently shook everyone at the time,' he added.

'Mr Lockwood, that is so sad,' Emma said sympathetically. 'My family has never spoken of any of this, and I'm now beginning to suspect there are other secrets that have been kept hidden,' she added.

'Recently, you may be interested to learn Mr Lockwood, I have come across a *Sydney Morning Herald* article from 1941 which suggested someone, perhaps from your family, may have contacted the NSW police asking them to investigate Mr Garland's fraud.

'I am wondering if you know whether it was your grandmother who made that request? If yes, then why were the police enquiries brought to a sudden end?' she asked.

For much of his life Roger had suspected that there was a lot more to the story and now realised that this young English woman on the line seemed determined to unlock the truth behind these questions.

'Emma, my family has always wondered why the case was never solved and I never knew the police actually had a suspect.'

He went on to explain his family thought it was poorly managed at the time and that the police may have bungled the case and failed to bring anyone to task.

Also, he told her his family retained very little confidence in the trustees, who it appears went to great lengths at the time to have the matter closed to save their good name.

As Roger was still known to the trustees and in view of what she had told him, he said he would contact its senior trust manager, Maxwell Marshall, whose name she had given to him.

'I will tell him to expect your call and ask him to reopen the Charles Garland file and provide the information you need.

'What do you intend to do with all this information when you get it?' Roger asked.

Unable to answer, Emma hesitantly responded, 'Right at this moment Mr Lockwood I am not sure, but when I am, you will be the first to know.'

*　　*　　*

Booking a private office at work a few days later, Emma nervously punched in Maxwell Marshall's direct number, realising she was about to tell the biggest tale of her life.

But the search depended on how well she delivered it.

Dabbing her moist brow with a tissue she heard his line ring.

'Marshall, Australasian Trustee, how can I help you?'

Taking the call in his modern office tower overlooking Sydney Harbour, the senior trust manager who had built a fine stockbroking reputation after graduating from Sydney University before joining the Australasian Trustee Company in 2009 as a trust officer, permitted his gaze to momentarily take in the sweeping views over the bridge and Circular Quay.

'This is Emma Childers here, I understand Mr Lockwood informed you that I would be calling.'

'Yes, indeed Miss Childers,' Mr Marshall reassured her, 'I understand it is about a Garland matter dating back to the 1940s.'

Emma had decided she needed to tempt him, so he would agree to give her the information she needed.

'Mr Marshall, I was informed that in 1941 a wealthy client of your firm was defrauded of a fortune. My family in England were closely involved at the time and have recently been contacted by the police. They said they have uncovered a paper trail from an account dating back to 1941 suggesting that the money may have belonged to the late Mr Garland, who at the time was a client of yours.'

Deliberately showing only a glimmer of interest, Mr Marshall carefully chose his words trying to avoid the worrying mention of the term "paper trail".

'My firm's present day management has only a vague knowledge of the matter you refer to as it was so far in the past.

'Should the firm agree to assist this new police enquiry, it is our normal procedure to only deal directly with them,' he said.

'So Miss Childers, if you would be kind enough to give me the details, we might be able to proceed on that basis.'

Emma was prepared, anticipating Mr Marshall would attempt to cold shoulder her request.

She came quickly to the point.

'My family has recently become aware of the circumstances surrounding the fraud that were no doubt a very great embarrassment to your firm's reputation in 1941, as it was to my family at the time, who for some reason have kept it secret ever since.

'In light of how poorly it was managed in 1941, my family retains little confidence in the Australasian Trustees Company, as it appears they went to great lengths to shut down the matter.'

Mr Marshall was taken aback with her bluntness, but he knew full well how close the trustees had come to losing everything when the Garland fraud had the Pitt Street banking scene awash with rumours of their massive stuff-up and it almost made it onto the front page of the Sydney papers.

'Mr Marshall, as a result of our lack of confidence, my family has decided to tread very carefully with this new development and judiciously consider to whom we might reveal any of it,' she persuasively added.

'The police have asked my family if we can lay our hands on any documents containing details of Mr Garland's bank accounts and the amounts involved to confirm their latest line of enquiry. I would also like the full name and details of the suspect who was never properly tracked down.

'This is the specific information that I am asking your firm to provide,' she said, leaning back in her chair to await his response.

As a senior manager, Mr Marshall felt obliged to ensure the debacle, which the firm's managing director at the time, Sir Kenneth Codrington, had unwittingly caused, must never be repeated, certainly not on his watch.

In the slim hope the firm might recover a part of the largest single amount of money it had ever lost, he offered to confer with his managing director and then the board to obtain their views.

'If they should agree, as the files are buried in our 1940s documents storage, it may take some time to locate them,' he added.

'Thank you Mr Marshall, my family would be grateful for all the help you can give and I will look forward to your call,' Emma said, concluding the conversation feeling slightly more confident she might obtain some of the details she needed.

*   *   *

In England, after Emma's mother hung up from her daughter's odd phone call about Charles Garland's Melbourne lady friend and in the days that followed, she continued to worry that a horrid part of the Swansons' past might be coming back to haunt them all these years later.

It was never spoken of, but the family always suspected Margie's Portuguese boyfriend had somehow got a sniff of Charles' money and helped himself to it.

Irene had often wondered why so much of her mother's war years remained a mystery, believing perhaps the trauma was too much for her to ever speak about.

The circumstances surrounding her mother's prestigious Florence Nightingale Medal was rarely mentioned either. Even on the annual 11th November Remembrance Days, Irene would plead with her to put on her medal and go out and march, but she never would.

She chided herself for not asking her mother more about the war before she passed away and now so much of the truth had gone with her to the grave.

Irene remembered when she and Peggy were tidying up her mother's possessions, they had noticed some cartons of old letters and photos, which they had only taken a cursory glance through in their haste to get the house ready for sale.

Irene wondered if Peggy had ever bothered to keep any of those memories.

If so, perhaps one day, when she had the courage, she might pore over them to see what they contained.

37. Returning to London

'Mum, I've discovered Granma had a baby before you were born. His name was Frank and I think he was adopted out.'

Emma's unexpected phone call had sent Irene's head into a spin. She had no idea about the existence of an out-of-wedlock child and she was shaken.

Irene tried to take in what her daughter was saying about some secret pages from a diary and her mother's love affair with someone called Emilio.

Irene had often wondered why the family had despised her mother's wartime boyfriend. It finally dawned on her this must be the reason.

'Mum, nothing you say is going to stop me flying home,' Emma declared.

In her confused and distressed state, Irene snapped.

'Emma, you have just started a new job. I beg you, don't throw it all away to chase some fanciful notion.'

Adding to Irene's confusion was the dreadful feeling of becoming trapped, knowing some of the story which was now coming out, she had only heard snippets of, and then there was the unexplained discovery of the baby booties after Margie's death, which she had never discussed with anyone and certainly not her daughter.

Emma was fast discovering how her mother could be unmanageable when asked about certain aspects of the family's past, especially Granma's and the war years. She couldn't believe that no-one knew of the explosive diary.

The electric tension down the line between South Melbourne and London was almost enough to power a whole suburb.

* * *

Becky's sleuthing on Emma's behalf turned up much more than expected.

Margie's baby, named Frank, was born in Plymouth in 1941 as Emma had suspected and had been adopted out to a couple by the name of Dalton, who had an older daughter.

Frank Dalton was a retired teacher, married with children and now lived in Portsmouth. Becky had obtained his latest address and number, which she said she would give to Emma when she arrived.

*　*　*

As her Skybus sped along the freeway to Melbourne's airport, Emma eased back, took a long, slow, deep breath and tried to relax.

She allowed her mind to wander pleasantly for the next short while, until she was brought back to the present when her phone rang.

It was Roger Lockwood.

In the frenzy of the last few days of getting away, she had all but forgotten he had promised to get back to her after meeting Mr Marshall at the trustee firm.

'Roger, so good to hear from you again. That reverberation you can probably hear in the background is the bus I'm on going to the airport.'

Roger told her he had just come from his meeting with the trustees.

'Having located my late uncle's file, do you believe Mr Marshall would not hand it over for me to read?'

'I explained to him you and I needed certain information to assist the police enquiry, which he said you had made him aware of.

'I assured him that what we wanted would in no way impinge on the firm's good name but he held out, so as a last resort I decided to show him a copy of that 1941 *Sydney Morning Herald* fraud report you sent me.

'As he read it, I indicated if his firm would not co-operate, my family would ask the NSW Police Ombudsmen to conduct an enquiry on the basis of what my grandmother had previously discovered, suggesting undue influence being brought to bear by the firm on the police to suspend their enquiries into the fraud.

'I decided to sit there and stare him down whilst he weighed up the alternatives and reminded him that you were also waiting to hear back from him.

'With the heat in the kitchen getting too hot, he finally relented, asking what specific questions we want answered.

'So when I read them out, he flipped quietly through the file looking for them and making some notes,' Roger said.

'How good is that!' exclaimed Emma.

'Absolutely. He provided the following info, which if you have a pen and paper handy, I will give you,' Roger offered.

Over the next five minutes Emma scribbled down Charles Garland's banking details, the value of the funds transferred to the false account in London, the reference number for the trustee's statement sent to Scotland Yard and the last known address in Oporto of the prime suspect, Emilio Bestillo.

'Roger, this is exactly what I need thank you so much. Apologies. I have to go now but I will keep in touch.' Emma's bus pulled to a halt outside the terminal.

As she leant down to grab her bag the last thing she heard Roger say was, 'Now you have this information what are you going to do with … '

Having her phone accidentally drop out, she felt a pang of guilt but knowing she didn't have an answer, for the time being she decided she would delay calling him back to answer his question.

*　*　*

Seated in the airport's international departure lounge, Emma patiently waited for the call to board her flight.

Balanced against her leg was her satchel that contained her tablet and a notebook with a list of the people she planned to see.

These included Jessie Tyler, who she hoped could tell her more about Margie's war romance and Aunt Peggy, who might have kept some of Granma's personal papers and perhaps, by some stroke of luck, Elizabeth's old letters to Charles.

She hoped Frank Dalton might tell her more of his life's journey and if time permitted, she may also need to go to Portugal.

Hearing the boarding call, she collected her satchel and as she waited by the gate, it occurred to her that the journey she was embarking on was being driven by forces buried deep within her proud family roots.

What was now creating momentum was that so many lives around her had been so deeply affected over many decades by the wartime scandals.

She was being caught up by the emerging trail of sadness and despair including Granma's grief, her bitter rift with Gertrude, her pregnancy and the impact of Charles' swindle, his untimely death and the subsequent impact of much of this on Charles' sister, Alice.

Capping it off, in Melbourne poor Elizabeth, madly in love with Charles, was unable to go to his bedside when he was injured and was powerless to do anything.

Tightening her seat belt, she leaned back to watch lines of baggage carts buzzing under the plane's wings.

She remembered not all that long ago she had been on this same tarmac, about to wing her way home to pay her last respects to Granma and deliver her eulogy.

She thought how differently she was seeing things now.

Then, she could never have imagined herself trying to unravel the family scandals that had wreaked such havoc.

So much had transpired in such a short space of time since she read the diary entries that her life had become a whirl.

She felt driven to get to the bottom of it all.

Suddenly her ears and senses were filled by the whine of the powerful engines firing into life that would shortly, during take off, thrust her pleasantly deep into the back of her seat.

Thinking about what lay ahead in the next weeks, she wondered who might hold the "magic key" and whether she could unlock the answers she sought.

38. Digging into the Past

Despite her advancing years, Jessie Tyler had steadfastly refused her family's suggestions to move into aged care.

Instead, typical of her, she had promised herself that in her latter years she would move to the seaside where she could enjoy the sea air and swim.

She found a freshly renovated studio on the South Coast overlooking Brighton's famous pier and was captivated by its panoramic seaside views and the English Channel in the distance.

It was only a short stroll to the St James' Street shops and perfectly suited her needs.

As a young woman Jessie had desperately wanted to marry, settle down and start a family. Tragically in her twenties these dreams were dashed when her wartime air force fiancé, Robert, was killed in a bombing raid over Germany in late 1944.

On the long, lonely train trip home from Margie's funeral she enjoyed many rich memories of their lifelong friendship.

With Margie's passing she was feeling her ninety-seven years and realised she had never been more vulnerable or alone.

When she got home, she took out her dusty, old photo album, which she hadn't looked at in years. She looked through for old photos of Margie and wistfully dreamed of what might have been if only things had turned out differently.

For most of Jessie's latter life she had kept up a daily exercise regime including long walks, special breathing and exercise techniques and more recently, summer swims.

Slightly stooped and far less agile, her face and twinkling eyes radiated a certain kindness and willingness to assist others in need.

*　　*　　*

Emma put in a call to Frank Dalton, who got a huge shock hearing from her after having only briefly met her at the wake. Mystified as to why she would want to come all this way to see him and suspecting she might have stumbled across his link to her family, he invited her to come down on Saturday.

*   *   *

Since moving to Brighton, Jessie's phone rang rarely. Calls were usually from the council's care team, the doctor's rooms or her family on her birthday.

So when it rang on an otherwise ordinary morning, Jessie had no idea who the voice could belong to.

'It's Emma Childers here, you might recall Miss Tyler, we spoke before and met at my grandmother's funeral. You told me about some of the amazing experiences you and she shared as schoolgirls and young ladies in London.'

'Emma, of course I do. You spoke so beautifully that day and did her proud.'

'The reason for my call, Miss Tyler, is that I have recently returned from Melbourne, having discovered some revealing information in some pages of Granma's wartime diary, which had been secreted away in an antique clock she left to me.'

Jessie remembered how fond Margie had been of that clock.

'Miss Tyler, I am doing some family research and have some questions I would like to ask you about Granma and her war years. If I caught the bus to Brighton, would you be willing to see me?' asked Emma.

'First of all Emma, please call me Jessie,' she suggested.

'And yes, of course I would love you to visit and we will have quite a lot to discuss. I have a spare room so you must stay the night and while you are here, I can show you around the village and we could have coffee on the pier.'

'That would be perfect,' Emma said, thinking to herself that she could fit in a visit to Brighton on her way back from Portsmouth where she was going to meet Frank Dalton.

'Jessie, I expect to be returning from Portsmouth next Saturday, would that suit?'

*   *   *

Hanging up from Emma's call, Jessie set out for her daily beachfront walk and for a change, decided to hike out to the end of the pier, all the while wondering how much of Margie's past Emma had stumbled over.

She felt it rather strange that some seventy-five years on someone might be interested in it.

Now that the Secrets Act no longer had a hold over her, as the fifty-year limit had passed, perhaps this eager young lady just back from Melbourne might be ready to hear the real story that no-one had ever heard.

Holding tightly to the rusted handrail to steady herself against the fresh sea breeze, she gazed out to the few ships passing on the hazy horizon. The spray from salty spume landed on her aged face, causing a chilled shudder to ripple down her spine as she thought about the years of guilt she had carried by not being able to save her best friend from that swindling Portuguese cad.

* * *

Peggy was intrigued when she heard her niece had returned unexpectedly to London. So when Emma asked if she could come over to look through Margie's old papers for something she was seeking, Peggy felt pangs of guilt for not having checked the cartons she had put under the bed in the spare bedroom ages ago.

When Emma arrived she explained to Peggy she was hoping to see if there were any wartime letters from Elizabeth to Uncle Charles.

Locating Margie's old diary was uppermost in Emma's mind, but she didn't reveal this in case it wasn't there.

Going to the bedroom, they dragged the sagging cartons out from beneath the mattress and lifted them onto the bed.

Opening the first carton, Peggy removed a set of folders and began quietly scanning through them.

On the other side of the bed, Emma removed the remaining folders and put them on the duvet.

Taking a closer look, Emma skipped through Margie's gardening notebook, her war press clipping files, a stack of humorous wedding telegrams and her Red Cross bravery citation. She flipped through heaps of photos in an old shoebox and found one of Charles and his batman which she put aside.

There was her old 1950s phone directory containing a list of numbers, several of which Emma took down.

Peggy finally came to a leather "Charles Garland' embossed folder which contained a bundle of Elizabeth's old letters tied up loosely with string.

She began reading aloud Elizabeth's letters leading up to the one Charles received just before the bomb accident.

Both sadly agreed that Charles feared he could lose Elizabeth's love which had added to his deteriorating state.

It quickly became clear to Emma, having read Charles' letters to Elizabeth, that the letter she wrote to Charles after he was injured was convincing proof of her undying love for him.

Although Emma made a thorough search, there was no sign of any diary, dashing her hopes of finding it sooner rather than later.

*   *   *

The following day she visited New Scotland Yard, but try as she might, she could not convince the officer on the front desk into helping her in relation to the Garland fraud.

He said that unless she could produce papers from his Executors showing there was an unsettled estate matter or a court order, Scotland Yard was unable to be of any assistance.

Disappointed, but not undeterred, she caught a bus to the Commonwealth Bank at Ludgate Hill, hoping the manager at least would agree to reopen the file and give her something new to get her teeth into or track down.

Whilst the manager listened to her persuasive story, in the end he said the bank was not in a position to provide any further information.

Two knockbacks coming one on top of each other caused Emma to wonder if her good luck had come to an end and her trip home was heading for the rocks.

*   *   *

Emma's hopes rose a peg when she finally met up with Frank Dalton in Portsmouth.

He felt shocked a distant relative, whom he had only met once at his birth mother's funeral, had contacted him out of the blue and was now asking questions of him in his living room.

She could see from his craggy, seventy-five-year-old features that he appeared to have lived a troubled life.

Over morning tea, she explained what she had learnt about him, and listened as he gave an insight into his life as a young lad before he had married Shirley whilst they were studying teaching in the late 1960s. They had two children.

He explained their youngest daughter, Clare, was born with mild autism that required special schooling. Now in her forties she still needed home care, which Frank explained was getting beyond what he and wife could cope with.

Then he admitted to Emma he hadn't discovered he was adopted until he had to produce his birth certificate for a driver's licence in his early twenties.

The original certificate revealed he was adopted and that his birth mother was Margie Swanson. No-one was nominated as his father.

'For over twenty years I was deeply tormented by this discovery,' Frank explained.

'I wondered why my mother had deserted me. It upset me so deeply that I needed to see a succession of counsellors to try and deal with my demons.'

'That is so wretched,' Emma whispered.

Frank went on, 'Then in my early forties, a psychologist suggested I should try and seek closure by meeting my real mother and father,' Frank confided with a deeply pensive look on his face.

'So how did that go and how did you feel?' Emma gently inquired.

'When I finally met your Granma, initially she seemed very wary and even denied that I was her son,' said Frank, tears welling at the hurtful memory.

'I showed her my birth certificate with her maiden name on it, and that caused her to break down in shame, offering a stream of apologies for all the hurt she had inflicted.'

Emma leaned across, placing a hand on his to console him.

'Then I asked her who my father was, what was he like, were there any photos of him and what happened to him.

'All she would tell me was his name was Emilio Bestillo and he lived in Portugal,' Frank concluded.

'Did she ever divulge to you anything about their romance?' Emma asked.

'She tried to explain it was one of those wartime things. She said when she met my father she fell deeply in love, then she fell pregnant and he panicked and fled to Portugal.

'I could see at this point my mother had become an emotional wreck, with so many dark disappointments she had suppressed catching up with her, I realised I had taken things a little too quickly.'

"How did you feel after that first meeting?' Emma asked.

Taking a deep breath, Frank took a few moments to find an answer.

'I had secretly hoped she would have welcomed me with open arms after all those years and we could begin to heal the wounds.

'But she seemed in a state of denial, which I suppose was because her husband Gordon and her two daughters Irene and Peggy had absolutely no inkling I existed,' Frank added.

'I felt so confused. On the one hand, I'd finally discovered my real mother and on the other, I had learned of the lie she had lived with for so long which she had become trapped by.'

Frank told Emma they had parted, promising to see each other again, with Margie saying that first she needed to sort herself out.

'What did you do then? Emma queried.

'I needed time to more fully process what it all meant. Having done that, I decided I wanted to find my Portuguese father and discover why he had disappeared off the face of the earth, leaving my mother and me in the lurch.'

Emma held her breath in excitement. 'Please tell me what you discovered.'

39. South Coast Research

Enjoying the lovely bus ride along England's picturesque South Coast to Brighton, Emma realised the key lesson from her search to date was to keep an open mind on what might come up next, because at every turn the plot kept twisting.

The trail of carnage she had discovered that had been wreaked upon her family was only getting murkier and continued to sadden her.

From what Frank told her in Portsmouth, she felt even more driven to hunt down the answers, more convinced than ever that the key to them lay hidden in Margie's old diary.

More than anything, Emma wanted to know why everything had been kept a secret.

Since she first laid eyes on those torn out pages that raised so many questions, she had acquired only half the answers. But she still didn't know why the pages had been torn out, who hid them in the clock and what the real story was behind Charles' swindle.

Emma suspected her mother knew more than she was letting on but decided not to confront her just for the moment.

Jessie gave Emma a welcoming hug at the Brighton bus station before they set off walking home, chatting furiously like old friends. On the way, Jessie proudly pointed out her favourite seaside features including the beach and the long, iconic steel pier in the distance, with a veritable circus of attractions under its white dome.

Arriving at her red brick 1930s flat just off the beachfront, Emma was captured by its neat white-painted windows and fragrant climbing roses beside the front door, saying, 'What a simply divine escape you have.'

After dropping her bags in the spare room, Emma went to the kitchen to find her hostess had prepared a delicious platter of Dorset cheddar and biscuits and was busy pouring white wine into a pair of crystal glasses that sparkled in the rays of the soft, afternoon light.

Settling at the kitchen bench, Jessie proposed a toast to Margie's memory.

As she was about to take a sip, Emma reminded herself that come what may, she mustn't place any undue pressure on this proud lady, who had so kindly invited her to stay.

She needn't have worried.

Before Emma could finish her next sip, Jessie asked if she was ready to hear about the war and its profound impact on Margie and her family.

In a soft voice, Jessie began.

'You will not have been aware, but for over seventy years, I've had to keep what I am about to tell you a complete secret.

'Early on in the war, your Granma learned I had taken a position with the Foreign Office, and she was very unhappy I could not tell her anything about what I was actually doing.'

'I had gathered something like that from Granma, who told me that you had worked at a strange place called Bletchley Park,' Emma said.

Jessie's tone became more cautious.

'I won't go into the details about that job, which came under the War Secrets Act, but it meant I could never tell anyone, not my parents or even my best friend, what I did.

'Since the war ended I had still been bound to silence by the Secrets Act, but now thank goodness, that restriction has been lifted.

'So I am now able to tell you the truth about my job at Bletchley Park, about your Granma and her boyfriend Emilio that led to all those dreadful developments in the early 1940s.'

Emma noticed Jessie seemed to be building up a "head of steam", causing the ninety-seven-year-old to become more articulate and visibly determined.

'Our section handled a stream of top-secret military messages. We knew about the spies by their codes, we knew when and where Britain was going to attack German cities and we even knew where the U-boat submarines had been ordered to wait to attack Allied convoys.

'Emma, would you believe in the next hut there was an odd sort of a chap, Alan Turing, and some of his university "boffins", who had developed a room jammed with top secret, whirring floor-to-ceiling machines, which I saw by accident once, that had dozens of spinning wheels and electrical wires running everywhere. I only learnt well after the war that it was the world's first working computer.

'Their astonishing room of machinery was able to crack the Nazi's unbreakable Enigma Code. The staggering intelligence it yielded, many say, helped shorten the war by two years and saved more than ten million lives,' Jessie concluded with a feeling of pride knowing the small part she had played in that huge story.

'That's quite extraordinary,' Emma exclaimed.

'Dear, during the early war years, your Granma and I were invited to a do at the swish Dorchester Hotel where we were introduced to a Portuguese wine salesman, who took an immediate shine to Margie.

'Even before we left the function, I knew she had fallen for him,' Jessie added.

She explained how she had taken an instinctive dislike to him at the outset, and before the night was over had a nagging thought she had heard his name mentioned somewhere before.

'When Margie revealed on the way home in the bus that he had asked to take her out, I decided I had to check him out when I returned to work.

'When I did, to my horror, I found he was someone I had read about earlier, who had been placed on a MI6 "watch list" as a possible Nazi sympathiser.

'Of course I couldn't breathe a word of this to Margie, but I did warn her in the strongest possible terms of the dangers that men like him posed to innocent young women like her.'

As Emma wondered where all this was heading, Jessie took a moment to slice off some more cheese and refill their glasses.

'I think your grandmother was desperate to find true love with someone who believed in her.

'In Emilio she thought she had found it, but I am sure her judgement was clouded.

'Her headstrong streak led her to defying her mother and she just threw herself "hook, line and sinker" at that foreigner,' Jessie added.

She explained that she read in Mr Bestillo's file that he had got a girl pregnant in his hometown then deserted her, and the girl's father had demanded a very substantial payment to keep a lid on the scandal.

'My dear, this was most likely the reason that cold-hearted cad stole her uncle's money. It was such a dreadful thing, which I'm sure sent Charles to an early grave.

'I read in his file, that as soon as he got his hands on the money, he fled London, not giving a damn about Margie or her uncle's plight.'

Jessie said when Margie discovered she was pregnant, all hell broke loose when she told her mother, which almost caused Margie to have a breakdown.

In the next while, as more of the remarkable story came to light, Jessie kept topping up their glasses.

She told Emma that Margie held so much respect for the way her Uncle Charles was finding his feet in England after his Australian parents had died tragically a year or so earlier. So when poor Charles was badly injured in a bomb blast, Margie was devastated and her caring soul came to the fore.

She really wanted to help her uncle and went out of her way to visit him regularly. In time, she took Emilio with her and in fact, Charles became quite friendly with him, which delighted Margie, as she desperately wanted their blossoming relationship to be accepted.

'It turned out she was unwittingly facilitating an appalling crime,' Jessie said.

'Ever since, I have felt so guilty and powerless that I couldn't bring a stop to their affair,' Jessie sadly mumbled as tears began to well in her eyes.

As the story had deepened, Emma saw Jessie's troubled face reveal the deep shame she had carried for too many years.

Emma leaned across and put her arms around her, 'It was not your fault, Jessie. It was your duty to remain silent and I am sure you gave Granma as much support as you could, but there were other forces at work you weren't responsible for. Under the circumstances, you did the best you could.'

The lifting of the weight of guilt she had borne for all those years suddenly became too much for Jessie.

Wrapped in Emma's caring arms, she broke down, knowing that finally the painful truth had come out.

Emma felt very emotional too, but knew in this moment she had to remain strong.

The one lingering regret Jessie still held was that she never had the strength to tell any of this to Margie and apologise for what she had done.

'Emma, two years ago I decided to tell her,' Jessie blurted out.

'But the right moment never came up and when I heard she only had weeks to live, it was too late because it would have upset her dreadfully.

'The biggest regret of my life is that she went to her grave never knowing the truth!'

Emma realised that the highly charged exchange had completely drained Jessie and suggested, 'I think at this point we should take a break.'

When Emma had gone to her room, Jessie allowed her thoughts to return to Margie's wartime affair, which she had always felt was doomed.

She reminded herself for the umpteenth time that if Margie ever found herself in any trouble, that domineering mother of hers would always "rule the roost".

And of course she did just that, sending Margie off to Plymouth for her confinement.

*　*　*

As Emma snuggled up in bed with her book after dinner, she listened to the unfamiliar sounds all around her.

Outside, the muted howl of the wind driving waves onto the beach was punctuated by the chatter of tipsy revellers heading home.

From the next room she heard Jessie pottering about preparing for bed.

Somehow, these sounds soothed Emma's troubled mind as she began processing all that Granma had gone through at almost exactly the same age as she was.

She realised in her life she had never faced the horrors of war or had to endure a mother like Gertrude or suffer the consequences of having a cad for a boyfriend.

She had never carried the guilt of having introduced someone to a close relative, resulting in the theft of a fortune.

Suddenly Emma felt herself being engulfed by the hardships Granma had endured.

How brave she had been and what grit she must have had trying to put it all behind her.

She began to wonder how much of this Granma had told her daughters or if she had kept it to herself.

*   *   *

The following morning, after Jessie reassured her that she had slept well, Emma steered the conversation towards her interest in the missing diary.

Choosing her words carefully, after being asked about Granma's journal, Jessie revealed, 'She told me once she had been given one. I expect when she discovered she was pregnant and told her mother, she would have written about her feelings and desperate situation.

'Before she left for Plymouth, she told me she suspected her mother had been sneaking into her room to read her diary. She thought that if she took it with her there might not be a safe place to keep it, so before she left she said she had hidden it in a very safe place.

'Do you know where that was?' Emma asked.

Jessie's eyes twinkled.

'Before we finished school, Margie told me she had discovered a spot under a floorboard in her corner wardrobe she had used to hide a friendship ring a boy had given her and keep her poetry. It's my guess the diary might still be there too.'

'So do you think Granma had torn out those diary pages and hidden them in the clock?' asked Emma.

'I think it very unlikely Margie would have done that because she had a safer place in her wardrobe,' Jessie suggested.

'Then did Gertrude find her diary and in a fit of rage, rip the offending pages out and hide them in the clock?' Emma asked.

'That's very possible,' Jessie concurred. 'But if they were that upsetting, why didn't she just burn them?'

'Perhaps Gertrude was worried what Margie would do when she discovered they were missing, and want them back,' Emma suggested.

Jessie explained that when Margie returned from Plymouth, she discovered a bomb had damaged her old home and her family had moved to another.

'Maybe Gertrude forgot about the hidden pages,' posed Jessie.

'That seems quite possible, Jessie. Now, one final thing before I head off to catch my train. Do you recall the Swansons' old street name and number? Emma asked.

'Oh goodness the street address, that's so long ago. Off the top of my head I don't, but it might be in my old address book over there in the writing desk, Jessie said.

'I suspect, Emma, you've got it in mind to go and take a look in that old wardrobe for it.'

*   *   *

As her train from Brighton approached Victoria Station, Emma turned her thoughts towards what lay ahead over the next few days.

Her stay with Jessie had proved deeply moving and she realised what a powerful impact the war had on her friendship with Margie.

Thinking about the Swansons' old family home in Dulwich Village, she had no idea if Margie's diary was still there. The only way to find out she thought, would be to make a "cold call" to see if the people living there would be willing to let her take a look in the wardrobe.

40. Meeting his Father

In Portsmouth, Frank told Emma that when he met his mother for the second time she opened up a little more about her life.

Apart from telling him about what she did after the war and providing more details about his birth, she admitted being sorry for having introduced his father to her uncle in the first place.

'I asked her why she felt so remorseful,' Frank said.

'My mother explained that my father had swindled her Uncle Charles out of a fortune at the worst possible time, when he was trying to recover from his blast injuries.

'When she met Emilio, she had absolutely no idea he was in desperate need of money to silence a girl he had got pregnant in Portugal,' Frank said.

'I had never heard this until now,' Emma stated in semi shock.

'My mother said the distress her uncle had suffered from having his inheritance stolen by someone he trusted was a gut-wrenching blow from which he never recovered, and it more than likely contributed to his demise,' he told her.

Frank then went into great detail about tracking down information about his elusive father, including spending weeks checking 1941 ship's passenger lists and digging up scant details from Scotland Yard's investigation into his father's alleged involvement in the Garland fraud.

Emma listened intently, making the odd entry in her notebook.

To this juncture, she had placed little emphasis on the lead-up to the swindle other than on why it had been kept quiet.

It wasn't until Frank disclosed that he had discovered his mother felt responsible for causing the fraud that her ears really pricked up.

'Mother also told me that she went to Oporto in 1951 with the intention of finding Emilio to try and bring closure to her broken heart by telling him about their child.

'At his old family home she was informed he did not live there anymore and that they would not reveal his whereabouts.

'Having seen a number psychologists myself, I realise that all the events around that time in her life led me to believe my mother was severely depressed.

'From the police records, which I was allowed to see, I discovered that after my father had returned to Portugal, the Lisbon police took him in for questioning at the request of Scotland Yard.

'At the time Portuguese law, I have learned, required a suspect had to be charged within thirty days of arrest and put before a judge or the person was set free.

'The Lisbon file indicated Scotland Yard was preparing a brief to have him charged with fraud and deception, but it was taking time, partly because they were waiting for the NSW police report of interviews with Mr Garland's family in Sydney and the full details from the Australasian Trustee Company.

'The irony is that the Fraud Squad's brief arrived a few days after my father had been released and had disappeared into the sunset,' Frank concluded.

'Do you know where he went?' Emma asked.

'Not really, his trail had seemingly gone cold, as had the investigations,' Frank admitted.

'So in 2001, I decided to finally go and look for him. I caught a Channel ferry and a train to Bordeaux then took the long bus trip to Oporto, or as we Brits call it these days, Porto,' he concluded.

*　*　*

Arriving in Porto, Frank had begun searching through the Bestillo Nacional business history in the town's library, where he was shown backdated newspapers copies of the *Jornal de Notícias*.

With the help of an English-speaking assistant he was told they contained several articles on the firm as well as a photo of his father, both when he was appointed managing director and when he announced his retirement.

Frank ran off copies of his father's photo.

From several articles the assistant read out, Frank wrote brief notes backgrounding his father's progress from salesman to managing director and that he had lived in Lisbon for many years after the war, before being recalled to Porto to take up a management role.

*　　*　　*

Taking a bus from Porto to the Bestillo Nacional vineyards overlooking the Douro River near the town of Castelo de Paiva, Frank spoke with a number of locals who had known Emilio after he re-joined the firm in the 1950s, at a time when it was facing great financial uncertainty.

Returning to Porto, Frank joined a wine tour group inspecting Bestillo Nacional. The warehouse and offices overlooked the world famous Rabelo moored sailboats that in the early 1920s carried barrels of port wine down the river.

He laid eyes on his father's offices for the first time and also noticed a sporty red Alfa Romeo in a parking space reserved for his father.

*　　*　　*

'How did it feel when you were about to meet him for the first time?' Emma asked.

'In my heart I held out the slender hope that he would reach out to me as a long lost son.

'I was nervous I would loathe him for all he had done. In a dark way I also found myself wondering whether I might want to look up to him, but thinking about all the water that had flowed under the bridge, I let these thoughts go.

'And I was apprehensive that he might deny he was my birth father, so I took the evidence with me.'

*　　*　　*

It took considerable effort for Frank to summon the courage to finally step into his father's imposing Bestillo Nacional offices the next day. Walking up its steps he checked if the red Alfa Romeo was in its allotted parking spot. It was.

Gritting his teeth Frank approached the front desk and boldly asked to see Emilio.

He watched as the receptionist phoned Mr Bestillo's secretary.

'Soon after she came out to the foyer and asked who I was and what I wanted to see him about,' Frank explained.

'I asked if she would kindly let him know a long, lost relative from England was waiting to meet him.'

'Believing his family had no such relatives, the secretary appeared flustered and asked to see some identification.

'From the corner of my eye, I noticed several staff at reception listening with increasing interest, wondering why a stranger was asking to see their highly respected managing director.

'So I summonsed the courage to say loud enough so they could hear that Margie Swanson's son is here to meet his father.'

'I could not miss the look of astonishment on the faces across the foyer, as the secretary turned abruptly and strode off to Mr Bestillo's office.

'That very moment Emma, was a small consolation for the years of sadness my mother had endured,' Frank proudly admitted.

Soon after, the secretary returned and ushered Frank into a timber-panelled boardroom where he found an elderly, grey-haired gentleman supported by a walking stick, looking stunned and pale.

'I could only vaguely recognise him from my mother's 1940 photo and the newspaper photos,' Frank recalled.

'His brown, deep-set eyes and facial features were a lot like mine, although more tanned, he was around my height but stooped in his advanced years.'

'Were you shaking in your boots?' Emma wanted to know.

'Yes, slightly. He guardedly shook my hand and we took our seats.

'Our initial conversation was respectfully guarded until he summonsed the courage to ask why I had come to see him.

'At that very moment I realised I held all the cards.

'I wanted to see his reaction to the name "Swanson", which he had probably not heard in sixty years. It seemed to jolt him.

'I anticipated he would try to test me before conceding an inch, which he did.

'I told him about applying for a driver's licence, for which I needed my birth certificate and discovering that I had been adopted and that my father's name was not on the certificate.

'He then asked what evidence I had that he was my father?

'I told him that when I finally tracked down and met my birth mother in Wimbledon, she told me all about her affair with him leading to her pregnancy and having me,' Frank explained.

Frank told Emma he could see his father become agitated.

'It was sinking in that a child he never knew existed was sitting there in front of him making these claims. This brought back disturbing memories of his unsavoury past that he had hoped would remain secret.'

'How did he react?' Emma asked.

'He asked what I wanted from him. I calmly told him I bore no malice and that I simply wanted to meet him, tell him who I was, find out more about my heritage and hopefully discover why he had deserted my mother.

'Hearing this he appeared to slightly relax, then turned the conversation towards my mother, wanting to know what she did after the war, about her family and where she was living.

'He also asked me about where I grew up, my adopted family, where I went to school and my teaching career.

'I asked him what he did after the war and about his family. He only revealed a potted version from the 1950s when he returned to Porto from Lisbon, got married, his children arrived and how he took over the firm and helped it recover from near financial ruin.

'When I asked him what he did in Lisbon, all he would admit was that he worked for a bank for a number of years before returning to run the family firm.

'It was at this point, Emma, that I decided to give up delving into his Lisbon years, but I knew there was a lot more to it than he had revealed.

'To lighten up our conversation, I asked him what the Alfa Romeo GTA I'd seen in his parking space was like to drive. For a fleeting moment his eyes lit up, revealing a rare glimpse into one of his real passions.

'It was obvious he was tiring, so I decided to conclude the meeting.

'Before I left, he asked if there was anything else I was seeking from him.

'I told him that I felt meeting him was a positive start. But more than anything, I wanted him to acknowledge that he was my father and that he cared about me.

'He had shown resistance to answering many of my questions in any detail, saying he was not yet sure about things and that meeting me like this had come as a huge shock and he needed time to think.

'Hearing this made me seethe with anger.

'In my mind I thought … If he was any sort of a man he should face up to his sordid past and "bite the bullet".

'However, as he was in shock I realised it would be more productive to meet another time.

'When I told him I planned to leave the next day, he surprised me by asking if we could continue our conversation in the morning over breakfast.

'So far he had admitted very little and had expressed no regret for abandoning my mother and me.' Frank concluded.

*　*　*

Following the breakfast meeting with his father, Frank went over his notes in his hotel room, highlighting some leverage points, noting a number of matters his father had refused to divulge.

Frank had deliberately not raised the issue of the Garland fraud, deciding to keep this explosive card up his sleeve for the right moment.

Instead of catching a bus back to Bordeaux, Frank decided to go instead to the São Bento train station and book a seat on a train to Lisbon.

*　*　*

The next day, as his train gathered speed after crossing the picturesque Douro River bridge it began winding its way south. Frank looked over his "Lisbon To Do List".

It included visits to the offices of the *Jornal de Notícias*, seeing the police records to check his father's 1941 arrest and find out what records the bank that had employed him might still have.

*　*　*

At the *Jornal de Notícias* offices he was shown to a visitor's computer to search through its backdated issues.

But the paper was written in Portuguese and he couldn't understand a word. Explaining his problem at the front desk, he was advised an English-speaking member of staff could assist for a small fee.

Knowing his father had been held for nearly a month in April 1941, he asked the interpreter if she could find any court mentions of it.

Soon she read out of what he was looking for, which he wrote in his notebook.

Police yesterday took into custody Mr Emilio Bestillo, an Oporto wine salesman who recently returned from England, at the request of British Police, who allege he was involved in a major fraud.

Appearing at his arraignment before a judicial magistrate, Mr Bestillo denied any involvement, claiming there was a mistake and that he was completely innocent.

The magistrate ordered he be held for thirty days whilst awaiting a brief supporting the charge to arrive from Britain to enable Lisbon Police to press charges.

He ordered a copy of the article and continued his search with the interpreter's assistance. Other than a short mention four weeks later that the police had released Mr Bestillo without charge, there was nothing further.

The interpreter then pointed to a social page photo of Mr Bestillo taken in 1945 that showed him in a tuxedo, with an attractive model on his arm beside an Alfa Romeo in front of the ritzy Hotel Palácio Estoril.

Frank later looked up Estoril in his guide and found it was a fashionable seaside resort town some 20 kilometres west of his hotel that attracted the rich and famous.

The guide said that during the war the Hotel Palácio was Europe's largest and most glamorous casino, attracting only the very wealthy from either side of the war, providing they could travel to neutral Portugal.

Frank realised it would have cost his father a small fortune to live the high life there but that is exactly what he had done.

He was about to pack up and head across town to Banco Espirito Santo, the bank where his father had worked, when the member of staff assisting him spotted a later 1956 article hidden amongst the financial pages.

Lisbon's leading business bank, Banco Espírito Santo, is set to announce it is prepared to underwrite the failing fortunes of Oporto's Bestillo Nacional Wine Company, which for many years has laboured under a series of losses and widespread unrest in its warehouses and vineyards.

An unnamed source told this paper that the bank is seeking sureties in the order of forty-three million escudos, which Bestillo Nacional's directors have to put up.

However with the firm's managing director ailing and no succession plan in place, Bestillo Nacional is desperately casting around for a white knight and a new manager.

Frank asked her what that amount of escudos would be worth in English currency and after consulting another clerk, she suggested around £200,000.

These two pieces of information helped explain the sort of life his father had led between fleeing London and his recall to Porto in 1956 to take up a senior role in the Bestillo wine business.

* * *

Arriving at Banco Espirito Santo's head office he asked to see the personnel manager. When he was ushered into a small meeting room, he explained that his mother was dying in England and he desperately wanted to find his long lost father, who had worked at the bank in the 1950s, to inform him of her plight before time ran out.

He didn't expect the bank would be of much help but anything which could help him join up the "dots" was being sought. He was told Mr Bestillo's last place of residence in Lisbon was in Avenida da Liberdade.

He then went to the Lands Registry Office to ascertain what properties his father might have purchased with his windfall, but there was nothing on record.

Next he visited the Directorate General Office of Justice and paid for a copy of his father's police certificate, which contained some revealing information relating to his arrest.

41. Unread Letters

Peggy and Emma had discovered, when they went through Margie's old papers, a photo of Charles in a wheelchair at Buckingham Palace on the day he received the George Cross Medal.

A man in uniform beside him was revealed to be his batman, Lance Corporal Kirk, from the writing on the back of the image.

Peggy explained that her mother had told her that he was very loyal to Charles and had been deeply affected by the bomb blast. He had spoken warmly about what a superb leader the Lieutenant had been.

Emma remembered that Charles had mentioned the batman in one of his letters to Elizabeth.

It then suddenly occurred to her that if he were still alive and she could find him, he would be the only person still alive who could tell her anything about Charles.

She used her laptop to search for possible links to retired military personnel, which eventually led her to Halsey House in Norfolk, which had a Lieutenant B. Kirk (retired) as a resident.

As the summer months approached along England's east coast, the longer days in Norfolk were encouraging Mr Kirk to venture beyond his Royal British Legion nursing home.

Mr Kirk's neat bed-sitter, with its southerly windows that let in the noon sun, was furnished with his favourite recliner brought from home, a small bookcase filled with books, folders and a number of family photos.

On the days Mr Kirk ventured into town, he enjoyed sitting in his wheelchair in one of his preferred pubs. Here, sipping on his ale, he could take in the views of Cromer Pier reaching out into the North Sea and watch bathers frolic in the waves and tourists stroll down the esplanade.

However, the slight-framed, frail, veteran still had a sharp mind and missed stimulating conversations.

* * *

When Emma called Halsey House and explained to the receptionist that she was researching her family history, she was hoping Mr Kirk would take her call and confirm one way or the other if he knew Lieutenant Garland.

Propelling himself across the room in his wheelchair to answer the phone, his face lit up when he heard that a very interesting young lady wanted to speak to him.

Since his wife died, few people ever called other than on his birthday or at Christmas.

'It is a pleasure to take your call Miss Childers,' he answered. 'I am not sure how I can help.'

Emma explained her family connection to the late Lieutenant Garland, telling him about discovering the Buckingham Palace photo and asking if he was the same Lance Corporal Kirk she saw in it.

'If it is you, would you like to see it? This would give me the opportunity to ask what you can remember about him.'

Hearing the Lieutenant's name spoken for the first time in seventy years astonished Mr Kirk, and brought back long, forgotten memories of the war and the dreadful bomb blast.

He could still remember the sound of the explosion and the blast of heat, which knocked him flat and deafened him for months. It brought back memories of the smell of acrid smoke and the awful sight of dead and bloodied bodies.

'You bringing this up has caught me somewhat offguard,' he told Emma in a wavering voice.

'Of course I remember, I was proud to be the Lieutenant's batman. You know, he was a thoroughly fine gentleman.'

'If you felt up to it Mr Kirk, I could catch a train from London to show you the photo and we could go out for something to eat and a chat,' suggested Emma.

*　　*　　*

After meeting in the Halsey House foyer, she wheeled Mr Kirk out towards the beachfront. She remembered her Granma telling her she used to push Charles like this around the park after he was injured and wondered if decades later she was somehow repeating what her Granma had done.

As Mr Kirk gave directions to his favourite waterfront café, they rounded a corner and the glistening, blue North Sea swept into view.

Having found a seat and placed their orders, Emma produced the photo and enjoyed seeing his proud expression as he carefully examined it.

'You know Emma, the Lieutenant told me that despite everything, receiving that medal was the proudest day of his life,' Mr Kirk revealed.

'I have never forgotten how he looked out for every man in our Section like they were his own sons. He always put his own life on the line to protect ours.'

Emma asked Mr Kirk if he recalled Charles speaking about his family.

'Mostly he kept those things to himself, but the Lieutenant did tell me of his deep affection for his niece, whom he said had been so kind to him, especially after the accident.

'I do know he would have done absolutely anything for her,' Mr Kirk added.

Hearing her beloved Granma spoken of so lovingly brought a delighted smile to Emma's face, which Mr Kirk didn't miss.

'Emma, there is something rather important your family will not be aware of from that time when the Lieutenant was in hospital,' he said.

'When I visited, he was heavily sedated and in very low spirits. His arm was in plaster, his head swathed in bandages and only his sunken, watery eyes and pale lips were visible through small slits.

'He asked me to take down a letter he wanted sent to a woman he loved by the name of Elizabeth.

As I began writing, the Lieutenant poured some of his heart out.

'He explained the extent of his injuries, which he said he would have to live with for the rest of his life.

'He described his concern for the sight in his right eye and that part of his face was disfigured and as a consequence he was no longer the loving, active man she had come to know.

'He had me write more, but I shan't go into that at this time.

'I realised he was honestly informing Elizabeth that they should end their relationship, for her sake.

'When I saw tears dampening the bandages around his sad, weary eyes I hated what he wanted me to do.

'When I arrived back at barracks that evening, as ordered I put his letter into an envelope and addressed it, fully intending to post it the next day.

'But I felt more than troubled, which caused me to sleep very fitfully that night, knowing his letter was about to ruin two lives.

'So the next morning I went to the chapel and asked for His guidance.'

Sitting opposite, completely spellbound, Emma asked, 'So what did you do then?'

'Despite the Lieutenant's order to post his letter, I did something dreadful.

'Instead of sending it to Elizabeth, I sat down and wrote to her explaining that due to the Lieutenant's injuries he had asked me to transcribe this letter.

'In it I gave her a more encouraging report of his condition, although I did mention his disfigurement and the grief it was causing him. Of course I added that he sent his enduring love and hoped that all was well with her in Melbourne.

'There is also something else you should know, Emma,' he continued.

'Before our Section went out on each day's assignment, the Lieutenant would leave a sealed, pre-written letter addressed to Elizabeth in the event he did not return.

'On the day of the bomb blast, after he was taken to hospital, his final letter to her was there in his room, taped to the mirror. It was never sent or opened,' he added as Emma listened intently.

'I have held onto both those letters ever since. With what you have told me today of your search for the truth about your distant great-great uncle, I now feel your family should have both of them.

'Mr Kirk, we had no idea those letters existed or the role you played. Thank you for telling me this.'

Returning to Halsey House from lunch, Emma's mind was in a whirl as to what the letters Mr Kirk was about to give her might contain.

She wondered if there was a possibility Charles had confided something very personal to his batman, such as the guilt he carried from causing the bomb blast or was it about having let Elizabeth down.

It seemed so unfair that the train was full and she would have to wait until she arrived back in London before she found a quiet place to read them.

She asked herself, in similar circumstances what profound words would she have chosen to write in a final goodbye letter to her sweetheart.

Just the thought made her shudder.

42. Opening the Letters

Returning home from Norfolk, her mother pestered her about what she had learnt. Knowing if she breathed a word of the letters, Irene would stamp her foot until she read them. The wait was becoming almost too much to bear.

Instead, Emma told her about her enjoyable scenic train trip, where they had gone for lunch and Mr Kirk's illuminating recollections of the Buckingham Palace medal investiture.

Irene was rapt to hear that Mr Kirk had said Charles simply adored Granma and would have done anything for her.

Emma wondered as she brushed her teeth that evening if the girl in the mirror was ready to tackle her mother with the remaining questions.

But first she still needed to read the letters Mr Kirk had given her and then tomorrow she and Becky were going to make a call at the Swansons' Dulwich Village home.

Emma needed to create some space so she could get away to read the letters, so after clearing away the dishes, she excused herself and headed to her room.

Tucked up in bed, she tore open the first envelope, and was surprised it only contained a single page in Charles' distinctive handwriting:

December 1940
Dearest Elizabeth,
I leave this letter in the event that in carrying out my duties in this war for my King, country and the Royal Engineers I might not return.

I hope this never reaches you, because if it does you will know I am dead.

Just because I do not return to your arms to hold you close does not mean I will not be there with you.

I want you to know I will always be looking over you.

So whenever you feel lonely, just close your eyes and remember I truly loved you with all I had and know you were everything to me.

But now I need you to push on with your life and face the fork in the road ahead.

I want you to go on and create a fulfilling life, knowing I will be proud of the path you select.

Yours forever,

Charles

Emma wondered how she would have felt emotionally if she had ever received something so sad yet in a way so beautiful from someone she loved so dearly.

She realised there must have been thousands of servicemen like Charles who wrote last letters to their loved ones, as a final farewell and tragic reminder of a life given to save their King and country.

In a perverse way, Emma was glad that Elizabeth never received it.

Regaining her composure, she imagined herself for the moment in Elizabeth's shoes, as she nervously opened the next envelope.

St Thomas' Hospital

February 1941

My dearest Elizabeth,

Due to my dire state, my batman has kindly agreed to pen my letter to you but I am afraid it might waffle on and make little sense.

I lie here in agony, sheathed in bandages, drifting in and out of sleep.

I wonder what happened at the site and feel enormous guilt that through my mistake one of my men lost his life and another remains badly injured lying in a bed in this ward.

The pain I bear for the accident is at times overshadowed by the sadness I feel that my body is wracked by injuries I may have to carry for the rest of my life.

I need you to know that despite surgery to my right eye and side of my face, I will have permanent disfiguring scars.

My arm will mend in time and the doctors are suggesting I may have a type of blast stress that will affect my concentration and balance.

I am told they may send me home next week, as they need my bed.

Elizabeth, you have only known me as a proud man.

I have only ever wished to be worthy of you, of my family and my country.

But now I feel I have let you and everyone down.

Given my situation, with such poor prospects, perhaps to make it easier for everyone, the best way out is to simply end my life.

This is what I wish.

Your loving

Charles

PS. It is my wish that this letter is kept confidential, as I do not wish for my family to ever know my inner thoughts.

Having read it a second time, Emma rested it on her duvet and stared out the blackened window to allow herself to absorb each and every word.

She now fully understood why Mr Kirk had disobeyed the order to post it.

Knowing that Elizabeth had been denied the truth and instead led to believe Charles was on the road to recovery, when in fact he was in a dreadfully depressed state and was prepared to end his life, caused Emma to feel profoundly sad.

She wondered why his batman had ignored the warning and hadn't informed someone.

Much of all this caused her to question if Granma knew Charles was suicidal.

Did Granma's parents subsequently learn about his suicide and keep it a secret?

And because of Charles' untimely death, did the police who were supposedly pursuing Mr Bestillo close the case?

Emma wondered if this was the reason the scandals had been kept secret.

Closing her eyes to shut out these thoughts, she listened to the soft patter of rain on the window and muffled voices from the TV seeping in from the next room that intermittently broke her silent weeping.

43. Under the Floorboards

The very thought of making a cold call at Margie's former home and asking if she could look in the wardrobe was proving very daunting for Emma, so she asked Becky to go with her.

Armed with a photo of Granma in her school uniform, the pair caught the bus to Dulwich Village and walked to College Crescent, where Emma had to find the nerve to step up to the front door of the detached brown brick house and knock.

They timed their visit for when they thought people would be home preparing dinner.

A girl in her teens opened the door and told them her parents were not there.

Realising the inappropriate situation and after explaining why they were calling, Emma asked her if she could call one of her parents and subsequently explained the extraordinary reason for their visit.

The girl's father told her he would be happy to show them the room when he returned from work, so Becky and Emma went back to the village to while away a couple of hours.

Returning and introducing themselves to the father, Emma showed him the photo of Margie.

'Would it be OK if we go up to her old room and take a look in the wardrobe?' Emma asked.

'I suppose,' the man said and led them upstairs.

Immediately seeing the corner wardrobe was still there, Emma asked if she could open it.

She dropped to her knees, buried her head beneath a row of dresses on hangers and began to search.

In semi darkness, wanting to get a closer look at the floorboards, she shifted a jumble of shoes aside, then asked Becky if she could shine her phone's torch light to see what was there.

After what seemed forever to Becky, Emma spied a single floorboard with bruised edges that hadn't been nailed down.

After trying to lift it, Emma called for a knife, which she used to prise the board free.

Looking into the musty cavity she immediately spied several dust covered photos, a small ring box and a parcel wrapped in paper tied with string, which she carefully picked up to look at more closely.

She removed the wrapping and to her delight she found it contained a very old, leather bound pocket size diary that was gold embossed and surely must have been the one that belonged to Granma.

Before opening it, she noticed its tarnished gold lock had been forced.

Flipping through a few pages, she immediately saw it was written in her Granma's neat script.

Looking up at Becky she breathlessly exclaimed, 'This is it!'

Emma then went back for another look in the hiding place and began to wonder what she should do with the other items.

'Beck, ought we take them with us or should we leave them here?'

'I would take them,' Becky suggested. 'They are of no value to anyone other than your family.'

Explaining to the father watching patiently at the door that they had found what they had come for, Emma asked if she could also take the other small items, which he had no objection to.

As his daughter held the front gate open for them on their way out to the street, she said she hoped the diary contained the answers Emma had come so far to find.

'By the way, you have just shown me a very cool place to hide my private stuff.'

*　*　*

Tripping down the crescent towards the village, with the diary tucked safely in her carryall, Emma could barely wait to get to the pub to celebrate their discovery.

Having found a quiet spot, they settled down on the bar stools to regain their breath. Then Becky slipped away to order champagne to toast their fruitful Sherlock Holmes afternoon's work.

Holding the diary, Emma let its energy flow into her hands and began to feel a wave of suppressed euphoria rising in her.

When Becky returned and they had toasted their discovery, Emma opened the diary on the table and suggested they should both have a look at it.

Becky thought otherwise, 'Emm, much as I would love to have a peek, you must be the first to properly digest what it contains. It might hold some surprises, which are none of my business. You can tell me all about them after you have read it.

'Right at this moment, I think it's like that James Bond film we recently saw together, *For Your Eyes Only*.'

Whilst Becky went to the bar to get a second round, Emma couldn't wait any longer to call Jessie and tell her the exciting news that the diary was exactly where she said it might be.

44. Emma's Inner Thoughts

Accompanying Becky back to her flat to stay the night to avoid another round of her mother's questions, Emma settled down to read the journal while her friend watched TV in her room.

Propped up with pillows on the sofa, Emma felt some trepidation as she held the small leather diary.

Her attention returned to the damaged gold lock. Whoever had broken it had not bothered to cover their tracks.

Opening the cover expecting the unexpected, she uttered a quiet prayer, 'Please Granma, make this as easy as you can for me.'

Scanning the first pages, she wondered where they were going to take her.

Soon she was reading of Margie's school days and her secret confessions.

Emma read that Granma was fourteen when she was given the diary and her early entries were mostly "one-liners" about New Year's Eve celebrations in 1935, happenings at school, what she had spent her pocket money on and the occasional sleepover at Jessie's.

When Margie took the diary with her on the Scotland trip, Emma noticed her account of the Empire Exhibition and her impressions of the places she had been were more detailed and engaging.

Emma's ears pricked up when the diary mentioned Jessie's flirting and beer drinking with some soldiers in a pub; what a far cry the teenage Jessie had been from the elderly lady she had more recently come to know.

Then the next dozen or so pages were causing her to nod off.

Suddenly she came across an entry that Jessie's Bletchley Park cover stories hadn't entirely fooled Granma.

Soon after was a more interesting entry when she met a man.

Tuesday 3 September 1940
Am on cloud nine after tonight's Dorchester function.

*Met the most handsome man who nearly swept me off
my feet. He even asked me to have afternoon tea with
him.*
*I know Jess took a dislike to him, but I think she might
be a bit jealous.*
*Am now holding my breath hoping Mr Bestillo calls
like he promised.*

The next pages covered the frightening days leading up to Sunday
7th September when she wrote that everyone had to scurry off to an
air raid shelter when Germany began bombing London.

Despite the brutality of war arriving in London, Margie appeared
preoccupied, anxiously waiting for Mr Bestillo's phone call.

Amongst many personal thoughts, some that Emma found slightly
embarrassing, was of Granma's growing feelings for Emilio and how
excited she was to be desired.

She encountered the dark memories that were confronting Margie
after her heroic rescue of two children from a fire and how the trauma
had deeply disturbed her.

Then Emma came across an entry in the second week of January
1941, in which she wrote how upset she was when she discovered after
driving a badly injured officer and a soldier to hospital after a bomb
defusing accident, that the unrecognisable officer turned out to be
her uncle.

<u>Friday 31 January 1941</u>
*Was shocked on my hospital visit to find Uncle Charles
still so weak and in low spirits. His medical clipboard
indicates the doctors are worried about his low pulse
and infected wounds, which I've noticed are beginning
to reek.*
*Tried to cheer him up, got a broad smile but it didn't
last long. He needs a miracle to get him better.*

<u>Sunday 2 March 1941</u>
Shocked that Uncle Charles is finding life so hard to bear.

If I were in his shoes I wonder how I would have
handled this happening to me.
Not sure what I can or should do.

The journal kept reminding Emma how much Granma had inspired much of her life, especially having encouraged her to go to Australia. Thinking of this, she thought she knew what she would have done if she had been in Margie's situation.

On the next page, she read about the Swanson family's thrilling invitation to Buckingham Palace where the King was to present her uncle with the George Cross Medal.

<u>Sunday 16 March 1941</u>
Emilio left a message for me apologising that he will
not be able join us at the palace tomorrow. Called him
back but there was no answer, which is strange, as we
haven't spoken in days.

Emma read Margie's amazing account of the Buckingham Palace investiture and how distressingly the day had ended when her uncle read that letter which was to shatter his world.

Emma could see from the diary that the next week became a blur for Granma, especially when the bank confirmed the worst.

<u>Tuesday 18 March 1941</u>
When I phoned Uncle Charles, I found him very upset
after the bank confirmed the money transfer from
Australia was missing.
He told me his bank had called in the police and that
he is going to provide them with a statement.
I have never heard him so upset before, not quite sure
what I should do.
Tried calling Emilio to tell him uncle's awful news, but
the line rang out, again.

<u>Wednesday 19 March 1941</u>
From a long conversation with Uncle Charles today he admitted if he has lost all his money he would have trouble funding his recovery.
I tried to encourage him to look on the bright side.
He disclosed there had been several times since the accident when he realised he might always be an invalid and permanently scarred and that he had considered what little was left of his life was hardly worth living.

Emma could see Granma had problems of her own and Emilio was avoiding her.

<u>Thursday 20 March 1941</u>
Today my life was turned hopelessly upside down when Uncle Charles told me the police have named Emilio as the prime suspect.
I apologised to Uncle Charles for having introduced Emilio to him in the first place.
I suddenly feel so guilty for having caused all this and am feeling crushed!
To think I trusted that bastard with my love and my body.
My heart now lies in a thousand pieces.

The diary revealed that Gertrude was still outraged after learning of Charles' loss and had exploded when she heard her daughter's boyfriend had been named the prime suspect.

Then Emma suddenly came across a whole bunch of missing pages, which she realised must be the ones found in the clock.

These she recalled, contained Granma's innermost thoughts when she had discovered she was pregnant and her wretched discovery that Emilio had left town, which didn't quite align with Jessie telling her that Emilio couldn't face the prospect of being a father.

Now wide awake and reading on, the final pages caused her jaw to drop.

<u>Monday 31 March 1941</u>
I feel unsure about having my baby but there is no other way.
I had felt guilty for deceiving mother but not any longer. I have discovered she has been reading my diary and broken the lock to access it.
Worse still, she has torn out a whole lot of pages. When I asked for them back she said NO, she was keeping them for my own good. No-one was to ever find out anything about the baby.
This led to another almighty fight.
I have passed the point where I can ever trust her again and I feel so sad it's come down to this.

Emma now had the proof that it was Gertrude who had ripped the pages out to ensure the baby scandal never came back to embarrass the Swansons.

<u>Tuesday 1 April 1941</u>
This is my last night at home before I catch my train tomorrow.
Feel very guilty and sad I'm leaving Uncle in the lurch with him struggling and needing my support and not knowing why I am going.
Am still beside myself Emilio has left me, never to know he is the father of my child.
As I am not sure I will have a safe place for this diary if I take it with me I have decided to hide it in my secret place in the wardrobe until my return.

As Emma snuggled deeper into the sofa, she wondered why Gertrude hadn't also torn the pages out that mentioned Emilio's fraud. Surely she would have wanted that covered up too.

Turning the light back on she found a pen and wrote in her notebook:
Was there someone else who wanted to sweep the fraud under the carpet? If so, who was it?

274

45. Outside the Square

Having thoroughly read Margie's diary, it incensed Emma that with all the havoc Emilio Bestillo had wreaked, he had got away with it unscathed.

Knowing a lot more about the fraud and its ugly aftermath, she had decided her journey ahead was to see that justice was finally done.

From the outset, Emma had never thought about profiting from what she had discovered, but only about returning some of Bestillo's ill-gained wealth to Charles' family.

*   *   *

After reading the diary she was still vague about the outcome of Frank's visit to Lisbon.

She dialled his number and while she waited for him to answer she doodled a clock face on her notebook.

'Frank, the reason for my call is to ask about something you only briefly mentioned previously. You told me that you had gone to Lisbon and discovered a whole lot more about your father.'

Frank pulled a chair over to the phone, knowing this conversation was going to take a bit of time.

'In Lisbon I discovered when my father died, that he had left a large inheritance to his wife and children.

'But I felt as his eldest son, he owed me something.

'I raised this with a retired solicitor in my Sir Francis Drake Bowls Club team. Under our law, he suggested that it might be worth pursuing.

'Far too late I discovered that Portugal's inheritance laws are very different to ours and I should have engaged a local solicitor to contest the Will instead of doing it myself,' Frank explained, sounding defeated.

'Do you know what it would have cost if you had gone through a legal firm in Portugal?' Emma asked, all the while thinking that route might not only have been expensive but also very risky.

'Emma I have no idea,' said Frank, knowing he should have gone into this more thoroughly at the time.

Hearing him say this, Emma remembered what Alex had told her to keep in mind:

"When you feel boxed in, think outside the square".

She now realised she might need to organise a visit to Porto herself.

46. Cards on the Table

When she was living at home, her mother knew Emma always came straight to the point if something was bothering her.

Since moving to Melbourne, Irene sensed her daughter had become more distant from her and was wondering how she could bring her concern up without Emma becoming defensive.

Irene asked herself if she had made mistakes of judgement in the past, but then as a mother, there were often things you didn't fully divulge to your children.

* * *

After discovering the diary pages, Emma had kept in mind Alex's sage advice to play her cards carefully.

He illustrated the point using a case in New South Wales where the corruption commission had forensically investigated two MPs, Eddie Obeid and Ian Macdonald, for ministerial misconduct, resulting in both being convicted of corruption and sentenced to lengthy jail terms.

The prosecutors had carefully "lined their ducks up" before making a move to crack open their main targets.

Emma decided this was how she was going to chase down the answers to her questions.

On the flight home to London, she reminded herself she was delving deep into murky family waters spanning over seventy years. The locks she was endeavouring to prise open were stiff with accumulated mistrust.

More than ever she realised Gertrude, Granma and even Jessie had personal reasons to leave things where they lay and she suspected her own mother had her own agenda.

Before she returned to Melbourne, Emma intended to fly to Portugal, to follow up on Frank Dalton's failed inheritance claim.

First, though, she needed to have a serious talk with her mother.

She wrote in bold letters in her notebook:
Why have all these matters been kept a secret?

*   *   *

She then joined her mum on the couch to watch her favourite TV show. As the end credits rolled, Emma asked if they could have a chat about why she had flown home and the amazing story that had unfolded.

While she went to get her notebook and the diary, it gave Irene a few moments to reflect on the hurt she had felt about Emma keeping her in the dark these last few weeks.

Since she was quite young, Irene had known there were gaps in her mother's life that she never really understood.

For instance, when she looked through the family album, her mother had never convincingly explained why there were so few photos of Gertrude or why she rarely ever talked about her.

Her train of thought was broken when Emma returned and settled down beside her on the sofa.

Emma was anticipating the conversation they were about to have was going to be challenging, but regardless it was time to have it.

She knew Irene often tried to over-manage their conversations and would not let her have her say.

It wasn't as though Emma distrusted her mother; it was more that she could be evasive or jump to conclusions.

Turning to look at her and taking a deep breath, Emma began.

'Mum, I know you are frustrated that I've been holding back on what I have been delving into but I have needed to save this conversation until now. Undoubtedly you will be wanting to know why.'

'Look Emma, I really don't know why you are making such a big deal of it. Can we just get on and discuss whatever it is you want?' Irene pressed.

'Because it is a big deal. The information I am seeking is pivotal to everything surrounding Frank's birth, Mr Garland's fraud, Emilio Bestillo and many of Granma's issues,' Emma shot back.

'And YOU are the only person who might have the answers.'

'Darling, you seem to be getting a little steamed up,' Irene suggested, trying to calm things.

'What I am hoping is that the two of us can work out some answers,' Emma said, recomposing herself.

Irene slowly pondered the point, and then much to her daughter's surprise tacitly nodded her agreement.

'Firstly, you know after Granma's diary pages were discovered I wanted to know who tore them out,' Emma stated.

'We now know it was Gertrude trying to cover up Margie's pregnancy and the affair,' said Emma.

'What I don't understand is why she would have hidden them in the clock? Mum, is it possible she forgot they were there or did she intend for them to be found after she passed?'

'I have a suspicion she felt too guilty to burn the pages and instead hid them in her clock, hoping they would never be discovered,' Irene intimated.

'I can imagine her doing that,' said Emma. 'But why did she need to keep everything, including Margie's baby, the fraud and even Charles' suicide a secret?'

Irene paused before explaining. 'When I was growing up, my parents would often say, "The neighbours would have had a field day" if ever they discovered I had done something really naughty.'

'But Mum, that doesn't get Gertrude off the hook,' interjected Emma.

'Darling, back in the 1960s we still had many of the same restrictions that ruled Gertrude's generation. My friends were the first to have pocket radios, rock'n'roll records, the top 40 and TV sweeping into our lives that introduced new ideas and totally reshaped our values.

'We were light years ahead of the very restrictive early 1900s in which Gertrude was raised, when it was all about keeping up appearances,' Irene explained.

Emma nodded. 'Granma's diary makes it clear that Gertrude kept her on a very tight leash, even after she left school. But I don't understand why she trashed her daughter's trust in her to achieve this and in doing so, became such a dragon.'

'My mother told me about how Gertrude grew up in a God fearing Sussex family and was sent to a private girls' school that ingrained in her very strict conventions,' Irene explained.

'But there has to be more to it than that,' Emma suggested.

'Yes, there is. When she was younger her family's standing in the village was ruined when the news got out that her older sister had eloped with a married Italian navy officer, and not long afterward found she was pregnant. That sent an earthquake through the village,' Irene said.

'Gosh, that would have been devastating,' exclaimed Emma.

'From this horrid experience, I can only assume Gertrude wanted to ensure that a scandal of that magnitude would never happen to her family ever again.'

'What I don't comprehend Mum, is why you haven't spoken of this before now. Is there something you want hidden too?' Emma asked.

'To tell you the truth,' Irene confessed, 'I have always hoped it would never come up and no-one would be the wiser about it.'

'So when did you first suspect Granma had Frank?' Emma suddenly asked.

The question caused a pained look to flash across Irene's face as she searched for the right words to articulate the truth.

'When she was alive, I never had any suspicions. It was only when I was clearing out her beloved mahogany writing desk after she died that I came across a small brown paper parcel tucked away at the back of a drawer.

'When I unwrapped it, there was a tiny pair of beautifully knitted woollen booties that looked like they had never been worn.

'They were exactly like the ones she knitted for me when I was a baby, which you can see here in this photo of me in Granma's album.'

'That is so very special, but what made you think they were for a possible third child?' asked Emma.

'I felt this could be the only reason my mother would have kept them.

'How I longed to be able to have talked to her one more time, to ask if the baby had died, or whether she had miscarried and if the baby was born before Peggy or me.'

Taking a few moments to recompose herself, Emma opened one of the letters that Mr Kirk had given her and read out a paragraph written by Charles Garland:

"Given my situation, with such poor prospects, perhaps to make it easier for everyone, the best way out is to simply end my life."

Emma asked, 'After Granma discovered Charles had taken his own life, what did she do with the news?'

'Knowing my mother was very honourable, I expect when she discovered the empty bottle of sleeping pills in his room, she would have felt obliged by her nurse's oath to inform the hospital,' Irene explained.

'I haven't read anywhere that Gertrude ever found out about his suicide. Do you think she ever did?' Emma queried.

'I suspect when the appalling news filtered out, and with all that was going on at the time, if Gertrude ever discovered it, she might have added it to her growing "never to be discussed file", Irene whispered.

Opening the diary, Emma began reading several entries in which Granma detailed her heartbreak surrounding her pregnancy and Emilio's betrayal of Charles and her.

'When you were a little girl, Mum, were there any signs that Granma might have been depressed by those happenings in her life?' Emma asked.

'I had no idea at the time, but then there were days when she stayed in bed and father would tell us to go outside and play because she needed to rest.

'On one of those days, when I went to give her a cuddle, I saw letters spread across her duvet which she hurriedly bundled up.

'I was too young to ask who they were from but they made me curious. Thinking about it now, she could have been suffering bouts of depression.'

'Did you ever find out who the letters were from?' Emma inquired.

'When I was a bit older, I was in her room when she went to the bathroom. I noticed a letter on the bedside table. My curiosity got the better of me and I couldn't resist taking a peek, discovering it was from Alice Lockwood whom I had never heard of.

'Mrs Lockwood wrote of her anguish at her brother's death and his fraud and how angry she was with a trustee company, who, she believed, washed their hands of the matter to save their good name.

'I have always remembered what she wrote in the last paragraph:

> *"If ever there is an opportunity to square the ledger,*
> *then please write and tell me."*

'I knew I could never ask my mother who Alice was or what she had meant by that offer. It took me years to work out she was Charles' Australian sister.

Irene then watched Emma write *"squaring the ledger"* in her notebook.

'Mum, all my life I've only ever known Granma to be a loving, caring person but knowing now she had Frank, why do you think she pushed him away and didn't welcome him back into her family?'

'I suspect she had some very deep-seated reasons,' answered Irene, feeling unsettled.

'Perhaps she didn't want to upset your grandfather who would have had no idea before they got engaged that she had given birth to Frank.

'You need to know that in those days having a child out of wedlock was considered socially shocking and if he had known, he probably would have called the wedding off,' Irene concluded.

'That was a tough decision she had to make,' said Emma.

'There is one further thing Mum, which I haven't told you about Frank's family. He has an older autistic daughter, Clare, who is in her early forties and is dependent. I'm wondering when her parents are gone how she is going to get by, as I expect she will need specialised care that is going to cost a serious amount,' Emma said.

She was surprised their conversation had flowed more easily than she had expected, revealing many raw insights into Granma's and Gertrude's lives.

Feeling the air between them was so much clearer and that they had developed a renewed level of trust, Emma sensed this was the right moment to pass the diary over to her Mum so she could gain a new insight into Margie's troubled past.

Feeling more connected to her daughter, Irene slipped on her reading glasses and, peering over the rims, gave her an adoring smile.

As she opened the diary, Irene casually intimated, 'When this is all done and dusted, why don't you write a novel about it?'

Emma leaned over and gave her mum a loving hug, and whispered, 'I might just be tempted to do that.'

47. Roof over Clare's Head

Picking up the phone in her Portsmouth home, Mrs Dalton was delighted to find Emma on the line sounding bright and cheery, wanting to speak to her husband, who was in the garden watering his herbs and flowers.

Walking to the back door to call him, she thought what a breath of fresh air this young lady had recently brought into their lives.

For too many years, Frank had seemed rudderless, carrying too much angst and sadness after discovering he was adopted, facing resistance when he had tried to forge links with his birth mother and experiencing nothing but anguish when he had met his father.

But since he had met Emma, Mrs Dalton felt his spirits had been lifted by her interest in their families' history and he seemed very excited with where she was taking things.

'Hello Emma, what a pleasant surprise to hear from you. What's been happening? Tell me your latest news,' said Frank, looking forward to what she was about to say.

'Frank, it is good to speak again. Since the last time, I have made some good progress and have just hatched a plan I want to discuss with you,' said Emma.

As he listened enthralled in the hallway she updated him on her discoveries, including finding the diary, which she suggested he might like to read, and the existence of Charles' unsent letters.

When she mentioned the possibility that his mother might have suffered depression after the war, which could explain her reluctance to openly accept him as her long lost son, she sensed Frank's emotions had taken a hit.

Changing the subject she asked, 'Can you tell me more about Mr Bestillo from your visit to Lisbon?'

Frank took her through, in much more detail, the banking and police information and documents he had obtained that clearly showed how his father had laundered Charles' fortune in the Lisbon casinos, then used it to secure loans enabling him to ruthlessly gain control of the family wine business.

Emma made a note to ask Frank at another time if he could make some photocopies of several documents she might need.

Then out of the blue she asked a totally unrelated question.

'How is Clare's new part-time job at that distribution centre going?'

'Thank you for asking. She's settled in well and is really enjoying the work and also making friends,' Frank proudly proffered.

'That's very reassuring, Frank. The plan I've been thinking about is to do with Clare.

'I hope you won't consider it rude of me to inquire how Clare is going to get by when Mrs Dalton and you are no longer able to look after her?'

Frank was initially taken aback with her question and as he tried to collect his thoughts he unwittingly let the line go quiet, knowing he was reluctant to discuss something as sensitive as this, but in truth he and his wife had been worrying about this for some time.

'Are you still there?' asked Emma politely, pondering the silence.

'I'm sorry, that question completely caught me offguard. Yes, I have to admit her future care is a big issue. The only way we think we would ever be able to afford it is to win the lottery,' Frank admitted.

Acknowledging this, Emma returned the conversation to Frank's attempt to be legally recognised as Mr Bestillo's son.

'If we could find a way to have Clare's future secured, would you and Mrs Dalton be interested in looking into it?

'Absolutely,' answered Frank.

Emma then told Frank about an offer Charles' sister Mrs Alice Lockwood made many years ago in a letter to Margie, offering assistance to "square the ledger" with the trustees.

'I can't see how that very old offer could be of any help, as Mrs Lockwood must have since died,' said Frank.

Emma then told him about her dealings with Mrs Lockwood's grandson, Roger Lockwood, who had become involved with her quest to discover the truth behind the cover-ups and the fraud, suspecting he might be willing to assist.

'Frank, if I could raise the funds to cover the legal costs for you to lodge a claim as Bestillo's son who is entitled to a share of his estate, would you be prepared to go through with it, for Clare's sake?'

'So this is the "hatched plan" you mentioned earlier?' Frank responded.

'Yes, it is,' Emma replied, waiting in suspense for his answer.

'Of course, my initial reaction is yes, but I will need to discuss any offer of financial assistance with my wife.'

Mrs Dalton, who had been listening intently from the kitchen, was relieved that finally there might be some light at the end of the tunnel for their very worrying problem.

Emerging after he hung up with a cup of tea for him, she asked, 'What's this about us getting financial help?'

48. Email to Roger Lockwood

The solicitor in Porto who contacted Emma after reading the short brief she had emailed him, said that if Mr Dalton's claims can be put before a Justice and proved, then he may have a legal entitlement to Mr Bestillo's estate.

Emma asked if he could give a cost estimate of what would be involved, fearing his answer was going to be way beyond Frank's limited resources.

*　*　*

With a figure in mind, Emma then wrote to Roger Lockwood:

Dear Roger,
I hope my email finds you well and in good health.
After all you did for me before I returned to England to pursue answers to the issues that arose from the diary pages, I thought you would like to know how I am progressing and to answer that question you left me thinking about.
Firstly, I have been to the Commonwealth Bank in Ludgate Hill, where Charles had an account, and met with the manager.
All he would tell me was that the file showed the stolen money was traced as far as Madrid, where it was transferred into a German officer's account, which was untouchable. From there the money trail went cold.
I will come back to this later.
Secondly, I was able to track down quite a lot about Mr Emilio Bestillo, who, as you know, was Margie's boyfriend at the time. Their affair ended when he fled London, leaving Margie carrying a child, Frank, who was adopted at birth by the Dalton family.
All this, together with the fraud, has been kept a family secret.
Since arriving I have met Frank Dalton, who told me he grew up never knowing he was adopted. He married in the 1960s and he has two children, including a daughter Clare who is autistic.

*Emilio Bestillo returned to Porto and died a few years ago leaving
a substantial estate.*

*Frank told me he had made an unsuccessful application to
be recognised as his son but he represented himself and was
ignorant of Portugal's complex inheritance laws, causing his bid
to fail.*

*Thirdly, discussing the scandals with my mum, she told me
of a letter she had seen a long time ago, written by your late
grandmother Alice to Margie soon after Charles died.*

*Mum told me Alice wrote of her pain and suffering at Charles'
untimely death and conveyed how angry the family remained that
the trustees had washed their hands of the fraud to save their
reputation.*

*Your grandmother also said if ever there was an opportunity to
"square the ledger", then to please ask for her assistance.*

*Roger, before I left for London you asked me what I was going to
do with the information you gave me.*

*At the time I wasn't able to answer your question, but now I know
what I want to do with it.*

I want to ask you for a huge favour.

*It appears Emilio Bestillo laundered the money he stole from
Charles Garland in Lisbon, which he used to prop-up, then
acquire control of his family's firm.*

*I have undertaken a search of Portuguese inheritance laws and
now believe Frank could legally argue he is the late Mr Bestillo's
son and heir and have a right to a share of the estate.*

*Frank's daughter lives at home, and will in the next few years
when her parents can no longer keep a roof over her head, need
to go into care, which will be expensive.*

The Dalton family could hardly be described as well off.

*Subsequently, when they die, there will be insufficient funds to
cover Clare's special care requirements.*

*But if Mr Dalton were able to mount a successful claim, resulting
in him being awarded a part of the estate, it would solve Clare's
needs.*

Email to Roger Lockwood

I hope you won't consider me impertinent, but on behalf of the Daltons, I am asking for your help to "square the ledger" as your grandmother suggested, by helping Frank mount a new legal challenge.
Over the seven decades this epic saga has run, Emilio Bestillo has never been brought to account. I consider our side owe it to Clare to see it closed, as her hour of greatest need approaches.

Yours truly and kindest regards,
Emma
London

49. Squaring the Ledger

Emma's email was waiting on Roger Lockwood's computer when he arrived at work.

Until he read Emma's request, he had no idea his grandmother had ever made such a bold offer to Margie Swanson to help if she was able to find a way to "square the ledger".

Although, from the way Emma had phrased it, he knew immediately that was exactly how his grandmother would have phrased it.

*   *   *

Before he answered her email, Roger placed a call to his London office to obtain some legal advice. After receiving this, he phoned Mr Marshall at the Australasian Trustee Company.

'Good morning, it's Roger Lockwood here.

'I am sure you will be interested to know I have had an update from Ms Childers, that bright, young English girl who was in touch with us both a month ago.'

'Yes, I recall her, what has she turned up?' asked Mr Marshall.

'She will have told you of the police line of enquiry and how the trail went cold after Mr Bestillo was arrested in Lisbon, only to be released.

'In her latest email she explained where police matters got to after the fraud and where the money trail ended.

'Her search has produced new evidence that after the war, Bestillo laundered much of the Garland money in various Lisbon casinos and then ended up putting quite an amount of it into his family's wine business.

'She has, in addition, recently discovered Bestillo had an English-born son, Frank Dalton, who as it turns out, was born out of wedlock to Bestillo's girlfriend, a certain Miss Margie Swanson.

'Emma has reported Mr Bestillo died a year or so ago from a heart attack, leaving a substantial estate.

'His son, Frank, who lives in England, wants to make a claim as Bestillo's son and heir on his father's estate with the proceeds to be used to fund his autistic daughter's future care needs.'

'Roger, I can't see how these developments involve us,' said Mr Marshall.

'Miss Childers has asked for assistance to enable Frank Dalton to mount a legal inheritance case in Portugal.

'Mr Marshall, in light of the very shadowy situation surrounding the Garland fraud, Frank Dalton's inheritance challenge gives you an opportunity to tidy matters up and make amends, even though it's decades late,' Roger proposed.

Mr Marshall was blindsided with his demand, but tried not to show it.

'Roger, if the board was ever prepared to consider such a request, what sort of figure do you have in mind?' he tentatively asked.

'For your information, Portugal has a system of *"forced heirship"* which means certain portions of Mr Bestillo's estate must be left to particular relatives, including his children, either biological or adopted. That cannot be overridden by his Will,' said Roger.

'Mr Dalton would have to produce irrefutable evidence that he is Mr Bestillo's son, which would involve expensive DNA paternity tests.

'My London office estimated the fee for preparation, serving papers and legal representation for a three-day contested application would be in the order of twenty-two thousand euros. For your information, this in Australian dollars is around thirty-three thousand.

'My family would cover any other costs over and above that figure,' he concluded.

On the end of the line Roger could hear Mr Marshall's heavy breathing but he said nothing for a few moments to allow for his demand to sink in.

'I am afraid that is a substantial amount and I am not at all confident I could get my board to agree,' Mr Marshall finally replied.

Expecting this pushback, Roger came firmly back.

'Mr Marshall, let's put this another way.

'The amount stolen from Charles Garland's account, in today's money, is worth a figure north of sixteen million dollars.

'Your board will be aware the shock from the fraud and subsequent loss was a contributing factor to Mr Garland's suicide.

'Mr Marshall, we both know that the Australasian Trustee Company played a pivotal role in this tragic saga and my family has received information that your firm had the police investigation stopped and reports in the *Sydney Morning Herald* quashed to protect its good name.

'What I am now asking is for Miss Childers' request be paid by your firm, as my dear, late grandmother had so aptly put it, "to square the ledger".

'What I am proposing to wrap-up this muddy case is less than five percent of your annual salary,' Roger finished.

A second uneasy silence came over the line as Mr Marshall weighed up his options, which would have unnerved someone less determined than Roger Lockwood.

'If you would email me the request, I will put it to the Board to consider making an ex-gratia payment, but on the clear understanding we do so without prejudice or admitting any legal liability,' said Mr Marshall.

*   *   *

As soon as he heard that the Board had voted in favour of the funding, Roger Lockwood replied to Emma:

> *Dear Emma,*
> *Thank you for you email. I am delighted with the good progress you have made in finding answers to most of your questions, to the point where you now know where those investigations were meant to take you.*
> *Your fine work has truly inspired my family and me. We are very grateful for the amount of time you have devoted to it.*
> *Like you, the Lockwood family seeks closure to the events surrounding Charles' fraud and what Bestillo did with the money.*
> *You asked for assistance to enable Frank Dalton to make a legal*

claim as a son and heir to his father's estate.
That is a very noble request.
I am writing to advise that the Australasian Trustees Board has made a decision to make an ex-gratia payment to help Mr Dalton conclude these murky matters.
Furthermore, it would give the Lockwood family great pleasure to support your initiative in any way we can over and above what the trustees are putting in.
I've had our London office make inquiries and we were given the name of a highly recommended Porto legal firm, with English speaking staff, which specialises in inheritance matters. Their name is Belzuz & Associados.
If you would ask Mr Dalton to contact them, they will commence proceedings.
Please inform him that twenty-two thousand euros has been lodged in a Belzuz trust account to cover the cost for the application and to engage a top barrister to appear on his behalf at the hearing.
I now hope this provides a way forward to ultimately bring all these matters to a close.
Both my family and the Board at Australasian Trustee Company ask if you could keep us abreast of Mr Dalton's legal progress. We are all stakeholders, like you and your good family, as well as Frank and his wife and children.

Best wishes for every success.
Kindest regards,
Roger

50. The Legal Team

Frank Dalton was over the moon when he heard the news of the funding of his application from Emma.

Things then began to move swiftly.

Knowing she only had a week to get matters in order for the application, Emma returned to Portsmouth to tidy up a host of loose ends with Frank.

They went forensically over his Lisbon findings, making notes and copies of various documents that covered Mr Bestillo's police case, his arrest, his extravagant playboy lifestyle, his spending on luxury hotels and society parties, his large plunges in the swish Hotel Palácio's casino and his money laundering.

The DNA paternity test Frank would undertake in Porto should prove his claim.

She hoped Granma's diary would demonstrate that in the early 1940s Margie and Mr Bestillo had a liaison that led to Frank's birth, but in the back of her mind Emma still thought they might need a plan B in case the Bestillos produced something that caused Frank's application to be dismissed.

*　　*　　*

At her mother's place Emma had seriously considered selling her antique clock to fund her possible return trip to London, but knowing its hundred-year history, she couldn't immediately bring herself to do it.

When she raised her dilemma with Alex, he had suggested by selling it, her Granma was helping to square the ledger. Finally heeding his advice she decided when she returned home she would reluctantly take it to Colman Clocks for them to sell.

By the time she got back from Portsmouth, she had almost run out of credit on her Visa card even though she had increased her limit for the trip.

Her only option was to return to work in Melbourne so she could get up to date with her rent and pay off her card, but she needed to go

with Frank to brief their new solicitors and then fly home from Porto
instead of from Heathrow.

* * *

Arriving in Porto, Frank and Emma caught the airport train into
town to meet Ms Inez Vitoria of Belzuz & Associados Solicitors, who
provided them with an overview of Portugal's inquisitorial justice
arrangements, which she explained was quite unlike the British
system.

She said that their judges had the freedom to manage proceedings
as they wished and were able to delve into matters well beyond what
the parties brought to the hearing.

When Emma asked about the legal road ahead, Ms Vitoria took
them through the preparation of the application that included naming
the parties involved and providing all supporting evidence, as well as
a copy of Frank's birth certificate. She asked about when and where
Frank had met his birth mother and father and what transpired. She
also went over the supporting evidence including photos, letters,
official records, Margie's war diary and meeting notes.

Never realising his application would require so much supporting
evidence, Frank panicked when he realised how much information he
would have to get together and send to Ms Vitoria when he returned
home.

Initially Emma was loath to give up Granma's diary but Ms
Vitoria convinced her it would be a vital piece of evidence that had to
be disclosed.

Ms Vitoria then mentioned that when Belzuz & Associados had
lodged Frank's application and sent a copy to the Bestillo family, there
might be a delay while they decided what to do.

If they chose to oppose the application they would have to file a
written response with their evidence to both the court and to Belzuz
& Associados.

* * *

After seeing the solicitor, they met the barrister, Mr Vincente Silvino,
who had been engaged to run their case and represent them at the
hearing.

295

He outlined how the presiding special court judge would order the court's independent DNA tester to take samples from both parties with the results to be presented at the hearing. The judge would also order both parties through their legal representatives to meet in conference with an associate judge to sort out the hearing dates and procedures.

Mr Silvino then explained to them how the court hearing would be conducted. He said a number of witnesses, including Frank, would be called to give evidence and be cross-examined by the defence's barrister.

The thought of having to take the stand considerably frightened Frank who had always felt uncomfortable speaking in public.

As the meeting was drawing to an end, Mr Silvino wondered if his new client would turn out to be a "gold-digger", given the well-known Bestillos were extremely wealthy.

Emma looked over her notebook filled with pages of "must do items" and began to feel uneasy that she and Frank had been launched into a shaky orbit where the outcomes in court weren't predictable, despite reassurances from their very expensive legal team.

Emma came to the conclusion Mr Silvino didn't appear to be embracing Frank's case like she had anticipated. He was explaining the legal procedures, but had asked few questions about the people involved and the background to the case.

Without the emotional side being tabled, she expected a favourable decision would be that much harder to achieve.

'Mr Silvino, I think you need to know the back story driving Mr Dalton's application,' she interposed, seeing immediately that Mr Silvino was put out.

The barrister had never had a client question how he conducted matters.

He quickly came to the conclusion that this English girl obviously didn't respect his standing on the top rung of Portugal's legal ladder. Yet she seemed willing to go the extra distance to achieve a positive outcome.

'Mr Silvino, this case is like a North Atlantic iceberg where only ten percent of it is visible, whilst the rest lurks menacingly beneath the surface,' said Emma unperturbed.

'What has brought Mr Dalton to Porto to make his claim is a very sordid saga perpetrated by his father, Emilio Bestillo, some seventy-five years ago.

It resulted in scandals, huge losses and secrets that have destroyed peoples' lives.'

Emma then recounted how Mr Bestillo had met Margie Swanson, what she had learnt of their emerging relationship, Margie's pregnancy, the events surrounding the fraud, Bestillo fleeing London with the police in pursuit, the money trail to the Lisbon casinos and Frank's attempt to get to know his father.

Mr Silvino quietly absorbed her profound and moving account and made a note how her fearless revelations might be used. He wished she were able to be at the hearing, knowing this English girl would have made a brilliant witness.

'You need to understand Emma, much of what you have just told me cannot be raised in court to support Mr Dalton's application,' he said.

'But what you have so eloquently explained has helped me understand that what you are seeking is a small sliver of badly overdue justice.

'That being the case, I want you to know, it is now my earnest desire to see justice is done.'

*   *   *

On her last day in Portugal, Emma continued to work on developing her plan B.

If she was forced to activate it, she suspected the Bestillos could not afford it to be leaked to the media because it could result in the tax office investigating Mr Bestillo's very shoddy financial affairs.

*   *   *

Relaxing in the taxi on the way to Lisbon's airport, Emma still worried about leaving everything to the solicitor and barrister to sway the judge.

She kept having nagging thoughts that the Bestillos would pull a rabbit out of the hat at the last minute.

Who in Porto would know how to counter that?

One thing was certain, she knew she couldn't afford to be there, as she had to return to her Melbourne job.

With the eleven-hour time difference, she realised how difficult it would be to activate and run plan B from such a distance.

But that was how it was. All the hard work she could do was done and now the case was in the hands of the gods.

*   *   *

When the Bestillos announced they would oppose Frank Dalton's application, a pre-hearing conference was called by an associate judge that was attended by Ms Inez Vitoria. She had carefully read Mrs Bestillo's affidavit and found that it contained much of what was expected.

*   *   *

Ten days before the hearing, when she got back to Melbourne, Emma sent Roger Lockwood a further update.

He called her as soon as he received it, saying, 'I've just finished reading your excellent account and thanks for keeping me informed. You need to know I think you are doing a fine job.

'Now I am aware you are fully resigned to being unable to be at the hearing and that you hope to receive daily updates from Mr Dalton's legal team.

'However, I've just decided, whether you agree with me or not, that you simply have to be there for the hearing.'

'But Roger,' exclaimed Emma. 'You know I simply can't afford to go and my firm would never allow it. I've used up all my holiday leave and I've got rent and my credit card payments to catch up on.'

'I fully understand all those concerns Emma, but absolutely no-one has the driving passion that you have, to see that justice is done,' said Roger.

'Now I want to tell you what I am arranging. My PA is organising flights for you to Porto and accommodation, which I will pay for. When we end this call, I will transfer $5,000 into your account to keep you above water and I've also realised you will need a translator if you are to follow the proceeding,' Roger concluded, knowing he had always expected to be called on at some stage after the trustees came on board to support this last and final bid for justice.

Absorbing the implications of Roger's offer from out of the blue, Emma was near speechless.

'What you have just offered is an absolute miracle! For the moment I'm lost for words, except that from the bottom of my heart, I want to say a profound thank you.

'I'm so happy it's brought tears to my eyes but I am praying that I don't let the Daltons and you down.'

After hanging up, as she walked towards her supervisor's desk, Emma wondered how he was going to react when she asked him for more time off to fly out to the hearing.

51. Day One: Before the Judge

'Your Honour, my client claims that he is the late Mr Emilio Tiago Bestillo's son born in England,' said Mr Vincente Silvino, standing at the right-hand side of the bar table as he opened his case before Judge Ulderico in Porto's General Jurisdiction Court.

'Under Portuguese law, my client is a legal heir and entitled to a share of Mr Bestillo's considerable estate.'

As he went further into Mr Dalton's claim, his self-assured, black-gowned frame was highlighted by the summer morning's sun gently filtering through the stained glass windows that bathed the tiled floor of the timber-panelled court with a patterned yellowish hue.

Mr Silvino confidently turned and tapped a pile of evidence on the table beside him, indicating his intentions to air it during the proceedings.

In preparation for today's hearing, Mr Silvino had spent long hours carefully reading the defence's "Declaração Juramentada" (affidavit), that included Mr Bestillo's son's birth certificate and he highlighted dozens of key paragraphs with yellow sticky notes for future reference.

Seated next to Mr Silvino was Belzuz & Associados' solicitor, Ms Vitoria, and in the row behind, dressed in their Portsmouth Sunday best, sat Mr and Mrs Dalton, anxiously sweating on every word, feeling out of their depth in a court so far removed from home.

On Frank Dalton's right sat an interpreter to help them follow proceedings and assist them when they were called to the witness box.

Next to the interpreter was Emma Childers, still feeling jet-lagged after her long flight, looking apprehensive but inwardly glad today had arrived and quietly optimistic.

At the rear of the court, amongst a scattering of visitors, sat a *Jornal de Notícias'* reporter, Teresa Olimpia, unobtrusively poised to take notes. She was drawn to this hearing having noticed that the well-respected Bestillo family was involved in the contested matter.

Initially it didn't appear to be very newsworthy, but she had noticed that the brilliant barrister, Mr Donato Sousa, was appearing for the Bestillos and was seated at the other end of the bar table attired in a pure wool flowing legal gown, jabot collar and wig that conveyed a sense of imposed importance.

Word around the courts was that he had a bulldog reputation in contested cases.

Ms Olimpia thought she might stay until he came on so she could have the pleasure of seeing him in full flight.

As Mr Silvino continued, Mr Sousa appeared indifferent to the proceedings as he awaited the call to launch his client's defence.

Sitting behind Mr Sousa was Emilio Bestillo's widow, obviously well into her eighties. She was accompanied by two of her four adult children, her eldest daughter Josefa and Aleixo, her youngest son, named after his great grandfather.

*   *   *

Earlier that morning before the hearing got underway, Mr Silvino had told the Daltons to try not to worry.

Regardless, Mr Dalton was a nervous wreck, knowing he would be called to the witness box to answer questions and be cross-examined by Mr Sousa.

Frank had never appeared in a court of any kind. The nearest was when he had failed to pay a parking fine on time.

No amount of dabbing his brow with his handkerchief was stemming the beads of sweat forming.

Then he remembered the last words Emma whispered soon after they had taken their seats.

'When the going gets tough, and we know it will, remember this hearing is not about you. You are doing it for Clare.'

Then he recalled his daughter's trusting smile when she gave him a heartfelt goodbye hug before they left for Portugal, knowing he was trying to secure her future.

Her unconditional love gave him the strength to stand tall and get on with what lay ahead.

*   *   *

After laying out the relevant inheritance laws, Mr Silvino decided to test the judge's tolerance for sensation and rouse Mr Sousa from his continuing indifference.

'Mr Bestillo was a serial womaniser,' he announced.

Immediately Mr Sousa was up on his feet, as expected, erupting with an angry challenge that saw the judge rebuke Mr Silvino and order him to withdraw the assertion.

The tactic had worked.

Suddenly Teresa Olimpia's wandering mind was taking an interest in the proceedings.

The judge then called Emma to the witness stand where, through her interpreter, she told the court of the existence of Miss Swanson's diary and the entries made about Margie and Mr Bestillo's relationship.

As she related how the affair had ended, a rustle of whispers rippled through the court while Mr Sousa slouched, stony faced, trying to appear uninterested, but Ms Olimpia noticed when it came to his turn to question Emma, it was clear he hung onto her every word.

'Miss Childers, please read again the entry for Saturday 22 October, 1940.'

As the interpreter told Emma his request, with an anxious look on her face, Emma turned the pages back to the entry and repeated:

'Awoke smiling this morning after he made beautiful
love to me yesterday.'

Mr Sousa then highlighted to the court that the entry made absolutely no mention of his client's name and strongly asserted that Miss Swanson could have been referring to anyone, not necessarily his client.

Looking unfazed, Emma asked the Judge for leave to correct the assertion, which was granted.

'Mr Sousa, if you reread Miss Swanson's entries before 22nd October and days after it, you will see that the only man she mentions being in her life and holding her heart, was Mr Emilio Bestillo.'

Emma asked the judge if she could read these aloud, and without waiting to hear the translation Mr Sousa quickly rose, conceding, 'That will not be necessary.'

At the other end of the bar table, Mr Silvino respected how skilfully Emma had stood up to Mr Sousa, who he well knew from here on would be on his feet at the slightest sniff of blood.

52. Day One: Character Assessment

The next witness to be called was the aging Mrs Luzia Valborga who many years before had a short relationship with Mr Bestillo.

Mr Sousa jumped to his feet and loudly objected to her being heard.

'Mrs Valborga has no material connection to this case and as such will be wasting the court's time.'

Unruffled, Mr Silvino rose to argue, 'Mrs Valborga's evidence will throw a light on the character and behavioral pattern of Mr Bestillo.' It was an argument which the judge accepted.

It didn't take long for Mr Silvino to lead his witness to the point where she revealed how her relationship developed with Mr Bestillo.

With her hands clasped nervously and eyes dipped, Mrs Valborga searched for the right words.

Sitting upright she bravely stated that when she was an innocent, young woman working at Bestillo Nacional she had started a relationship with Mr Bestillo that resulted in a pregnancy.

'He took off on a ship to England leaving me to fend for myself and my unborn child.'

'At any time did Mr Bestillo acknowledge he was the father of your child or offer any support?' asked Mr Silvino.

'Not until my father pressed him for a payment,' answered Mrs Valborga.

'Do you remember how much that was?'

'It's so long ago but I recall it was around fifteen million escudos.'

Hearing the amount, Teresa Olympia's gaze quickly shifted to Mrs Bestillo, who was hiding her teary face in a hanky.

At the other end of the table, Mr Sousa's florid face bristled with rage.

As the day neared its end and Mrs Valborga concluded her evidence, try as he might Mr Sousa feared he could not dislodge the clear perception that had been successfully established – that Mr Bestillo was a womaniser.

*　　*　　*

When the court rose, Frank Dalton went into a huddle with his legal team to go over his testimony for the next day, while Emma went to find a café, where she found herself sitting opposite the woman who had been taking notes in the rear of the court.

'Excuse me,' said the woman in English.

'I saw you in court today. Are you part of the Dalton family?'

The journalist leaned over and offered her hand. 'Hi, I'm Teresa Olimpia, a reporter for the town's daily paper.'

Emma froze, wondering if the woman would start asking her questions. At the same time, she was glad to discover Frank's application might get some publicity that might threaten to bring a level of shame upon the Bestillo name.

As she calculated how to handle this sudden encounter, Ms Olimpia took the lead by shaking her hand, giving Emma her business card and suggesting if she would like to talk to give her a call. She then quickly departed, saying something about being on a deadline.

*　　*　　*

On the *Jornal de Notícias* editorial floor that evening as the print room's deadline loomed, Teresa Olimpia's editor was in a grumpy mood.

When she approached to tell him she had filed her story in the system, she quipped, 'It could be slightly juicy.'

As he read it, he uttered, 'Damn, damn and damn!'

He well knew there was an editorial rule that no-one could print anything critical of the Bestillos without the paper's owner giving his consent, as he was an old family friend of theirs.

With urgent messages to the owner going unanswered by the time the paper went to press, Ms Olimpia's story was "spiked".

53. Day Two: High Drama

'Would you tell the court what your father said when you introduced yourself to him as his long lost son?' Mr Silvino asked Frank Dalton through the interpreter, when he had nervously stepped into the witness box.

Frank had filed his father's exact words carefully away after their meetings.

Mr Silvino asked, 'Mr Dalton, why did you think Mr Bestillo was your father and how did you tell him?'

'I told him I had tracked down my birth mother who told me who my father was,' Frank said.

'Mr Dalton, what else took place when you first met your father?' asked Mr Silvino.

'During that meeting I could clearly see he was slowly coming to the realisation that the fully grown man sitting in front of him could be his son.

'I thought that my presence was bringing back some of the unsavoury past that I believe he wanted to keep secret,' Frank said.

'Mr Dalton, what did he say after he acknowledged he was your father?' Mr Silvino asked.

'He asked what I wanted from him.'

Frank considered them to be amongst the most distressing words he had ever heard because his father showed no feelings whatsoever that he was his eldest son.

Having to repeat them here in this court was like reliving the nightmare again.

'How did you answer him?' asked Mr Silvino.

'I told him I bore no malice, but I simply wanted to meet him, tell him who I was, find out more about my heritage and hopefully discover why he had deserted my mother and me.'

Mr Silvino picked up two documents from his evidence pile and sought the judge's permission to show them to the witness.

The judge indicated he could proceed.

'Mr Dalton, would you please read out the names on each of these documents and tell the court how they relate to you?'

Mr Dalton took only a brief moment to recognise the first was his original birth certificate and the second showed when he was adopted and his surname was changed to Dalton.

He verified both were his.

'I seek leave to table these two documents as proof of Mr Dalton's birth and his adopted name change.

The judge then asked Mr Dalton to read out the name of his father on the birth certificate.

'There is an empty space for that with no name, your Honour,' replied Frank.

The judge nodded, knowing that under Portugal's paternity law, DNA testing is required if a birth certificate of a child does not show the identity of the father. When paternity is established, it usually leads to the father being made responsible for child support and more.

The judge then looked at Mr Silvino who advised he had no further questions of the witness.

*   *   *

With Ms Olimpia's editor having been given the green light to report the case by the paper's owner, she arrived in court for day two to follow developments in this increasingly tantalising hearing shortly after Mr Sousa had begun questioning Mr Dalton.

'Can you produce written evidence that Mr Bestillo admitted he was your father?' asked Mr Sousa in an intimidating voice.

'Well, no.' said Frank.

'When you claim Mr Bestillo conceded he was your father, was there a witness present?'

'There was no-one present,' said Frank, as his heart beat rapidly.

'Based on there being no written agreement, or any witnesses, Mr Dalton your entire claim gets down to your word versus his,' Mr Sousa asserted.

Sensing he was being led towards troubled waters, Frank searched back into his memory.

'Mr Sousa, the notes in my daybook, which I kept when I met my father will address your concerns.'

Frank looked expectantly at Mr Silvino, who picked up Frank's spiral notebook from his evidence pile and took it to him in the witness box.

Thumbing open to the chapter marked "Porto meeting with my Father", Frank looked up at the judge, seeking permission to read out selected entries, which was given.

> *'At the meeting with my Father in his office today he appeared visibly shocked and unsettled at me being there.*
>
> *Given his age I realised it would be more productive for us to leave today's meeting where it rested and for us to meet another time.*
>
> *When I informed him I was leaving Porto the next day, he surprised me by suggesting we should continue our conversation in the morning.*
>
> *So far he had admitted very little and had expressed no regret for abandoning my mother and me.*
>
> *He appears to want to keep his past a secret to ensure no-one in Porto knows of his past life.'*

'Mr Sousa, my father's office diary, of which you have a copy, confirms our second meeting, instigated at my father's request, which bears out what I recorded in my daybook.'

Hearing this, the court fell silent.

Mr Sousa looked down at his notes, and in low voice indicated he had no further questions of the witness.

*   *   *

Opening the Bestillo case, Mr Sousa called Mr Espirito Santo Junior to the witness box. He was the adult son of the late Mr Ricardo Espirito Santo senior, the former head of the powerful Santo Banking group and a lifelong friend of the Bestillos.

'Mr Santo, can you please tell the court what you recall of the late

Mr Bestillo, when as a university student he boarded with your family in Lisbon?'

'In the 1930s, he lived with my family whilst he went to Lisbon's university. During these years we became good friends.

'My father provided Mr Bestillo with a part-time job at his bank and it's my understanding the branch was disappointed he didn't continue with them after he graduated.'

'Did he ever mention to you any children he bore out of wedlock or ever meeting Mr Dalton?' asked Mr Sousa.

'He never made mention of any children other than the four Mrs Bestillo presented him with, nor spoke of ever having met Mr Dalton,' Mr Santo concluded.

Mr Sousa sat down knowing his star witness had neatly avoided a "can of worms" being opened.

*   *   *

When the afternoon session resumed, the clerk called the court's DNA expert to take the stand to give her findings.

The judge asked Ms Fabienne Wanetts to tell the court the names of the two parties she had tested.

'They were Mr Frank Dalton of Portsmouth and Mr and Mrs Bestillo's fourth child, Alexio,' she answered.

'Your honour, as is the normal procedure, I took saliva swabs from both, which I sent to the state approved Labco Noûs laboratory in Lisbon, who completed the tests and issued the results.'

'Ms Wanetts, can you give this court an outline what the test results might look like?' the judge asked.

'In the DNA parentage test, the probability of parentage is typically 99.99% when the alleged parent is biologically related to the child.

'The result when the alleged parent is not biologically related to the child is zero.'

'Would you please inform this court of the result of the Dalton-Bestillo tests? asked the judge.

In the silence that followed, you could have heard a pin drop, as all eyes and ears keenly anticipated what Ms Wanetts was about to reveal, knowing everything the court had heard to date had built to this single electric moment.

'Your Honour, the probability of Mr Bestillo being Frank Dalton's father is zero.'

As the word "zero" swept through the court, the Dalton camp froze in shock and disbelief.

The gathering of Bestillo supporters broke into loud applause, drowning out the last of Ms Wanetts' evidence.

One of Mrs Bestillo's daughters leaned forward and congratulated Mr Sousa, lightly tapping him on the shoulder.

Judge Ulderico angrily banged his gavel to bring the pandemonium to order.

When it was restored, he abruptly announced he would hand down his decision in the morning.

At the rear, Teresa Olimpia realised she now had a "Goliath slays David" scoop and was flat out keeping up with the consequences of the shock result.

Shifting her attention to Frank Dalton, Teresa noted he looked like a bus had just hit him as his interpreter explained that the tables had been turned.

Hearing the decision, Frank slumped dejectedly into his seat, burying his head in his hands.

Next to him, Mrs Dalton broke down into tears and was being consoled by Ms Vitoria, who looked pale.

Teresa then observed Emma's white knuckles gripping her notebook as she stared disbelievingly at Ms Warnetts, apparently holding back tears.

Realising she couldn't crumble, Emma pondered how Frank's test could have produced zero, because in her heart she knew it was not possible.

Feeling a rising anger that the Bestillos had just pulled a rabbit out of the hat that she had always feared, she asked herself how they had been duped.

Without an answer, she knew now was the time to activate her plan B and run hard with it. She and the Daltons had nothing to lose.

At the bar table, Teresa saw a stunned Mr Silvino wearily rise from his seat to begin gathering up his papers.

He was wondering what he had overlooked as he faced the probability the judge would most likely dismiss his client's application the next day.

After this afternoon's stunning revelation, he doubted that any new evidence could be uncovered which could save the case.

Knowing a high profile loss of this magnitude could weigh heavily on his hard-earned reputation, Mr Silvino feared that when the decision was announced he would be cornered by the *Jornal de Notícias'* reporter, who would want to know if Mr Dalton would appeal.

*   *   *

Trying to remain supportive, Emma accompanied the Daltons from the court. Outside on the street, she suggested they might join her for a cup of tea to calm their nerves. Instead they said they wanted to go back to their room for a quiet rest after the afternoon's turn of events.

Leaving them to walk to the hotel, Emma decided she needed a coffee to steady her shattered nerves and think.

Returning to the same café she went to the day before, as she waited for her espresso, she ran into Ms Olimpia who, seeing how pale Emma looked, asked if she was okay.

'Honestly, I'm devastated. I never saw that DNA result coming,' Emma confessed.

'Presuming the judge dismisses Mr Dalton's application in the morning, where will you take things?' Ms Olimpia asked.

'I am going to discuss it with the Daltons tonight,' was all that Emma would say.

Trying to lighten the conversation, Ms Olimpia changed the subject.

'What do you know about Aleixo Bestillo? I need some more background information on him for my article.'

Hearing Aleixo's name again, Emma's eyes unexpectedly lit up like a 500-watt light bulb as the penny dropped.

It had suddenly dawned on her that Alexio's birth certificate in the defence affidavit was a photostat copy, and at the time she had not thought it odd that it was dated some time after his birth. Suddenly she realised no-one on Frank's side had sighted a certified copy of the original.

As Ms Olimpia enjoyed the last creamy sips of her coffee, from out of the blue Emma suddenly asked, 'Ms Olimpia, where is your births and deaths registry office and do you know when it closes?'

'Why do you need it?' Ms Olimpia asked, as she fumbled on her phone to look up the address.

Scribbling it down Emma assured her, 'I will tell you after I've got what I'm looking for,' as she began a dash to the Conservatória do Registo Civil at Sá Bandeira, knowing it closed in thirty minutes.

54. Late Night Conference

At the Conservatória, Emma watched nervously as the clerk accessed the file to Alexio Bestillo's original birth certificate on a computer and send it off to the printer.

Anticipating a short wait, she called Ms Vitoria.

'Inez, I have a question regarding the judge handing down his decision in the morning. What would happen if something unexpected came up tonight that completely overturned the Bestillos' position?'

'Whilst the judge is making his decision, there is no avenue for anyone to approach him,' explained Ms Vitoria.

'Then, what if the Bestillos were somehow forced to withdraw their objection to Frank's application?' Emma asked.

'If their side was to inform the court before the day's hearing commenced of their decision to do that, the judge might allow their barrister to make a statement to the court before his decision was handed down,' Ms Vitoria explained.

'But Emma, why on earth are you asking me this?'

'Inez, you know the Bestillos are a very hard-nosed family that haven't got to where they have in business by always playing exactly by the rules.

'And during Mr Bestillo's lifetime he certainly didn't care what rules he broke and I wouldn't put it past Mrs Bestillo to have learnt a little of her husband's street cunning,' explained Emma, as she focused on one thing, securing justice for Mr Dalton and the only way to do that was to win at all costs.

'Inez, you have known from the outset of Frank's application, I have prepared a plan B should the legal avenue bomb.

'What I am asking you to do after this call is to arrange two meetings tonight to put my counter plan into play.

'For the first meeting, you and I need to meet with Mr Silvino.

'Then somehow I need you to find a way to convince Mr Silvino to arrange an urgent second meeting with Mr Sousa in his chambers, to put an unexpected matter before him.'

'What unexpected matter has arisen that might cause Mr Sousa to agree to your request?' asked a doubtful Ms Vitoria.

'Trust me, shortly I will have something that overturns the Bestillos' position,' said Emma.

*   *   *

Completing the call, Emma realised the clerk had returned and was waiting with the certificate at the counter.

Thanking him as she slipped the envelope into her satchel, she hurried towards the doors where an attendant was waiting to shut them for the day.

Once outside on the portico, before heading down the steps, she couldn't resist taking a sneak peek inside the envelope, slipping the certificate out just far enough to read what was written in the space reserved for Alexio's father's name.

'Harrumph!' she exclaimed loudly not caring who heard.

'Just as I had thought!'

Reaching the foot of the steps she heard her phone ring.

Ms Vitoria was on the line saying Mr Silvino was not happy having to cancel an appointment to attend the meeting. Further, he has refused point blank to arrange the meeting with Mr Sousa until he was satisfied that whatever startling new evidence Emma claims she has warrants it.

'Please inform Mr Silvino that I have just obtained explosive new evidence that completely overturns the Bestillo case. It could also lead to Mrs Bestillo being found guilty of deception and worse, lying under oath to the court.

'This is why I am demanding that Mr Silvino see what I have and then urgently meet with Mr Sousa – tonight.'

*   *   *

In his chambers, Mr Silvino waited for Ms Vitoria and Emma to arrive, thinking how this had become no ordinary case.

He wondered if this eleventh hour meeting would confirm that Emma had turned up substantive new evidence.

Was Emma hoping that the threat of an investigation into Mr Bestillo's tax avoidance or his role in the Garland fraud being published might cause Mrs Bestillo to cave in?

Had something else arisen of which he had no inkling that would turn the tide against the Bestillos?

*   *   *

At his gentlemen's club as he perused the menu, Mr Sousa enjoyed a second soothing double malt whisky, which he had taken with him into the dining room.

Tuesdays were his club night, where he enjoyed conversing with captains of industry, legal eagles and influential family patriarchs over dinner and drinks.

Tonight was a little more special as he looked like he was heading for a big win in court in the morning.

From behind Mr Sousa's chair appeared a tuxedoed waiter who leaned politely over his shoulder and whispered that there was an urgent call for him in the manager's office.

Annoyed at having his pleasant night disturbed, Mr Sousa unhurriedly rose and stomped off to take the call, where he found Vincente Silvino waiting on the line.

'I apologise if I am interrupting your dinner Donato, but a grave matter has arisen regarding today's case that requires us both to meet urgently,' explained Mr Silvino.

'What on earth could be so important to justify that?' demanded Mr Sousa. 'I've just sat down to eat.'

'Donato, when you see what I have, you will agree the matter must be resolved before the court sits in the morning,' said Mr Silvino.

*   *   *

It was after 9.30 pm when Vincente Silvino finished the meeting with Emma and Ms Vitoria, then drove with the explosive evidence to Mr Sousa's chambers.

Seated nervously at his upstairs antique desk, Donato Sousa heard the car pull up outside.

He watched through the window as Vincente strode across the street with a satchel tucked under his arm.

Inviting his guest to take a seat, Mr Sousa moved to his side of the desk, unconsciously hoping it might save him from what he suspected could only be bad news.

'Vincente, calling me to a meeting at this unholy hour better be important,' Mr Sousa declared.

Trying to keep things on an even keel, Mr Silvino looked briefly at his file, then looked directly at Mr Sousa before he began in a low voice.

'Donato, we have known and respected each other for a long time and have come to enjoy each other's company on various occasions.

'Down the years I believe we have both prided ourselves regardless of whatever side we were on, that we have always been "straight shooters".

'Absolutely,' replied Mr Sousa, becoming more distrustful of what Mr Silvino had up his sleeve.

'In my first meeting with Ms Childers she informed me of Emilio Bestillo's womanising and of the two children she knew he had sired out of wedlock.

'She also spoke of his explicit greed for money and provided evidence of the fortune he stole from Mr Garland, which he laundered through Lisbon's casinos.

'As we both know, only a little of this carries any weight on this week's paternity application.

'In ordinary circumstances, as you and I well know, Mr Dalton's claim rests on your client's relationship with Mr Dalton's mother and the DNA paternity test.

'Today, our side was stunned that the DNA tests returned a zero paternity result.

'Vincente, we know all this. You still haven't given me a good enough reason to drag me back here tonight,' said an angry Mr Sousa.

'Donato, after what I am about to reveal, you will have no option but to phone Mrs Bestillo tonight. I don't care if she is in bed. Have someone wake her, as she needs to hear what you must do.

'You need to tell her that in the morning when the court resumes and before the judge delivers his decision, you intend to inform the court you intend to withdraw your client's objection to Mr Dalton's claim.

'Vincente, why in Christ would I ever instruct her to do that?' Mr Sousa spat back.

In that moment, one could have cut the air with a knife, as Mr Silvino took the copy of Alexio's original birth certificate from an envelope and after unfolding it, carefully laid it on Mr Sousa's polished desk.

He then read out where his index finger was pointing.

'There, you can plainly see that Alexio is not their child!'

'The Bestillos adopted him and changed his name and ever since have papered over the truth!' bellowed a triumphant Mr Silvino.

As Mr Sousa absorbed the shocking reality staring up at him from the desk, it began to dawn on him that the certificate Mrs Bestillo had provided for Alexio was a fake.

Only the slow ticking of the clock on the mantelpiece broke the otherwise deathly silence.

Any thought Mr Sousa had of feeling hungry had well and truly flown out the window.

With a wry smile, Mr Silvino leaned across the desk and tapped Mr Sousa's phone, waiting impatiently for him to pick it up and make the call.

Vincente was anticipating the great pleasure he was shortly to savour when he phoned his chambers to advise Ms Vitoria and Emma that the Bestillos had withdrawn their paternity contest.

55. Day Three: The Final Outcome

With a favourable decision expected in court, the number of Bestillo supporters attending the following morning was noticeably larger and noisier.

In her customary rear seat, Teresa Olimpia waited to record how the Bestillos received the decision and where her story might go from there.

Checking around the court she noted that the parties had resumed their usual places, except Mrs Bestillo had not yet arrived. Surely, Teresa thought, she couldn't be running late.

Then when the judge arrived, after the clerk had conveyed a message to him from Mr Sousa, she observed his body language seemed very different from the previous days.

Waiting pensively until the court was fully quiet, the judge gave Mr Sousa leave to make a statement.

A peculiar silence rippled across the court as faces turned expectantly towards him.

They watched him rise with sagging shoulders and an ashen face as he took hold of the lectern to steady himself. In a low modulated voice that was a far cry from his confident bluster on the previous days, he delivered a terse one liner:

'Não constestaram as acusações.'

As the unexpected bombshell spread like wildfire across the court, all but sucking the air from the room, the Bestillo supporters gasped loudly followed by a loud questioning roar.

Leaning over to her interpreter, Emma asked what exactly the barrister had said.

'Mr Sousa declared his client pleads no contest. This means the Bestillos have withdrawn their objection,' said the interpreter.

Ignoring the din, Judge Ulderico quickly adjourned the court.

As he rose and turned to depart through the rear door, a shocked

Teresa Olimpia caught a glimpse of his craggy face that seemed to show a hint of disbelief.

She watched the small Dalton contingent on their side of the court rise and delightedly hug each other, knowing justice had finally been done.

Teresa Olimpia could see the relief on Emma's smiling face as she watched Frank Dalton bury his teary face on his wife's shoulder, knowing his fifty-year wait for justice was over.

As Teresa packed her satchel, the reality struck home that this case had suddenly become for her an international "David slays Goliath" story instead.

Epilogue

Frank Dalton
The Daltons were shocked with the outcome, but delighted. Frank was grateful justice had finally been served and, more importantly, the future care of his daughter was assured.

Before leaving Porto, he contacted Mrs Luzia Valborga (nee Felloni) to thank her for appearing, and expressing that he would like to share a part of his inheritance with her family.

Jessie Tyler
When she heard the good news Jessie felt that in some small way a little of the guilt she had carried since the war had been lifted.

Roger Lockwood
Roger celebrated the news of Frank Dalton's win with his wife and children and made a point of updating the family's album with a series of press cuttings from the case that Emma had sent him.
He knew his grandmother, Alice, would rest easier now that the 'Ledger' had finally been squared.

When she returned to Melbourne, he invited Emma to Sydney to stay with his family.

Teresa Olimpia
Having finally sighted Aleixo's correct birth certificate, Teresa Olimpia researched the Bestillo history, discovering Mrs Bestillo had few prospects of producing a son, which led to the Bestillos adopting Aleixo, who was expected to take over the firm.

Teresa's subsequent series of in-depth articles in the *Jornal de Notícias* covered the gripping story of the Dalton-Bestillo case, which took many turns and won a European Press Prize for best "Investigative Reporting".

Emma Childers

Later that year as Emma started her new position at Garland International, an offer made by a grateful and impressed Roger Lockwood, she found time to reflect that what were once "Margie strokes" were most definitely turning into a new tranche of "Emma strokes".

The Porto decision was a huge relief and it helped her feel vindicated for the immense emotional effort and time she had devoted to finally lay open so many secrets from her family's past.

Finally, over seventy-five years later, justice had been secured and a portion of the family legacy had been rightfully restored.

And in a strange quirk of fate, Emma's clock had failed to sell and she was able to reclaim it.

Acknowledgements

As the humble author of the *Fractured Trust,* my creative efforts alone could never have produced this novel. I am very fortunate to have been surrounded, supported and egged on by a caring creative team to whom I would like to convey my heartfelt thanks and deep appreciation.

To my editor, Elissa McCallum, whose sustained, creative oversight kept the story on the rails. Thank you for always asking the hard questions, demanding plausible answers and causing numerous rewrites that finally enabled the novel to reach a level where it could be published.

To Bonnie Wilson, whose final editing helped raise the novel to the next level and her creative ideas helped shape the book's cover design.

To my devoted wife Sallie Sabey, whose support over thirty months has inspired and kept me from straying too far by helping keep the plot together through her unfailing patience and dedicated subediting of reams of drafts and rewritten copy.

My thanks to my good colleague Jervis Ward and his team at The Creative Parrott for developing the cover design and doing the typesetting that seamlessly transformed my manuscript into a finished tome.

A special thank you to Maryanne Gall, who inspired me to create the character of Emma. She gave me a glimpse of what it is like to leave London behind and set up home in Melbourne.

I am grateful to a number of my good friends, especially the Moorhouse Marauder cyclists, who participated in the research to ensure the novel would have appeal and from whom several character traits have been borrowed.

To Gordon Moffatt, whose germ of an idea led to the novel in the first place and his overview that ensured his long held idea has finally been produced.

To Heather Power, who contributed ideas along the way that helped link the generations and edited the manuscript prior to publishing.

To Stuart Adam, a former Australian Army officer who provided a real insight for the plot and Charles Garland's enlistment in the Royal Engineers.

To Ben White, a former Army officer, whose expert bomb disposal and technical advice was invaluable in shaping Charles Garland's role in the bomb disposal section.

To Jo Sabey, for many insightful and creative comments outside the square that led to certain characters being introduced and developed.

To Sam Sabey, whose savvy backroom work developed the novel's website.

And John Schultz and his energetic team at Waymore Distribution, who gave me valuable advice at the formative early planning stages for the book.

Finally, my express thanks to Kerry Collison of Sid Harta Publishing, who took on my novel. He has given me such fine advise and arranged all the distribution channels.